Falling Down

A rockstar novel

ROCKSTAR

Anne Mercier

COPYRIGHT
Falling Down

Editor: Nicole at Proof Before You Publish
Cover Design: Anne Mercier
Interor Design: Cassy Roop of Pink Ink Designs

DEDICATION

To my dad who has always been a tough disciplinarian. It took me becoming an adult to realize he was strict because he believed in me even when I didn't believe in myself.

Quotes That Inspired The Rockstar Series

"I just try not to subscribe to the ways of the celebrity. I'm not a celebrity, I'm a working actor. A lot of the events – the parties and the premieres that people go to, to get noticed, I'm just not into it. I'll hang out with my friends, go see punk shows, read at home. At the same time I have a production company which is a lot of work."
~Milo Ventimiglia

"Oh my God. Nothing against the [teen] magazines because they definitely have their purposes, but I don't want to answer questions like, 'Do you have a girlfriend?' and 'What is your favorite color?' Answering more adult questions is more intriguing and that's the vibe I'd like to give off."
~Milo Ventimiglia

"I don't seek attention. If anything I'd rather blend in, remain anonymous."
~Milo Ventimiglia

"Be yourself and like what you like and fuck everyone else."
~ M. Shadows, Avenged Sevenfold

"The best revenge is being yourself."
~ Zacky V., Avenged Sevenfold

"The most important thing you can ever do is follow your dreams."
~ Jimmy "The Rev" Sullivan, Avenged Sevenfold
(RIP Rev. You are missed.)

Chapter

one

Lucy

Our flight's delayed which isn't a surprise. Thank God for iPhones and headsets or I'd have to endure the incessant chatter of Regina Russo. Yeah, that's my mom. The chatterbox who is now talking my brother's ear off. The difference between Joey and me is he likes to talk as much as my mom. I'd much rather enjoy solitude.

Sera and I are listening to a random playlist on Spotify. She chose the Today's Top Hits playlist, which is okay, but I'm not into a lot of the rap-type music whereas Sera loves it. It beats out listening to Regina any day.

Sera taps my shoulder and I pull one earbud out.

"Stuck in Chicago, of all places."

"Could be worse. We could be stuck in Kansas."

"Or Texas."

"Truth. Let's go get something to drink and see if maybe they have some decent magazines with His Sexiness in the gift shop."

Sera snorts. "His Sexiness."

"What? He is."

"He's alright. His brother's seriously hot too."

"Oh yeah. Mom, we'll be right back."

"Don't be too long. I have a feeling we're going to be up in the air soon."

"We won't."

We head through the concourse of Chicago's O'Hare International airport. Tons of people are traveling today. I wonder if it's like this every day or if Thursdays are busier than most.

"Ugh," Sera says. "If I get bumped one more time I'm going to throat punch someone, I swear. It's so rude. I mean, how hard is it to walk around someone instead of into them?"

"Swap," I say, tugging her to the right so she can walk along the wall.

I'm not a fan of being bumped into, but I don't have a hair-trigger temper like Sera. Let me tell you a little about Serafina Manzini. Her mom, Lily, was my dad's sister. She was a Russo. Tommy Manzini married a Russo, which caused some major feuding. Mr. Manzini refused to get involved in his brother's "family business." Who could blame him? Who wants to get involved with the freaking Chicago mafia? Hell to the no thank you. Well, his brother didn't take too kindly to being told no and after multiple threats and multiple "fuck you's" from Sera's dad, they killed Sera's parents execution style. When the hit was carried out Sera was on vacation with us, which is the only reason she's still alive. Now, she's protected under my family as our grandpa Giovanni and my uncle Emilio are involved in the "family business". We aren't directly involved in any of that crap. My grandpa respects my dad's decision to go legit and raise us outside the rules of the mafia, which I am thankful for every day—though we will never be one hundred percent outside. That's just not possible. I've seen my cousins Nico and Bella both with guns tucked in the waistband of their pants and I've been told they can hit moving targets better than some of their most seasoned veterans. Bella can't participate, being a girl and all, but that doesn't stop her from trying. Not something I'd want to participate in. This was going to be the life for Sera had her uncle succeeded.

Oh, and just so you know, my grandpa "took care of" those who killed Sera's family. I shouldn't be happy about that as revenge doesn't solve anything, but now those thugs won't be able to do that to anyone else. Go gramps! (He'd have a fit if I ever called him gramps to his face.)

Now, you're probably wondering what that has to do with Sera's temper. Well, before her family was killed, Sera was bubbly and fun. She was always positive but with the loss of her family, she's become bitter, angry, and, at times, hostile. She just has no patience for anyone's bullshit anymore—her words, not mine. So, you can imagine after she's been bumped into five or six times how she'd react. It wouldn't be pretty. It'd range from yelling and swearing to possibly punching someone in the face and, as she mentioned, throat punching someone. Well, let's just say it would have been ugly.

"Oh! Starbucks!"

"Hell yeah," Sera says, following behind me.

"What do you want? My treat."

"Caramel macchiato, Venti, triple shot."

I raise my eyebrows. "You're going to be hyped on the plane."

"All the better for playing Candy Crush."

"Oh my God. You and that dumb game."

She flips her long brown hair over her shoulder. "Whatever. You only think it's dumb because you can't get past level 96."

"Suck it."

"If you had something to suck…" She breaks off with a shrug and a smirk as we step up to the counter to order.

I order Sera's large cup of caffeine and for myself I order an Americano with vanilla syrup, extra sweet, with two creams.

As we wait for our order there's a commotion in the center seating area near the flight boards.

"Huh, I wonder which celeb is flying today," Sera questions.

I shrug. It's not uncommon to see celebrities pass through Chicago, I've just never seen one up close and personal.

"Maybe it's someone sexy like Taylor Lautner." She wiggles her eyebrows at this and I can't help but smirk.

"Doubtful. It's probably some old dude or a model," I start to ramble as I hand Sera her coffee and pay. I head off to the side to stir in extra sugars and creamer. "Maybe it's Miley. Or the Biebs," I say with a snort.

Sera taps my arm a couple times.

"What?" I look over at her. She's standing there with her coffee halfway to her mouth, her mouth hanging open and her eyes wide.

"What's going on?"

"L-look," she points.

I turn and I nearly drop my coffee. All the air in my lungs has been sucked out in some sort of vacuum and I can't breathe. I grab Sera's arm and make some incoherent sound that sounds like, "unh". She must get what I'm saying because she responds with, "I know!"

"Unh!"

"*I know!* Wow. Did you conjure him up looking for His Sexiness? You should go ask for his autograph."

No way. Uh-uh. I, Luciana Russo, am a chicken. I can't even move at this point. Hell, I can't even speak. I'm sure he wouldn't understand "unh".

"You have to, Lucy. You've wanted to meet Jesse Kingston since we were in seventh grade! This is your one and, probably, only shot."

She's right, but I can't move. I don't even have a pen. I must be talking normally now because she thrusts a pen and paper in my face. Then she grabs my arm and drags me to where he's standing.

"Unh." Guess not, she just knows.

Okay, you're probably wondering who the hell Jesse Kingston is and what the big deal is. Let me tell you. Jesse Kingston is People Magazine's Sexiest Man Alive the last three years running. He's tall, dark and delicious. He's sex on a stick. He's the lead singer of Falling Down and has the sexiest voice I've ever heard. I kid you not, his voice is deep and gravely and sends chills down my spine, goose bumps all over my body, and moisture between my thighs. Oh yeah, that's Jesse Kingston. Okay—back to the hottie that has my mouth and body in zombieland.

I wipe around my mouth, checking for any signs of drool. Oh God. My heart is going eleventy billion miles an hour, I've got tummy flips going on, and my girlie parts are tingling—all this because he's within twenty feet of me? If he touches me I'll likely spontaneously combust.

"Jesse!" Sera calls out.

Unh. She tugs me along behind her as she walks over to him. Oh. My. God.

"Ladies. How are you today?" Oh that smile.

"Good, we're good," Sera says as she smacks my arm. I give some semblance of a smile, which I'm sure looks hideous. I'm such an idiot. His mouth kicks up into a grin—dimples!

My gaze zeroes in on his piercings. He's got a hoop in his eyebrow and another through his bottom lip. Could he be any sexier? Yes, yes he could. How you might wonder? Well, he's wearing a tight black Chevelle t-shirt and worn, faded, and ripped jeans along with a pair of scuffed black boots. Hot! Both of his arms are full of tattoos that I wish I could focus on, maybe trace with my tongue, but, well, zombieland and I'm not so sure my tongue on his body would be welcome at this point.

Sera rolls her eyes at me. "You're traveling alone?"

He nods. "The band is in L.A."

She pouts. I know she was hoping to see Falling Down's lead guitarist and Jesse's brother, Ben Kingston. Sera started crushing on him in tenth grade when they came out with their third album that was a bit harder than their previous ones. Her favorite song to date is *My Fantasy*, which was the title song off of that album and spent thirty-seven weeks at the top of the charts.

"My friend, Lucy, would like to get your autograph." I stand there frozen.

"Is that so, Lucy?"

Still frozen. I refuse to try to speak. I don't want to "unh" in front of him. This is embarrassing enough.

He reaches out to take the pen and paper from my hand and as he leans forward he whispers, "It's okay, Lucy. I won't bite. Well, unless you want me to, of course." He flashes those straight, white teeth and winks. Whiskey-colored eyes dance with humor and I sigh on the inside because I seriously can't snap out of this, whatever it is.

He signs the paper, taking his time. He caps the pen and places it and the paper in my hand, closing my hand around the items so I don't drop them. He doesn't let go of my hand and my eyes zoom in on that. Holy hell. Jesse Kingston is holding my hand—it was just for a few seconds, but he held my hand! His fingers are slightly callused, no doubt from playing his guitar and wow, am I starting to sweat?

"Are you going to be alright, Lucy?"

"Um…" Hey! It's better than unh.

Sera sighs in exasperation. "She'll be fine. She's just had the biggest crush on you forever."

I register what she said and vow that as soon as I can move I'm going to kick her ass. And here it comes—the blush. It creeps up my neck to my face. I'm sure I'm a lovely shade of red right now and red is so not my color.

"Really?"

"Oh yeah. She's been following your career since you went national your junior year in high school."

"Wow," he says with a smile at me. "That's a long time."

"Yeah, it is. She ran around screaming when your first album debuted and when your video came out she threw a party."

"That's dedication."

He's still smiling. I stare at those amazing lips. I want to lick them. Nibble on them and tug on that lip ring a bit with my teeth.

I manage to blink.

"Hey, I think she's coming out of it," he says.

I shake my head. "Oh my God. I'm so sorry."

He flashes those pearly whites again—and those dimples. "No worries."

"I'm Lucy."

"Nice to meet you Lucy," he says, that callused thumb caressing my hand as he shakes it, sparks zinging up my arm, more moisture pooling at the apex of my thighs—I am a hormonal teenager and let me tell you this man makes them rage. He reaches out and tucks a strand of my brown hair behind my ear and I don't think my heart can take it.

"Nice to meet you too." I thrust the pen and autograph toward Sera who takes them.

"Let's walk and talk. I think my flight might be ready."

"No private plane today?" Ha! Look at me talking normal.

"Nah. Not for just me and the big guys," he says, pointing to his bodyguards. "When the band travels then we take the jet."

I nod. God. To have a private jet. Better yet, to be on *their* private jet when they're all on board. Heaven.

"So you're a fan."

"Mhmm." We're walking super close, so close our arms are touching as we walk. When our hands brush against one another, he winks at me.

Winks! He's seriously tall. I mean, I know from his bio and from going to the concerts he's six-three, but compared to my five-three, he's a giant. His shoulders are broad and I swear I can see his muscles ripple in his stomach as he walks. Another place I'd like to lick. Is it hot in here?

I look at Sera out of the corner of my eye. She's grinning and she fans herself. Definitely hot in here. Like the bodyguards trailing behind us aren't going to tell him she did that? I just bite my bottom lip then grin wide.

"Where are you headed?" he asks.

"L.A."

"I'm headed back there myself."

"Oh, were you at Comic Con?"

Jesse's involved with a company that makes comics, ones based on rockers, of course. He heads to as many Comic Cons as he can—I know this because I stal-, uh, follow him online. I would never stalk him. Okay, I do follow him closely sometimes. I sigh. Alright, alright, I follow him closely all the time. I've even got a Google alert. That doesn't make me a stalker. It just makes me a die-hard fan. That's all. I'm sticking with that so shush.

"Good guess. I was. There was a great turnout. It's part of what I love about the Midwest. People have passion and they're not afraid to go the extra mile to show their dedication."

"Hmmm," was all I could manage.

"Excuse me while I check in." He squeezes my shoulder gently, then walks up to the counter, the same counter we checked in at, and the airline chick all but puddles at his feet. Who can blame her? With his wavy, dark hair that touches his collar and those whiskey-colored eyes that had me captivated. Jesse Kingston is a walking, talking bundle of testosterone. A woman's equivalent to a man's walking wet dream.

"Do you think he's on our flight?" I whisper to Sera.

"It looks like it. Holy shit! Jesse Kingston!"

"I think I just fangirled all over the place."

Sera laughs.

"I can't believe this is happening. This has got to be a dream."

Sera pinches me—hard.

"Ow! What the fuck?"

"Not a dream. Just proving it to you."

"You're so violent."

She shrugs and snaps more photos of Jesse. I didn't notice before, but I think she's been snapping away since she first saw him. I need her to send me those photos. Every single one. I don't care if it's of the back of his head.

Oh, here he comes. His gaze zeroes in on mine and I can't help the smile that pulls across my face. Oh, he is seriously beautiful.

"Looks like the flight will be ready in a few minutes," he says as he stands in front of me.

"Can I get a picture with you?"

He smiles. "Of course."

I hand Sera my phone as Jesse leads me over to a less crowded area. He puts his arm around me and, oh my God, does he smell good. Like the ocean and sandalwood and yum. He pulls me closer to him and I wrap my arm around his waist. Oh my, even his side is hard and muscular. Damn. I rest my head against his chest. I'm sure I've got some goofy smile on my face but I honestly don't care.

"All done?" he asks Sera.

No! Keep holding me close.

"Yep."

Damn.

He turns to face me and there's about an inch of space separating our bodies. Oh this works, though I'm tempted to take that baby step and press myself up against his hard body, maybe even do a little rubbing.

They call for boarding and I can't look away, I'm mesmerized by his gaze, those amazing golden eyes with tiny flecks of green and brown. *No! Don't go. Please don't go, or if you do take me with you!* He doesn't look away until one of the big guys clears his throat signaling it's time to go.

"Lucy. It was really great to meet you."

I want to shout that he can't leave me, howl at the moon, or flop down at his feet and beg him to never leave me. I can honestly see myself wrapping my arms around his leg and him having to drag me along behind him.

He's holding my hands, both of them, in both of his and I really, really don't want to let go.

"Thank you. And thanks for the autograph and photos."

He brings my hands to his lips and kisses them. My breath stalls in my chest. "Honestly, it was my pleasure."

He tilts his head to the side just a bit as if he's trying to figure something out.

"Have we—" He pauses then shakes his head. Then he smiles that panty-melting smile. He runs his knuckles gently down the side of my face and with that he's gone.

I feel like I'm going to cry. How stupid is that? I mean, he's Jesse Kingston and he was just being sweet to a fan. I get it. I know it, but the sting of tears won't stop.

Sera knows and she pulls me into a hug.

"God, Luce."

I nod and sniffle, blinking back ridiculous tears.

"Girls, we need to board," my mom calls.

"Dude, was that Jesse Kingston?" Joey asks.

I nod.

"I bet Lucy needs a change of panties."

Even though he's totally right, I reach over and punch him in the arm. "Pig."

"Joseph Anthony Russo you will watch your tongue."

Sera hands me the autograph and pen. I look at her.

"Did that really just happen?"

She nods. "And you have proof."

She hands me my phone and there's a picture of me and Jesse. My breath catches. We're staring into one another's eyes as he caresses my face.

"Oh my God, Sera." This time there's no holding back the tears.

"I know," she says and throws an arm over my shoulders as we board the plane, pulling me in for a half-hug. "The electricity was zapping around you two. I thought we were going to be electrocuted."

I sigh.

Sera looks around to see if she can spot Jesse.

"He's likely in first class."

"Yeah, probably," she says, taking her seat.

I sit next to her and look out the window. I can't believe this. In two days I audition for a major starring role in a movie that would make my career if I land the part, I'm moving to Los Angeles *and* I met Jesse Kingston, touched him, and he kissed my hand—a hand that's still tingling from his lips.

"We should have let mom upgrade us. Do you think we can sneak up to first class?" Sera asks.

I smile softly. "As much as I'd love that, I'm not a stalker and I don't want him to think I am. I'm going to hold on to what he's given me today and keep it close." See? I'm not a stalker.

She nods. "I can see that."

"Maybe one day…"

"Maybe."

We sit in silence for a minute as the flight attendant tells us about the emergency exits, my mind blank as if it can't comprehend what just happened.

The jet engines fire up and we're lifted off the ground.

"You going to send me those pictures?"

Sera smiles. "Already done, darling. Already done."

"Perfect."

"I got an amazing picture of his ass."

"Only one?"

She gives me a look of exasperation. "Please. Try twelve."

"Twelve? Why twelve?"

She grins. "A dozen hot buns."

I laugh. My sister totally rocks.

Chapter
two

Lucy

Six Years Later...

"*Please Micah.*"

"*You made your decision, Maggie, when you were snuggling up to your ex.*"

"*It was just a hug goodbye.*"

"*I know what I saw, Mags. That wasn't just a hug.*"

"*It wasn't,*" *she says with a lone tear sliding down her cheek, her head hanging in defeat.*

"I hate that Maggie had to hurt Micah in the end," I say with a sigh as Sera and I reread some of the final lines from "Always You", a movie I just got done shooting.

As we head to downtown Los Angeles Sera shrugs. "She ended up with her happily ever after soulmate and Micah found his happy with Becca in the end. They were just using each other to get through the shit until they could get back to the place they each belonged."

"True. I really am glad that movie is done though and if I never have to work with Aiden Jensen again it'll be too soon."

"Don't even get yourself worked up."

I nod. "I won't. The cokehead."

Sera looks at me.

"That's all I'm going to say."

"Mhmm."

I never said I wouldn't steam on the inside. Let me tell you about Aiden Jensen. He's a phenomenal actor and when I got up there as Maggie and he got up there as Micah, we sizzled. But he was a nightmare. He ruined what started out to be one of the most fun and beautiful movies I've ever been a part of. See, Aiden's addicted to cocaine so he's twitchy, bitchy, constantly hot and sweaty, and an all around pain in the ass. He set us so far behind our deadline, I barely got any time off in between jobs. Jackhole.

As we pull into the lot where we're going to be filming the music video, I breathe a sigh of relief that my mother is in Paris right now. She calls incessantly when she knows I have a new project starting and if she was here instead of in Paris, she'd continue to throw her objections at me over this project.

This will be the first time that Sera and I will be working together in nearly nine months. Sera gets on film, just not for movies or television. She mostly models but she gets on camera for music videos too. If we decide to get involved in a video, we always do so together. It's our one way of connecting to music together like we used to in high school. Sure we still jam out in private but it isn't the same. We'd both give anything to be up on that stage singing and performing to tens of thousands of people, to hear them singing our lyrics back to us. Yeah, that's my goal and my mother knows it.

Regina Russo wanted what she wanted and expected everyone else to fall in line and I've done so all my life—until now. I'm twenty-three years old. I'm an adult. It's time for my mom to cut the freaking cord already and let me live my life. She can focus on Joey's career. He's a phenomenal actor and he loves it, all of it—the fame and fortune, the media attention—whereas I look at it as merely a job. Yeah, I'm successful but it isn't what I want to do for the rest of my life.

"Did you ever find out what band the video was for?"

"No. Irene was supposed to get back to me but she's been dealing with the Aiden fiasco." Irene is my agent and she's nothing less than sensational. I pity her having to deal with Aiden as a client right now.

She nods. "It doesn't really matter. Irene and Cage only let us do videos with big-name bands anyway."

"True that. I don't mind going in blind so long as we get to jam a little."

"I heard that."

We get out of the car and make our way inside the studio. There are multiple scenes set up for filming. Looks like this is going to be a really good video. It must be a massively popular band. I just hope it's rock and not rap. I love all kinds of music *except* for scream metal, techno/rave, and rap where every other word is fuck or bitch.

We're greeted by a familiar woman with a headset and clipboard dressed in a navy pencil skirt with a white short-sleeved straight-line sweater and an amazing pair of navy slingbacks.

"Miss Russo. Miss Manzini. I'm Marci Benson. It's a pleasure to see you again," she holds out a hand and both Sera and I shake it in greeting.

"Marci. Call us Lucy and Sera."

She nods at me. "The crew is here and setting up. The band won't be arriving until later. I'll take you back to the conference room where they'll let you know what their plan is for the day."

We trail behind as she continues to talk.

"There are no trailers for hair, makeup, or wardrobe. Since Mr. Nichols purchased the building, he added rooms in the back for all of that."

"Nice," Sera chimes in.

"There's coffee and some pastries available so feel free to help yourselves. If there is anything you need throughout the day, don't hesitate to ask someone to get in contact with me."

"Thanks."

I see movement out of the corner of my eye but I'm too late to see who it is.

"Holy God, Lucy. Did you see who that was?"

"No. Who was it?"

"I can't be sure but it looked like Xander Mackenzie."

"From Falling Down?"

She nods.

"I don't think so. Kennedy is seeing that model. There's no way they'd need us if that were the case."

She tsks. "You of all people believing what they read in a gossip rag."

"It's not from a gossip rag. They were on Entertainment Tonight doing some red carpet thing. They even talked to the reporters together and confirmed they were on a date."

Sera shrugs. "Well okay then. It just looked like him, but then again there are a lot of rockers with tattooed arms and black hair with an amazing ass."

"True that." Jesse Kingston comes to mind. Yum.

We head into the conference room, which is empty and I'm actually grateful. It's seven-thirty in the morning and I've only had one cup of coffee. This morning, all Sera and I managed was to get up, shower, and throw on comfortable clothes. I'm not a morning person and if I have to be up this early, I better be receiving a source of caffeine on a regular basis. I don't care what I look like before I get on set so no one better bag on my yoga pants and Deftones concert shirt either. That was one hell of a concert.

I head straight for the coffee, mix in some French vanilla creamer and sugar. Ah, thank God for Cage. He knows what I like. I pull back one of the plush black chairs at the table and take a seat. Then, only then do I savor the first sip of coffee. Oh my God. It's so good. It's strong, just the way I like it.

I must moan aloud because Sera starts laughing.

"Good?"

"Oh yeah." We're both sitting at the table, nibbling on pastries and drinking coffee. It's when I start to drink my third cup that Cage Nichols walks in with three people trailing behind. I elbow Sera who wiggles her eyebrows.

Cage Nichols is one of the most amazing video directors ever. He's also so super hot that women pant when he walks in the room. Take Sera for instance. Panting, right now.

His hair is cut short and he's semi-casual today in dress pants and a dress shirt. His body is to die for. I've been lucky enough to see him shirtless and the man is ripped. His dark brown eyes are twinkling as he walks over. I get up from the chair.

"Oh my God!"

He chuckles and gives me a hug. "No, darlin', just Cage."

I snort and Sera mumbles, "God works."

Pine. He smells like pine and soap and man. It's a comforting scent.

He smiles and I swear I can hear Sera's heartbeat speed up. "Sera, my love."

He pulls her into a hug and she jumps up, wrapping her legs around his waist. I burst out laughing.

"If I was your love, Cage, I wouldn't be single," she says with a pout, then lays a loud smacking kiss on his lips.

We've worked with Cage at least half a dozen times on different videos with different bands and he's always made it fun for everyone and the videos were phenomenal.

Sera protests lightly when he sets her down and takes a seat at the head of the table.

"You remember Amanda, Dave, and Gina."

Sera and I nod. "Great to see you all again."

"Likewise," Dave says. Cage has amazing assistants who are loyal, professional, and I would love to steal them from him.

"So, ladies. We've got a special video we're going to start shooting today."

We both nod.

"I gave you a half hour to fuel up on your caffeine, Luce," he says with a wink. He looks at his watch. "The crew's already setting up and the band should be here in a little over an hour. I figured you both could go get all prettified before they get here so they don't have to wait."

"Temperamental artists?" I ask.

"Nah. There's just no reason for them to sit around here."

"You're awesome like that," Sera says with a purr. Cage winks at her.

"Get a room already. Sheesh." I'm not sure why they haven't already hooked up for as hot as they are for each other.

They both look at me blankly. Yeah, uh-huh. We all know. As if they're fooling anyone.

"It's eight-fifteen in the damn morning. How the hell you two can be up for flirting, I have no clue."

Gina gets up and gets me more coffee.

"Bless you."

She smiles. "You're welcome."

"Dave, pass me that jelly-filled doughnut."

Sera laughs.

"What?"

"You're going to hate yourself later when you've got to run extra to burn off those calories."

"Hell no. We're going to be shaking our asses out there for the video, right Cage?"

He nods. "Oh yeah."

"Well, there you go. Exercise. Calories and doughnuts burned off." I take a big bite then lick the raspberry filling.

"Pig," Sera says with a laugh.

I take another bite.

"Alright, ladies. We start filming at ten. Head on over to makeup and get yourselves made up for our rockstars."

"Whose video is it? "I ask.

Cage smiles. "All I'm going to say is they're a big name and I know you definitely like them. I'll let you be surprised."

"Hmmm."

With a wink, he and his assistants leave the room.

"Well, let's get started."

Chapter
three

Lucy

We're waiting in robes for hair and makeup to arrive. Sera's in the room next door looking through the clothes on the rack, clothes they're likely going to have us squeezing into and hanging out of. I took a quick peek at them. Skimpy.

"We're going to look seriously hot," Sera says.

"Like seriously hot *hookers*."

"Oh come on, Luce. When have we ever looked like hookers in any of Cage's videos?"

"True. It's just there's barely any material to those outfits. I'm afraid my hoohah is going to be showing."

Sera laughs. "That's what panties are for."

I'm ready to tell her that I don't want the world to see my panties when the hair and makeup team walk in.

"Ready for primping, ladies?" Spenser asks, perky as ever.

"Spenser! It's been too long!"

"Don't I know it. I've missed your gorgeous faces." He air kisses both cheeks then does the same to Sera.

Spenser Clarity is the best makeup artist I've ever encountered. Spenser is the best because he's worked long and hard to get there and he has natural talent. No one takes care of my skin and hair like Spenser. No one.

I note he has two new people working with him and wonder how he likes that. Spenser hates incompetence and is a perfectionist.

"New girls?" I ask with a raised brow.

"Yes and they're amazing. I got so lucky with these two. They were interning. Interning! If you can believe that. I saw what they could do and immediately snatched them up. Come here, girls."

The two gorgeous redheads walk up smiling.

"You've got to meet Lucy and Sera. We've got it made today. These two don't require much work at all, they're so naturally beautiful."

"Nice to meet you, I'm Simone and this is Carmen."

I smile, "A pleasure."

Sera mumbles incoherently around her pastry.

"So, what's on the agenda today? Looks like skimpy and slutty?"

"Oh, no. No. Definitely skimpy but never slutty. Not for you two. We always keep it classy."

"Thank God."

"Do you know who we're working with?" Sera asks.

Spenser grins then closes his lips and pretends to turn a lock and throw away the key.

"Secrets. I promised."

I huff. "You know me, Spense. I'm going to go crazy not knowing."

"We'll just have to distract you. Let's get started."

An hour later we're made up and my hair is primped and curled and slightly sprayed. That's what I love most about Spenser, he doesn't spray an entire can of lacquer hairspray onto whatever style he gives us, and what he does spray is unscented for which I'm very grateful. The scented stuff makes me sneeze.

"Ah, here's Gina. Wardrobe time!" Spenser claps. "I can't wait to see what they've chosen."

"Let's go, ladies," Gina says with a smile. She leads us over to the wardrobe area and immediately heads for the racks of clothes.

Turns out we aren't going to be rockstar hookers after all. They dress me in a red corset top that ends with red ruffles just above my belly button. The straps are a bit wider than spaghetti straps. Laces thread through on the side and behind the laces is a lacy, see-through fabric. What I love about it the most is the bustline. It's white with red polka dots which contrasts nicely with the red straps and bottom as well as the red ruffles that line the top bustline. All in all it's pretty conservative. My boobs are, of course, pushed up to within an inch of their life giving me some pretty rocking cleavage for someone who only wears a C-cup. The ruffles seem to enhance the boobage, which I think is pretty awesome. They pair the top with a pair of super tight white crop pants that stop just below the knee. With the pants being white, it brings forth one of my worst enemies.

I hold the pants up to Spenser and he raises a brow.

"You know what this means, don't you?"

"Luce, if the worst of your wardrobe is the white thong that you'll be wearing *underneath* your other clothing, don't bitch about it. They could have you out there in a bikini that is the equivalent to three triangles and a few pieces of thread."

"Valid." What can I say to that? He's right. I suck it up and head behind the dressing screen with Gina.

"Can I keep these shoes?" I ask Gina. They're a pair of three-inch crisscross, strappy, ankle-wrap sandals that are amazingly comfortable and easy to walk in.

"You can keep anything you want. You know Cage's policy."

Yay! Shoes!

She finishes accessorizing me and Spenser runs up and spritzes me with my favorite perfume.

"Why the perfume?"

"Trust me. You'll be glad I spritzed you when you see who's here," he sing-songs.

"We're here for a video not a date, Spense."

He just tsks. Who the hell could it be? There are a handful of bands that would elicit that sort of reaction and I just can't imagine any of them wanting me and Sera for their video. We're conservative compared to a lot of the models and actresses who do videos, which puts us on many of the bands' short list.

Sera steps out from behind her screen wearing a spandex-type black dress with short cap sleeves, black stockings with a seam running up the back of her legs, and a pair of black lace overlay peep toe pumps. Her brown hair is swept up into a fancy up-do with curling tendrils framing her face.

"Bitch."

She laughs. "What's your problem?"

"First, I've got a thong up my ass crack and you know how I love that."

She laughs again, louder.

"Second, I hate you. I hate that your ass is smaller than mine."

"Truthfully, Luce, I should be calling you a bitch and hating on you because I envy your curves."

"You can have them."

"Trade."

If only.

We head back to where Spenser is to chat him up a bit but he and the girls are busy.

"Hmm. We've got thirty minutes to kill. What do you want to do?"

"After I put your lipstick on," Spenser says, throwing a cape over my shoulders and chest before dabbing my lips an amazing shade of red.

"Yeah, after that."

"Let's go check out the set. Maybe we can figure it out," Sera says adjusting her dress as Simone steps up to whip a cape over her and uses a slightly darker shade of red on Sera's lips.

"You two are gorgeous and those boys are going to swallow their fucking tongues when they see you, aren't they girls?"

They all murmur their agreement.

"Do we have wardrobe change?"

Spenser rolls his eyes. "Since when don't you have wardrobe change in a video?"

"A girl can hope. Let's go peek, Sera."

We head out into the studio, over to where there's a faux stage set up. Any and all graphics that would lead to our discovery of who our mystery band is are covered with black fabric.

"Ugh, Cage," Sera says with a laugh.

"Agreed. There's really no point to going any further."

Sera walks over and reaches for a guitar.

"Sera! What are you doing?"

"What does it look like I'm doing?"

"It looks like you're touching what is likely a temperamental musician's guitar! Put it back."

"Fuck that. We have thirty minutes. Let's jam."

I nearly bite my bottom lip then remember the lipstick. Glancing over to the guitars, I can't resist. I pick up the other acoustic guitar knowing full well someone's going to be pissed we're playing their instruments.

"What should we play?"

"P!nk?"

"*Just Give Me A Reason*. Let me get to the piano," I tell Sera. Piano. I love playing the piano and it's been entirely too long.

I take a seat and flex my fingers. "It's been a long time."

"That it has. Ready?"

I nod. "Count it out."

She does and we start playing and singing as if we haven't missed a day. When that song ends I go back for the guitar as Sera heads to the drums. I grin.

"We're going to be in so much trouble."

She grins and shrugs.

"*Who Knew*." Sera counts us off and we give it all we've got. We play a couple more P!nk songs, then I call for some Red.

"Last one. *Never Be The Same*."

"Nice," Sera says.

We lose ourselves in the music, the lyrics, the feel of the beat pulsing through our bodies. If we'd been paying attention, we'd have noticed them walk up, but we didn't and they don't stop us.

Out of nowhere an electric guitar starts up and a very recognizable

Falling Down • 28

male voice joins with mine. I nearly piss my pants. I'd know that voice anywhere but my eyes fly to my left to make sure my ears aren't playing tricks on me. When I'm met with a very sexy and smiling pair of whiskey-colored eyes I return their twinkle with my own.

When the song ends, my eyes are still wide and staring and I'm shaking slightly. Holy! Shit! Mother of God... I'm going to kick Cage's ass.

I hear Sera's gasp. She must notice Xander standing next to her, his arms crossed, grin on his face.

I can't speak, just stare.

"Well, say something. We know you can sing so we know your voice works."

Oh boy. Jesse Kingston. He doesn't sound all that amused even though he has a smirk on his face.

"Um…"

He tilts his head to the side then looks at Sera as she walks up.

"Yep, it's us."

He bursts out laughing. "I'd know that 'um' anywhere."

I thrust his guitar out toward him. "Here. Sorry." I stand up from the stool and smooth down my pants, flipping my loose curls over my shoulder.

He takes the guitar with one hand then throws his other arm around me, pulling me in for a hug. Holy Mother of God.

"Lucy."

Huh? He remembers me? I breathe him in. God, he smells the same. Ocean and sandalwood and yum. His muscles are larger and he has a lot more sexy tattoos. I stand there stiffly and he steps back.

He quirks up a brow. "Really?"

"Huh?" is all I could come up with.

"Again?"

Sera sighs. "She only gets like that around you."

He gives her a disbelieving look and she shrugs.

"Seriously."

"What's going on?" This comes from the sexy magnificence that is Ben Kingston.

"Holy Mother of God," I say under my breath.

All five of them, six including Sera, start laughing.

"Um, sorry we touched your precious," I say, pointing to his guitar.

He chuckles. "Normally I'd want to break your fingers but since you knew what you were doing and used her for good instead of evil, I'll say it's no problem."

"What constitutes evil?"

"Taylor Swift."

I laugh.

He nods. "Why are you two not in a band? You're fucking terrific."

I shrug. "Long story."

"They always are."

Cage walks up. "Well, I see you've already met."

"Sort of," Sera says.

Cage smiles. "I heard you both. I'm going to talk you out of that shitty acting and modeling and into music if it's the last thing I do."

"We were just goofing around. It's been forever since we've done any serious playing," Sera tells him, handing me a bottle of water.

"Thanks." My throat's tender. It's been too long since I've used my voice regularly.

"It didn't sound like it. It sounded like you've been doing this forever," Xander says.

Jesse hands me a peppermint Life Saver.

"Helps," he says motioning to my throat.

I nod. "Thanks."

"Cage, dude, Jesse's met these hotties before," Xander says with a grin.

"Is that right?"

I nod. "A lifetime ago."

Jesse frowns. "It hasn't been that long."

"It has. I was untainted by the wicked ways of Hollywood."

"Not true, Luce. You'd acted before," Sera interrupts.

"Those were shit parts and that doesn't count."

"It *all* counts in Hollywood, darling," Ben says.

"So you're all tainted now, huh?" Jesse asks with another lift of his brow.

I shrug as Spenser comes flitting up. "Damn you Luciana Antonia

Russo."

"Oh, now you've done it. He three-named you." This comes from Ethan, the bassist.

I send him a scared look and he chuckles.

"It's not that bad, Spense."

"Woman, you don't have a mirror and I have my eyes right on you. You've chewed off your Stalker Red lipstick."

Jesse laughs.

I gape. "Is it seriously called Stalker Red?"

Spenser rolls his eyes then cuts a glance to Jesse. "No, but that would have fit with her girlie crush on you, right?"

I gasp.

Spenser waves his hand. "It's really called Make Out Red."

I just blink as Jesse opens his mouth. I point. "Not a word."

He laughs as does the rest of the band.

"I'm not sure which is worse."

"Stalker, definitely stalker," Spenser says with a shudder. "Yours isn't so bad. Sera's is called Smitten Lovey Dovey."

I smirk and Sera rolls her eyes.

"I don't care what it's called, let's just fix it so we can get started," Cage says with a laugh.

"Spense, I love you."

I was going to hug him but he pushes his index finger into the middle of my forehead. "No."

"I just wanted to hug you."

"No. You'll mess up what we," he says, pointing to him and the girls, "just fixed after you and Serafina Rosalie Manzini decided to play rockstar."

"Hey," I say with a huff. "We could be for real if we wanted."

"Not if your mother has anything to say about it," he retorts as he clips closed his makeup case and sashays away.

I turn back to the band with a bland look. They are all smirking so I narrow my eyes. They just smirk even more. Ugh, rockstars.

"Don't render me speechless by staring at me with all your rockstar hotness."

"It'll happen," Sera says with a shrug. "Jesse's here."

I nod and they all grin and look at Jesse who's smiling. "It's a curse."

He frowns. "Hey!"

I laugh. Goodness, the butterflies have set up a pretty wicked cadence in my stomach. Jesse fucking Kingston. Are you kidding me! Holy shit! My crush, the rocker I lust after, and the one man who can, indeed, render me speechless. *Keep it cool, Luce. You got this.*

"Let me introduce you to everyone though likely you know who we all are, if I remember correctly."

Sera whispers, "Stalker fangirl."

I elbow her side and blush.

"My brother, Ben Kingston on lead guitar, Ethan Ashcroft on bass, Kennedy Caldwell on rhythm guitar and boards, and Xander Mackenzie on drums. Guys this is Lucy Russo and Sera Manzini. We met a few years back in the Chicago airport of all places."

"That we did," Sera says with a grin. "I still have a magnificent picture of your ass on my cell."

Jesse throws back his head and laughs. "That doesn't surprise me. Not at all."

Sera shrugs. "Since Lucy was a bit wrapped up," she gives us a pointed look, "someone had to take the pictures. Memories and all that."

"Uh-huh," Ben says with a grin. "Sounds like spank bank pics to me."

"God," Sera says with a laugh. "Women don't have 'spank banks'."

"Then what is it you have, because we all know women rub them out just as much as guys do."

I laugh and mouth "rub them out" to Sera who laughs.

She nods. "We do. There's no denying it, but unlike most, Lucy and I have photographic memories."

"Enough said," Ben says with appreciation.

"And with the right vibrator, you don't even need an image—though I'm sure Lucy still conjures up Jesse after all this time."

"This is the oddest moment of my life," I say aloud to no one in particular.

"If you're done?" Cage asks, smiling.

Xander wiggles his eyebrows. "Damn, Cage. You got us our very own movie star and model."

"Dude," Ethan says and they fist bump.

I turn to face Cage and feel Jesse's hand rest on my lower back. Oh God. A shiver runs through me and I thank Gina in this moment for using those boob cup thingies so my hard nipples aren't poking through my top. Jesse begins circling his thumb and I'm ready to puddle at his feet. What is he doing?

Unh. I'm almost there to the unh stage.

I turn to look at him and he's looking at Cage, a falsely innocent look on his face.

"So, what's the plan Cage?" Jesse asks.

Cage outlines the overall storyboard for the shoot, then runs through the sequence it will be captured to minimize wardrobe and makeup changes.

"It should take a couple days, maybe more to get it just the way we want it."

"Cool," Xander says and taps his drumsticks together. "Let's get to it."

Chapter *four*

Lucy

The day was long and grueling and somehow Sera and I managed to get through it without doing the whole squealing fangirl thing. I even managed to avoid "unh". I'm pretty impressed with us if I do say so myself.

When I heard Jesse start singing, my heart dropped into my stomach. I swear it stopped for a minute before it kicked into high gear. Then when he touched me? Holy Mary Mother of God. Instant wet panties... well, thong. Thankfully I was able to change out of that shortly after we began. Cage decided to do the shortest of the takes first so what started out as a conservative outfit, turned into bootie shorts and tank tops cut low enough so our really pretty lacy bras were showing. Add to that the kick ass black boots, the heavy makeup, crazily styled hair (lightly sprayed thanks to Spenser's tricks) and we were kicking ass.

When the band began playing their new song *Back To Then* I almost stopped and stared instead of playing my part. Jesse noticed, smirked, and sent me a wink. The timing of that couldn't have been more perfect. As he winked, I winked back and leaned forward, touching my toes, my ass cheeks peeking out of my shorts—all part of the routine. I threw him a wicked grin over my shoulder and his nostrils flared. When we cut for a lighting adjustment, Ben walked up and smacked me on my ass with a laugh.

"That was awesome."

"Why, thank you. Thank you very much. The timing couldn't have been more perfect."

""You're not the same shy, frozen girl you were six years ago. I don't think my big brother was expecting that."

"It's different behind the camera. For me, anyway. I can be anyone they need me to be and today I'm a rockstar's girlfriend slash dancer."

He nods with a smile. "I smell trouble."

"Smells good, doesn't it?" I laugh. "Seriously, it's only a few days. How much trouble can we get into in that amount of time?"

Ben raises his eyebrows. "Watching you two? A whole fuck of a lot."

"It'll be fine."

"Girl," he says shaking his head. He never finishes the sentence as we take our places once again.

Now, after stripping off the slut-wear and unzipping and pulling off these seriously sexy but feet killing boots, I let out a moan and rub my aching feet. I change back into my comfy clothes, move to sit in this amazingly relaxing chair, just before setting my feet into a foot massage basin.

"I really, really love you Spenser."

"Oh, I know it, gorgeous."

"Not just for the foot massage or the fact that you spritzed me with each wardrobe change."

"Mhmm."

"But mostly because you didn't lacquer my hair and you never will. It's amazing that Simone can brush through this and whip my hair up into a bun like that without it being sticky. How do you do it?"

"I'll never tell."

"I want to hire you to go everywhere I go. I'll take you with me to every movie and tell them to fuck off with their makeup and hair people.

I'll have my Spenser."

"I'd follow you anywhere, Luce."

"I'm not kidding, Spenser. You have no idea what damage those… those… *people* do to my hair when we're filming."

"Oh, I see it and I wasn't kidding either."

"Seriously?" I perk up, nearly kicking water all over the floor.

"Seriously. But I'm not cheap."

"Well, that's a given. I'll pay you double. You're entirely worth it."

"Woman, you're crazy. You'd have had me at this rate."

"You're worth more than that to me. That means you, Simone, and you, Carmen, will be with us forever and ever and ever."

They cheer happily and Sera snorts out a snore. We all burst out laughing.

"Regina's going to be calling soon to talk me off the rocker ledge."

"Jump, Lucy. Do it. Just jump. You're an amazing actress, but your heart is music. I heard it and saw it when you sang."

"It's not that easy, Spense."

"It *is* that easy. You're a grown-ass woman now and your mother needs to back the fuck off. It's your life. Let her glam it up with Joey. That's all she needs. He's top tier."

"I know. I know. I don't understand why it's such a big deal."

"Control. She doesn't know shit about the music industry so she can't manage you there."

"Hmm. That's true. I don't have any movies lined up for a while. I'm taking a break. I was back to back for the last five years with only a short break in between. Except for this last one."

"What happened?"

"Aiden fucking Jensen happened."

"Don't even get her started," Sera says through a yawn.

"Well if it isn't Snorey McSnorelson."

"I was awake."

"You snort-snored."

She flits a hand in my direction. "We're going to do it, aren't we?"

"I want to but we need to see what there is out there for us first."

Sera nodded. "Irene will know. She's always got the hookup."

"That she does."

"I'm on hiatus until further notice from modeling."

I turn to her. "You didn't tell me that."

She shrugs. "It's not what I want to do. Sure, it's glamorous and makes me feel sexy but I want to eat a cream-filled donut. If I want to eat the entire pint of Ben & Jerry's Salted Caramel Core, then I'm going to eat the entire fucking thing."

"Damn right you are! You can have a fat ass like me."

"Cupcake, your ass is anything but fat."

I stare at Sera for a minute with wide eyes, then take a deep, calming breath.

"Jesse Kingston, what are you doing back here? We could have been naked," Sera says with a grin.

"A man can hope."

"How disappointing for you," I say with a grin.

"Not so much. You're still here."

I suck in a breath. Oh my. No. Yes. No. Oh my God. I wasn't prepared for Jesse Kingston today. I'm not prepared now. Truth be told, I will never be prepared for the hotness that is Jesse Kingston. What is he doing? Here. With me.

He flops into the chair next to mine and Ben strolls over to the sofa. Next come Kennedy, Ethan, and Xander.

"Sera?"

"Yeah, Luce?"

"Why? Why is it they come back here when we've just gotten our makeup scrubbed off and our hair thrown up in messy buns while we sport our yoga pants and t-shirts? We looked fucking amazing no more than ten minutes ago."

Sera lets out a loud sigh. "It's our curse."

I nod and press my lips together. "We have a lot of curses."

"True story," Sera murmurs.

The guys just stare like we're freak shows.

"Stop staring! I know I look like shit, okay? Makeup-less Lucy isn't a great sight to behold."

"Oh, I don't know," Xander says. "I think you look just as hot without makeup as you do with it. Maybe hotter since it's real."

Jesse lets out a growl and my eyes widen. Xander grins and Ben winks at me.

"Did he just growl?"

Ben winks again.

"Well, thank you Xander for the compliment. That's very sweet of you to say."

"Great shirt," Ethan tells me with a wink.

"Thanks. Deftones put on an amazing concert."

"Avenged Sevenfold?"

"Yeah baby."

"Nice."

"M. Shadows is so damn sexy."

"Oh my God," Sera moans. "There are no words. M. Shadows," she says with reverence and I grin.

"Mmm," I groan, leaning back in my chair, wiggling my toes.

"Is that a moan for M. Shadows or do you have sore feet?" Jesse asks.

"Sore feet. Killer boots."

Jesse places a towel on his lap then lifting one of my feet and massaging.

I close my eyes and moan out loud. His hands still. "Oh, don't stop. That feels so good."

He starts rubbing again and everyone in the room starts laughing.

"Shut up. I know what it sounded like and I just don't care."

I peek through one eye at Jesse and he grins. I close the eye again and just relax into my chair.

"Your hands are amazing."

Silent pause.

"Again, I know what it sounded like. Get your minds out of the gutter. You all can see he's rubbing my *feet*. Pervs."

"Yeah, pervs," Jesse says with a hint of laughter in his voice.

"Don't think I don't know you're smiling over there, Kingston."

"Oh, hell yeah I'm smiling. I'm thinking if this is the kind of reaction I get when I'm rubbing your feet, what kind of reaction am I going to get when you're naked and underneath me."

"Hmm. You're assuming a lot with that statement."

"How so?"

"First, you're assuming I'm ever going to be naked when you're around. Second, you're assuming you'd be on top. Third, you're assuming you'd be able to touch me in such a way that would cause me to moan as I did when you rubbed my sore, overworked feet."

"First, I've no doubt I'm going to see you naked, it's a matter of when. Second, the first time I'm definitely going to be on top, after that we'll play it by ear. Third, I guarantee I can make you moan longer and louder than you just did *and* you'll be screaming my name."

The first time? Wow. Screaming his name... I'm all for that if he's inside me while I'm doing it.

Sera snickers, Spenser lets out a frustrated noise, and the guys are murmuring amongst themselves.

"Hmm. Guess we'll have to wait and see but I'm not going to bet the ranch."

He stops rubbing and taps my shin so I'll look at him.

"Challenge accepted, Cupcake."

"Do you realize you just laid down a challenge to Jesse Kingston?"
"I didn't. He just took it as one."
"Same thing, Luce."

"I'm not worried about it. We're only on set a few days and I doubt we're going to find ourselves in a situation where any of that will be possible. Besides, he was just saying those things because everyone was there and he wanted to best me."

"You didn't see his face."

I shrug. "Again, not worried."

"I sure as hell would be. We're talking *the* Jesse Kingston."

"Besides, why are they being all friendly with us? The bands have never done that with us before. It's just surreal."

"Did you ever stop to think they might think you're a big deal?"
"No."

"You should. Hollywood actress appearing in their video? It's got to be a major deal for them."

"Meh, maybe. But I'm really no one. Just some chick doing a job."

Sera nods. "And they're just guys, doing their job. But due to fame and the hype that goes with it, you all think the other is a big fucking deal."

"I am certainly not a BFD."

"You are to them."

I shrug and my phone rings. "Why did I have to let you drive home? If I drove I wouldn't have to answer this call from Regina."

"Just get it over with."

"Yeah." I sigh. "Hey mom."

"How was your shoot?"

"It was good. A lot of fun."

"What band did Cage pick for you this time?"

I bite my lip knowing my mom is going to know this is a huge deal for me the minute she hears the name but there is no talking around this one.

"Falling Down."

Silent pause. "Isn't that Jesse Kingston's band?"

"Yep."

"The one you've had a crush on since seventh grade?"

"Mother. That was a long time ago."

"Hmm. Was it? I remember your reaction when we ran into him in Chicago. Don't think I've missed the fact you've also gone to multiple concerts of his as well."

"Their music is fucking awesome mom." I throw the F-bomb in to piss her off a bit.

"Luciana Antonia Russo. Watch your language."

"Yes, mama." I grin at Sera who grins back.

"Now, tell me, what you have lined up next."

"Nothing."

Another silent pause. "What do you mean?"

"I'm taking a break and so is Sera."

Again, silence. "You realize you're doing this at a time when your career is just skyrocketing. This could potentially lose the momentum you've just gained."

"I'm aware of that. After the last movie with Aiden Jensen, I need a break. It was a nightmare, mama. I am not exaggerating. Even Mel lost it."

"Well, that's saying something then, isn't it? Mel's the most laid back director I've ever met."

"I know! I'm telling you, mama, it was the worst. I was stressed out nonstop. My hair started falling out again."

"Oh Luciana. Did you start taking your vitamins again?"

"I have." God, I hated this job.

"That's good then. Hopefully being away from that situation your body will recover quickly."

"I hope so. I don't want to be a patchy baldy twenty-three year old."

Sera snorts out a laugh and my mother tsks.

"You all think I'm kidding. You've seen it, Sera."

"I have. I admit. It wasn't pretty, mama." I love that Sera calls my mom, mama. She is, after all, like a sister to me.

"I think I found a way to fix that problem though."

"Oh? How is that?" my mom asks.

"I hired Spenser and his two assistants."

"Oh!" My mother shouts out a girlie happy sound. "I'm so happy. Spenser is the most amazing artist."

"That he is and he doesn't lacquer me."

"You're so hung up on that."

"Mother, why do you think my hair fucking falls out?"

"Language, Luciana."

"Yes, mama."

Sera sends me a grin and I grin back. We're such bratty daughters.

"I'm glad everything is going well for you both. We'll discuss this hiatus again later in the week. I need to call Joey and see how his movie is coming along."

"He's likely in the middle of filming, mom. It's only a little after four here."

"True. That gives me time to run down and have some coffee and pastries. Talk to you soon darlings. I love you."

"Love you too," we both murmur into the phone and I press the End button.

I lean back into the car seat and turn my head to Sera.

She glances at me out of the corner of her eye. "What?"

"Jesse fucking Kingston, Sera. Can you believe this? Falling Down. This is insane."

She nods and smiles. "Feels kind of like a dream, right?"

I nod and we're both silent and lost in our own thoughts.

It does feel like a dream, but it's real. Shit.

"Jesse fucking Kingston."

Chapter
five

Lucy

"We're going clubbing, right?"

I groan at Sera. My feet are killing me from dancing in those damn leather boots. I'm just glad I get a wardrobe change tomorrow and those boots can be history. Honestly, those boots are hot. They would be great boots for normal outings and things like that, but to dance in for hours while making a rock video? Not so much.

"Seraaaaa," I whine.

She sits down next to me where I've flopped out on our sofa.

"I'll let you wear the Jimmy Choo's."

"The black Mary Jane's?"

She nods. Damn her.

"You fight dirty."

"I know. It's a gift. Chinese for supper?"

"Yeah. The usual."

"Okay, I'll call it in now. That'll give us time to shower before they get here."

"I'm not showering. I'm sitting in my Jacuzzi bath and soaking my tootsies."

"Poor baby."

"Fuck off. You got to wear strappy sandals that had padding." I pause. "Whore."

She laughs. "It's not my fault."

"Whatever. It's always your fault."

"I know, I know. Whereas my bribing skills are a gift, things always being my fault, is a curse."

"Damn straight it is," I say as I hobble toward my bathroom.

I turn on the water, adjusting for temperature and pour in some bath salts. Yes, they are the effervescent kind. And yes, the bubbles feel amazing. I'm worked up, I admit this. I mean, hello! Jesse Kingston just talked about getting on top of me and making me scream out his name. Seriously. I'm in need of an orgasm and self-induced is my only option right now. This is why I have a waterproof vibrator. His name is Raul and he never lets me down. With Raul I'm guaranteed multiple orgasms every single time.

Twenty minutes and two toe-curling orgasms later (thank you Raul) I'm slipping on my robe when I hear the doorbell. I'm so hungry I might just eat the entire quart of moo goo gai pan. I snag one of the vegetable egg rolls and moan aloud as I take a bite. I didn't eat much for lunch—I never do when I'm on set. I'd rather be hungry than eat too much and feel sick or actually puke all over the place.

"Cage and the guys are going to meet us at Sunset."

I pause my chewing. "By 'guys' you mean Jesse Kingston-type guys? Falling Down-type guys?"

Sera nods and smirks. Oh boy.

"How is this my life?" So much for not being in a situation where I've got to worry about the challenging rockstar hottie. I'm honestly not sure I'm up for this. I mean, I am but we have to work together for a few more days at least and I don't want to be all flustered around him. I get pretty nervous around guys I have to work with after I've slept with them. I'm not sure why. I guess my ideal one-nighter is just that—one night and then never having to see them again. I learned early on in my career to not sleep with my costars.

It's eight o'clock and I'm in a simple black and pink spaghetti-strap tank top, black Capri pants, and Sera's black Mary Jane's. These are the most comfortable pair of three-inch heels I've ever encountered, with the red strappy sandals I wore at the shoot today coming in a close second. My lip curls as I remember the torturous boots.

Whenever we go out, we always have someone drive us (that'd be Max—we love Max) and we never go anywhere without a bodyguard. You just never know. My bodyguard's name is Frank. He's a very large man. He's a good six-four and over two hundred-fifty pounds of solid muscle. He's got a beautiful face to match his beautiful body but don't make the mistake of thinking because he's pretty that he's soft. Frank will do what he needs to do to keep me and Sera safe no matter what. He's a very sweet thirty-something-year-old married father of two. He adores his family and I'm happy that we have him as part of ours. None of my employees are considered "staff". They are family.

We walk into the club and it's pretty packed for a Tuesday.

"Let's grab a drink and see if we can find Cage," Sera says.

I nod and follow behind her. I get stopped by a group of college kids who ask me for my autograph and some pictures. I wave Sera off when she looks back. I don't mind taking time for the fans, after all they take time to come see my movies, right? I like letting them know I appreciate them and their support.

After about fifteen minutes, Frank steps up signaling the autograph session is over, as is our routine, and I smile and thank everyone. Frank follows discretely to the bar where I order a Captain and diet Coke. I ignore the stares from the onlookers. I'm not that big of a deal. Honestly. I've been in a couple movies. So what? I'm just a person like they are, which is why I don't understand why everyone blows things up to "celebrity status". Now I understand why Milo Ventimiglia said he's not a celebrity, he's a working actor. I ascribe to that very same philosophy.

I pay for my drink and turn to see Sera waving me over to the dance floor.

"I'll be right over here, Luce."

"Thanks Frank."

He winks and nods.

Sera and I start shaking our asses as Enrique starts singing about dirty dancers. I swivel my hips and roll my body. Sera and I are laughing as we let ourselves go. Honestly we don't let ourselves go very often, but we need to blow off some steam.

The music segues into Push It and I grin. I set my now empty glass on a nearby table and Sera sends me a wink.

I barely start dancing again when I feel a pair of very large, masculine hands wrap around my waist. I know who it is without looking. I can smell him—ocean, sandalwood, and yum. It is trouble in the form of one sexy rocker. How do I know? I know because Sera's laughing, or she was until Ben walked toward her.

Ben was right earlier, he did smell trouble. He just didn't tell me it was with a capital T.

They must have some pretty great security with them if they're not being mobbed. Jesse presses himself close, wrapping his arms around me, his hands resting on my lower abdomen. He leans in and whispers, "You look fucking hot, Lucy."

I grin and wiggle my hips and slide down his body to a crouch, then touch my toes, straightening my legs and lifting my ass up against his ever-growing erection before slowly sliding my hands up my body as I stand up fully. I turn my head to look into his amazing face. Yeah, same move as earlier today and it worked again. Jesse's seriously sexy—all tall, dark, and dangerous. He is a bad boy personified and I couldn't be more turned on.

Ciara and Justin Timberlake take over next singing about love and sex and magic. This song could have been written about Jesse Kingston. Women fall in love with him, have sex with him, and they think he's magical. I may be tempted by two of the three. Love isn't in the cards for me. I'm not looking for anything too serious, which is a good thing because Jesse Kingston doesn't do relationships.

He turns me around and lifts one of my legs up toward his hip, grinding his hard cock against my belly, sliding his leg between mine as he pulls me tight against him, hands on my hips, guiding me to circle my hips with his. I slowly slide my hands up his chest, pausing when I feel the nipple rings. That's seriously sexy. I look up at him through my lashes. He is, of course, grinning. I run my fingertips over the rings, gently tugging on them and he groans aloud. After that, the music fades out and all I hear is my heavy breathing.

My hands continue their ascent to rest on his chest. I'm not tall enough to wrap them around his neck. His thigh rubs between my legs with every swivel of my hips. I raise my arms, arching my back I lift my hair up off the back of my neck, then slowly let it fall back down as I ride his thigh the same way I would ride his cock.

He's not grinning now. Oh no, there's no grin. He is the poster boy for sex and sin. His eyes darken to the color of chocolate, his lids slightly closed. I step closer to him again, standing on tiptoe to try and reach him. He bends slightly and I trace my index fingertip over his lips, his lip ring, my mouth parting as I do.

His mouth opens and I slide my finger inside. He licks then sucks it gently into his mouth. I very slowly pull it out. My gaze flicks up to his and there is no doubt in my mind he wants me. Given the chance, if we weren't in public with everyone watching us, he'd probably fuck me right here—and I'd let him. I get even wetter at that thought. I'm sure he feels the heat and maybe even the wetness between my legs but I'm too turned on to care.

He tucks me in close, his hand on the back of my neck pulling my head to his chest and I note the music has slowed down. His heart beats furiously beneath my ear, I can feel it on my cheek and I know mine is beating just as fast.

Do I want Jesse Kingston? Yes, yes I do. Does it go against my rules of no sex while working with someone? Yep, it does. Am I going to ignore that rule tonight? This is, again, Jesse fucking Kingston. The man I've been lusting after since seventh grade. The man who took a little piece of my heart in that airport six years ago. The man who is now running his fingertips up and down my spine and nibbling on my ear. My answer is a resounding *you betcha baby*.

He pulls back a bit then dips down to press a kiss to my forehead. My eyes close of their own volition. He takes advantage and presses light kisses to each eyelid, then to the tip of my nose. Next, one kiss to each cheek, my jawline, my chin until finally he slowly and softly presses his lips against mine.

All breath and rational thinking leave my body. I swear I feel my brain short circuit. If someone were to ask me what two plus two was right now I wouldn't be able to answer. The kiss is no more than a flutter at first. He takes my bottom lip between both of his and sucks gently, the metal of his lip ring biting into my bottom lip I let out a moan as his hands come up to cup my face.

He tilts his head ever so slightly and takes my lips in a breath-stealing kiss. His tongue slides along the seam, demanding me to open to him. There is no room for argument. I know he will accept nothing less than my full submission to his request. I open for him and his tongue slides against mine. I push closer to him, wrapping my arms around his waist, pulling him closer to me as he slowly and thoroughly fucks my mouth with his tongue. It is exquisite. It is bone melting. It is everything I imagined it would be and more.

We kiss and kiss and kiss for what feels like forever when it hasn't been more than a few minutes. He whispers against my lips something I can't hear. I don't think I'm supposed to.

With his hands still cupping my cheeks, he looks directly into my eyes. I'm not sure what he's looking for but whatever it is I'm pretty sure he finds it. His lips come down hard, his tongue dueling with mine as we sway slowly to whatever the hell song is playing. I'm losing myself in him and it feels delicious. I'm not going to lie to myself or to Jesse. I want him. In a very bad way. I'm sure by my responses to him he's already figured that out by now. Just in case he hasn't I whisper to him that I do.

He kisses along my jawline to my neck, up to my ear. Oh God. Behind my ear. My secret spot and he zeroes right in on it. I shiver and I feel his lips curve into a smile against my skin. He sucks gently on my skin then kisses his way back until his mouth meets mine once again.

I'm floating and it feels amazing. I give way to my body, my lust, my desire. I drag my fingernails down his back and he groans into my mouth. And that's when it happens.

A flash. Then another and another and another.

"Shit," I whisper against his lips.

He runs a hand through his hair. "God damn it."

Frank comes walking up, telling the patrons to put their cameras away but the damage is already done. I can already see the headlines. *Straight-Laced Actress And Bad-Boy Rocker Get It On, On The Dance Floor.* Shit. Shit, shit, shit.

"I have to go, Jesse."

"I know. Hand me your phone, Luce." His fingers fly over the screen then he hands it back to me and digs his own out of his pocket.

"You've got my number and I've got yours. Use it."

I tilt my head to the side unsure what he wants of me. I step up on tiptoe and he leans down to meet me for a quick, soft kiss.

"I'm sorry," I whisper.

Before I fully pull away he whispers in my ear, "Next time we're doing this in private where no one can interrupt us and I can get you naked."

His words send a shiver through my body and he winks as I pull back, letting Frank lead me and Sera out of the now insanely rowdy crowd. Frank must have called in backup because there are two more men flanking us and the car's already pulled up to the curb.

We all get into the car and I flop back with a sigh.

"God damn it!" I shout. No one bats an eyelash at my outburst. They know how much I hate the invasion of my privacy, the gossip, the bullshit. I blame my mother for this. Sure I'd have to deal with some of the same if I'd gone the musical route but nothing like I have to deal with now, as an actress.

"That fucking sucked, Luce."

"Ya think?"

Sera raises a brow.

Frank hands me a bottle of water and I take a long drink.

"Sorry. I'm just… fed the fuck up with this life."

"It could have been worse. At least there weren't many paps outside."

"Doesn't matter at this point and you know it. Those pics will be sold and online within the hour with some sleazy headline to go along with them."

"It's not that bad." Frank tells me, trying to reassure me.

I give Frank a bland look. "Frank. You saw us. It was far from innocent. I lost myself."

He nods. "You never let loose like that."

"I know. I just—"

"Oh for fuck's sake," Sera said. "It's Jesse Kingston! Who wouldn't lose themselves in that hot, delicious hunk of man, especially if they've been crushing on him forever?"

"True, but the world doesn't need to know about it. Or see it."

"But they will. And that means Reggie's going to be calling."

I nod to Sera. "And with her being, what, nine hours difference this'll hit the internet just in time for her Google alert to go off during her breakfast."

"You're an adult."

"I am. And, as I keep saying, I'm tired of this life." I turn to Sera. "I'm giving up the acting. I can't do this life anymore. Maybe if it's some amazing part and we aren't touring or making music or recording, but other than that I'm done and Regina's going to have to learn to deal with it."

Sera lets out a whoop.

I reach out to take Frank's hand. "Will you stay with us, Frank? If I switch things up a bit?"

His hand squeezes mine. "I'm not going anywhere and neither will Max, Gio, or Mike. We're family." They nod their agreement.

"I love every one of you and appreciate you more than you know."

"Baby girl, we know." This comes from Mike who barely ever speaks.

I'm about to get all sappy and mushy when my phone rings.

"Wow, that's got to be a record." I look at my watch. "Only thirty minutes and she's already circling on her broomstick. There had to be a plant in there. There's no way they could have gotten the story and pics up that fast without putting someone in there or paying them off outside before they came in."

"Likely," Frank nods. "You gonna answer that?"

I didn't answer it the first time she called and she's calling right back.

"I suppose."

I press Talk.

"Good morning, mother." I hold the phone away from my ear knowing full well she's going to say all three of my names very loudly.

"Luciana Antonia Russo. What have you done now?" She then breaks into a stream of Italian, which, unbeknownst to her, I fully understand.

She's calling me a foolish girl. Something about my crush on the dirty rockstar. Dirty! He's not dirty. She's got some nerve.

"Are you done yet?" I ask blandly.

"Don't you take that tone with me, young lady."

"In case you've forgotten, I'm twenty-three years old. That makes me an adult. That means I can take any damn tone I want. I am tired of this Regina. I am done."

"Regina? This is how you speak to your mother?"

"Right now it is because you're not my mother right now. You're my manager."

A pause. Frank raises his eyebrows. "What are you done with exactly, Luciana?"

"Acting. I'm finished."

She laughs. "Darling, you're just upset about the reporters again and right after you've had such a hard time with Aiden Jensen." She tsks. "Your father is here."

"Hi Button."

"Hi daddy."

"You okay?"

I sigh. "I will be."

"You indulged yourself tonight and now the media will have a field day but it will die down in a couple of days and things will be back to normal." My mother. Always trying to rationalize me into agreeing and doing whatever she says.

I move the phone to my other ear.

"You don't understand, Regina. I. Am. Done. Acting. No more movies. No more television shows. No more anything. Done. Done, done, done."

"You can't mean that. Your career is at its peak right now."

"Then it'll take a long time for it to plummet to the bottom, right? I can't do it anymore, mom. I just can't. I never wanted to act. I did it because it made you happy, but I'm a grown woman and I need to do what makes me happy before I'm old and gray and miserable."

"Luciana—"

My father cuts her off. "Enough Regina. Are you sure this is what you want to do, Button?"

"It is. You know I've wanted this for a long time."

"Yes, we know. And you're correct. You are an adult. This is your life so these are your decisions to make." My mother tries to interrupt him and he shushes her. "You do what makes you happy, Button. We will support you in your decisions."

My mother is cursing in Italian. I just know my father is giving her "the look" because she immediately shuts up. I want to laugh, but I'm sure that won't go over well.

"Luciana, you and Serafina are set on doing this rock thing?"

"We are mama."

She sighs. "Then I will do what I can to help you if you wish for me to continue being your manager."

"We do—until we find one we can trust who knows the music industry. But no decisions for us, mama. Sera and I make our own decisions and will consult you in any major ones we need to make."

My father says something to her I can't hear.

"Fine," she huffs. "I'll notify Irene and she will have to draw up new contracts and one for Serafina as well."

"We'll meet with her whenever they're ready. Just have her give me a call."

"I will."

"Thank you both for supporting this decision. Sera and I just want to do what makes us happy."

"And that is why I'm not fighting you on the decision."

"That and the fact that daddy's right there."

She grumbles. "He is very demanding. But I knew this day would come sooner or later. To be honest I'm surprised it took this long. I'll call you in a couple of days. Maybe if you get the band together soon you could work on a soundtrack for one of Joey's movies."

"Maybe, mama. We'll see where this goes. We don't even have a full band yet."

"You will. I have faith. Take care of yourselves."

"You as well. I love you both."

"We love you too."

The call ends and I sit there for a minute or two just staring at my phone.

Without looking up I ask, "Did that just happen?"

"Yep," Sera says.

"That was too easy."

"That's because dad was there."

I snicker. "That certainly did help. She would have tried to talk us out of it if he hadn't been. He saved us about an hour of unnecessary chatter."

"That he did."

I look to Sera and she's already looking at me.

"We're going to do this. For real."

"For real."

"It's time," I say and we start squealing like high school girls. Frank and the guys smirk—they very rarely full-on smile or laugh but this is one time when they cave and enjoy the moment with us.

Everything from earlier with the press slips away from my mind as we celebrate our new path. This is one of the happiest moments of my life and I intend to enjoy it.

Chapter
six

Lucy

"Hey, hey I wanna be a rockstar," Sera sings as she walks into the kitchen.

"A little Nickelback for breakfast?" I ask with a grin.

She twirls in a circle. "I'm so happy right now, Luce. We get to start living our dream."

"I know," I say. I can't stop grinning. I have been all morning. I barely slept last night. I was too excited.

"We should ask Jace if he wants to play with us."

"You know he'll be on the next plane out, Sera."

She picks up her phone and calls him. "I'll book his ticket. He can stay here. I'll let Max and Frank know."

She nods. "Jace! Mr. Sexiness! How would you feel about starting up a band with me and Luce?" Pause. "It's for real." Pause. "No shit. For real." Pause. "Luce is on her laptop waiting to hear how soon you can get away and—" She laughs. "Book it. Soonest you can get."

I laugh. "I love you Jace!" I yell.

"He loves you too and he says it's about fucking time, woman."

I nod. "I know."

I've never been this alive at six in the morning. Well, not including the day after I met Jesse in Chicago. That was… yeah.

"Wait a second, Sera," I say as an idea takes over my brain. I walk over to where she's standing. "Speaker please. Hey Jace."

"What's up sexy Lucy?"

"I'm wondering, what about Luther and Tommy? Do you think they'll want to join us?"

"I'm not sure. Luther's got a steady girl and Tommy's married with a baby on the way."

I'm a little disappointed but I understand.

"No worries. We'll find someone to fill the spots. I'm not sure how, but we'll get it done."

"Hello!" Sera says. "We have connections to Jesse Kingston. He'll help. I'm sure of it."

"I can't ask him to do that."

"Why the hell not? You heard them yesterday. They want us to do this."

"True. Okay, I'll see what he says. I'll talk to him and Cage together today. I'm so excited to see you Jace!"

"We're going to rock the hell out of it, you know this, right Luce?"

"I know it," I nod to Sera.

"Anything you can't take on the plane that you want to bring, box it up. I'll have someone come take care of it for you."

"Thanks Luce."

"You betcha baby. Just pick up your ticket at the counter. You're all set. I paid for extra luggage so you can bring an extra bag."

"Woman, I'm not like you and Sera."

I laugh. "I know, but this is forever, Jace."

He pauses. "Forever."

"I've got to get in the shower but I'll see you tonight. Max will be there to pick you up."

"Thanks, both of you. Not just for the ticket or the car, but for including me."

"You're the best bass guitarist we know," Sera says. "There's no one we want more."

"Cool."

"I'm off," I say as I head toward the shower before I start to cry. Our dream is starting to come true.

When we get on set, we're met by an extremely enthusiastic Spenser.

"What's up, Spense?"

"What's up?" he asks incredulously. "Are you fucking with me right now, Luciana Russo?"

I just stare.

"You haven't seen the internet or turned on a television, have you?"

"Oh shit," Sera says.

"Uh, no." Shit. Last night. Club Sunset. Flashes. Paparazzi. Me and Jesse. Mmm, me and Jesse. A familiar ache settles between my thighs as I remember how it felt to touch and kiss him.

"Come with me," he pulls me along with him, Sera following on our heels. He heads to an office and turns on the television. It's seven-thirty and all the morning news and talk shows are just getting started and there we are. The first channel.

Me and Jesse pressed as tightly together as we can be, my arms around his waist, my nails digging into his back. His hands are cupping my face, his thigh between my legs. Jesus. We look as hot as it felt.

"They're speculating. No one has any idea what's going on between you two or how you connected," Spenser says.

"After all that last night, we went home and grabbed our stuff and we stayed at a hotel. We didn't have to deal with the paps but you can bet your ass they're camped out at our front gate," Sera says with an arch of her brow.

"Well, hell. We need to change it up for Jace. He can't go to the house. I won't subject him to that."

"He can stay at the hotel with us. We booked the entire floor."

I nod at Sera and put a call in to Max and Frank.

I glance at the computer and see Spenser has pulled up a video of me and Jesse. A video. Holy God.

I make a strangled noise and Sera tells Spenser to play it. It starts from the beginning of my dance with Jesse and ends with the flash. It's the entire thing. It's sexy and it's hot and I want to do it again.

"Oh my God," I breathe out.

"It's sexy as hell," Spenser exclaims.

"Hell yeah it is," Jesse says from behind me. I whip around to see him leaning against the doorframe, arms crossed over his chest, feet crossed at the ankles. He appears to be completely relaxed, rather blasé about the whole bullshit media gossipfest.

I huff. "Honestly Jesse."

One side of his mouth lifts in a smirk.

"Don't you smirk at me."

So he does.

"I can't help it. This is amusing. You're amusing."

"I'm amusing. Are you kidding me right now?"

"Lucy, you're taking this too seriously."

I tamp down my temper. Too seriously, he says. I narrow my eyes.

"Oh hell, Jesse. Now you did it," Sera says.

"What?"

"Her eyes are narrowed, her nostrils are flaring, her lips are thinned out. She's pissed. She's going to blow any second."

"She can—"

"You better not go there right now, hot stuff," Sera tells him with a laugh.

"You're probably right."

I take a deep breath. "So you saw the video, then?"

He nods.

"You know what?"

He looks like he's unsure whether he should respond or not. Sera, knowingly, stays quiet as does Spenser. Jesse follows their lead.

"For as hot and wet as I was last night on the dance floor, we should have just fucked right there."

Sera laughs, Spenser coughs, and Jesse's eyes darken.

"Perhaps we should have."

I shrug. "We may as well have. The only difference would be if we were naked because we were all but fucking in that video."

Jesse steps forward, tucking a strand of hair behind my ear. "Lucy, trust me. If we were fucking you'd know it. I'd be buried so deep inside of you, you wouldn't know where you ended and I began, and I can guarantee it wouldn't be over as quickly as that dance was."

I lick my lips and more moisture gathers between my thighs. His lips are hovering just over mine and I am severely tempted to kiss him right here, shove Sera and Spenser out the door, and have Jesse Kingston fuck me up against the wall.

He smirks as if he knows what I'm thinking and I lift a brow. He winks then leans in and presses a soft kiss to my lips. "Soon."

"Not soon enough," Spenser says. "Jesus, you two. Even I need a cold shower after that."

"And Lucy's going to need some dry panties," Sera blurts out.

Jesse's smile grows.

"Do we need to do damage control?"

I shrug. "Nope. I really don't care anymore. I just hate my personal life being scrutinized, speculated, and dissected."

He nods. "The life of a movie star."

"That's not—," Sera says with a smile until I cut her off, shaking my head. Out comes the award-winning Serafina Manzini pout.

"Awww, why not?"

"Later. We need to get ready or Cage is going to get cranky. You know very well that a cranky Cage is not a good thing."

"True enough," she responds.

"Jesse, can I talk to you later? Not about," I wave a hand at the television and computer, "that but something else."

"Of course."

I nod, my gaze unable to move from his lips. "I've got to go."

He nods. I start to stand up on tiptoe and he meets me halfway for a lingering touching of our lips. He pulls back and rests his forehead against mine.

"This is so going to complicate things."

"I hope so," he says with a pat on my ass. "Now go get ready."

I squeal when he smacks my ass again and laughs. I grin the whole way to hair and makeup. I lick my lips, savoring his taste. Oh boy. Jesse Kingston.

The day is long and tiring. We get through a lot of filming and I'm ready to get back into my yoga pants.

"You said you wanted to talk about something?" Jesse asks.

"Yeah. Actually," I say looking round. "Cage? Guys? Can Sera and I talk to you all in say, twenty minutes? I'd like to wash the mask off my face and get out of this ridiculous leather dress."

"It's fucking hot," Kennedy says. It's the first time he's ever directly spoken to me and I thought he was mute or just hated me.

I laugh. "Thanks. It really is hot. It's making me sweat under my boobs and that's just gross."

He laughs. "Too much information, girlie."

I nod. "Twenty minutes?"

They all murmur their agreement.

Sera jumps up and down a bit as we walk back to the changing room. "We're really doing this. I can't believe it," she says twirling in a circle.

"We are." And I'm scared shitless. What if we suck? What if we fail? What if we can't find decent band members? What if the ones we choose get hooked on drugs? What will the rules on the bus be if we tour? There is so much to think about and my brain is overloading.

"Stop it," Sera snaps.

"What?"

"You know what. Knock it off. We haven't even gotten started yet and you're freaking out about shit you don't need to be freaking out about."

She knows me so well.

"Unh."

"Oh boy. You're 'unh'-ing?"

"I'd 'eh' but people make fun of us for doing that."

"Valid."

"You've been reading Jay McLean again, haven't you?"

"I have. Logan Matthews is such an asshole hottie. I can't get enough."

"Agreed."

I stand behind the changing partition and slip off the heat suctioning torture device known as a black leather dress and breathe a sigh of relief. Then I proceed to stomp on it.

"Gross."

"What?" Sera asks.

"Boob sweat. I need a washcloth."

"Well go get one."

"I'm naked and I'm not putting that sweat trap back on."

There's a knock on the other side of the partition and I gasp, pulling the leather up to cover my nakedness.

There's a low chuckle from the other side and then a hand appears at the top with a wet washcloth.

"Oh my God."

"Yeah, you'll be saying that to me a lot, Cupcake."

"I can't reach, can you just drop it?"

"Sure."

The washcloth drops and I catch it, dropping the dress and washing beneath, around, and all over my breasts.

"This feels amazing. God, Jesse, you have no idea."

He chuckles again. "You'll be saying that a lot too, but I'll have an idea because I'll be making it happen."

I snort. I don't bother to deny it. I am definitely going to be sharing some fucktastic moments with Jesse Kingston. What red-blooded woman with a pulse would deny herself that pleasure? Certainly not this one.

I pull on my sports bra, yoga pants and t-shirt then sit on the bench with my shoes and socks.

"It's safe to come back here now."

Jesse comes around the side and eyes the leather dress on the ground.

"Did you trample it?"

"Yes," I say with venom.

He smiles. "Why?"

"It sucked all the fluids out of my body and pushed them on and around my boobs and any crevices it could find. It's made of evil."

He chuckles. "That bad?"

"And then some." I tie my second shoe and sit up. I meet his gaze, there's humor there. "Sure, sure, laugh it up at my expense. It's all fun and games until I'm dehydrated and pass out and need you to resuscitate me."

"Oh baby, I'll resuscitate you anytime you want."

"Pig."

"Oink."

I laugh. "See? This is why."

"Why what?"

"This," I say waving my hand around, "is why I think you're cute."

"There's way more to it than that, Lucy. Stop lying to yourself. It'll make things easier in the end."

"What things?"

"You accepting that you're mine."

My eyes widen. "Yours?" I squeak.

He nods, lips pressed together in a thin line.

"You don't seem too happy about it." I hop in the chair and Spenser helps me take off my makeup.

"I wasn't happy about it six years ago in Chicago and I'm not happy about it now."

"I have no idea what you're talking about."

He grunts and I wipe makeup from my face, just quietly thinking of nothing.

"You do. You felt it just as I did in Chicago. I saw it."

"That was a fangirl crush, Jesse."

"Nope. It was more and you can deny it all you want."

"I won't deny my attraction to you."

"That's a good thing. You're sexy as hell so we're on an even playing field."

"As far as that's concerned, yes."

"I figure we'll just fuck it out," he says and I laugh. Spenser snorts. I laugh hard, so hard I'm doubled over. I snort in a very unladylike manner and Sera comes over.

"What's so funny?"

Jesse shrugs and I point at him, tears running down my cheeks I'm laughing so hard. Oh God, it's hurting my stomach.

"Fuck it out," I say and fall off the chair onto the floor laughing. Jesse narrows his eyes then slides down, his legs on either side of my hips, grabbing my arms, pinning them above my head.

I try to stop laughing, I really do, but giggles keep bubbling up. He's not pleased that I found his statement funny.

"I'm sorry, Jesse," I say, trying to catch my breath. "It's just… the way you said it." I giggle again.

He lowers his face to within an inch of mine. "I guarantee you, Luce, you won't be laughing when you're naked beneath me—not unless I want you to. You'll be moaning and writhing and clawing up my back and shoulders. You'll be calling out my name as I make you come over and over again with my fingers, my tongue, and my cock."

All laughter has fled and I instantly get wet just from his words.

"Jesus."

He nods. "You'll be calling for him too."

Oh yeah, it'd be easy to get lost in Jesse Kingston but I can't allow that. I know all about guys like him, where their cocks fucking rule their world, where emotion doesn't enter into the equation. Been there, done that, don't want a repeat.

"Not so funny, now is it?"

I pause. He really is full of himself and taking a whole lot for granted. Yeah, I think he's hot as hell and I've wanted him for a long time, but his? I don't think so. I belong to *me*. He can play that game with his little groupie whores.

"You're mine and it's not a joke."

"I don't even know what that means."

"Neither do I, but we'll see how it plays out, yeah?"

"Yeah, I don't think so," I say as panic fills my chest. I push him off of me and stand up. "Nope. No. Can't do that." Can't allow that. I grab a wet towel and finish washing my face.

"What?"

The shock is evident on his face and I hide my panic and shrug.

"The whole fangirl crush thing I had going on when I was younger? Sure it's still there and I'd be lying if I said I didn't want you in my bed. But yours?" I shake my head.

"Yeah, *mine*."

"I'm pretty happy being just me."

He just stares. I see disbelief, anger, and frustration in his gaze. Good. Not every woman is going to bow down to him. He's not used to the word 'no', that much is evident. That's probably because this is Jesse Kingston. Rockstar extraordinaire. Player. Manwhore. He can have anyone he wants and usually does, only this time he wants me… as his? I don't think so. That'd be a very big mistake.

"If that's how you want this to go, I'll play along."

"Jesse, this isn't a game."

"Sounds like you're making it one."

"No. *You* are making it one. We barely know one another."

"So what? We'll get to know one another—in and out of bed."

"How do you propose we do that when we have one more day on this shoot and then we go our separate ways?"

"We'll figure it out."

I shake my head. "I'm not going to deny my attraction to you. That's just stupid, but that's it. Attraction, lust, want, desire. That's all."

"You keep telling yourself that, Lucy."

"It's the truth."

"Uh-huh."

Frustrating, arrogant, egotistical rockstar!

"They're waiting for us. We need to go," he says as he grabs my hand, pulling me down the hallway. Spenser laughs behind us. What the hell? As we near the conference room, I struggle to pull my hand out of his and he just clings.

"Let go."

"I don't think so."

"Jesse. Stop."

He meets my gaze, looking for something. He must see whatever it is he was searching for because he nods slightly.

He lifts our hands and presses a kiss to our knuckles. "I'll let you go. For now."

He releases my hand and I roll my eyes.

"I'm not going to be yours, Jesse."

"You already are."

With that, he walks into the conference room, leaving me standing alone in the hallway.

"What the hell is wrong with that man?" I ask to no one in particular.

No. I. Am. Not. I am not his. Crushing on him, lusting after him—yes. He's got an ego problem if he thinks he can claim me after working with me for two days. I've come across his kind before and that's how I learned to keep me to *me*. Jumping into something because of the attraction, because it feels good—some people are built for that, but I'm not. I've learned the hard way that broken hearts never truly mend, never become whole again. There are always a few missing pieces left behind with the careless one who did the breaking and they don't even appreciate your sacrifice. Those remaining pieces are their trophy.

I won't make that mistake again.

Chapter
seven

Lucy

"What's shakin', doll?" this, from Xander, Falling Down's drummer and the smoothest talking man I've ever met.

"Hey," I say with a smile as I take a seat. "Sera and I would like to talk to you all about…"

"Our total life change," she interrupts.

"What? You're getting sex changes?" Ben says with a chuckle.

"No, smart ass," Sera glares.

Jesse hands me a diet Coke and takes a seat next to me. I force a smile. "Thanks."

"No problem, Luce." He opens the top of his Coke bottle and takes a long swallow. I get caught up in the movement of his throat as the liquid flows from his mouth and down into his throat. His mouth—that mouth, those lips—pressed against the rim of the bottle. I want those lips on me.

"Jesus, Lucy. Look away from the hottie and let's get to business."

Jesse grins, I blush. "Uh, yeah. Sorry. So I was saying—"

I get cut off when the conference room door opens.

"What's up, fuckers?" Jace exclaims and Sera and I squeal and run over and hug him. I jump up, wrapping my arms and legs around him, and he smacks my ass.

"Oh my God, we weren't expecting to see you here!"

"Max said you were still here, so here I am."

"This is awesome," Sera says with a laugh.

There's a clearing of a throat and I turn to a frowning, stern-faced Jesse. Oh boy. Mine. I roll my eyes.

"Everyone, this is Jace. He grew up with us and he's come out here to play with us."

"Play?" Jesse says with a scowl. I want to laugh. Jealousy is a different look for Jesse.

"Yeah," I say, walking back to my seat. "You see, after the whole club incident, I realized I was completely done."

"What do you mean 'done'?" Cage asks.

"Acting. Unless some phenomenal part with an amazing costar—"

"Milo Ventimiglia," Sera interrupts with a smirk.

"Yeah," I breathe. "Milo." I take a moment of silence to appreciate all that is Milo. I'm so distracted by the hotties today I can't even focus. "I was saying, unless some really great part I can't pass up falls in my lap, I'm done."

"Same with me for modeling," Sera adds, meeting Cage's gaze with a smile.

Surprised murmurs fill the room.

Cage raises his brows. "What does Regina say?"

I laugh. "She was *not* happy at first and was trying to talk me out of it until my dad jumped in."

"Excellent. Good man," Cage says with a grin. "Does this mean what I think it means?"

"It does."

"What does it mean?" Jesse asks.

I lean forward and look around the table at the rockstars seated here, the award-winning producer that is Cage, and I realize in this moment that I'm blessed. My acting got me here, in this moment, but it's time to do what I love, what makes me whole.

"It means that as of yesterday, well last night, I'm no longer an actress and Sera's no longer a model and Jace no longer works at his dad's accounting firm. It means that we're going to come together—with a few others that we still need to find—and share our music with the world."

"You're going to rock?" Ben asks with a grin, his dimples winking at me. Whew, those Kingston dimples.

I nod. "We are."

Everyone goes nuts. From "that fucking rocks" to "holy shit". The room is loud and boisterous and it's nothing like I expected. They're excited for us.

"Lucy, this is cool as fuck." I laugh as Jesse pulls me into a hug. "Are you sure?"

I nod. "One hundred percent."

He lets go of me and shakes his head.

Cage gets everyone to quiet down.

"What do you need to make this happen?" Always the businessman.

"First I'd like to say I'm not sure why you've done it but you've befriended us and you barely know us."

"We know enough," Xander says. "You're hot, you're talented, and you're sweet and classy chicks. We like you."

"Just like that? You're *rockstars*."

"And you're an Academy Award-winning actress and let's not get to the nominations," he retorts. "Why are *you* befriending us? You don't have to be our friends to get in Jesse's pants."

That pisses me off and he knows it. He smirks. "I wouldn't use you like that. That's just rude—" He grins. "You totally played me."

"I did. You're really sexy when you're fired up. Now, as Cage asked, what do you need to make this happen?"

"Band members," Sera blurts out.

"*Reliable, nondrug-using* band members," I correct.

"Well, shit. That's easy," Ethan chimes in.

"Easy? Even the nondrug-using part?"

He nods. "We know a lot of people and I, personally, know a few guys and girls who are looking for a good band."

"But we're not established and you know a lot of people are going to turn their noses up and really criticize because of who I am." I look to Sera and Jace apologetically. "They're going to see an actress not a musician."

"Fuck them," Jace says.

"Exactly," Jesse agrees. "Fuck 'em. Look at Jared Leto."

I snort. "Jared Leto is in a class all by himself. He just stands there and women fall at his feet—add in his talent and you've got a phenomenal talent like no other."

"So you'll be in a class all of your own. It's the talent that gets you there, the voice, the band, the music. You've all got it."

Sera sighs. "Jared Leto. Wow, those eyes of his and his smile."

"Oh boy, Jared. Do you happen to know him?" I ask.

Jesse frowns when Ethan tells me he can introduce me sometime. Sera and I wiggle our eyebrows at each other.

"Mmm, Jared."

"Back to the topic at hand," he says with a pointed look. "Just let us know what spots you've got open and we're on it." Jesse looks to Cage who nods. With the band and Cage working together, we can't go wrong.

"Well, it depends. Sera do you want to drum full-time?"

Xander laughs.

"Find something amusing, drummer boy?" Sera grits out.

"Yeah, your skinny arms drummer girl."

"I was skinnier than this in high school and not nearly as toned."

"Flex a muscle, darlin'."

She does and I'm pretty impressed. He raises his brows then reaches over and squeezes underneath her arm. She rolls her eyes.

"Please. As if I wouldn't firm that shit up. It's a woman's weak spot."

Jesse squeezes me in that spot and grins.

"Smart ladies."

"We started out with a trainer who was like Hitler on crack. He taught us a good regimen *then* wanted to tell us what we could and couldn't eat and that was it for me," Sera tells them.

I nod. "There is no messing with my food. I eat what I want, how much I want, and when I want. Don't be trying to take away my peanut M&Ms or I'll cut a bitch."

Jesse chuckles and rests his arm behind me on the arm of the chair, his hand resting on my lower back. Jace notices and his eyebrows go up. I roll my eyes at his public touchy-feely display and Jace grins.

"I think you forgot something, Lucy."

"I did?"

"You did. You forgot to introduce me to the best damn band ever."

"Oh my God! Please forgive my error." Sarcasm is my friend, I embrace her with love. "At the head of the table down there is Cage Nichols, multi-business owner, record and video producer extraordinaire." They greet each other with a nod.

"Next is Ethan Ashcroft, bass guitarist for Falling Down. Then we have the ever quiet Kennedy Caldwell on rhythm guitar, the bratty Ben Kingston on lead guitar, and the ever critical Xander Mackenzie on drums. Next to me, currently groping my ass is the man with the sexiest voice around, none other than Jesse Kingston. Guys, meet Jace Warner, bass guitarist for," I pause and look at Sera and Jace questioning and they both nod. "Blush."

"Fucking perfect," Xander says with a clap. "That is fucking perfect for you. Blush."

I blush then and he points and laughs.

"Fuck off," I say with a laugh. "It was the name of our band in high school."

"Where are the other members, Lucy?"

I sigh and look at Jesse sadly. "They've got responsibilities and lives and kids and good jobs and… strings they don't want to tug on."

He nods. "Got it. Sera's got drums? Or are you going on guitar?"

I can see she's torn.

"It's easier to find good, reliable drummers than it is guitarists—but only because I know more of them." Cage nods to Jesse in agreement.

I bite my lip and Jesse reaches out and smoothes it with his thumb. "Don't."

"I can't help it. Nervous habit."

He ignores my statement and looks to Sera for her answer.

"Rhythm guitar."

"Good choice. You being up front with Lucy will bring in the guys. Jace and whoever we get, if it's a guy, will bring in the girls."

Sera pouts. "Drummers bring in people."

"Fuckin' A we do," Xander exclaims.

"I know it, but honestly, can you see it, Xan? These two up front, Jace in the middle."

He nods as do the rest of the guys and Cage.

"I see it and I'm liking it," says Kennedy who never speaks.

"Oh my God! He speaks!"

He scowls. "I'm a man of few words. It'd be cool if you could get one more chick in the band. Doesn't matter if it's guitar or drums. It'll even out the guy-to-girl ratio. We've got so many chicks at our shows there are no tickets left for the fucking guys unless it's their boyfriends."

"True that," Ethan says.

"I'm sure none of you complain," I say with a pointed look to Jesse. His brows lift and I look away, jealousy flooding me at the thought of him fucking the long line of groupies he's gone through. My teeth grind together in irritation. Fucking groupies. Fucking rockstars. Jealousy does not look good on me.

"So we need lead guitar and drums?"

"Sera, why aren't you taking lead?" Jace asks.

"It's been too long."

"Yet you were willing to tackle drums?"

She huffs.

Ben stands up. "Come on. Let's go see what she's got."

"What? No," she protests.

"Suck it up and let's go. You should be lead," I whisper, "and you know it."

We get to the part of the set that is a faux stage and Xander hands Sera his sticks. "Let's hear the drums first so we judge correctly."

She nods. "What do you want to play?"

The band picks up their instruments. Xander taps his chin with his index finger. "You up for a challenge, doll?"

She narrows her eyes and he grins. Sera's always up for a challenge and calling her 'doll' will only make her more determined to win.

"I thought so. Let's see how much stamina you've got. *Nightmare* by Avenged Sevenfold."

"Oh boy," I say to Jesse with raised eyebrows. He just shrugs. "I can't really sing this one with you. Ethan's better for this one."

"That's why you're not backing me up. You're singing it with me. I've heard your rasp."

"Whatever, I can't sing like a dude," I say, knowing I'm going to sound like shit singing this song. This is a total guy song. I'm all for equal rights, but there is no way a woman's voice can compare to Matt Shadows.

"Let's do this."

Sera whips her long brown hair up into a messy bun and takes a seat, adjusting for the height difference. She looks up and counts it off on her sticks and we're rocking.

Jesus, I think to myself. *She's still incredible.* She looks amazing, so natural and a pang of guilt floods me. If it hadn't been for my acting, we'd have already been playing and Sera wouldn't have had to settle for modeling when music is *her*.

I close my eyes and lose myself in the lyrics, the music, the beat. This feels incredible. *This* makes me *feel. This* is what I'm meant to do. Not acting. I open my eyes and see Jesse's are closed as he sings the fuck out of this song. God, he's incredible. He's beautiful, truly, in a very rugged, rough, bad-boy way. Maybe it's the bad boy thing that is attracting me to him. It wouldn't be the first time.

My voice does nothing for this song. His—well, his challenges it in different ways than the original. He opens his eyes and winks just as the song ends.

"Fucking killer," Ethan shouts and fist bumps Jace. The two bass players were having a good time it seems.

Xander nods at Sera, his grin wide. She hands him his sticks. "You kicked ass. How do you feel?"

"Like I could keep going."

"Could you keep going for two hours solid? Maybe with a couple small breaks."

She tilts her head to the side and wiggles her eyebrows. He grins again. "I was talking about drums, darlin', but if you're heading in that direction we can always find out together."

She laughs. "I could keep playing for two hours. Maybe not at that pace the entire time, but I could do two hours."

He nods. "There's always a few less heavy songs mixed in the albums so if you wanted drums, you'd be great."

"Thanks. That means a lot coming from you."

It really does. He's one of the best drummers out there right now. It hasn't escaped me that this is one of the most popular rock bands who are topping the charts and these moments with them seem so surreal.

Xander just nods.

"The question is," Jesse says, "do you want to be back there or would you rather be up here?"

"First, let's see what she's got for the chords," Ben says.

I smirk and Jesse raises a brow. "Just watch," I whisper and head over to grab rhythm guitar.

"Whatcha got going on here?" Kennedy asks as I pick up one of his guitars.

"Relax, oh silent and sexy one. I won't wreck your precious. I just know what she's got in mind and I need to do rhythm for her. Well, I don't need to, I want to because this is going to be epic."

"What's she got in mind?" Ethan asks.

"The same thing she always has in mind whenever someone challenges her on guitar," Jace says with a grin. "The only question is which song."

"My new favorite," she announces and I raise my eyebrows and my mouth forms a small o.

I hop up on a stool. I prefer to sit while I play guitar, even rhythm. Most people prefer to stand but I hate the guitar strap. I just feel too restricted. I'm weird and I admit this freely.

"You're gonna have to sing this one solo, hot stuff."

Jesse nods, grabs the mic and stool, and plops himself right next to me. "What is it?"

"You'll know it as soon as the first note is played."

He nods again.

"Ready?" I ask.

Sera nods and Jace winks.

Sera strums the first chord of *Hail To The King* by Avenged Sevenfold and all brows go up and grins appear. Sera jumps in to sing her part as do

Jace and Xander. Kennedy matches me, Ethan matches Jace, and Jesse blows the vocals away.

Ben stands in front of Sera and watches her while his fingers work the fret, grinning. She's not even paying attention. Her eyes are closed and she's in the zone. Give that girl a guitar and she's gone.

When the last chord is struck, the studio is completely silent. Sera's head comes up and she grins at me.

Ben shakes his head. "Fucking *Hail To The King*."

She shrugs. "I do so love a challenge and I'm glomming on A7X right now."

"Obviously you've been playing some if you know that song."

"Well, yeah. I'm a musician. I have to play even if I'm not in a band. Lucy and I had jam sessions."

"Good. It seems you get to choose what you want to do because you're fantastic at both," Ben says.

She grins at him. "Thanks, Ben."

He nods. "I mean it. That was incredible."

Another extremely flattering compliment for my girl. I can't help but smile.

"It's up to you. If you do drums, you'll be in the back and likely someone else will have to sing backup. If you choose lead, you get the spotlight. If you choose rhythm, you get a lot of spotlight but not as bright," Jesse states.

"First, would you be content back there? People know who you are as a drummer, I mean, look at Xander. The women are nuts for him even back there," I say.

"Probably not. I'd prefer to move around the stage a bit."

I nod. I thought so. She feels too much when she plays to sit still for that long.

"That leaves lead and rhythm. Would you be content with rhythm or do you want to continually challenge yourself?"

Jesse looks at me with a knowing smirk. He knows what I'm doing and what she's going to pick.

"I, of course, want the challenge," she says with a grin, her brown eyes, so much like mine, flashing with humor and excitement. We may be cousins but to me she is my sister.

"Then you're it, woman," Jace says with a grin.

"So we're looking for rhythm guitar and drums. You need anyone for boards?" Jesse asks.

"Nope. I got that."

"No shit?"

"No shit. Why do you sound so surprised?"

He shrugs.

"What, only Sera can be a musical prodigy?"

"I never said that."

"They must have missed our P!nk performance yesterday," Sera explains.

I nod. "Must have. And now I feel like I have something to prove," I say heading to the piano. I flex my hands and fingers, cracking my knuckles. Jesse sits next to me on the bench with his microphone. God, he's so pushy. He's not going to give me space at all to deny his claim. Well, I'll just ignore it and keep going like nothing's out of the ordinary. I adjust the mic on the piano.

I start playing *Your Song* from Elton John and everyone joins in on their cue. Jesse sings the first verse. I join in on the chorus and take the second verse. Jesse leans forward catching my attention and sings the last line of the second verse to me. *Yours are the sweetest eyes I've ever seen.*

Oh boy. I smile and we finish out the song.

"Well done, Cupcake."

"Thank you, thank you," I say with a laugh.

Cage stands from his chair in front of the stage. I forgot he was there. Oops.

"You want my opinion?" he asks.

"Always." I have the utmost respect for this man who came from nothing, lived on the streets, and managed to make himself into a business mogul as well as someone everyone in the music industry respects and admires.

"Sera, take lead. Luce, just sing, do acoustic when you want, during breaks or whatever. Piano if you need to. Focus on working the crowd, engage them. Jace is perfect." Cage shakes his head and laughs. "I knew you'd be sensational but I wasn't expecting this."

His words warm me all the way to my heart. He's seen many, many bands—rock, pop, rap—you name it, he's seen it, and he thinks we're sensational. There is no greater compliment.

"So we find rhythm and drums and get you set up in a studio. You've got songs, right?" he asks.

I laugh. "Are you fucking with me right now?"

"Yep," he laughs.

I throw a guitar pick at him, which doesn't go very far.

"Yeah, we've got songs. Books upon books of songs."

He nods. "You know I own a company that produces records."

"No, had no clue at all," I tell him, pointing at Jesse and the guys to name one of the many amazing bands he's got on his label.

He laughs. "I've got the company studio and a private one. You can use the private one any time you want, but in a couple weeks I want you in the company one recording your album."

"Holy fuck," Jace says. "You're *that* Cage Nichols."

He nods. "I am."

"Oh yeah," Sera says walking up to him and jumping on his back. Piggy-back time. "We're going to be on sexy Cage's label." She leans forward and kisses his ear.

His arms reach back and cup her ass, holding her up.

Jesse puts his arm around me. "I'll help you. Whatever you need."

"Thank you, all of you, for this." They all nod.

I meet the whiskey-colored eyes of a man I've crushed on and admired since I was a teenager. "Please know that I don't expect it from you, but I am grateful for every single thing you do."

"I know, Lucy. If I thought it was anything else, you wouldn't be *mine*."

I lean in and whisper to him, "I'm not yours, Jesse."

"You will be before the night is over."

Desire rushes through me and I'm instantly wet at the thought of Jesse's hands and mouth on me, his cock deep inside me. It's been a long time since I've had sex. I do a mental calculation—holy shit, over a year—fourteen-plus months. That's just sad. I tilt my head and consider for a second. I'm not sure if I should give in or hold out. I think waiting until we're done working on this project together is the smart choice, so I ignore his last statement.

I stand up. "I've got to say, boys, I'm pretty surprised you knew that last song."

"What?" Kennedy asks. "If there's a musician out there that doesn't know that song, they are a disgrace."

"Agreed. I just figured you guys were too hardcore to know Elton John."

"Fuck no. It's a classic. Layla. Lola. Shit, they're the best," Ethan says.

"Truer words were never spoken," Jace replies.

"Well all right. We need to get Jace settled in at the penthouse—"

"Penthouse?" Jesse asks.

I nod and blow out a breath. "Suites really."

"Why are you staying in a hotel?" his brows pull down and he frowns.

"Well, Mr. Sexy Rockstar, I can't go home. It's surrounded by reporters and when I say surrounded, I mean surrounded. It's gated, but that means stopping and risking someone getting in when the gates open and I can't be bothered to hire additional security. I've never had to before, and I'm not starting now."

Jesse nods, lips pressed tightly together again. I'm coming to realize he does that a lot when he's upset or annoyed or pissed off.

"So where are you staying?"

"I've got an entire floor booked at the Beverly Wilshire. Once filming is done, we'll stay in the house in Santa Monica."

"I'm sorry, Lucy. I didn't realize the reporters were on you that bad."

I shrug. "It's par for the course."

"They weren't nearly that bad at my place."

"Gated community?" He nods. "Yeah, mine's not. I haven't had a need for it."

"Until now," Sera says.

"You're a movie star," Xander says. "How could you not need a gated community?"

"I've always stayed under the radar when I've gone out—avoided temptation, so to speak. It's not that we haven't been looking already, we just never made it a priority."

"Guess we will now, huh?" Sera says and I nod.

"We're taking Jace out for drinks," Kennedy says and I groan.

"Really? His first night here?"

"Is there a better time?"

I sigh. "He's got his own suite I'll give you the key, Jace. I rented out the floor so we have privacy. You all can party there if you want just keep the skanks to a minimum please and over on your side of the building. I don't want to hear that shit."

I look around and there's no Sera. "Where'd Sera go?"

"She took off with Cage," Jace replies.

I nod. Not surprising.

"Do you have a car here?" Jesse asks.

"Max."

He nods. "I'll take you home."

"Okay. That's probably better. Then Jace and the boys can have Max or Gio drive."

He nods. I hand Jace his suite key and tell him they've got the car for the night if they want it but they decide they're going to party anywhere within walking distance and Jace's suite.

"We'll drop their cars off and Max can take us to the hotel."

"Sounds good. Stay out of trouble," I tell Jace as I give him a hug. I mimic a Robert De Niro as I point and squint my eyes at the other guys who just grin.

Damn rockstars.

Chapter eight

Lucy

"You're not going to invite me up, are you?" Jesse asks.

I shake my head. "No, I'm not. We've still got to work together."

"Just one more day... more like half a day. There's not much left to shoot."

"Jesse."

"Lucy."

I can't help but smirk a little. He's something else. Jesse freaking Kingston. I shake my head.

"What?"

"Nothing."

"Oh come on. It was something."

I turn in the passenger seat of his red brand-spanking-new Mustang to face him. "You really want to know?"

He glances over for a second before looking back at the highway stretched before us. "I do."

"I was just thinking 'Jesse freaking Kingston'."

He grins. "Yeah, that's me."

"It still seems surreal."

"I could say the same Miss Hollywood actress. Luciana freaking Russo."

I wave him off. "I'm not anything but a mediocre actress at best."

He laughs. "Oh really. This coming from the woman who got nominated for an Oscar after her very first film."

"Please. It was best supporting actress and I didn't win."

"Still nominated *and* you won the actress Oscar for your last film so don't tell me you're mediocre."

"Meh. I don't feel like I deserve any of that. I'm just Lucy and I go play other characters sometimes."

"You work hard, learn all the lines, get into that character, make it believable."

"Great scripts help."

He chuckles. "Would you stop? You can't admit you're good?"

"I just don't see myself like that. It's just a job… acting. Now music… That's going to be something I really want to succeed at."

"I have no doubt you're going to. It might be a little slow going at first, but I honestly don't think so. Not with Cage's backing."

I nod. "I have to find a new manager, though Cage said he would step in for the time being. I'm not sure how he can find time for that with everything he's already got going on."

"I'm sure it has a little something to do with Sera."

"Probably."

"How'd you meet Cage?"

I smile at the memory. "Well, it wasn't long after I'd met you that Irene, my agent, had lined Sera and I up to be in a music video for Crashed. My mom hated it. I mean *hated* it. Anyway, when we got there, his assistant Marci greeted us just like she did yesterday and took us into the conference room. There sat Cage and a few of his people as well as all the band members from Crashed. It was all Sera and I could do not to squeal like stupid little fangirl groupies." I shake my head at the memory.

Jesse chuckles. "Go on."

"I'd never worked on anything like the videos so we were essentially virgins—that's what Cage called us. I was offended at first but didn't say a word. I mean, it's Cage Nichols. At least that's what I thought back then. Anyone who isn't in the industry, I've noted, doesn't see anyone who *is* in the industry as just a person. They're all hyped up to be OMG Mr. Rockstar or Miss Actress."

"Kinda like you just thought of me a few minutes ago?"

"Yeah, but I know you're just a guy who loves music who gets to do what he loves for a living. But that's not how we saw it back then, Sera and I. So we were pretty awed by everything. Then we got on set and it was so much fun. God. So much more fun than acting in a movie or television show. The music, the lights, the sound, the stories that Cage creates for the videos—but mostly it was the music. Sera and I lose ourselves in it and we weren't prepared for being in a video."

"Uh-oh. I sense something bad is going to happen."

"Not bad, just super embarrassing."

"What happened?"

I pluck at an imaginary piece of lint on my pants. "Well, we got out there and Crashed started playing. Sera and I did our ass wiggling as we were supposed to but when they got into it, so did we. We were dancing around singing the lyrics at the tops of our lungs," I laugh out loud at myself. "It was just horrifying to do that in front of all these professional people."

"How hard of a time did they give you?"

"That's the thing. They didn't."

"No?"

I shake my head. "They knew we were being weirdoes but they didn't stop playing. They let us get our goofy dancing and singing out of the way, they laughed a bit, and told us we were a lot of fun. Cage—he just sat there in his chair, leaning to one side, elbow bent upward so his chin was resting on his hand—you know what I mean."

He nods.

"So quiet and stoic, I thought we were fired for sure. Then he gets up from his chair and walks over to us, just me and Sera, and pulls us both into a hug and starts laughing, telling us what a breath of fresh air we are, that everyone is always so serious. Well, that set the tone for that shoot and our relationship with Cage. We started hanging out with him a bit, I took his advice on movies and things—he's good friends with Irene, by the way."

"Of course he is."

"I know, right? Anyway, so we just became friends and whenever we can, I should say whenever my schedule allows for it, we work on videos with him. I'm not sure how many we've been in. Five? Seven? All I know is that Cage is one of our best friends and there's something between him and Sera that they are in such denial of and I'm afraid they'll never act on."

"I've seen them together. There's no way they'll be able to hold out much longer."

I shrug. "Maybe. I hope so. They'd be happy together but Sera's... different."

"There's a story there."

"There is but one very personal and private."

Jesse nods. "I can respect that."

We're both quiet for a couple minutes, a comfortable silence before Jesse breaks it.

"What did you think when they told you, you were going to be doing a video with us?"

"Ha! They didn't!"

"What do you mean?" he asks with a confused grin.

"Sneaky fuckers, all of them. Cage, Irene, Spenser, all the assistants... none of them told us who it was, just that it was some big-name band and we'd be happy. It was a 'surprise'."

"So you didn't know until you saw us?"

"Not a clue. Not until Ben strummed his guitar and you sang with me. Talk about a heart-stopping minute."

"We heard you when we walked in the building. You were singing some P!nk song and when we got halfway to you, you started in on Red. We all just kinda stopped where we were and listened. None of us said a word. Your voice," he shakes his head. "It was an incredible thing to hear and then we started toward the sound and when I turned the corner and saw you, I couldn't believe it."

I grin shyly. "Yeah, well. I thought for sure we were going to get bitched out for touching the guitars and Sera on the drums."

"There was no way, after what we'd heard. No way. And then seeing it was you, well, who can yell at you?"

"Oh you'd be surprised," I say with a laugh.

"Bastards, every one of them," he quips. "Seriously though, I knew you were going to be there but I thought it was part of the crew fucking around." He shakes his head. "To turn the corner and see you and Sera caught up in the music like we do…"

I just nod. I can't think of anything to say.

"Little Lucy who couldn't even speak was standing there singing her heart out six years later."

I turn to look at him a little confused as to what he's trying to say and he glances in my direction.

"You're going to make it. It's going to happen fast, too. You need to prepare for that."

I nod. "I'm not sure how, but we'll try. I mean I know the fans and stuff are going to be much different than they are at movie premieres and things like that. I've been to concerts but I've never been backstage or a VIP or anything so I'm not sure how that all goes."

"It's completely different from what you're used to, Luce. There are so many fans, and they all want a piece of you. They'll reach up on stage to try to touch you and there are days you just don't want to be touched. You just want them to enjoy the music—not you—you know?"

I nod. "Well, from what I've heard you have no issues with the fangirl groupie whores."

He raises a brow. "From what you've heard?"

"Oh yeah. It's common knowledge that you're a manwhore. Jesse Kingston, the man with a new girl every couple hours." I nod. "Yep, it's not news."

He grins. "Really. That's what's being said?"

I nod and twist my fingers in my lap. I hated reading about that, hearing about it from people we've worked with. Manwhore Kingston. I cringe inwardly. It shouldn't have bothered me. He was just my crush and he was nothing to me, but it did. It bothered me on a personal level, which was utterly ridiculous. I knew it and I tried to not let it get to me, I tried to avoid the gossip, and I was successful until our next video shoot. I turn and look out the window as Jesse pulls onto the exit ramp in silence.

He pulls into the parking lot of the hotel instead of in front and I know he's going to talk. I don't want to hear it. I really don't. It's not my business. It's not like I was chaste, though I didn't fuck everything with a penis either. I sigh and turn to look at him.

"What Jesse?"

He raises a brow. "Well that put a damper on your mood, didn't it?"

I shrug.

"Look Lucy, I can't change my past, what I've done or who I am. Yeah, what they said was true for the first few years we were out on the road, but that gets old after a while."

"So it's just one girl a show then," I say with intended snark.

He sighs and runs a hand through his hair. "You're going to find out and it may not be the same for you, but after a show, the adrenaline rush..." He shakes his head. "You feel on top of the world. I mean, you just got to do what you love and rock it out in front of fifty-plus-thousand fans and they fucking loved it. It's like no other feeling I've ever experienced."

I just nod and look out the windshield at nothing in particular. A palm tree. Some desert plants that have quite impressive survivability in the rainless and super dry state of California.

"You don't want to lose that feeling. Then there are the women throwing themselves at you—"

I hold up a hand and look at him. "Stop. I don't want to hear this. You owe me nothing, Jesse. I'm not sure why you're trying to explain yourself or your actions to me. I'm nobody to you, not really. It doesn't matter."

"That's not true—"

"It's true. Thank you for driving me home, Jesse."

He nods, his jaw clenched. "What are you going to do for the rest of the night?"

"First, I'm going to take a nice long shower and rinse off the gross dried leather boobage sweat." I curl a lip. "Then I'll probably put a movie in and turn into a Tijanette for the night."

"A what?"

"A Tijanette."

"What the fuck is that?"

I laugh. "Okay, something you might not know about me. I love to read. I read every day in my spare time. If I'm not working, I generally read all day and lounge by the pool or whatever. I just—read. It's my escape."

"Okay, what does that have to do with Raisinettes?"

I laugh out loud, so loud and hard that I snort. "Not Raisinettes, *Tijanettes*. You see one of my favorite author's names is Tijan and her fans or street team is called Tijanettes. I love her stories and there are a couple I haven't read yet, so I'll download it to my Kindle, grab a bottle of wine, and lounge on the oversized sofa with a pillow and blanket because Sera probably set the air conditioning too low and I'll freeze my ass off."

"What movie are you going to watch?"

I shrug. "A chick flick probably."

He cringes. "Well then. Maybe when we've wrapped up everything with the video tomorrow, you'll let me take you out to dinner."

While I'm mulling this over, Jesse starts his car and pulls around to the front of the hotel. I look at him, at the gorgeousness that is Jesse Kingston, and I know what I'm going to do. The potential for heartbreak is high. The potential for love is low. But it's Jesse. I lied to him earlier. I did feel something when we met in Chicago. The zing. The electricity. The heat. It's all still there, stronger than ever and getting stronger every minute he's near me.

"Alright, Jesse. Dinner it is."

He nods, seeming a bit surprised, then a genuine smile blooms across his beautiful face. I can't bring myself to smile. I'm afraid. I'm very, very afraid.

"We'll work the details out tomorrow. We've already exchanged digits so you can call me anytime."

"And you can call me. Convenient how that worked out for you."

He chuckles. "I admit it. I wanted your number."

I smirk. "And now you have it. Do you know how many squealing fangirls would kill for this phone number?"

"Don't even think about it."

I laugh. "I wouldn't."

"Look, Lucy. I'm sorry. I didn't mean to bring up shit that upsets you. It's just, I don't know. I feel like I need to explain."

"You don't. As I said, you owe me nothing."

"Maybe not but it feels like I do. Anyway, you're going to have guys in your band and I don't know how Sera is or if you'll get another girl, but I know for sure the guys are going to get wild for a while. Hell, you might."

I nod. "I doubt I will but I'm anticipating others will. There will be no skanks on the bus. If they want to fuck skanks either they fuck them backstage or in a motel or hotel when we're stopped long enough, but I am not going to listen to groupie giggling all fucking night."

"Wow. That was a lot of fucks and skanks. Hot button, Luce?"

"Fucking yes it is. These women are pathetic. Okay, not all of them, but a lot. See, I'll be as straight up with you as you were with me, Jesse. I would have gone backstage with you or wherever to fuck you, I admit that." Both of his brows raise at this admission. "But, here's the difference between me and a lot of the others. While I would be with you, that's it for me. I wouldn't go to the next band and fuck that singer or guitarist or drummer. I wouldn't fuck anyone else from your band. You get what I'm saying? I love the entire band of Falling Down, the guys are seriously hot, but while I'm their fan, I'm mostly yours. You were inspiring to me when I was growing up and I crushed on you big time back then. So, while a lot of others aren't discriminate, they just want a band member, it doesn't matter who, because whoever they get is famous and that means they can brag to their friends or whatever they're using them for, that's not me. Now I'm not talking about the women who might be young or for whatever reason are in a rebellious stage—I'm talking about the ones who make that their *life*. That's pathetic. Where's their self-respect? They use you all and while you think it's okay because you get to get laid regularly and use them in return, I just can't think it's okay. Everyone has a right to their own opinion."

"I get it."

I nod. "Good. Now it's time for me to go wash this gross dried boob sweat off. I hate leather. Just putting that out there in case you missed it the first fifty times I mentioned it."

"Glad you reminded me. I think I forgot." He smirks then leans over and presses his lips softly to mine. My eyes flutter closed and then it's over. I open them to find him looking at me, so closely that I can see those brown and green flecks I noticed in Chicago.

"I know you're a good girl, Lucy. You're beautiful and classy. I think maybe you thought I had you labeled under the groupie category. But, Luce, you don't fit into that category. I know that. Hell, you don't fit into any category but your own. Okay?"

I nod. "Okay."

He gives me another quick kiss and motions to the valet who opens my door.

"I'll see you in the morning, Jesse."

"See you then, Cupcake."

I head into the hotel feeling lighter in some regards and a whole lot heavier in others with just a dash of confusion. I'm glad he knows I'm not a groupie in spite of my fangirling. I almost hate myself for that—almost. But I can't because even though I didn't know Jesse at that time, I admired him. While I think he's a whore, I admire his personality and his love of music.

I put the keycard into the elevator slot for our private floor and check myself out in the mirrored walls. Ugh. I look like hell and yet he called me beautiful. The man needs glasses. I sigh as I step off the elevator and head to my suite. I walk to my bedroom and toe off my shoes and sit on the bed.

What a day. Seven hours of ass shaking is a lot of work and seriously tiring. I'm starving. I call down to order room service, a big fat cheeseburger and fries. I just step out of the shower when my phone beeps. Jesse. I grin.

Jesse: *I'm glad you let me drive you home. I want to get to know you, Lucy.*

Why? For how long? And what's the point? Yet...

Lucy: *I'd like to get to know you too, and that's the truth. I don't know you personally, I only know things second-hand from what I've read or heard or seen, and I think first-hand would be so much better. Oh yeah, double entendre. *winks**

Jesse: *I think there's a whole lot of bad girl underneath that good girl, Lucy. I hope you let her come out and play with me sometime.*

Lucy: *She might be around tomorrow night.*

Jesse: *I look forward to meeting her too, if she decides to show up. If not, then another time. Goodnight, Cupcake. xx*

Lucy: *Goodnight, Jesse. Sweet dreams xoxo*

Jesse freaking Kingston. I am in so much trouble.

Chapter *nine*

Lucy

The last day of filming lasts four hours so we're done at noon. Everyone decided to go to lunch, which was a great way to wrap things up. I love working for Cage and even though I'm on hiatus from acting, I'll help him out anytime.

Sera's disappearing act last night lasted well past the time I passed out reading about Samantha Stratton and her nutso mom. I thought my mom was controlling. Sheesh.

Tonight—in about an hour—is our date. Oh boy. I already know what's going to happen and I'm prepared for it. Jesse's going to get me in his bed and we're going to have amazing, toe-curling sex. I'm not going to complain about it or make excuses. I'm going to enjoy every second of it because in all honesty it's been over a year and I have no idea when I'll be having sex again. Not to mention this is Jesse Kingston. Opportunities like this don't happen every day.

I thought about this last night and I'm okay with the idea of Jesse and a one-time thing. He doesn't do relationships—ever. Okay, I lied. One time won't be enough but if that's all I can have, I'll take it. I have no idea what I feel for him but I know I want him. Who wouldn't?

Since we're done filming, we're staying at the house in Santa Monica due to the paparazzi. I know it's stupid to be going out with Jesse tonight, but I'm not going to be a prisoner. Yes, they're going to jump to conclusions because we were just seen together and will be again tonight. I shrug. I don't care. Nothing they print about me or say about me on the internet is true anyway. Okay, that's not true either. Maybe ten percent is true.

I'm putting on the finishing touches of my makeup when Sera walks in.

"Tonight's the big date, huh?"

I raise a brow. "How did you know that?"

She rolls her eyes. "We all know about it. It's not like Jesse's keeping it a secret. Are you trying to?"

She reaches for my curling iron and starts working on my hair.

"No, I'm not trying to. I just… I'm trying to keep it low-key. We've already got paparazzi following us, blocking us from our home. I'd rather they didn't get wind of this before we get wherever Jesse is taking me."

"I can understand that. Are you ready for a night with Jesse Kingston?"

I can't help but grin. "I'm nervous and excited at the same time. I mean, sex is obviously in the plans for tonight—it *is* Jesse after all."

Sera nods. "Are you going to be okay knowing Jesse doesn't do relationships?"

"I'm good with that. I've mentally prepared. Done some mind voodoo."

Sera grins. "You're so weird. I can't believe you still believe Nana Russo's able to put hexes on people."

"She can! Didn't you see when she put the juju on Norman Brown? His hair fell out! Eyebrows, eyelashes, head, chest, arms, legs… all of it!"

"He was in his seventies, Luce."

"Yeah, but all the hair on his body was gone in a matter of hours! That is not age. That is Nana Russo's juju. I'm telling you."

"According to Nana, that stuff doesn't work if you do it on yourself."

"It can't hurt to try. If it fails and Jesse pisses me off or hurts me somehow, I'll make a voodoo doll and use it as my new pin cushion."

"You don't use pins for anything."

"I'll take up needlepoint."

Sera laughs. "Okay, okay. You're covered with your side of birth control, right?"

"Yep. I got the shot two months ago. I have an alarm set on my phone for my appointment with Dr. Brickner for next month." Not that I'll be needing it for probably another year after this sexcapade with Jesse.

"Good. Monday is when we meet some of the people the guys lined up for Blush."

"Yeah. I'm anxious to get started."

"Are we going to use the song?"

"Oh. I don't know. I'm sure it'll be fine if we do. Jesse won't be around while we record or tour so it won't be an issue. He may hear it on the radio or something if we get that lucky."

The song. After I met Jesse six years ago, I wrote a song about him and our chance meeting. If he heard it, he'd know it was about him.

Sera nods. "Hair's done."

"No spray."

"Okay."

"I want to keep it light and airy that way it won't stick to my head when we have sex."

"Ah, good thinking. Did you pack a bag?"

"Do you think I should?"

Sera shrugs. "I don't know. I'd ask Jesse though. You never know what he's got planned."

"True. Ugh. I don't want to ask him that. He'll know I'm anticipating spending the night with him."

Sera laughs. "He already knows that, I'm sure."

"And he may not want me to sleep over."

"Please. He knows who you are and what you're about. He knows a sleepover is going to happen."

"Probably but I really don't want to affirm his assumptions."

"Just call the man," she says, thrusting my phone out at me.

I huff. "Fine."

Lucy: *Just wondering if I need to bring anything with me…?*

While I wait for a response, I go into my room and choose a simple black sleeveless dress outlined in red. As I'm putting my shoes on, my phone beeps.

Jesse: *Yep. I plan on keeping you in my bed tonight, maybe even tomorrow so bring what you need.*

Lucy: *You're assuming a lot, Jesse.*

Jesse: *Don't bother fighting it. It's going to happen. You know it and I know it.*

Really, what is the point of resisting when I want it as bad as he does? Might as well give in and make my dream come true... multiple times. Good God. Just thinking about it has me squeezing my thighs together.

Lucy: *One night won't be enough. I'll pack for three just in case.*

Jesse: *Three. Nice. I'm looking forward to it. I should be there in ten.*

Lucy: **gasp* Are you texting and driving? Stop before you hurt yourself or someone else!*

Jesse: *Cupcake, I've got a driver tonight. I'm safe. Thank you for worrying though.*

Lucy: *See you soon.*

"You're wearing sexy lingerie, right?" Sera calls out from the living room. Jeez. Jace is here with Ethan. How embarrassing.

"Come look!" I call back.

"Coming," Ethan shouts.

I laugh out loud. "No way, pal!"

"Awww, you're no fun!"

"Sure I am. Ask Jesse how fun I am when I'm through with him."

I hear Ethan and Jace laugh.

"Alright. What do you have on?" Sera asks from the doorway.

"Black lace and garters."

"You're good. Pack extra in case you go somewhere, then seduce him again with the lingerie."

"Already packed."

"Wow, you really are ready for him, aren't you?"

"I am. I've been fantasizing about this for eleven years, Sera. *Eleven years.*"

"Probably not *this* kind of fantasizing when we were twelve but I get what you mean."

The doorbell rings. Oh boy. There goes my belly. Butterflies.

"I'll get it," Sera sing-songs.

Oh boy again. More butterflies swarm when I hear his voice. Jesse. Kingston. Is. In. My. House. If someone had told me this would be possible five years ago, hell even a week ago, I'd have told them they were full of shit.

I press a hand to my stomach and take a deep breath. I got this. No problem. Be sexy. Be seductive. Be confident. Another deep breath. With a nod I pick up my weekend suitcase and my purse.

There he stands. Oh my. He looks seriously sexy in his black dress pants, black boots (he's a rocker, I don't think rockers do dress shoes), and a red and black polo shirt. He's dressed very little like Jesse the rockstar and he went out of his way to do this for me. I sigh. I don't want him to think he has to be someone else for our date. But I'm not going to say anything. I don't want to offend him.

"Wow," he says with a wide grin.

I match his grin with one of my own. "Hey. You've seen me all fancied up before."

He nods. "I have, but never for a date with me. That makes this special."

I blush and he chuckles as he steps forward to take my bag. He presses a kiss to my cheek.

"You look beautiful," he whispers against my ear, his breath sending shivers down my spine.

"Have a good time, you two," Sera calls out as she locks the door between the den, where Jace and Ethan are, and the living area, where we are. I hear rattling and I laugh.

"What's going on?"

"She's protecting us from Jace and Ethan."

He grins. "You're a good woman, Sera."

"I know it. Now go before the gorillas pick the lock."

"Have a fucktastic time!" Ethan shouts through the door and I laugh again.

We step outside and it's still unbelievably hot at seven pm. That's Cali for you.

"Nice digs," Jesse says nodding toward the house.

I shrug. "We needed a place away from the city. It was the beach or the hills."

"I prefer the beach, too."

Jesse hands my bag to the driver, who Jesse introduces as Victor, then opens my door. I smile and slip inside. He closes the door and walks around to the other side.

I smooth my skirt, which has ridden up a bit with sitting. It sits just above the knee when I'm standing. I didn't factor the sitting part in. Oh well. It covers just enough so he can't see the garter. I take a deep steadying breath while I have a few seconds to myself. *You got this, Lucy.* I do. I do. I nod to myself.

Jesse slides in and the driver closes his door. He slips his sunglasses on and I reach into my purse and do the same. Good plan. He won't be able to see my eyes so he won't be able to read me as easily.

He reaches for my hand and pulls me closer.

"Come sit next to me, Luce. Remember, I don't bite unless you ask me to." He presses a kiss to the side of my neck and I can't help the intake of air at both the statement and the sensation. He said the same thing to me six years ago when I was in my state of "unh". I squeeze his hand and give him a smile.

"I remember."

"So you could hear me, but you just couldn't speak."

I nod, embarrassed that I'd frozen like a statue.

"I'm not sure what came over me. The minute Sera pointed you out, my brain stopped functioning."

He's grinning that sexy, confident, I'm-so-hot-and-I-know-it grin. It's cocky and it's a total turn on.

"You were hot for me. You thought I was sexy and amazing."

I roll my eyes. "Well, yeah. You already know I had the crush on you. Sera pretty much told you everything."

"Mhmm," he says leaning in, running his nose along my jawline. "You smell amazing. All feminine and floral." A shiver runs through me and goose bumps break out over my body.

"Thanks." I turn my head and his lips are right there, just a breath away. Neither of us moves. We just sit there staring at each other's mouths. Oh to hell with this. I lean forward and press my lips against his. His hand squeezes mine gently and his other hand slides under my hair to the back of my neck.

I can't help the breathy sigh that escapes any more than I can help the fact that I am wet and wanting.

He doesn't deepen the kiss, just sips at my lips with his. It's sexy and sweet and erotic at the same time.

He pulls back and looks at me. Just looks. He tucks a strand of hair behind my ear, his fingertip swirls around my ear and I shudder.

"What was that for?" he asks.

"Well, I have a theory."

His smile widens, his dimples wink at me, and I want to lick them. I am so going to later.

"What theory?"

"Since this is our first official date and all, there's all this tension and nervousness—at least for me. You seem fine, which isn't fair. But, anyway, I thought if we got the first kiss out of the way now, then I could relax."

"Hmm. Are you relaxed now?"

I laugh. "Not really."

He chuckles. "You don't have to be nervous, Lucy. I'm just me."

I nod. "I know." That's the problem. Jesse Kingston, my life-long crush and tonight I'm going to fuck the hell out of him.

"You are, are you?"

"Oh my God." My face turns red, I can feel the heat. "I totally didn't mean to say that out loud."

He laughs. "I figured, but it's honest and that's good."

"Jesse. That's not the only reason I'm going out with you—the crush thing I mean."

"Oh, no worries, Lucy. I know that."

I raise my brows. "You do?"

"I do. If it was the whole crush thing, you'd be immobilized, unable to speak let alone kiss me. You'd do the shy schoolgirl thing which is hot in its own way, but I prefer the grown up Lucy for our date tonight."

He's just too sweet and he knows entirely too much. He keeps touching me. Little touches. Sexy touches. Seductive touches.

He leans in and places a kiss on my jaw, then another, and another. He works his way back to my lips and kisses one edge, then the other before trailing his tongue across my lower lip.

"Mmm. Strawberry. I've never come across a lip gloss that tasted like anything other than flavored wax until yours." He runs his tongue along my upper lip and I can't hold back the moan. My eyes drift shut and my hands grip his shoulders, pulling him closer.

His tongue slowly, teasingly slides between the seam of my lips, asking for entrance and I grant it willingly. Oh my God. My heart is going to beat out of my chest.

His tongue thrusts into my mouth meeting mine, tangling with mine, moving in and out. He slides both hands into my hair, threading his fingers through, pulling me to him. My arms wrap around his neck as I lean into him and he lets out a groan.

He breaks the kiss and trails kisses along my jawline again.

"Jesse." It comes out as a breathy whisper.

"Mmm," is his reply. He presses one soft, lingering kiss against my lips then pulls back. His gaze meets mine and I can't look away. Our breathing is ragged and I know I'd like nothing more than to take that shirt and those pants off of him and have my way with him right here, right now.

His thumb glides around my lips, removing the smeared lip gloss. I grin and reach up to his lips.

"Not my shade?" he asks.

"Ha. Not really. I think a pretty pastel pink would be more your color."

"I know something pink that's my color," he says with a wink.

I gasp. I can't believe he just said that—or that it's totally turning me on when he talks like that. As I wipe his lips clean of my lip gloss he reaches up and slips off my sunglasses.

"I need to see you."

He crooks his finger at me, coaxing me closer. I lean forward, my ear right up to his lips.

"I want nothing more than to strip that fucking sexy-as-hell dress off your body and see what you've got on underneath. Then I want to take off your bra, your panties, your shoes, and I want to kiss my way down your body, spread your legs wide so I can see how pretty your pussy is. Next I'll run a finger up your slit to see how wet you are. I bet you're wet as fuck right now, aren't you?"

I am so turned on right now that I'm dripping, so yeah, but I don't respond. His fingers tighten in my hair slightly. I'm having trouble breathing, my body nearly shaking. I want him so much, the excitement, the anticipation.

"Aren't you, Lucy."

I nod.

"Mmm, I thought so. That's fucking hot."

He pulls back and meets my gaze. His hand makes its way up my thigh, under my skirt. He grins when he comes across the garters.

"Nice."

I let out a breathy sigh when his finger slides against the outside of my lace panties. When he presses it harder against me, I can't hold back the moan that slips past my lips. Thank God for privacy screens in limos.

When he slips his finger underneath the edge of my panties I gasp and grab his shirt in my tight fists. He slowly slides it inside me, a little at a time.

"How does that feel?"

I hope he's not expecting me to answer at this point, especially when he slips a second finger in and his thumb starts circling my clit.

"Fuck, Lucy, you're so tight."

"Ah," I say breathily, "It's been a while."

"Hmm." He works his fingers deeper. "Lean back, Luce, and scoot down to the edge of the seat."

Oh my. I'm embarrassingly wet and as soon as I'm moved down, he thrusts his fingers in deeper.

"Oh God."

"Mmm," he whispers. "Do you like my fingers fucking you, Lucy? Is this one of your fantasies?"

"Uh, recent yeah. But… oh, right there… oh my God… with the crush I was too young… Jesse." His name comes out as more of a moan.

"You weren't too young when we met. Did you think of fucking me then?"

I nod. "Yes. God, Jesse." His fingers are moving faster now and he's curved them so they hit my G-spot. I'm going to come so fast.

"Right there… mmm."

I can feel his smile against my cheek as the tingles begin and start to spread. Jesus.

"It feels so good, Jesse. I can't—" I let out a cry of pleasure.

"That's it, baby. Just let it happen."

One, two, three more thrusts and I'm moaning long and low, panting as the orgasm crashes into me. Wave after wave washing over me, it keeps going on and on and feels like it's never going to stop. My entire body tingles, my toes curl, my pussy pulses. I can't… it's so much. I gasp for air, unable to breathe, the pleasure hits me so hard.

He presses his lips against mine, swallowing my cries of pleasure, keeping them for himself. He continues working his fingers in, circling my clit, drawing out every possible second of pleasure until the shudders stop and my body stills against his hand. I'm limp. I'm a rag doll. There's no way I can move from this spot.

He breaks the kiss and I open my eyes to meet his gaze. His eyes have gone from the bright gold to a deep whiskey color. He slowly slips his fingers out and brings them to his lips.

"Fuck, Lucy, you smell incredible. Let's see if you taste as good as you smell and sound."

He slips his fingers coated with my release into his mouth and his eyes roll back in his head as he sucks them clean. He blinks his eyes open and stares at me.

"Delicious."

He's so… just… wow. So sexual, so overpowering, so sure and confident.

"I didn't intend for that to happen here in the car."

I just nod.

"You kissed me. You look so sexy. I just couldn't help myself. I had to touch you. I wanted to make you come."

"Well," I say, "at least I know you're not a selfish lover."

He grins. "Most of the time, I am. You're different. I want to make you come over and over and, fucking hell, Lucy, tonight I'm going to. It won't be gentle the first time. I'm sorry, but I want you too badly. I'll make up for it. I promise."

"I have no doubt, and hard and fast works for me."

He curses under his breath. "You can't say things like that to me Lucy."

"Why not? You want honest, right?"

"Yeah, but—"

"But nothing. When we get to your place, I don't want you to be gentle. I was kind of hoping it'd be one of those rip-each-other's-clothes-off-and-fuck-against-the-wall moments."

"Were you now? That can be arranged."

I nod and lick my lips. He reaches out with a finger and traces my lips.

"I can't feel my legs."

He chuckles. "Good. I need a minute." He sits back and closes his eyes. I look to his lap and see his extremely impressive erection.

I bite my lip. "Um, Jesse..." I say and reach out to touch him. He gently grabs my wrist and brings it to his lips for a kiss.

"I'd love if you touched me later but right now was for you."

"But I can—"

He shakes his head. "For you."

I nod and he presses a kiss to my forehead.

"We're going to my place. I made you dinner. I just have to heat it up when we get there."

"You cook?"

"In and out of bed," he smirks.

"Oh boy. Lame, Jesse. That was lame."

"I thought it was pretty good."

I meet his gaze. "Jesse. Thank you."

"For?"

"Privacy." Stupid paparazzi assholes.

He nods and pulls me to him, my head resting on his chest.

"God, what am I going to do with you Lucy?"

"Hopefully all the things you told me before."

He chuckles. "Oh, those will definitely happen. Many times."

"I'm all for multiples."

He grins and taps a finger to my nose. "Mmm."

The car slows as we pull up to a gated community, the driver is passed through and we continue driving. A group of reporters stand around hoping to get a look. Tinted windows save us from their scrutiny.

"We're here."

I sit up, looking out the window. "Which one is yours?"

"The one at the end."

Of course. He's got a house on the beach... in Malibu. I sometimes forget just how rich and famous Jesse is.

"Jesus, Jesse. It's freaking huge."

He grins.

"Oh my God. Ha. Your house."

"It is. The guys stay here."

"Ah," I nod. That's not a house. That's even more than a mansion. That's the biggest house I've ever seen and I've been to parties of many rich and famous.

"Let me get your door for you." He presses a kiss to my lips then exits the car. He walks around to my side and opens my door. He holds out a hand, helping me out. I grab my purse and tuck my sunglasses back into my purse. He takes my suitcase from the driver and thanks him. Victor has got kind eyes. I like that.

We walk up the steps and Jesse opens the door to what is a massive freaking mansion. Christ. You could fit hundreds of people in here. He probably has at some of the parties he's notorious for.

"Welcome to my home."

The foyer is huge with one staircase splitting off into two going in opposite directions. His color scheme isn't a surprise: Black, white, and red—the same color scheme for the Falling Down logo. A black and white checkered floor—I love that. The iron railings leading up the staircases are black, curved, and with an intricate design. There's random artwork that I don't even bother looking at right now. I'm just getting a glimpse because there is *so much*.

"How many rooms are in this house?" I look to Jesse who has one shoulder resting against a doorway, his arms crossed over his chest, his legs crossed at the ankles. He looks completely relaxed and I'd believe it if it weren't for the tic in his jaw. It's his giveaway and I'm not going to tell him I know it. Already. Ha! But—if I know his, he likely knows mine. Unh.

He shrugs. "A lot."

I nod.

"You hungry?"

I turn to look at him. "Yes," I say breathily and he knows I don't mean for food. He straightens from the doorframe and slowly walks toward me with his gloriously tall and muscled frame.

His hands cup my face, his thumbs gently caressing my cheeks, and I look up to meet his gaze. Desire flares bright and hot within him as it does in me.

I lift my hand and press it to his chest, just over his heart.

"Take me to your bed."

With that, he bends down, leans over, and whips me over his shoulder in a fireman carry. I squeal and I can't help the bubbling laugh that escapes.

He smacks my ass as he carries me up the stairs and I reach down and smack his in return.

"I'm not much for spanking unless I'm giving them out."

"Awww," I coo and slide my hands into the back pockets of his pants, cupping his ass and giving it a gentle squeeze.

He starts taking the stairs two at a time.

"Hang on, baby, you're in for a bumpy ride."

Chapter
ten

Lucy

"Did you just use a keypad to unlock your bedroom?"

"Yep."

"Why on earth...?" I ask as I'm hanging upside down, considering biting his tight ass.

He gently sets me to my feet, holding me up while I get reoriented.

"We used to throw tons of parties—"

"Not anymore?" I interrupt.

Jesse walks over and relocks the door and I fight the urge to press a hand to my belly to calm down those freaking butterflies mosh pitting in there.

"Sometimes. Not nearly as much as we used to."

"Let me guess. Women like to go into your room and snoop, take things, or lay there naked waiting for you."

Jesse grins. "Lucy, I really love the way you think."

"Are you trying to tell me I'm wrong?"

"Nope."

"Good, because if you did I'd call you a liar."

His grin fades fast. He walks closer to me and runs the pad of his index finger down my cheek. "There's one thing you'll learn about me, Cupcake. I don't lie."

"Oh come on, Jesse. Everyone lies."

"Not about stuff like that. Not about the important stuff."

"Who decides what's important?"

"Well, right now that'd be me and I'm deciding that it's really important for you to press that body up against mine so I can get you naked."

I walk up to him and do just that—press myself against him. He's close to a foot taller than me, even with my three-inch heels, so I'm not able to wrap my arms around his neck as I'd like to. I rest my hands on his chest and I just can't believe this is real.

I'm standing here with Jesse Kingston—the six feet three inch rocker, schoolgirl crush, and one sexy motherfucker. I do a mental headshake.

His finger rests gently under my chin and raises my face so I'm looking at him. He looks so serious. I suppose this *is* serious.

"I like when you look at me, Lucy. I want you to watch me while I make you mine," he leans down and kisses my lips. My eyes drift closed when his tongue slips in and tangles with mine. He tastes so good. He smells fantastic with his signature Jesse scent of ocean, sandalwood, and yum.

His hands drift to my back, sliding up and down, down, down until he cups my ass and pulls me closer to him. I let out a soft moan and he breaks the kiss.

"The noises you make are so fucking hot."

I blush. I can't help it.

"I don't want you to help it. I want you to keep doing it."

Shit. I didn't mean to say that out loud.

His hands slide up my back and his lips lick, kiss, and nip at my neck and jaw. I can't keep my eyes open but I don't think he minds right now. He can't see me anyway.

What if he finds my body lacking when he gets me naked? I mean, I'm not really big-chested like a lot of the fake groupie whores he's been with, I'm sure. I'm a very modest C-cup—meaning I could get away with a B-cup if I had to, depending on the fit.

"I don't think I'm doing this right if you're still thinking," he murmurs against my neck.

"I'm sorry."

"Uh-uh. No need for sorries no matter what, alright?" he asks meeting my gaze. I nod and he nods back. "Do you want to talk about it?"

I try to look away but he won't let me.

"No hiding. You've got no reason to hide here, Lucy. It's just me and you."

I blow out a breath. "That's just it."

"What?"

"*It's you.*"

"What do you mean?"

I step back and walk over to the table next to the bed and kick my shoes off. I throw my arms up. "It's you!"

"Yeah, and?"

"Jesse, come on."

"I'm just a guy, Lucy."

"No, you're not. You were my schoolgirl crush—a fantasy. Now here you are standing in front of me, ready to get naked with me. On top of that you're this mega rockstar who has had so many women that you probably lost count years ago. You're a rockstar who probably knows more about pleasuring a woman than—than the women themselves."

He folds his arms over his chest and watches me pace, his face void of any expression.

"Go on," he encourages.

"Ugh, you want me to spell it out?"

"Please do because I thought we'd been over this already."

"We have been. But…" I break off as I stop, head down. I'm just going to blurt this out, get it out there. I hate making myself vulnerable but maybe he can fix that if I tell him what I feel.

"But…"

I look up and meet his gaze. "I feel inadequate, Jesse."

His eyebrows raise and his surprise couldn't be more evident. "What? Are you kidding me right now?"

I shake my head and bite my lip.

He steps forward and tucks a strand of hair behind my ear. I love when he does that. It makes me feel sexy.

"Lucy, you're beautiful—beyond beautiful."

"Not just that, Jesse," I whisper.

"Inadequate sexually?"

I nod.

"I really don't think that's going to be an issue, Lucy."

"I'm not a virgin but I'm not all that experienced either. I mean, oh you know what I mean."

"Again, likely not an issue, not with the chemistry between us."

"But—" He presses his index finger to my lips, cutting me off.

"Why don't we address these issues one at a time?"

I nod. What else can I do with his finger against my lips than be quiet and let him take over? I'll admit, him taking over sends a little thrill zinging through my body.

He steps back and sits on a padded bench at the end of his bed. He starts unlacing his boots and removes them and his socks. When he's finished, he walks up to me, standing behind me. Then he reaches up and starts unzipping my dress and my breath falters.

You've got this, Lucy. You can do this. You want this. You're sexy, you're smart, and this incredibly sexy rocker that you've lusted over for nearly half your life wants you. You! You can give as good as you get. Give it, Lucy.

When the zipper presses against my lower back, he doesn't push the dress off my shoulders and I don't hold it up, yet it doesn't fall. He walks around in front of me and crosses his arms and I look up at him from underneath my lashes and wet my lips with my tongue.

He meets my gaze. "Shrug."

I do and the dress falls. He blows out a breath that is more of a hiss. "Holy fuck."

He steps forward and traces a finger along my collarbone. "Lucy."

"Huh?" is all I can manage when his finger dips down into the cup of my bra and rubs against my nipple.

"It's a crime for you to hide this body."

He steps forward and presses his lips to mine, giving me close-mouthed kisses, no tongue, but it doesn't detract from the passion he brings me. His hands cup my breasts and gently squeeze.

He steps back.

"Your belly button is pierced."

"Uh-huh."

"I thought it was part of the costume for the shoot."

"Nope."

"Fuck, that's sexy."

"I'm kind of disappointed you took your lip ring out."

He grins. "I didn't want to wear it on our date. Had I known it turned you on…"

He trails off and just stares.

"Know what?"

"Hmm?"

"I think we're going to go with your earlier suggestion."

I can't remember what I said. What did I say? Oh…

"Really?" I squeak.

He nods. That's one way to break the tension. No thinking, just rip-each-other's-clothes-off-fuck-against-the-wall sex. I nod back and then our mouths crash together, tongues tangling and our hands are everywhere. He's unhooking my bra as I'm lifting up his shirt. He pulls his shirt over his head and throws it across the room where it lands next to my bra.

I'm unbuckling his belt and he's sliding his hand between my legs. I moan as his finger rubs against my throbbing clit. I unbutton his pants and unzip them. He backs me against the wall.

"I want to leave your garters on this time," he growls in my ear as he tears my panties off. Tears. Them. Off. Oh my God.

I push his pants and his boxer briefs down his legs and he steps out of them. I'm not wasting time here. I want to know what he feels like and I am dying to have him inside me. I'm liking this no-thinking thing.

He leans down and pulls a condom out of his wallet. Oh yeah. Now we're talking, I think… then I look down and my eyes widen. There is no way that's going to fit. No way. I've had sex before but wow. I try to back up but I come up against the wall.

He rolls the condom on. "It'll fit and we'll go slow until you get used to me."

"I'm not so sure…" The man is huge. If he were anyone else and I didn't want him so much, I'd be outta here.

"Trust me, Luce."

I nod, eyes wide but full of desire. He cups his hands under my thighs, lifting me up and I wrap my legs around his waist, my arms around his neck, and press my mouth to his. I want him to have no doubts as to how much I want him. That was never in question.

He slips his finger down between my legs, gliding down my slit to my opening. I should be embarrassed that I'm dripping wet for him but when he slips a finger inside, I lose all train of thought.

"You're so tight, Lucy," he says, sliding a second finger inside. "Let's get you ready."

A moan is all I can manage for a response as his fingers glide in and out of my pussy, slowly but deeply, deeper than he went in the car.

When he starts pressing kisses to my neck again, I can't hold still. I want more, I need more. I want to feel him inside me.

"Jesse."

"Not yet," he says against my neck then licks me there.

His fingers move faster, harder, and I can't hold myself still. I start moving against his hand.

"There you go, Lucy. Take what you need. I want to feel you come all over my fingers." He begins circling my clit with his thumb and I'm teetering on the edge.

"Oh God, Jesse."

"You're so close. I can feel it. Let go."

I throw my head back and continue fucking his hand. He presses his thumb harder against my clit and I moan louder.

"Yes, just like that…" I moan.

He chuckles. "You're so fucking sexy."

I moan again when he circles harder.

"Come for me, Lucy. Come for me so I can slide inside you."

Those words alone throw me over the edge and I cry out. "Jesse!"

"There we are, give me all of it. Jesus, I can't wait to feel that around my cock." He works my pussy and my clit, drawing out every possible second of pleasure until I stop moving. Then he rubs the tip of his erection against my clit causing my entire body to jerk. I'm still sensitive from my recent orgasm.

"I could get you to come again just from this but I want to feel you squeezing my cock when you do."

He positions the tip against my opening and meets my gaze.

"Slow."

I nod, eyes wide because I really don't know how he's going to fit.

The head slips inside and I gasp.

"Okay?" he asks, watching me intently.

"Mmm, it just feels good." God he's huge.

He smiles. "Good. A little more." He pushes upward and lets me slide down at the same time, slowly, inch by inch, stretching me more than I've ever been stretched before. It burns, the stretch, but it hurts in a good way.

"Jesus, Jesse."

"You okay?"

"Mmm, yeah, you're so huge."

He grins. "I told you you'd say that."

I moan when he slips in further. "Mmm, yes you did."

"Almost there, can you take more?"

I nod. "I just need a second." Holy Jesus. I'm stretched so full with him inside me… I've never felt anything like it before.

He pauses and kisses below my ear and flicks his tongue against my lobe. He meets my gaze.

"I'm not hurting you?"

I shake my head no. Need is taking over and oh my God I want him all the way in me now.

"I want to feel all of you, I need more, Jesse." I feel full but it's not enough. I want everything. Every last inch of him buried inside of me.

"You've got a greedy pussy, baby," he says, pushing into me quickly until his balls press against my ass. "Fuck, Lucy. You feel incredible."

"Unh," is all I can manage. I need him to move so I clench my pussy around him. He's so thick I can barely move.

"Fuck, if you do that I'm going to lose control."

I thread my fingers through his hair, tugging a bit until he looks me in the eyes. "Do it."

"I don't want to hurt you."

"Only the best kind of hurt. Move Jesse," I say sternly. He just stares at me. "For fuck's sake Jesse, fuck me already."

That's it. He snaps. "You want me to fuck you? Hang on, baby."

His lips meet mine and his tongue aggressively duels with mine. He pulls out and slams back in. Oh my God. I've never felt anything like it. I've never been so full. He starts moving at a steady pace and it feels so good, I feel my orgasm building already. Incredible. I usually have issues coming a second time.

"Oh my God, Jesse."

"Harder?"

"Yes. Faster," I say as I tilt my hips and he slips in even deeper. He groans and I cry out. His hips thrust faster and harder and when I can't stand it anymore I reach up and grab hold of his shoulders and start to raise and lower myself, meeting his thrusts. With this motion, my clit rubs against his abdomen, my nipples against his chest, and the tingles begin.

"Lucy," he moans. "Watching your tits bounce, your head thrown back, while you ride my cock is the sexiest fucking thing I've ever seen."

I moan back in reply. "I'm going to come."

"Come for me, Lucy. I want to feel that incredible pussy squeeze my cock."

Jesus, he's good at the dirty talk and it's turning me on even more.

"Look at me."

I force my eyes open. A few more brushes of my clit against him, a few more thrusts and the tingles become a dull ache and then I'm coming, so hard, so incredibly hard, I can't catch my breath. Maybe I can't catch my breath because I'm screaming out his name. I suck in gulps of air as he hammers into me faster and harder, his fingers digging into my ass. He's so incredibly fucking sexy in this moment, his gaze locked with mine, and then he lets go with a long, loud groan. His hips keep moving as he comes and comes and comes, grunting with each spurt of his release. I continue moving my hips, wanting to milk every drop of cum I can out of him.

He presses his head into my neck and just rests there, his breathing as heavy as mine. I run my fingers through his long hair, my cheek resting against the back of his head.

Jesse lifts his head and meets my gaze, his expression somber. I'm not sure what to make of this so I just wait. I think he's still processing what just happened and I haven't even begun. My brain is scrambled.

"I'm going to be honest with you, Lucy."

The tone says he's disappointed. I nod, already feeling tears brewing at the back of my eyes and I breathe deep to force them away. I don't need to do that. Not now. Not here.

"You were worried about your body, about you not being hot enough or sexy enough. You've got the sexiest curves I've ever fucking seen, Lucy. That's no lie. I knew you were hot but under the clothes…" he shakes his head.

I feel better hearing this. But now…

He reaches up and cups my face with his hands.

"You were worried, feeling inadequate?"

I nod.

He blows out a breath, closes his eyes, and slowly presses his lips to mine, lingering for a few seconds before pulling back and walking backwards. He sets me down on the bed, slips off the condom and throws it into the trash. He turns the bedside lamp on and a warm glow fills the room.

Oh God. It was awful for him. He can't think of how to tell me. I look up at the ceiling and blow out a breath, willing myself not to cry. God, I'm such a baby.

Then he pulls back the blankets on his bed, lifts me into his arms, placing me on the bed, head resting on the pillows, his chest lying on top of mine and the rest of him is between my legs. He's propped up on his elbows, staring into my eyes, and I don't know what to think.

I reach up and tuck his hair behind his ears so I can see his face and he smirks.

"I don't have words."

What? My brows pull in as I frown.

"I know, right? A rocker and songwriter who can't come up with a few words."

"What?" I'm a little more than confused.

His gaze drops to my mouth and his finger traces my lips. "That, what we just did? It left me speechless. I'm not fucking around either. You stole my breath."

I just watch him, unsure what to say. *I didn't totally suck!* Inside I do a crazy happy monkey dance.

"You're so fucking sexy, Lucy. God, you're just incredible." He drops a kiss to my lips and rocks his hips against mine. My eyes widen. He's hard again.

"I want you again, Lucy."

I nod. He opens a drawer and grabs a foil packet. He rips it open then sits up and rests on his knees as he rolls it down his thick length.

He looks up at me again. "Do you want me, Lucy?"

"Yes," I nod.

"Let's see." He dips a finger into my wetness and hums. "So wet." He slips a second finger in then slides down the bed, kissing my thighs and calves as he repositions himself, his head between my legs.

Oh my God. I'm fighting the urge to squeeze my thighs together. He can see everything down there. I've never had a guy go down on me with the lights on.

"Such a pretty pussy. I'm going to taste you now, Lucy. I've been dying to do this for days and I can't wait anymore." His tongue snakes out and runs up between the lips of my pussy and then down to my opening. He pulls back, closes his mouth and his eyes, and swallows.

"You taste so sweet." He circles his tongue around my opening, then gently closes his lips around it, licking up my juices. He lets out a hum and my eyes roll back in my head when his tongue laps at my clit.

"Jesse," I whisper.

"So good," he whispers and continues licking, lapping and sucking at my pussy. When he slips two fingers back in, I can't hold back my moan of pleasure, and when he curves them just right and they hit that secret spot, I reach down and grab hold of his hair.

I can feel his smile against me but I don't care. It feels too good to care if he's smug right now. I am losing my mind. I have never, *never* come four times—including the car. Ever, and I'm getting really close to doing just that.

"Jesse." My breath catches and he looks up and meets my gaze. He takes one last lick then moves up my body. He sits on his knees and pulls me forward, draping my legs over his thighs. Then he thrusts smoothly into me.

He groans and his eyes close as he holds himself still. He opens and meets my gaze.

"You okay?"

I nod.

"Sure?"

I nod. "Just… fuck, Jesse."

He chuckles. "Mmm. Feels fanfuckingtastic." With that he begins moving, slowly at first, then faster and harder. His hands slide beneath my hips and he tilts them up.

"Christ you're so hot and wet. So fucking tight."

With each thrust, he grinds his pelvis against my clit and soon, too soon, I'm hovering on the edge of the orgasm I thought was lost.

"There we go," he whispers. "I want you to come again, Lucy, because I'm getting close." His hips are slamming into me, hard and fast, his gaze locked on mine.

"I can't control myself when I'm inside your body, when you squeeze my cock and grip it so tight."

I moan and he grins. Oh, that grin, it's devilish. He drops his head to my neck and starts licking and kissing, moving faster and harder, his hips pistoning into me, his balls slapping against me and I am lost. The orgasm overtakes me and I call out to Jesse, each pulse stronger than the last and then he calls out my name with a roar, then bites my neck—yes, bites me!

"Your pussy… fuuuuck… takes everything from me." His body jerks against me, our bodies prolonging each other's pleasure until we're both left panting and limp.

"Holy fuck," he says against my neck.

"Unh," is all I can manage as I thread my fingers through his hair, my head resting on the pillow, my eyes closed.

We lie there in silence a few minutes and then I feel his lips curve into a smile. He lifts his head and I open my eyes to look down at him.

He disposes of the condom then lays back against me, his elbows on either side of my chest, his mouth kicked up in that oh-so-sexy half grin.

"Lucy?"

"Jesse?"

"You were worried you'd be inadequate?"

I nod, biting my lower lip. He reaches up with his index finger and smoothes over my lip. "Don't. Your lips are too pretty."

My lips are pretty? No one has ever said my lips were pretty before. My eyes, sure. My hair, yeah. But my lips? I'm oddly flattered.

"You're far from inadequate. If you were any better I'd be dead."

I roll my eyes. Whatever. Typical guy response.

"Don't roll your eyes at me. I don't know how to do this, Lucy. I don't normally talk to the women I've fucked."

I nearly flinch, but stop myself before I do.

"So, I'm trying because you're nothing like them." Okay, that's better. "All I can think to say is your body is perfect, the sounds you make are sexy as fuck and turn me on to the point I could come within seconds. Just thinking about them is starting to get me hard. And I'm not going to bullshit you. I've fucked a lot of women."

"Groupie whores," I snarl.

He grins and nods. "Groupie whores. But it's never been like it is with us."

"Which time?" I ask.

"All of them. Fucking mind-blowing."

"Hmm."

He lifts a brow in question.

I lift a shoulder and deadpan, "It was alright."

For a few seconds a look of disbelief freezes on his face, then he throws his head back and laughs an all-out, belly-rolling laugh in a way I've never heard or seen before and it's beautiful watching him laugh.

He tickles my side. "You are a brat."

I squeal. "No tickling, please, please, Jesse."

He kisses my lips softly. "You hungry?"

I nod. "Starved."

He gets up from the bed. "Stay there a minute." He walks beautifully naked into his bathroom and I now see the tattoos covering his entire back and shoulders. I knew he had them up his arms, but I didn't know they went that far. I need to touch those nipple rings later—after I lick his tattoos. When he comes back into the room I note he has one down his left thigh as well. I'll have to thoroughly inspect them later.

Jesse pulls the covers back. "Open."

"What?" I'm asking as he gently presses a warm, wet cloth between my thighs cleaning me. It's the sweetest, gentlest gesture and so uncharacteristic of what I'd expect from Jesse. He is such a contradiction. Such a bad ass rocker, tough and rough, tattooed bad boy, but then he's got a soft side that he's slowly starting to reveal.

He tosses the cloth into the hamper. He opens a drawer and grabs a shirt. He walks over, pulls it over my head, and I slip my arms through. The sleeves go down to my mid-forearms and the length nearly reaches my knees. It is, of course, a black, awesomely designed Falling Down t-shirt.

"It's a little big."

"You already told me that, but you adjusted," he grins.

"Oh my God."

"You already said that too. Multiple times, in fact." He pulls on a pair of black boxer briefs and a t-shirt.

"Jesse!"

"Oh yes, you screamed that out many times as I told you, you would."

All I can do is laugh as he stands there, looking so seriously smug. I walk over to him and climb up his body. His hands lift me and rest under my ass.

I cup his face in my hands.

"Jesse Kingston."

"Luciana Russo."

"You are incorrigible."

He nods. "I am."

I laugh again and he grins. I press a kiss to his lips.

"Feed me!"

"Oh, I'll feed you… food first. Cock after."

"Incorrigible!"

Chapter
eleven

Lucy

"Oh my God, Jesse, this is amazing," I say around a mouthful of beef and broccoli stir fry. The rice was the only thing he had left to make—well, and he had to reheat the stir fry. "Where did you learn how to cook?"

He takes a drink of his beer. "My mom. She was an equal opportunity mom, meaning it didn't matter if you were male or female, everyone did the same chores."

I nod. "That's how it was in my house too. There was no difference between me, Sera, or Joey. We had a chart and we followed it. I'd mow the lawn or wash the car and Joey'd do dishes or laundry, same with Sera and every day it changed."

"More wine?" he asks, holding up the bottle.

"Sure, thanks."

He nods. "How did Sera come to live with you?"

I frown. It's definitely not a happy story and I hate telling it, but I tell Jesse—not all the details, just the main points. He doesn't need to know that our families are freaking gangsters.

"Damn, that's rough."

I nod. "It was so hard on her. She's not the same as she was before... well, before."

"I can understand that."

"We don't really talk about it so..."

"No worries. I won't bring it up. At first I thought she was your sister but then you mentioned being cousins yet I knew she grew up with you and calls your mom her mom."

"My parents are her parents, my brother is her brother, and she's my sister. That's how her parents would have wanted it and so that's how it is."

"As simple as that?"

"As simple as that."

We hear a car rumble up and car doors close. I adjust my t-shirt to cover as much of me as I can.

"That shirt covers way more than enough. You wore less in the video."

"True, but I'm bra- and panty-less," I whisper as if it's a sin.

He shrugs. "They're not going to make a big deal out of it."

"Hmm."

Ben and Xander come strolling out onto the terrace where we're finishing our meal by candlelight. Jesse lit a bunch of candles while I was using the restroom and surprised me when we came out here to eat.

"What's going on?" Ben asks.

"We're eating, what does it look like?"

"Looks like Lucy's half naked," Xander says with a snicker.

I blush what I know has to be a deep scarlet if the heat that's burning my face is any indication.

"Dude. Don't fuck with her about it."

Ben punches Xander in the arm. "Don't be a dick. You know better."

"Jeez, it was just a joke."

"Well, keep that shit to yourself. Lucy's different," Ben says, grabbing three beers from behind the outdoor bar.

"I know she is. What the fuck?"

"Oh my God, you guys. Just let it go. It's fine," I reassure them.

Jesse scowls. "It's not, but we'll discuss it later."

Ben hands a beer to Xander and another to Jesse.

I fork my last bite of stir fry into my mouth and pretend nothing's out of the ordinary. I have no idea what just happened here or why these guys are acting so retarded to each other so I'm going to ignore it.

"Seriously, Jesse. This was so good."

He smirks, another innuendo on the tip of his tongue.

"Don't even go there."

He chuckles and Ben says, "Dude." And they fist bump. How did he get that out of what was said? Xander reaches over and fist bumps him as well.

I roll my eyes and take a sip of my wine.

"There's pie for dessert if you're interested."

I press a hand to my stomach and groan. "I'll let this settle a bit first."

He nods. Ben and Xander dig in to the stir fry without a word and I wonder what life is like here at Casa Falling Down.

I tuck one leg beneath me and rest my elbows on the table.

"So, tell me. What's a typical day like here at Casa Falling Down?"

Ben chuckles and Jesse and Xander smirk. "Casa Falling Down?"

I shrug at Ben. "Well, I can't call it Casa Jesse or Casa Kingston because that doesn't include everyone. Casa Falling Down seems appropriate."

I take a drink of my wine enjoying the cooling night air, the slight breeze, and the company.

Ben nods at that. "A typical day. Well, it depends really on what we've got going on. Some days there are interviews, either TV or radio. Other days there's studio time. There are days we just stay in and go into our studio in the back and write songs and make music."

"You have your own studio?"

They all nod like it's no big deal.

"It's the first thing I had done when I got the house," Jesse says.

"Sorry Jesse, but I've got to say it. Lucy you look so fucking beautiful sitting there right now, all mussed and in the candlelight," Xander says.

"Wow," I whisper. "Um, thanks."

"You're just so relaxed. You look now like you look on film. Relaxed, carefree. Happy."

"Huh." What do I say to that?

Jesse crooks a finger at me. I lift a brow but go over to him. He pulls me onto his lap and I wiggle to get comfy. He toys with the back of my hair.

"Do I normally look uptight?"

"Far from it. It's just different seeing you away from work and family and all your responsibilities," Xander tells me.

"Sometimes what's routine can weigh harder on us than we think," Ben adds.

"I don't mind taking care of Sera and Jace. And now that we're going to be making music, I won't have to worry about acting."

Ben nods. "You take care of more than Sera and Jace. I admire it. It's just nice to see you in this light."

I'm not sure what he's getting at. "Well thanks. It's nice to be in this light."

Jesse gives me a squeeze.

I smile. He runs his fingers up and down my thigh innocently. I rub the back of his neck with the hand I have resting there.

"You're staying a couple days then?" Xander asks.

I shrug. "Just playing it by ear."

Jesse frowns. "No."

"No?"

"No. You're staying the weekend."

"What? Jesse it's only Thursday. You want me here that long? Don't commit to something you'll regret later. Let's just take it as it comes."

Jesse ignores everything I just said, as does Ben, apparently, when he looks up and says, "The weekend?" His surprise evident.

Jesse just looks at him, Xander looks at Jesse. No words exchanged, no expressions altered, just a silent stare. Ben and Xander both nod at the same time as if they're communicating telepathically, which they could be. I mean, they've been around one another for so long, they probably can already read each other's minds.

"I don't know what was just mentally exchanged there, but it's kinda creepy how you do that."

"I'll never tell," Xander says.

"Traitor," I tease.

"Where's Ethan?" Ben asks.

"Last I saw him he was at the beach house with Jace."

Ben nods. "Cool."

"Yeah, it's like they're long lost friends or something."

"Ethan's like that," Jesse says. "He gets along with everyone and no one is a stranger."

I nod. "He seems nice. He didn't talk very much while we were working."

"He's all business when it's work time. When you see him off the clock you'll see the real Ethan."

"Kennedy's the same," Ben says and Jesse agrees.

"Kennedy is so quiet."

"Yeah, he doesn't say too much. His mind works a mile a minute so he's constantly thinking," Xander explains.

"Ah. Okay. I wasn't sure if I should take it personally or not."

"No way. All the guys had a great time working with you and Sera," Xander elaborates.

The other two murmur their agreement.

"Good. I had such a fun time, even if the boots killed my feet the first day and the leather caused massive amounts of boob sweat the second day."

They all chuckle.

"Whatever," Xander says. "You both looked fuckin' smokin' hot. That video is going to kick ass."

"I hope so. It's not the first video we've done but it really is one of the most important since it's going to kick off your new album."

"True that," Ben says, sliding his chair back and picking up all the plates.

"I can do that, Ben," I say. "Jesse cooked so I can do the dishes."

Ben raises a brow. "You're a guest, so thank you but I've got it." He winks and heads into the house, Xander grabs the rest of the dishes, waves and follows.

The minute they leave Jesse kisses me. Just a brush of his lips at first, a caress of his hand up and down my back, then his tongue traces the seam of my lips and dips inside. I moan softly and wrap my arms around his neck, turning my body so my torso's flush with his. The hand resting on my thigh slowly works its way up to my breast. He squeezes gently then rubs his thumb across my nipple through my shirt.

"Jesse," I whisper against his lips.

"You're so beautiful," he murmurs as he kisses his way along my neck. "I can't stop looking at you or touching you. I have to have you again." Without warning he lifts me and twists me so I'm straddling his lap. I tug at my shirt.

"Don't worry. They won't be back out here. They're over on the other side of the house."

"Are you sure?" I ask breathlessly as he begins to lift my shirt.

"Positive. Lift," he orders and I lift my arms. He pulls the shirt over my head then does the same to his. Both of his hands cup my breasts and he watches as he squeezes and caresses them.

"You've got the perfect body, you know?"

Nope, I don't know. It's just alright. I'd never think of it as perfect but if he wants to think that, far be it from me to argue. I mean, if Jesse Kingston thinks my body is perfect, my fantasy man come to life, then I'll let him.

His head dips down and he licks a nipple before sucking it gently into his mouth.

"God, Jesse," I sigh. That lip ring against my nipple, digging in... holy hell. It feels so good. His mouth is hot and wet and tugging just right on my nipple so I can feel it between my legs.

"Mmm, your noises. Your moans and sighs are so fucking sexy they get me instantly hard."

He grabs my hair in one hand and pulls my head back. He kisses his way up my chest to my neck and to that spot that drives me crazy just behind and below my ear. I shiver and I feel the grin against my skin.

"I can't get enough of you." Join the club.

I slide a hand between us, under the waistband of his boxers and wrap my hand around his erection. He groans and I begin to slowly stroke his length. Still suckling on my nipple, he drops a hand between us as well and thrusts two fingers into me.

"Fuck, you're so wet for me. Your pussy is so hot and tight. Fucking perfect."

That dirty talk. Hot. As. Hell. I moan as he thrusts his fingers in and out of me as I stroke him with the same rhythm. I slide my thumb over the head of his cock, wiping the precum collecting there and bring it to my mouth.

"Mmm."

"Holy fuck."

"I want to taste more of you, Jesse," I whisper into his ear.

He grunts. "You drive me fucking crazy. Later you can, now I need to fuck you."

He lifts me up and carries me over to the bar, fumbles around in a drawer, then looks triumphant as he produces a condom. I lift a brow.

"Not my stash but it'll work." He tugs his boxers down and I cling to him like a monkey while he bends over. He sits back down in the chair.

I grab the condom from him and tear it open with my teeth. I've never done this but I've watched it so I'm going to try. I do as he did before, pinch the tip then roll it down slowly. He moans as I take my time.

"This is going to be hard and fast."

I nod. I'm all for hard and fast. He lifts me and positions his erection at my opening.

"All you," he says, letting me take him inside me as fast or slow as I need to. I'm afraid to go too fast. I mean, the man is huge. Not just length, but girth. His dick is really intimidating.

I sink down, taking him inside. I'm so wet he slides in easily. When he's almost fully inside me I push down hard.

"Fuck, Lucy."

"Yes, that's the plan. You fuck Lucy."

He chuckles and starts to lift and lower me with his hands on my hips. It isn't long before we're fucking hard and fast, his cock touching my cervix over and over causing moan after moan to escape my lips.

His hips come up as mine slam down and I cry out. He stops. "Did I hurt you?"

"No. Jesus, Jesse. Don't stop."

He laughs, outright laughs, and starts thrusting again.

"You're so god damn tight, Lucy. Your pussy drives me crazy."

I moan again. His dirty talk turning me on even more than I already am. We're moving faster now, frantically reaching for our release. My clit starts to throb and my walls clench.

He groans. "Yes, God, Lucy. I can feel you. So good. Squeeze my cock, baby. Come all over me."

The only sounds out on the patio that I can hear are our heavy breathing, our moans, and our bodies slapping against one another. He pulls my bottom forward causing my clit to slide against his pelvis with each hard and fast thrust.

"Come for me, Lucy. I want you to come with me."

"Almost…" I moan and less than a minute later my walls squeeze his cock and my orgasm slams into me full force. His hips don't slow and I don't stop meeting his thrusts as he groans out his release. "Jesse," I whisper, as a new wave of pleasure overwhelms me. I keep coming and coming. It's never-ending pleasure and I think if I died right now I'd die extremely happy and beyond satisfied. A long moan tumbles from between my lips.

When the spasms subside, I rest my head on Jesse's shoulder and he rests his on mine.

"Holy shit," I whisper.

"Yeah."

He's going to ruin me for all other men. What do I mean going to? He already has I'm sure. Damn it. I shouldn't have done this, but it's too late now. If I hadn't I'd have regretted it for the rest of my life.

"I'm going to be sore."

"How long's it been?"

I shake my head. It's too embarrassing.

"No hiding, remember?"

I sigh. "Fourteen-plus months."

He pulls back and looks at me incredulously, eyebrows raised.

"What? Is that so hard to believe?"

"Well, kinda. Yeah."

I laugh. "Why?"

"You're gorgeous. You're a fucking movie star. You can have anyone you want whenever you want, I'm sure of that. There wasn't anyone you worked with that you wanted to just fuck when you were horny one night?"

I look at Jesse wryly. "My last movie was with Aiden Jensen."

He just looks at me blankly.

"Cocaine addicted Aiden Jensen. Asshole Aiden Jensen. Unprofessional as all fuck Aiden Jensen."

"Wow. How do you really feel, Luce?" he asks with a laugh.

"That movie took too much time, entirely too much time, and before that… it doesn't matter." I shrug. "I'm picky and I can't really just pick up a guy in a bar. I can just see someone taking pictures of me naked or making a video with their phone. If I thought the video of us grinding on the dance floor was too much, can you imagine what I'd have to put up with, with a sex video?"

"Hmm." He scoops me up and I wrap my legs around his waist. He slowly slips out of me then tosses the condom into the trash. He sits back in the chair, keeping me straddling his lap, reaches for a napkin and dips it into his water glass. He moves to wipe between my legs and I gasp at both the cold and the soreness between my thighs.

"Sore?"

I nod.

"Let's go take a bath."

"That sounds perfect."

He leans down and picks up both of our shirts, slips mine over my head and his over his head. I push my arms through the sleeves just in time for him to stand and I cling to him like a monkey again. He chuckles as he bends down, drawing a squeal out of me as I hold on tighter so I don't fall, and pulls up his boxer briefs.

He carries me up to his bedroom, punches in the code, and carries me to his bathroom where he's got a ginormous Jacuzzi. He sets me on the counter next to the sink and leans down to turn the water on. When we look for a new house, I want a tub just like this.

"That's going to take all day to fill."

"Nah, it doesn't take that long."

"What time is it anyway?"

He raises a brow. "Why? You got somewhere to be?"

"Shut up, no. I'm just curious how long you've put up with me and haven't gotten sick of me yet."

He steps close and kisses the tip of my nose. "Cupcake, I'm not even close to being sick of you."

"Hmm. Give me time. I'll drive you crazy."

"You already do," he says and wiggles his eyebrows.

"Ha. You drive me just as crazy."

He winks and walks into his bedroom.

"It's 1:15 a.m. and I've already given you five orgasms, counting the multiple you just had out on the patio as one."

I laugh. "You're counting?"

He nods. "Fuckin' A. I've got to keep you happy and pleasured."

"You do, huh?"

"Yep. It's my goal."

"Well, you're doing a great job so far. Such a good job, in fact, that I'm going to have issues walking today."

He grins, all proud of himself, and I roll my eyes. Men.

"Let's get you in the hot water. It should help a bit."

"Okay." I reach down to pull my shirt up and Jesse moves my hands aside.

"That's my job, woman."

"Get to it then."

He takes my shirt off, then strips off his shirt and boxers. He scoops me up and steps into the tub. He sits back with me between his legs. I lean back against his chest.

I moan softly.

"Feel good?"

"Mmm. Yes." I close my eyes and relax against him. "Sing for me."

"You want me to sing?"

"Mhmm."

"What would you like me to sing?"

"Anything. I'm not picky. I just love listening to your voice."

He presses a kiss to the top of my head and starts singing one of their older songs called *Forever Blue*.

Why did you walk away, where did you go
I've been looking for you, but you never show

Your heart is empty, you left me behind
Your soul is broken, do I ever cross your mind

You left me alone, something I never thought you'd do
You walked out the door and left me forever blue
You turned away, why, I haven't a clue
You broke my heart and left me forever blue

His voice is so strong and deep and his growl is incredibly sexy. He continues to sing the song and I wonder which one of the guys wrote this song and got their heart broken.

"Sing with me, Luce. I know you know the words."

I nod and we sing the chorus.

You left me alone, something I never thought you'd do
You walked out the door and left me forever blue
You turned away, why, I haven't a clue
You broke my heart and left me forever blue

If I ever see you again, I hope you're whole
If you ever find love again, I hope he touches your soul
If he loves you like I did, you'll never be sad
Mine will be the purest love you've ever had

You left me alone, something I never thought you'd do
You walked out the door and left me forever blue
You turned away, why, I haven't a clue
You broke my heart and left me forever blue
Forever Blue.

"I can't wait 'til you get up on stage and blow the crowd away," he says as he turns me to straddle his lap.

I wince slightly.

"Sorry."

"Don't be sorry, I'm not," I say with a laugh.

He smiles that sexy half-smile that tells me he's feeling smug. "I'm not going to lie. I think it's sexy as fuck that you're sore and it's from me."

"Are you going all caveman again?"

He nods. "I think I might be."

"So long as you don't drag me around by my hair, we're good."

"Nah. A little pain with the pleasure is good but that? No."

"Hmm. Spenser would kick your ass if you ripped out my hair."

"He fucking would too. That guy," he says shaking his head.

"We hired him, you know?"

"You did?" Jesse grins. "You stole him out from under Cage?"

"I did. No one can do hair and makeup better than Spenser and his girls."

"You took the girls too?"

"Damn right. They're incredible and we're going to have a band that's going to need attention."

He laughs out loud. "If it was anyone other than you, Cage would be pissed. He spoils you two."

"He totally does. It's part of why I love doing videos with him."

"Yeah, he's cool. We're only going to do ours through him from now on since we're signed with him now. Me and the guys like how he set everything up, and for as intense and detailed as that video is, it didn't take long to make at all. Three days isn't shit. Our shittiest video took longer than that."

"Which was your shittiest?"

"Our first, of course."

"I love your first one."

"You had a party to celebrate it, you weirdo."

I shrug. "I was crushing on you and the band."

"You crushed on more than just me?"

I nearly laugh at his tone. He almost sounds wounded.

"Don't pout. I could never crush on anyone as much as I crushed on you. You should have seen my bedroom."

He chuckles.

"It was Jesse Kingston fandom and I was the president. And now I'm sitting on your lap, naked, in your bathtub because you fucked me raw," I shake my head in disbelief. Crazy. Seriously crazy.

"What?" he asks when I remain quiet.

"If someone had told me when I was twelve or when I met you six years ago or even last week that I'd be sitting here with you like this, I'd have told them they were crazy."

"Hmm. Well, you're here." He presses a kiss to my forehead and I rest my head on his shoulder and wrap my arms around his waist.

The tub is nearly full and Jesse leans forward to turn off the water then hits the button to turn on the Jacuzzi jets.

I moan when the jets hit me crosswise across my lower back.

"Right?" he asks as he settles back with me clinging to him.

"Mhmm."

This moment feels so surreal. I close my eyes and kiss Jesse's neck. He runs his fingertips up and down my spine and I sigh. It's a very intimate moment and I'm glad that I've not given in to my emotions. I'm keeping them tamped down and staying strong. If I don't, I'll be in very real trouble because if I let my emotions run free, I risk the very real mistake of feeling more for Jesse Kingston than I know is safe.

He doesn't do relationships and I know it. It's why I'm guarding myself. I know better than to think I'm the exception to his rule no matter how differently he's treating me from his usual groupie whores.

I knew he was a sweet guy even when I was twelve. You can't hide that and he never really tried to. I imagine he does hide that side of himself when he's fucking the groupie whores. I bite back a snarl. I've got no right to react like that but I can't help it. Even before he knew I existed I reacted like that.

Jesse starts singing again, this time one of his ballads. With the jets on my lower back, Jesse's soft singing, his fingertips caressing my upper back, and my head resting on his shoulder, I try hard to stay awake. I really do. But I'm so comfortable and so relaxed that I drift off to sleep in his arms.

I swear I smell apples. I'm dreaming. I have to be because when I open my eyes, Jesse Kingston is kneeling above me with a forkful of apple pie hovering over my mouth.

"Unh," is all I can manage and he chuckles.

"Wake up, Luce. We've got pie to eat."

"Jesse," I whine.

"Lucy," he says in an equally annoying tone. "You know, you're going to hurt my feelings."

I give him a skeptical look.

"I made this pie and you don't want any of it. That's harsh and hurtful."

"I was sleeping."

"You're not anymore."

"Thanks to you."

He grins that sexy grin of his and I sigh. I hold the sheet up to my breasts and sit up.

"Here," he says, moving the fork of pie toward my mouth and I open. The taste of sour apples and sugar and cinnamon bursts on my tongue. "This is so good."

"I know."

"Wow. Arrogant much?"

"Nah. I just know I make damn good pie."

"Hmm," I say, snatching a plate of pie away from him. "I think maybe your mom's recipe has a little something to do with the awesomeness of this pie."

"True. But I still made it."

"Mmm," I moan as I take another bite of pie. "Your mom's a genius."

With this, Jesse frowns. He's actually pouting. He is too cute.

"Turn that frown upside down, mister. You've baked a fabulous pie."

"I'm not sure I want your compliments now."

"Awww, poor Jesse. I didn't stroke your ego hard enough?"

He looks at me. "I've got something you can stroke."

I laugh. "Let me eat my pie and I'll do just that. On second thought..." I break off, setting the plate down on the bed and leaning forward. "Lose the boxers, Jesse."

He raises a brow and smirks.

"Whatcha got in mind, Luce?"

"You'll just have to wait and see."

Jesse strips his boxer briefs off and sits back, resting on his elbows, legs stretched out, his cock semi-erect.

I lift a brow when I see it and he shrugs. "I've been sporting a semi or full hard-on since I saw you singing on that stage."

"Well, let's take care of that for you, shall we?"

I lean forward and Jesse rests his hand on my shoulder halting my progress.

"What?"

"I thought you were sore."

"I am, but what does that have to do with me giving you a blowjob?"

Jesse raises his eyebrows. "Nothing, but I don't feel comfortable leaving you unsatisfied."

"Yeah, pretty sure that's not an issue, Jesse. How many orgasms did you say you gave me?"

"Five."

"Right. And how many did you have?"

"Two."

I nod. "There you go then." I push his hand off my shoulder and reach a hand out for his cock, wrapping my fingers around his rapidly-hardening flesh and giving it a gentle squeeze.

Jesse lets out a soft grunt then lays back on the bed and folds his hands under his head. Awesome. His body is mine, and what a sexy body it is. He's muscular all over. His legs and calves are thick and well defined. His abs sport more than a six-pack, I count—a solid eight-pack. His arms are large, so large I can't wrap two hands around them, but not so large they look disgusting. I really hate overdone muscles, especially when they get all veiny—like when the veins stick up all the time. Gross. I saw Jesse's back and ass earlier—perfection. His body is nothing short of yum.

I stroke his cock slowly. He really is a very big boy. It's no wonder I'm sore. Over fourteen months of no sex and then I get a guy with a porn star cock. Yeah, I'm a lucky girl, but ouch. Soreness.

I climb up and straddle his legs. Jesse watches me and I don't break his stare as I slowly lower my head and swipe my tongue across the tip of his cock. His eyes drift closed and a low moan drifts between his lips.

I want to please him as he pleased me. When his eyes open and his gaze locks onto mine, my lips envelop his cock and I slowly take him into my mouth, wrapping a hand around the base. There is no way I'll ever fit that bad boy in my mouth no matter how far I can deep throat.

I work his length as best as I can, using my other hand to stroke, and I must be doing something right from the sounds Jesse's making.

"Sweet Jesus, Lucy. Your mouth wrapped around my cock is fucking incredible."

His fingers thread through my hair and I know he's going to take control soon. I relax my throat and take him as deep as I can.

"Fuuuuuuck."

I stifle my grin. Yeah, I thought he'd like that. I do it again and again until Jesse's hips start to thrust. I slide my free hand up and gently tug on his nipple ring.

"God damn, Lucy. Your mouth is so fucking good."

I stroke his cock with each thrust of his hips, with my hand and my tongue. I tighten the suction and he groans louder.

He thrusts deeper past the resistance of my throat over and over, his fingers tightening in my hair. I slide my other hand between his legs and gently cup his balls. He lets out a grunt.

"Holy fuck. You suck me so good and so deep."

"Mmm," I hum and he groans again. I slide my tongue along the underside of his cock while I suck now and his breath catches.

"Fuuuuuuck. Do that again."

I do and he moans long and loud.

"I'm going to come."

"Mmm," I hum again.

"You might want to move, Lucy."

Move? Is he kidding? That doesn't give him the ultimate pleasure. Besides I'm dying to know what he tastes like.

"Lucy—"

I roll his balls gently with my fingers, tug harder on the nipple ring with my other hand and that does it.

"Fuuuuuuck," he groans out, his hips jerking as his release hits and his cum splashes into the back of my throat. I continue to bob my head up and down, keeping him deep while I swallow every drop of his semen.

"Fuck."

Don't get me wrong, I'm normally not a swallower, but this is me fulfilling fantasies. I likely won't get another shot after the next few days so

I'm taking everything—and I want to leave him with memories he won't soon forget.

I lick his softening cock clean and sit back on my heels. Jesse's eyes are closed and he's got a smirk on his face. I crawl up next to him and snuggle into his chest, taking for granted the fact that even though I want to snuggle, he may not.

He wraps his arm around my back and his fingertips start running up and down my arm.

"I really like your bedroom."

"I really like you in it."

His bed is, of course, a California King, and so amazingly comfortable. The color scheme throughout the room is hunter green, black, and royal blue. There are a total of four doors in this room, all cherry wood, as are his dressers, tables, and anything wooden within the room. I love cherry wood. How he found perfectly matching accenting rugs to go throughout the room, I have no idea. Likely an interior decorator.

One door leads to the bathroom. When you first enter the bathroom there's the sink and long countertop and all the way down is a door to where there's a toilet and standing shower. On the opposite wall is the Jacuzzi.

The second door is an amazingly huge walk-in closet. It's more like a room inside a room. It's crazy and he doesn't even have it halfway filled up. It's sacrilegious and I made sure to tell him so.

A third door leads to a sitting room with a sofa, loveseat, and two La-Z-Boy loungers. There's a huge TV, a game system, and a media center. The room is tricked out.

"Your bad girl came out to play," Jesse says, pulling me from my thoughts.

I nod. "She did."

"I wasn't sure if you'd let her."

I shrug. "She deserves to have a little fun, doesn't she?"

"Mhmm, she does."

"Well, there you go."

He remains quiet for a few minutes and I can't help but wonder what he's thinking. I hope he's not thinking this is a normal thing for me—

swallowing and blow jobs because that couldn't be further from the truth.

"Stop."

"Hmm?"

"Stop."

"Stop what?"

"Thinking."

"I'm—"

"Yes, you are and you need to stop."

"You don't even know what I'm thinking."

"I'm sure it's not good."

He rolls on top of me and looks into my eyes. He starts playing with my bottom lip with his index finger.

"I don't know what's going on in that pretty head of yours, but it needs to stop."

"I—" Jesse cuts me off with a press of his finger to my lips.

"You're in there," he taps my temple, "putting yourself down because you let yourself do what you wanted. Second-guessing yourself, thinking that I think bad things because you are really fucking good at giving head."

I shrug. Bullseye.

"Best blow job of my life, by the way. You have nothing to be ashamed of, Luce. You were fucking amazing. There is no shame in enjoying sex or being good at it."

I huff and he lifts a brow.

"I hardly ever do that, just so you know."

"I never thought you did. I'm sure you keep that bad girl locked up pretty tight but I'm glad you're comfortable enough to let her come out and play with us."

I nod.

"Okay?"

"Okay."

"Good, because holy fuck woman, you blew my mind," he says, rolling onto his back, his arms flopping over his eyes. "I still can't feel my fucking toes."

I smirk then sit up and grab my plate of pie and finish eating it. I reach over for the bottle of water on the bedside table and take a long drink.

I eye his plate of pie laying on the bed by his feet, then look at him. He's not looking. I want that pie. It's so good. I look at him again, still not looking. I quickly swap my empty plate for his and start eating again, giggling.

I'm on my fourth forkful when he eyes me. I give him a smile and take a sip of water. He smiles.

"You're liking my pie, huh?"

"Mmm, so good."

"Yeah?"

"Mmm. In fact, it's so good," I say forking another bite into my mouth, "that I'm eating yours."

He stills. "You—what?" He sits up and sees the empty plate by his feet and then looks at mine, which only has the back part of the crust left so I pick it up and take a bite.

"What the fuck, woman? Now I gotta go all the way down to the kitchen to get more pie."

I shrug. "You should've brought the entire pie."

"I would have if I'd known you were a pie stealer."

I laugh. "I have a weakness for sweets."

"Good to know."

"Planning on using my weakness against me?"

He smirks that devilish half-smile. "Only in the best possible way."

"It's 4:30 in the morning, I'm sitting in bed, naked, with the hot and sexy rockstar that is Jesse Kingston, filled up on apple pie that he made from scratch, sore from phenomenal sex—I'm not sure there's anything that could top this moment."

"I've got the next three days to work on that."

Jesse gave me a half-day reprieve from the fuck-a-thon we had going on before he pounced and I certainly wasn't complaining.

The weekend was filled with seriously amazing sex, lots of laughs, good conversation, and delicious food. Jesse is a culinary genius. Too bad he isn't relationship material. He'd make for a great boyfriend.

I stuff the last of my clothes into my weekend suitcase. The time went by too quickly and now it was time to say our goodbyes.

Jesse steps up behind me, wrapping his arms around my waist and kissing my neck.

"You don't have to leave so early, Luce."

"I do," I say, tilting my head to the side giving him easier access to drive me crazy. "I've got a lot of things to do before we get caught up in the whirlwind of Blush."

"Mhmm. That's what it'll be too." He bites gently on the skin where my neck meets my shoulder and I sigh.

His hands drift up to cup my breasts. "Jesse," I whisper.

"I have to have you one last time."

I'll be walking funny for days but it's going to be oh so worth it.

Jesse turns me around to face him and cups my face in his hands. He stares at me long and hard, his head slightly tilted to the side and it's like a feeling of déjà vu from six years ago. It's like he's searching for something but I don't know what.

"What is it?"

He shakes his head. "Nothing."

He leans in and gently brushes his lips across mine, slowly increasing the pressure, then his tongue is sweeping inside my mouth to slide against mine. He's ruined me for all other men. Not just because his cock is amazing and he can bring me to orgasm like no one else—including myself—but because his kisses are magical. Sometimes slow and sweet and other times intense and passionate.

He pulls my camisole over my head and drops it to the floor. Next goes my bra, then shorts and panties.

"You should've just stayed naked."

Like he did. God, he's beautiful. I never did get a chance to trace all of his tattoos like I wanted. I'd start then Jesse would roll me underneath him and sex me up.

He walks me backwards toward the bedside table and reaches for a condom. He tears it open and rolls it on.

He dips his fingers between my legs testing to see if I'm ready. I'm more than ready.

"Your pussy is always dripping for me, Lucy. It's fucking sexy as hell."

"Mmm," is all I can come up with as he circles his fingers around my clit. When I start to get close, he pulls back and I let out a cry of frustration. He chuckles.

"Not yet. I want to take my time and enjoy this last time with you."

I nod.

"Crawl on the bed, Lucy, and stay on all fours."

I love how deep he gets when he takes me this way. He positions himself behind me and slowly slips inside me, pulling out and then pushing in a little further.

"God, Jesse."

"You feel so fucking good. You're so god damn tight. I've never felt anything like it."

I feel the orgasm he cut me off from starting to rebuild and I push back to meet his hips. He smacks my ass with his hand and I yelp, looking back at him in surprise.

"Stay still."

Oh my. The more he thrusts inside me, the more I feel the need to move, to search for the orgasm lingering on the horizon.

I gasp when he plunges deep and holds himself still, circling his hips. He lets out a groan. The sensations feel overwhelming, so good, I need to move. I arch my back and press back into him. He smacks my ass again, harder this time and I yelp again. He rubs his hand over the sting.

"I told you to hold still, baby. Don't disobey me or I'll have to tie you up."

I meet his gaze over my shoulder. "Seriously?"

"I'd find something to tie you up with."

"You're into the kink?"

"Not usually, no."

"What? I bring out the caveman side of you?"

He chuckles. "Something like that."

He smacks my ass again and my pussy clamps down on his cock. He groans and rubs his hand over the redness covering my ass.

"You like being spanked, huh, Luce?"

"I've never been spanked before."

"Your pussy gets so tight and you gush with each slap. Your body loves it and that's really fucking hot."

His thrusts get a little faster, a little harder and I moan. I'm so close. My clit is throbbing and tingling. One little brush would send me over the edge.

I reach between my legs and almost get my hand to its destination when Jesse smacks my ass again.

"I told you to be still. That means no bending down and touching, no moving. You don't get to rub your clit. Only I get to. You'll come when I'm ready to let you."

"Savage."

Jesse laughs then spanks the other ass cheek and pulls my hips even closer. He holds himself deep, pulling back just a little before pushing back in fast and hard. Each short thrust wrings a moan from my lips.

"Jesse, please."

"Please what, baby?"

"I need to come."

"Not yet."

"Brute."

He laughs again. "Let it build up so high and tight that when I touch your clit and slam my cock deep into you, you explode."

"Fuck me harder Jesse."

He grunts and obliges. His hips slamming against my ass, his balls slapping against my clit with each push of his hips, and it has me hanging on the edge again. I need to move. Just a little so when his cock goes in hard and deep, his balls hit my clit just right.

I can't help myself, I shove back to meet his hips, searching for that orgasm that has me desperate for release. He feels so good fucking me, but I need to come so bad.

Smack. My pussy tightens around his cock and he grunts.

"Jesus, Lucy."

"More, Jesse. Please."

"Soon, baby. Soon. Let it build."

"I can't wait."

"You can and you will."

I growl in frustration and he laughs. I see nothing funny about this situation. He has me desperate and writhing and he won't let me come. Cruel-hearted man.

I wiggle my ass, remember how it drove him crazy when I did it before, and he grunts. Smack.

"Your ass is going to be too sore to sit on if you keep disobeying me, Lucy."

He's rubbing his hand over my heated flesh as he takes his time fucking me, going slow, then fast. Going gentle, then hard. It's so inconsistent that it's driving me crazy.

"Please, Jesse."

"How bad do you need to come?"

"So bad, Jesse. Please." I can't stand it anymore. My head hangs down.

"You want to come now?"

"Yes!"

He grunts. "Okay Lucy. I'll let you come. But you're going to come again because it feels too good when you squeeze my dick tight inside you."

"Oh God."

He grunts. "Hang on, baby."

He thrusts hard and fast, his hips pistoning into me, his balls finally hitting my clit in just the right spot. In less than a minute I'm coming so hard and long that I can't catch my breath. It spreads throughout my body, going to my toes and the top of my head. I tingle everywhere as my walls convulse around Jesse's really fucking magnificent cock.

"Fuuuuuuck, that feels so good. Come on my cock, Lucy."

His dirty words turn me on even more and I'm still coming and I can't catch my breath.

"Holy shit. Oh my God," I cry out and I feel another orgasm right there. "Jesse."

"Oh yeah," he says hammering into me, "you're going to come again aren't you baby?"

"Yes, oh God, yes," I scream out his name as the second orgasm slams into me harder than the first, each wave crashing fiercely.

"God damn, your pussy grips me so tight. It's all I can do not to come."

"Come, Jesse."

"Not yet. You're going to come again."

"I can't Jesse," I tell him, my weight resting on my elbows now, my forehead pressed against the bed.

"You can and you will."

"Jesse—"

Smack. "You can and you will."

He pulls out and flips me over. His eyes are glazed over with desire, passion, lust.

He lifts my legs up over his shoulders and slides back inside me. He grunts.

"You feel so fucking good. I could come right now but I want you to come with me and I'm really enjoying the way your pussy feels around me."

"I don't know if I can."

He smirks. "You can."

He grips my hips tight and starts thrusting deep, so deep I feel the tip of him touch my cervix. "Oh God, Jesse," I groan.

"There you go, baby. You like it when I nudge you deep?"

"Yes," I hiss. I can't stand it. I'm so wet I can feel it dripping down the crack of my ass. I have no idea how the hell he gets my body to respond like this, but shit.

He groans. "You're getting close again. Your pussy's squeezing me. Fuck yeah."

He thrusts deep and hard and with each nudge deep inside, I get closer and closer to the edge. So, close.

"Jesse, please."

"Almost there."

He fucks me and fucks me and fucks me some more and just when I think I can't take any more, he slams into me so hard he starts pushing me across the bed. He pulls me back to him and slams into me once, twice and I'm flying, screaming his name and I really don't care if they can hear me on the other side of the house. My toes curl, goose bumps pop up all over my body, my nipples tingle, and the orgasm goes on and on.

One more hard, deep thrust and Jesse lets out a shout of, "Fuuuuck Lucy." Then he grunts and breathes heavily with each spurt of cum that my pussy milks from him. He keeps moving and coming and I see the surprise on his face. Now he knows how I feel and I'm so fucking glad he found that with me.

"Christ," he says and thrusts one last time before flopping down on top of me. I slip my legs off his shoulders, down to either side of him. His face is buried in my neck, his breaths coming fast and furious. "What the fuck was that?"

I giggle. Yes, I actually giggle. "Now you know how I felt with that last one. I couldn't even breathe."

"I love when you scream my name like that. That's what made me lose control."

"Mmm, happy to help."

"Shit. I don't want to move." But he gets up and disposes of the condom, then climbs back between my legs and on top of me. I wrap one arm around his back and toy with his hair with the other hand.

"I can't believe you spanked me."

"You fucking loved it. You keep surprising me."

"Do, uh, you do that a lot?"

"What? Spank?" he asks against my neck.

"Mhmm."

"Nope. Lucky you."

"My ass is still burning."

"But your pussy is singing."

I laugh. "It was more like screaming."

"Screaming for more of my cock."

"More like begging for mercy. I'm going to be so, so sore."

"Your pussy and your ass. Hell yeah."

"Caveman."

"Fucking A. You'll remember who fucked you good and hard all weekend and who spanked that sexy ass until you came all over my dick."

"Jesus, Jesse. The dirty talk gets me all horny."

He chuckles. "Yeah, I know."

"I can't go again. I'm so sore."

He grunts. "Good."

I try to think back and count how many times we had sex over the last four days, not limiting it to penetration, and I can't remember. I'm sure Jesse knows since he's been counting my orgasms.

"How many times did we have sex?"

I feel his smirk against my neck. "Why? You going to write it in your diary?"

"I might. There's lots of stuff in my diary about the hotness that is Jesse Kingston."

"Twenty-three."

"How did I know that you kept count? Seriously twenty-three?"

"Mhmm."

"My vag is never going to be the same."

"Nope. You'll always remember these last four days."

I sigh. That's what I'm afraid of. I'm never going to get over him and as he lays here on top of me, his breaths wafting across my neck, I know that what was once a crush is so much more than that. I'm all kinds of fucked up over Jesse Kingston. Sex complicates everything. I may not be in love with him but I'm pretty fucking close. This is so not good. Really not good.

I keep running my fingers through Jesse's hair as his breathing evens out, and he falls asleep. I could get used to lying just like this with this man. I could love him. It's just too bad he can't love me back. I sigh inwardly. How am I supposed to get over him now?

There'll be distance. Likely I won't see Jesse up close and personal ever again and the thought of that sends a pang to my heart. It hurts to know that. Why the hell did I think I could handle this with him and walk away unscathed?

Yeah, the things he did to my body have been glorious but my heart got involved somewhere along the way—likely in seventh fucking grade. I've probably been in love with him for the last eleven years. Can you be in love with someone you don't really know?

What the fuck am I thinking? In love? I'm not in love with him. I could be and probably would be if I had even just a little more time with him, which is why my having to leave is a blessing. It's going to save me and keep me from breaking.

"Jesse," I shake his shoulder gently.

"Hmm."

"I need to use the restroom." And then I need to run like the fires of hell are blazing on my heels.

He rolls to the side and I pad to the bathroom. I do my business and wash my hands. I splash some cold water on my cheeks. My face is flushed and glowing. Shit.

I twist my hair up into a messy bun and head back to the bedroom to get my phone. I need to call Max for a ride.

Jesse watches me as I do, his expression unreadable. My heart is pounding so hard I honestly feel like it's going to jump out of my chest. Fear. Pain. Anxiety.

Jesse meets me at the end of the bed where my clothes litter across the floor. He's eyeing me warily.

"I'm going to take a quick shower, if that's okay?"

"Of course."

I turn the water on. I don't need to turn around to know Jesse's standing behind me. I step under the spray, leaving the shower door open knowing he's coming in with me.

He grabs the body wash and squeezes some into his hands. He works up a lather then motions me forward. I step toward him and he begins washing my body, starting at my neck, working down the front of my body, then paying the same wonderful attention to my back. I look up at the ceiling and blink back the tears I don't want him to see. I rinse my body off. Then, being the masochist I am, I take the body wash and wash his body. While we're in the shower not one word is muttered yet each time our eyes meet there's so much being said.

I don't want you to go.

I have to.

I wasn't expecting this.

Neither was I.

Lucy.

Jesse.

I rinse my hands and Jesse steps under the spray. I step out of the shower and dry myself off quickly then wrap the towel around my body. I step into the Jacuzzi room and stop in front of the mirror. I look like shit. Ugh. There's not much I can do about it now. I walk into the bedroom with

Jesse right behind me.

He slips on his boxer briefs and picks up my lavender lacy boy shorts and holds them out for me to step into. He gently and slowly tugs them up my legs and over my hips. Next he stands and slides my arms through my bra straps, positions the cups, then hooks the back. He straightens the straps and even adjusts my breasts. I should be embarrassed by this but after everything Jesse's done to my body over the last four days, I can't even muster a blush.

"Your underwear is so hot. Do you always wear that? The lacy and sexy shit?"

"Mhmm."

"Damn. I'm going to be picturing that every time I see you on TV or in a magazine."

I step into my shorts as he holds them, then slides them up my body, his fingers caressing my thighs as he does. He buttons then zips them. He pulls my camisole over my head and pushes my arms through each hole before tugging it straight. His gaze locks onto mine and I feel the telltale prickles starting behind my eyes. *No. I can't cry. Not here. Not now. This can't happen.* My nose twitches and he smirks.

"Itch?" he asks, itching my nose for me.

Shit. Why is he being so sweet? I can't handle this.

"I should go, Jesse."

He nods. "I know you have things to do before tomorrow."

Oh God. I close my eyes for a brief minute.

"I do."

I slip my sandals on and stand there looking at him as he stares at me.

He steps forward and pulls me into his arms, holding me close. Oh God, oh God, oh God. Tears blur my vision. No. No Lucy. No. Look up and breathe. Just make it out of here before you lose it.

"Lucy."

He presses kisses along my forehead, cheek, jaw, chin and finally to my lips. Just a soft brush of his lips against mine and he pulls back, his thumb and forefinger hold my chin and I know he sees the shimmer of tears in my eyes but he doesn't say anything.

"Jesse," I breathe. "Thank you for this weekend."

He nods.

I step up on tiptoe and press my lips to his, my hands framing his face. I hold my lips to his, lingering, before I step back. I grab my suitcase and pull out the handle so I can roll it out. A lone tear rolls down my cheek and I brush it away. I head to the door before more tears fall. Pressing the code quickly, I open the door. I can't help myself, I look back.

I'll never forget this moment as Jesse stands there silently watching me, meeting my gaze as tears threaten to spill over. When I feel the first one start to fall, I smile and whisper, "Bye Jesse."

"Lucy," he says, taking a step forward. "This is 'see you later'."

I shake my head. I gasp for breath as I fight the tears building, racing down the stairs to the front door where Max is waiting for me.

I wish that were true, Jesse, but sadly I think this is the last time I'll ever see you. Thank you for everything. You're an amazing man and I'll never forget you or this weekend. I press a kiss to my index and middle fingers and blow it to him as the car lurches forward and takes me away from this dream and back to my reality.

Goodbye Jesse.

Jesse: *You saying goodbye doesn't work for me.*

Lucy: *What?*

Jesse: *Your goodbye isn't accepted and that means we're not done. I'll see you soon, Lucy. This is far from over.*

I don't respond, I just rest my head back on the seat, close my eyes, and hope like hell I can make it out of this in one piece.

Chapter *twelve*

Lucy

Still more than a little sore and confused from my weekend with Jesse, Monday brings new challenges. I work hard to push aside the complexity of feelings for Jesse—meaning the fact that I wish it could be more than just a weekend but I know the score. He doesn't do relationships and I've accepted that. Besides, I won't be seeing him again for—well, probably never unless we meet in some unlikely place.

Sera sighs. "Stop pouting."

"I'm not pouting. I'm nervous."

"Uh-huh."

"I am. You should be too with who Cage said was coming for the interview slash auditions."

"Are we really going to have them audition?" Jace asks.

"No, just play a couple songs with us and see if we get a good vibe. If not, then we'll jam with the next one on the list."

Jace yawns and takes a drink of coffee. "I'd die without Starbucks Americano."

"Same," I say and take a sip.

"I could go for a coffee IV on a regular daily basis. I wonder how wired a person would get from that," Sera says, looking out the window.

I snort. "I think we'd be bouncing off the ceiling like Mario."

"Ha! Likely," she replies.

Frank smirks. "This is the weirdest conversation you've ever had at seven-thirty in the morning."

"Well, it's probably due to the fact that *it's seven-thirty in the morning*," I scold, giving Sera a pointed look.

"Hey, don't blame me. I didn't set this up."

"He's kinda your boyfriend. You should've influenced him to set this up for late morning."

"I can't control the man and he's not my boyfriend."

"I said kinda."

"Still not."

"Denial: it's not just a river in Egypt," Jace says with a grin.

"What are you grinning about manwhore in training?" Sera says with clear disgust on her face.

"What?" Jace replies, feigning innocence.

"You *know* what."

"Yeah, Jace," I say, my tone laced with sarcasm. "How many skanks did you screw this weekend?"

He rolls his eyes. "Whatever."

Sera looks at him with a smirk. "Interesting. He's already evading and we aren't even on tour yet."

"What's your problem?" he asks us both.

"No problem. I'll adjust and not give you shit about it… eventually," I try to reassure him.

He grunts and takes another sip of his coffee, looking out the car window as we head to Cage's studio.

"We really don't care, Jace. Just don't be a prick, cover your dick."

I snort. "No glove, no love!"

Sera giggles. "Don't be silly, cover your willy."

More giggles. "Don't be a chump, cover your stump."

At that one, we burst out laughing.

"What the fuck?" Jace says, clearly exasperated. "I don't have a stump. Trust me."

"Yeah, yeah, stumpy," Sera says, taunting him.

"I suit up every time."

"Good boy."

He smirks at that. "Weirdos."

Max pulls the car around the back of the building as Cage instructed and we all head inside. I don't really think we need Frank and Max to protect us inside Nichols Records but I'm not going to argue the point. Frank's been pretty insistent with all the paparazzi around lately. I sigh inwardly. We need to find a house closer to the city so we don't have such a long drive when we have appointments. I'll talk with Sera and Jace after we finish things up today.

We walk inside the gold-mirrored building and I head to reception in the middle of the lobby.

"Good morning—" the woman pauses, her eyes widening.

I smile. "Good morning."

"Miss Russo, Miss Manzini, Mr. Warner. Mr. Nichols is ready for you. If you take the gold elevators up to the fourteenth level, you'll find his assistant, Marta."

"Thank you so much," I pause and look down at her nametag, "Elise. Have a lovely morning."

"You as well, Miss Russo."

We walk toward the elevators. There are three doors: black, silver, and gold. I can't help but wonder what the difference is. Weird. We step into the gold one and the doors close.

"I'm so glad Cage hires professionals," I breathe.

"Me too," Sera says.

"I wonder if it'll leak we're here," Jace ponders.

"I hope not."

Frank and Max don't look too worried about it. Truthfully, I can never be sure anymore.

The elevator doors open on the fourteenth floor and there's Marta, all ready for us. "Miss Russo. Miss Manzini. Mr. Warner. If you'll follow me, Mr. Nichols is expecting you."

The thin, dark-haired woman, dressed in a sexy but professional business suit, leads us to a conference room and Jace looks at me a little confused. "I thought we were doing studio stuff."

I shrug. "Likely we'll end up there. Mr. Meet-Me-At-The-Ass-Crack-Of-Dawn probably doesn't have the musicians coming for another hour."

Jace just grunts.

Cage greets us and we all take seats at the table.

"Was it necessary to have us here before the roosters were crowing?" I ask.

He grins. "It's really not that bad, Lucy."

"For who? I need coffee," I say as I head over to the coffee station. "Awww, you have my creamer. You're forgiven—almost."

Cage chuckles. "As long as it's almost."

"What are we doing here?" Sera asks.

"We need to discuss contracts and as your acting manager I can't advise you on these because I'm also the owner of the company."

"Lovely."

"It's not a big deal. Irene is also representing Jace, correct?"

"Mhmm."

"Good. I sent copies over to Irene and she'll have your attorney look them over."

"Oh, thank God," I whisper as I plop back into my chair. "Trying to decipher legal mumbo-jumbo is a total pain in the ass." Besides, I am not signing anything without Irene's okay.

"I just wanted to review everything with you before we head to the studio."

"Cool," Jace says, opening a bottle of cola and taking a drink.

"Is there anything else you need, Mr. Nichols?" Marta asks.

"No, thank you Marta."

She nods and exits the glass doors of the conference room.

We review the contract in detail, Cage explaining all the legalese in terms we can understand. It sounds like a pretty amazing contract, actually.

There are so many perks included in the contract as well as the impressive money. This can't be normal.

"Wow, Cage. This is extremely generous. You have a lot of faith in us."

He shrugs. "If I didn't believe in you I never would have let you think otherwise. I know good talent when I hear it. I'm positive you're going to be topping charts very quickly."

"No pressure or anything," Jace says with a chuckle, running his hand through his hair.

"Absolutely there's pressure. Think of it as incentive."

"Fair enough."

"Are there any questions?"

I look to Sera and Jace who both shake their heads no.

"Looks like that's a 'no' all the way around."

"Alright then, let's head to the studio and find you some band members."

When we enter the studio, we're greeted by another sweet-natured but, again, efficient woman at reception. As we head back through the hallway, I spot a really hot-looking guy. His hair is brown and messy-stylish, he's lean but muscular. His jeans hug well-toned thighs and what I'm sure is a very firm ass. His black t-shirt stretches across his chest and biceps outlining some pretty impressive muscles. Oh my.

"Whoa. Who is that?" I ask Cage.

"Hussy," Jace teases.

Cage chuckles. "Let me introduce you."

"Coffee and hotties, breakfast of champions," Sera says with a snicker.

"Damian, I'd like to introduce you to the members of our newest band, the one I told you about."

"Fantastic. Welcome aboard."

"Damian Black is one of our road managers among other things. Damian, this is Lucy, Sera, and Jace of Blush."

He shakes hands with everyone and I feel a little tingle when his hand clasps mine—it's no Jesse Kingston zing. He gives me a wink and I grin, trying to fight the blush that's starting to stain my cheeks.

"Pleasure to meet you. You're interviewing?"

"We are," I nod, my hand still clasped in his, neither of us move to pull away.

"What is it that road managers do?"

His green eyes hold my gaze steadily.

"We're responsible for checking in with the venues and setting times for setting up, booking hotels, securing cars if needed—usually if we're staying more than a couple days in one city. We also take care of anything and everything that you need on the bus from the absolute necessity to the ridiculous. We also are in charge of the crew. We make sure things are set up correctly and on time as well as packed up. Last but certainly not least, we handle any transactions that are needed at the venue. Generally this is an automatic thing, but some venues prefer the old fashioned methods of payment—especially the smaller venues."

"But Damian isn't just a road manager," Cage tells me and Damian sends him a look.

"Sounds like you're pretty important."

His grin widens and he flashes amazingly white teeth. Oh boy. "I can be *very* important."

Jace chuckles and I send him a glare.

"If you're done flirting with the new talent, Damian, we need to get started."

Damian just laughs. "I'm far from finished, but let's go."

"Oh, you're going with us?"

He places a hand on my lower back as we walk further down the hall.

"I am." He leans in and whispers, "I've been assigned to you."

"Oh boy," is all I can think to say and he chuckles again.

We enter a room off to the right and I let out a gasp. There he sits. The man I wasn't expecting to see ever again. My fantasy come to life. My dream come true. The best sex of my life. Jesse Kingston along with Ben, Xander, Ethan, and Kennedy.

"Well, this should be fun, huh?" Sera says.

I let out a sigh. "Fun, fun."

The guys are chatting and laughing when we enter the room but Jesse's smile fades as he notes Damian's hand on my back. I inwardly shrug. No strings. That was the deal so he has no right to be glaring at me like he is right now.

"Damian, you know the guys," Cage says.

They all murmur greetings as we all take our seats.

"What are you doing here?" I ask Jesse.

He flashes his signature half-grin. "Helping, of course."

"Of course. You didn't think to fill me in on this over the weekend?"

He shrugs. "It never came up."

"Oh, it never came up," I mumble under my breath.

"Nope, the only thing that really was up was my cock, if I remember things correctly." He, of course, says this loud enough for Damian to hear.

Sera snickers and I hiss and send her a glare. "What? It was funny."

I roll my eyes. "I think you could have mentioned it, oh, say, when we were saying our goodbyes and you let me believe I wouldn't be seeing you again anytime soon."

"I never said anything of the sort. If you assumed that, it's on you."

Ben's head is zinging back and forth between me and Jesse like he's watching a tennis match.

I sigh.

"Why are you pissed?" Jesse asks.

"I'm not pissed. I'm just… surprised."

"Obviously not in a good way," Ben says before taking a drink of his soda.

"I just wasn't expecting it, is all." After my long ridiculous girlie cry I indulged myself in last night, I started forcing myself to accept the fact I wouldn't see him again and here he is. I flip my hair over my shoulder and look at Damian who winks at me and tugs on a strand of my hair.

I swear I hear Jesse growl and when Ben starts laughing I know for sure he did. I don't look over at him. I can't. I'll get lost again. I'll long for more and I can't want that because it's something I just can't have. I want more than sex and that's all he's capable of. Without the possibility of a relationship, I can't be with him again.

I rest my elbows on the table and drop my face into my hands. *Breathe, Lucy. Just breathe.*

Sera rubs her hand over my back and I look at her.

"Okay?" she asks.

"Yeah," I whisper.

I note the frowns of the men across the table. Whatever. I don't have time for this now. I've got business to handle.

"We've got a few people lined up today," Cage begins just as there's a knock on the door. "And here's our first one now."

I turn to the door and my jaw drops, Sera gasps, and Jace says, "Are you fucking with me right now?"

"Pretty sure no one's fucking with you right now," Ethan says with a laugh. "You'd know it if they were and if you didn't, then you're doing something wrong."

"Holy shit," I murmur and elbow Sera. Her jaw is still dropped and I reach over to wipe the side of her mouth.

"What?"

"You had a little drool right there."

"Well can you blame me? That's Trace fucking Styx."

"Hell yeah it is," Jace says, getting up and walking over to the amazing drummer. We all murmur our greetings, shake hands, do our fangirling—much to Cage's amusement, and then we get down to business.

Trace is direct and informal, telling us about why he left his last band—drugs. Their use not his—and while he enjoyed drinking and partying, he didn't want to be mixed up in that shit. Who could blame him?

"Let's go jam," Trace says.

We head into the sound room where instruments are already set up for us. Trace picks a Flyleaf song and I smirk at the challenge.

I stand facing away from the window and meeting Trace's gaze. He counts it off and Jace leads us, I add the betrayingly sweet vocals at my cue, and Sera, Jace, and Trace come in as I growl out the lyrics. Trace's eyebrows go up and he smiles as he beats the hell out of the drums.

I turn around and note Cage, Damian, the guys from Falling Down, and another guy working the boards watch with straight faces. Sheesh, hard crowd today. I close my eyes as I reach deep and just lose myself in the music.

When we're done Trace belts out, "Cage, dude, where'd you find these guys?" He fist bumps with Jace.

Cage grins. "I'll let them fill you in on that."

We all walk out of the room and into where they're all standing. Jesse's grinning.

"Crazy vocals," Ben says and smacks my ass. I yelp. My ass is seriously sore from yesterday. Jesse smirks.

I laugh. "Thanks. Seems Trace wasn't the only one being tested today."

Trace shrugs. "If I'm going to sign on with a no-name band, they better be fucking good and I needed to see it for myself. No offense to Cage or you, X."

"None taken," Cage replies and Xander shrugs.

"Fair enough," I say. "I don't think I'd respect you very much as a musician if you didn't want to see what we were capable of."

He nods. "I'm in if you all are."

"Fucking A," Jace says and Sera and I laugh.

"Sera?" I ask.

"Oh yeah."

I nod. "Absolutely. Let's do this."

Trace grins.

Cage shakes his head. "Somehow I knew that'd be a perfect match. Good suggestion Xander."

Xander shrugs. "Only the best for our friends and that goes both ways."

"Oh Xander, I love you so much right now," I say dramatically and run and jump hug him, wrapping my legs around his waist. He's laughing so hard he nearly drops me and then he smacks my ass (the same cheek as Ben, mind you) and I squeal rubbing my ass.

Jesse smirks again and I narrow my eyes. I point my finger at him and his grin widens. "Don't do it."

He holds his hands up, palm out as if saying, "Hey, I didn't say a thing." He may not have said anything, but his smirk said enough. That man. Everyone's snickering.

On impulse I ask, "Trace, why don't you stick around and help us pick out the guitarist?"

"Legit."

Cage talks into his Bluetooth headset and tells Marta to cancel the other drummer he had scheduled for this afternoon.

Jesse walks up and slings his arm around my shoulders.

"How are you doing, Cupcake?"

"Pretty damn good. As Sera would say, Trace fucking Styx.

Unbelievable."

Jesse grins. "As I keep telling you, you guys are going to kick serious ass."

I slip my hand into the back pocket of Jesse's jeans. I really, really like his ass. "It doesn't seem real."

Sera shakes her head. "It doesn't. Joey's going to go all girlie when he finds out Trace is joining us."

"Oh my God, I never thought about that. Trace, my little brother is your biggest fan. He's going to go crazy over this."

Trace grins. "It's cool. I'm a fan of his too."

Sera groans. "Don't tell him that. His head is big enough as it is."

"True that," I say.

"I'll be honest," Trace says. "When Cage and Xander came to me and told me about your band needing a drummer then telling me who you were, I was skeptical."

I shrug. "I would be too. An actress, model, and accountant starting up a band? Yeah, there'll be plenty more jumping on that bandwagon and even more who will hate us out of sheer principle."

"Fuck 'em," Jace says.

"That should be our motto," Sera says.

"We'll work that into the logo."

I hear footsteps coming down the hallway and when I turn I want to fangirl all over the place. Sera actually does let out a fangirl squeal and the guys all laugh as Cage greets one of the best guitarists ever.

"Oh my God." I shake my head and rest my forehead against Jesse's shoulder.

"What's wrong, Luce?"

"This can't be real," I whisper. "It feels like the last week has been a dream and I've still not woken up."

Kennedy steps up and pinches my ass.

"Hey!" God damn! My ass is so freaking sore.

He shrugs. "Just letting you know you're not dreaming."

"Did you have to pinch my *ass*?" I say, rubbing the same damn cheek.

"Yeah, I did. Everyone else is spanking it. I felt the need to touch it."

I laugh. "Perv."

"You have no idea." Kennedy wiggles his eyebrows showing us he does have a playful side. I think maybe he's finally comfortable enough to let loose?

Cage steps up. "Alright. Layla Harper, meet Blush." He introduces us individually and for a minute I wonder if Sera's going to hump Layla.

"You hooked up with them already, Styx?" Layla asks Trace.

He nods. She looks at us, probably checking us out and assessing us in her own way.

"Let's jam," Trace says.

We head into the sound room and everyone takes their spot.

"Same song?" I ask.

Same band, different song. He names the song and Layla raises her brows. Trace laughs.

Same as before, Trace counts us off and by the time we're done with the song Layla has a grin so big I think her cheeks must hurt.

"That was kick ass," she says.

Trace nods, "Fucking killer."

She doesn't look at me, Sera, or Jace—only Trace. I'm not sure what I think of Layla. She seems kinda bitchy and judgmental. I'm not as excited about her as I was about Trace, especially when she notices Jesse and they share a kiss on the lips and a hug. They're very familiar with one another and it's no surprise. They toured together years ago when Layla was with Kickz.

Jace isn't as excited about Layla either. Sera's come out of her fangirl trance and doesn't seem all that thrilled. Cage notes our demeanor and nods.

"I'll give you a call and let you know, Layla."

She nods. "Sounds good. Nice meeting you all. Give me a call, Jesse," she all but purrs.

Yeah, I'm not her biggest fan and it's not just because she's hitting on Jesse.

When she's left the building, Ben asks, "Not going with her?"

I shrug. "I just didn't feel it. Her behavior tells me she's going to treat me, Sera, and Jace as less-than-equal and that doesn't work for me."

Sera nods. "Sadly, me either. She didn't feel like she fit in or that she even wanted to. She only gave a shit what Trace thought. There goes the fangirl feeling after seeing the attitude."

Trace is leaning back against the wall with his arms crossed. "Layla's not really a team player."

"Yeah," Sera sneers. "I suppose unless you're famous and have a cock, she's not really into being your pal."

"Noticed that, did you?" Ben laughs.

I nod. "I don't want to have to deal with that shit."

Jace agrees so that's a unanimous "no".

Cage looks at Ben. "I told you."

Ben shrugs. "I didn't think so either, but you never know."

"You knew it wouldn't be a good fit?" Jace asks.

Cage nods. "Her personality is completely different than yours."

"Well, who's next?" I ask.

"That'd be me, bitches."

"Are you shitting me!?" I squeal. I turn around to see the tall, model beautiful Megan Melody with her multi-colored rocker hair.

"Meggie!" Sera squeals and squeezes her in a hug. Jace and I join in.

"Huh," Kennedy says. "I guess they know each other."

"Oh my fucking God," Meggie says. "Get the fuck out of here with these bitches and then Falling Down. I'm going to need a dry pair of panties. For real."

I laugh. "We know Megan from high school."

"No shit?" Jesse asks.

"For real," Jace says. "She was in a rival band two towns over. We fought for gigs."

"How come you're not still with Taunt?" I ask.

"Ugh. Nothing but a bunch of cokeheads and manwhores. With me being the only female, it was just too much for me to have to listen to them fucking their sluts while I was trying to sleep."

"Gross," Sera says with a shudder.

"Huh," I say looking over my shoulder at Jesse and the guys. "That'd be kinda like having to live on the Falling Down bus."

Jesse lets out a laugh and shakes his head. "Tsk, tsk, Lucy. Always so judgmental."

"It's not judgmental if it's fact."

"Valid," Megan says.

"Holy shit, do you read Jay McLean?" Sera asks.

"Yes! Logan fucking Matthews, bitches."

I let out a laugh. Logan fucking Matthews.

"Let's jam, bitches," Meggie says with a bounce in her step.

"Yeah, fuckers, let's go," Jace says with a grin and fist bumps Megan.

As we head into the sound booth I hear Cage mutter, "We've got bitches and fuckers. This is going to be one hell of a ride."

We don't stop after one song. We go into two and three and then four. I notice Cage on his Bluetooth, likely cancelling the rest of the interviews, which is perfect.

With Trace and Megan, Blush is perfect.

We walk back out to where everyone's standing and I hug Cage. "I'm so excited, you just don't know!"

He chuckles. "I can guess from the smile on your face and that weird happy dance you and Sera are doing right now."

"Don't knock the dance," Sera says, grinning.

"Alright, business before we head to lunch. You all share the same agent, so this will be easy as far as contracts go. I'm sure Irene's going to want to talk to you all about a group contract with her. Right now you've only got individual and for different purposes. She'll have to modify Trace and Megan's and write one up for Jace." Sera and I nod.

"That's pretty freaking handy," I murmur.

"Irene is a goddess," Trace says.

I nod. "That she is."

"I want you all back here in two weeks to start recording," Cage tells us.

Meggie bounces on her toes.

"We've got a shit ton of songs to choose from between all of us," Jace states. "We can pick the ones we want and modify them to fit our style."

"Wicked cool," Trace says.

"You can use my private studio to practice and there's office space if you want or need room to work through the song choices."

Meggie whispers loudly, "Just how well do you know Cage?" and I smirk.

"Not as well as Sera."

Everyone snickers and Cage winks.

"All right. If you need me, you know how to get a hold of me. I'm sure I'll be seeing a lot of you."

I look around for Damian and he's nowhere to be found. He must have taken off when we were jamming with Meggie. Bummer. I would have liked for him to come to lunch with us.

"Let's go get some food," Ethan says. Everyone murmurs their agreement and as we're walking out of the building, I shake my head again. I just can't believe this is happening and it's happening so fast.

Jesse puts his arm around my shoulders again. I'm sure it'll hit me later, when I come down from my rocktastic high, how touchy-feely Jesse is with me, but right now I'm just floating on cloud nine.

"It really does feel like a dream, Jesse."

He presses a kiss to my forehead. "It's your dream coming true, Luce. Enjoy every fucking second of it."

"I intend to."

Ethan reaches out and pinches my ass. "You're not dreaming."

I squeal and give Ethan a look. He laughs and tries to hide behind Jesse. I chase him down the hall.

"You can run, but you can't hide, Ethan!" I yell.

He stops, turns, and looks right at me. "I don't want to run from you, Lucy. You can pinch or smack my ass any time you want." He wiggles his eyebrows.

Jesse frowns. "No pilfering, Ethan."

"Pilfering. Did you get a word-of-the-day app on your phone?" Ethan chuckles.

"Shut the fuck up."

As they continue their banter, I take a deep breath, rubbing my ass. This is it. This is real. This is our dream, my dream. I can't wait to get started.

We are Blush and we are ready to go.

Chapter *thirteen*

Lucy

"Jesse?"

"Yeah?"

"Why do you keep touching me?"

He shrugs. "Because I can."

I blow out a breath.

"I never gave you permission to touch me."

He shrugs. "You gave it to me the first time you screamed my name."

Jesus. He's been touching me all day. How can I get over the man when he keeps touching me? How can I get past the weekend of fucktastic sex when he follows me home? Yep, seriously. He followed me home. We all went to lunch and afterward, he invited himself over. His reasoning is to help pick out songs but we're not even doing that today. We're going house hunting, or we were. I'm not sure how that's going to happen unless Jesse's bored enough to tag along.

"You remember I told you Sera and I are going house hunting, right?"

"I do. Ben and I know of a few properties that are available for a decent price."

"It doesn't have to be anything as extravagant as Casa Falling Down. I doubt I'm going to have the entire band living with me."

Jesse chuckles. "Sure you will. You, Sera, and Jace already live together. You're good friends with Megan so she'll for sure move in and Trace being Trace will move in because he's going to want to be with his bandmates."

"I don't know. I'm sure Trace is going to want privacy when he brings home his girlie friends."

"He'll likely keep a fuck-pad for that."

"Well, hell," Sera says.

"Oh boy. Okay, so we'll need at least five bedrooms, plus two just in case mom and dad and Joey stay, plus two for whoever's on duty. Okay, yeah. And I want to put in a studio. Half Casa Falling Down size it is."

Ben snickers.

"Max will drive us. Some of the paparazzi followed us here," Frank tells us.

"Followed us all the way out to Santa Monica? Are you kidding me?" I ask.

Frank shakes his head. "Afraid not."

Great. Now they know where *that* house is too. "Well that sucks great big hairy donkey balls."

"That it does," Frank says with a smirk.

"Donkey balls?" Ben asks.

"Don't ask," Max tells him.

Frank grins. "You're better off not knowing."

Ben nods. "You're probably right."

I send Ben a wink. "Okay then, let's go house hunting."

"Well that sucked," Sera says. "True story," Jace replies.

I just sigh. Ben's on the phone with their realtor but I'm just not in the mood for any more house hunting crap.

"Looks like I'll be renting out a floor in the hotel again."

"Meh," is Sera's response.

"Max? Can we stop at the house?"

"Can do, Luce."

"I need to pick up some more clothes and shoes."

"Me too," Sera replies.

Ben hangs up the phone. "She said she's got a couple that fit what you're looking for, gated community and all that. She's going to look around for more and get back to me in a couple days."

"Oh, thank God. I didn't want to go anymore today."

"Fuck no," Ben agrees

I sit up higher in the seat, straining to see out the window. "Frank, any press hanging out at the house?"

"There were only one or two yesterday but I didn't see any at all today."

"Well, we're about to find out," Sera says as we turn the corner.

Jace whistles. "Nice digs, Luce."

I shrug. "Thanks. Too bad we can't stay."

"There's no one here."

"Right now. But the minute they find out I'm here, they'll show up. It's how they roll."

"And to think, you and Jesse hadn't even fucked yet."

"I know, right? Kind of a shitty deal there. Alright, let's go in so I can get my stuffs."

"Stuffs?" Jesse asks.

Sera pats him on the arm. "When it comes to clothes and shoes, Lucy goes into her 'stuffs' zone."

Jesse just raises a brow.

"If you want the ten cent tour, I'll be happy to show you around," Frank says.

"Perfect. Thanks so much, Frank."

"You got it, Luce."

"I'm going to go up and pack."

I head up the white-carpeted stairs and hold on to the black wrought iron railing—the one thing Jesse's mansion and my home have in common.

I grab a suitcase out of my closet and put it on the bed.

"Need help?" Jesse asks from the doorway.

"Hmm, maybe."

He hands me a diet soda. "Figured you'd be thirsty."

"Figured that out, did ya."

"Mhmm. You were singing and it's hot and dry out today. Plus you were singing under your breath all day. Makes for a dry throat."

"Seriously dry. I just always sing. I never notice I'm doing it." I take a long drink of the soda and recap the bottle, setting it on my dressing table.

I walk into the closet and grab a bunch of tops and some jeans and Capri pants.

I lay them on the bed and start folding them and packing them into the suitcase as Jesse takes a seat on the bed, his elbows resting on his knees.

"What's going on, Jesse?"

He takes a long drink of his soda then toys with the label.

"I was thinking…"

"Oh, don't do that, Jesse. That'll be painful," Sera says with a laugh as she walks in my room and flops on my bed.

Jace and Ben follow, but stand near the door with their beers.

"Need help?" Sera asks.

"Shoes."

"On it."

"What were you thinking, Jesse?" I ask as I follow Sera into the closet to get more tops and some dresses. He's about to speak when my phone rings.

"What's up, Max?"

"There's press all over the fuckin' place, Luce. We better get a move on."

I blow out a long breath. "Okay. We'll hurry."

"Press?" Sera asks.

"Yeah. Lots from what Max said."

Jesse nods from where he's leaning against the wall, arms crossed. I signal to him to hold his arms out and lay my clothes across them.

"For just a second."

"No problem."

I grab a few more tops and we all head into the bedroom where Jace and Ben are talking with Frank.

"Fuck, Frank."

"Yeah."

"Okay, what were we talking about? Oh, Jesse. What were you thinking about?"

He places my clothes on the bed and I start folding them. Jesse runs a hand across his two-day beard and it makes me want to bite him—strange urge.

"You know if you stay at the hotel, they're going to find you eventually. The staff doesn't get paid enough to keep those kinds of secrets and they all know that the paps pay well."

"They kept it quiet so far."

"Something's going on for them to pop up out of the blue," Sera tells me. "You can't expect them to stay quiet if it's more than just a you-and-Jesse thing."

"That's true and that sucks. I don't want to drive all the way from Santa Monica every day."

"They already showed up there today," Jace reminds me.

"That's true, too. This is such bullshit."

Jesse nods. "I agree. Which is why I was thinking you all should stay with us."

"What?!" I practically shout.

He shrugs.

"It's a good idea," Ben says. "We've got plenty of room and if Trace and Megan decide they want to hang out, we've got room for them too, as well as Frank and Max or whoever is with you for the day."

"Yeah, sounds good," Jace says.

I sigh and look at Sera. "I have to agree with them, Luce."

"Of course."

"I don't get it, Lucy," Jesse says. "You just stayed with me for the weekend. It's not a big deal to stay until things die down."

"It *is* a big deal," I whisper, continuing to fold clothes.

"Luce."

"It's a big deal to her, Jesse, because Lucy doesn't fuck around. Lucy is a relationship kind of girl because she wears her heart on her sleeve and, from what I've seen, with some time she'll be in real danger of losing her heart to you," Sera tells him.

"She's not the only one in danger of that," Ben says.

My gaze zeroes in on Ben's as I place a white eyelet sundress into the suitcase.

"What do you mean?" Sera asks.

Ben looks at Jesse for a brief few seconds then back at me and Sera. "Well, Jesse doesn't fuck good girls. Jesse doesn't have ladies stay in his room. Ever."

"He had Lucy in there."

Ben nods. "A good girl, right? Think about that. Another thing. He never gives out his code to his room or to the house for that matter."

I stand up straight and tilt my head to the side as Ben continues. I hear Jesse shift behind me.

"Jesse doesn't do sleepovers. Ever."

"And he had Lucy there for more than a weekend," Sera says, looking past me to Jesse.

Ben nods. "So, as I said, she's not the only one at risk. Plus, you can use our studio so you don't have to leave the house if you don't want to deal with the shit outside the gates."

I look down for a second. Wow. Okay. Well. Um. I've got no idea what to say, but I slowly turn to face Jesse anyway, meeting his whiskey gaze with mine. His face is riddled with the same vulnerability and uncertainty, hope and fear, that's mirrored on mine.

We just stare at one another and I don't know what it is that calms me by looking at him, but something does.

"Really?"

"Really."

"Wow."

"Yeah."

I blow out a breath and he smirks.

"How—"

He shrugs.

"But you don't—"

"I don't."

"So?"

He shrugs.

I nod and he nods.

"Don't break my heart, Jesse Kingston."

"Don't break my heart, Luciana Russo."

"You should pinky swear," Sera says.

"What are we twelve?" Jace asks with a laugh.

"Fuck off, it'd be romantic."

Jesse holds up his pinky and I hook mine to his. He pulls me into him and he holds me, both arms wrapped tightly around me.

"This is scary, Jesse."

"No shit."

"All this from a weekend?"

"Nah, not just a weekend."

I pull back and step on my tiptoes to press a kiss to his lips.

"Okay."

"Okay."

"Let's do this." I turn around and note Sera's got all my stuff packed.

"We're going to have to get the stuff from the Santa Monica house."

"Already in the works. I texted," Sera says. "Also let Max and Frank know."

"Damn, you're so good to me, sissy pants."

"Hell yeah I am. Don't forget it either."

Jesse pulls me back into his chest as Jace and Ben grab the suitcases.

"We'll meet you downstairs, Luce," Sera says.

I turn to Jesse. "Are you sure? This is a huge deal, Jesse. It may be weeks before I can come back here or until we find a house—"

He presses his index finger to my lips.

"I'm sure."

I blow out a breath against his finger.

"This is some scary shit."

He nods. "That's no lie." He gives me another soft kiss and I lick his lip ring.

"That's so sexy."

He chuckles. "Let's go fight our way out of here."

We head down the stairs and out the front door. We can't see the gate from here with the curved driveway but they're there.

"I can hear the vultures circling," Max says.

I nod as I get into the car with Jesse behind me, Ben on the other side of me. Sera, Frank, and Jace across from us. Yeah, we took the limo today and will likely have to take this or more than one car from now on with as many people as we're going to have with us.

Jesse grabs my hand, lacing his fingers with mine. I turn to him and he presses his lips to mine softly.

"We got this."

I blow out a breath and the car lurches forward.

"Lucy, is Jesse Kingston in there with you?"

"Are you and Jesse Kingston involved?"

"Is it true that you're giving up acting for music?"

"What. The. Fuck." Sera says.

I just rub my forehead.

"Are you going to be joining up with Falling Down?"

"Are you and Jesse Kingston an official couple?"

Jesse squeezes my hand gently. "I'll never tell them the answer to that last question but I'm going to say here and now that I hope we can get to that."

"Me too. Oh, God, Jesse. You can't want to get messed up in this."

I lean forward and put my head between my legs, taking deep breaths. He rubs my back.

"She alright?" Ben asks.

"Yeah," Sera says. "She's in danger of falling for Jesse fucking Kingston, the press is up her ass, we're finally getting our band together, and last but certainly not least, she's going to have to call Mama Russo."

"Yikes," Jace says.

"Not helping, fucker," I tell him and everyone chuckles. "What time is it?"

"Early," Frank says. "You can still probably catch Regina awake."

"Great, but much better than waking her up."

"I'm surprised she hasn't called you yet," Sera says as my phone rings.

"What the hell, Sera? How many times do we need to have this conversation? She's got radar for when you say that shit!"

"Sorry, but you were just about to call her anyway."

"I needed a few minutes to breathe and find my calm before I called her. Fuck."

"Wow," Ben says. "Potty mouth when she's stressed."

Frank laughs. "This is nothing. Wait."

"Hi mama."

"Luciana, have you seen the news? Listened to the radio? There's new rumors."

"Well, I haven't had time for television or radio but the paparazzi outside the house were a pretty good clue that new 'rumors' as you put it is going on. What is it now?"

"We need to be on speaker. Your father wants to talk too."

"Mama, it's not only Sera, Frank, and Max with me."

Pause. "Who else is with you?"

"Jace Warner—"

"Oh! Jace! I've missed him," she interrupts.

"Let me finish mama."

"Oh."

"Jesse Kingston and his brother Ben are here as well."

Complete silence and I cringe.

"Oh boy, that's not good," Jace says.

I jump when she drops the phone and starts swearing in Italian. My dad tries to calm her down, but calming Regina Russo down when she gets like this is impossible.

"Button!"

"Hi daddy."

"Your mother needed to—catch her breath."

I snicker. "Okay. We can do speaker. I heard mama tell you Jace, Jesse, and Ben are here."

"She did. You okay, Lucy?"

"Yeah daddy. Just overwhelmed."

"Okay, speaker then."

"We're going on speaker everyone," I say as I push the button.

"Hi dad!" Sera says.

"Serafina, my baby doll. How are you?"

"I'm good, daddy, but the vultures are bothering our Lucy."

"Yes, I saw on the news. This is starting to piss me off."

"Get in line dad," I tell him.

"You should have seen it, Mr. R. It was insane. They were everywhere shouting questions at the limo, trying to take pictures through the tinted windows."

"Jace, my boy. Hollywood is crazy. This is why Luciana wants out."

"It won't be much better being a rockstar," my mother chimes in.

"Mama."

"What? You know it's true."

I just sigh.

"It's good to hear your voice, Jace. I can't wait to see you again. It's been too long."

"It has. A long time."

"Mama, daddy, let me introduce you to Jesse Kingston. Jesse, these are my parents, Regina and Anthony Russo."

"Hello Mr. and Mrs. Russo."

"Ah, don't call me Mr. Russo. Mr. Russo is my father and he's trouble."

"And then some," Sera adds.

"Serafina," Regina scolds.

"Yes, mama."

"Ben, meet my parents, Regina and Anthony Russo."

"Nice to meet you," Ben says.

"And you both as well," my dad says. "We need damage control, Lucy."

"There's no damage done, daddy. It's bullshit and you know it. I want to know who leaked the band stuff."

"I'm not sure. We're going to look into it. Where are you staying?"

"Well, that's the thing, dad. If we stay in the hotel, the media will be there within the hour and we can't stay in Santa Monica because we've got work in the city this week with the new band and a few reporters were already outside the house today."

"I see, I see. That's a problem. You could stay with Joey—"

"NO!" Sera and I both yell at the same time and my dad laughs.

"I had to say it just to get the reaction."

"Harsh, dad. But I think we have where we're staying worked out."

"Good, good. Tell me."

"We're going to be staying with Jesse and Ben and the band at their mansion."

Silence, then cursing from my mother in the background.

"That's not good," Jesse whispers in my ear.

"That's not even bad."

He raises his brows.

"Tell me more, Button."

"They live in a gated community and their house is gated with high tech security," Frank interjects.

"Frank, my man."

"What's up, Tony?"

"What a shit storm."

"Yeah, but our girl's handling it."

"Of course she is. She's a Russo, isn't she? So she'll be safe with them?"

"She will. She'll have us there if she needs us as well. There's plenty of room from what Ben's told me."

"Yes, sir—"

"Anthony."

"Anthony," Ben corrects. "We have over thirty rooms in the house. They can have their own wing if they choose or they can stay in the same wing we're in. I think the latter would be better security-wise, but that's up to them."

"True, true. This sounds good. Lucy."

"Yeah daddy?"

"Are you involved with Jesse?"

"Yeah, I am."

"Hmm. I thought so. So those rumors aren't wrong."

"Those stem from when we were in a club."

"Practically fornicating on the dance floor," my mother says.

"Whatever mom."

"It's the truth. The video doesn't lie."

"I'm a grown woman, mother."

She tsks. "I just spoke with Irene."

"Is that where you were? Managing two phone calls at the same time?"

"Yes, you know I am good at multi-tasking. Anyway, she thinks it might be a good idea for you to do a press conference."

"What? No! Why can't she just put out a press release?"

"The rumors are out about you leaving acting and starting in music. There's speculation that you're joining Jesse's band. There's speculation you're also joining a few other bands. They're going to want to hear it from you considering the big topic of discussion is you and Jesse. "

"Of course it is," Jesse says.

"This is the life of a movie star."

"So I'm learning. I just wish none of this was going on, for Lucy's sake."

"We all do."

"I have to agree with your mom, Lucy, about the press conference."

"What? Traitor!"

He chuckles.

"You just don't know, Jesse. They're brutal. When I called them vultures, I meant it. They're vultures, piranha, and any other flesh-eating beast there is."

"We'll have to talk to Cage first and get things set up and coordinated between Lucy, Cage, and Irene."

"I like him, Lucy. He's intelligent."

Jesse chuckles.

"Oh Lord. You only like him because he's agreeing with you."

"It shows his intelligence that he agrees."

"Alrighty then. Carry on discussing the press conference that's going to put me in my grave."

"Dramatic much?" Jace says and Sera smacks him.

"You don't know, Jace. You'll learn and you'll learn fast. It's not like it is with rockstars or on TV when they see someone come out of a restaurant. They are harsh, accusatory, and vicious," Sera tells him.

Ben and Jesse both look shocked. I sigh.

"What do we have to do, mama?"

"Just do what Jesse suggested and coordinate everything with Cage and Irene."

"Okay. Cage is our acting manager until we get everything worked out. He may stay on during our first tour."

"I would prefer that," my dad says.

"I'm sure he'll be in touch with you soon, daddy. He faxed Irene the contracts."

"Good, good. Things are moving along then."

"Two weeks from today we'll be in the studio recording. Oh my gosh! Guess who is playing rhythm for us?"

My mom and dad mutter they have no idea.

"Meggie!"

"Meggie!" my mother shouts. "Oh, this makes me happy. Very happy. Meggie is a good girl. Weird and a bit rude but a good girl."

I laugh. "I agree."

"Who is your drummer?" my dad asks.

"Brace yourself."

"We're braced."

"Trace Styx."

"Oh! Joey is going to be crazy."

"I know, which is why I'm holding off telling him until we all get a chance to know Trace a little better."

"I can understand that," my dad says. "Ah, your mother is opening her wine."

"Oh boy. I'll talk to you as soon as I know anything about the press conference."

"You better," my mother shouts from across the room.

"Love you mama."

"Love you mom," Sera says.

"Hmm. Of course you do. I love you too."

"Thanks daddy."

"You're welcome, my babies."

"Love you daddy."

"Love you dad."

"Love you too. We'll talk soon. Your mother has two bottles of red open and breathing. It's going to be a long night."

"Have fun, dad."

I hang up and Sera plugs her ears as does Frank. They motion for everyone else to do the same and Max rolls up the privacy window.

"PRESS FUCKING CONFERENCE! ARE YOU FUCKING KIDDING ME! Motherfucking cocksuckers!"

I lean forward and put my head between my knees taking deep soothing breaths. Jesse rubs circles on my back.

"You okay, Luce?"

"Do I look okay, Jace?"

"No, actually."

"Well, there you fucking go then, huh?"

"Whoa," Jesse says, chuckling.

"Laugh it up rocker boy. You're not the one on the press chopping block."

"It really can't be that bad," Ben says.

I sit straight up as if a spring was released and Sera cringes.

"It can't? *Really*?" I screech. "Well, it just so happens that I have my laptop packed so I'll let you see what my press conferences are like and I wasn't even fucking the guy they were accusing me of fucking! We barely knew one another. We had three scenes together in a movie and we were rehearsing lines outside. We were laughing and just having fun sitting under a tree while rehearsing. Somehow that equated to a relationship that included sex—all kinds of sex because said actor was seriously into the kink. I'm not into that shit! And even if I were, it wouldn't be with him of all people! He's a nice guy but I've heard where his dick has been and there is no going near that shit. Ever."

Sera shudders as she names the celebrity.

"Dude," Jace says.

"I know, right? As if that's going to happen. I need a minute."

Head between knees. Breathe. Air in. Air out. Air in. Air out. Air in. Air out.

"What makes it worse for Lucy is—well, Jesse you know how she was both times she met you?"

"Frozen and speechless?"

"Yeah. Well, imagine frozen, not quite speechless, but if she doesn't have notecards she's fucked. So picture her on a podium giving a conference and the Santa Ana's being really strong that day."

"Oh hell," Ben says.

"Mhmm. Sweaty palms. Sweaty upper lip and forehead. Hyperventilating. Mumbling. Rambling. Saying things that made no sense and some things that made things ten times worse. It was brutal. And knowing she was in that state, they kept on badgering her. We were young and they abused her vulnerability."

I raise my hand and Sera and Frank plug their ears. I tick off one, two, three fingers.

"Asshole fucker shit ass bitch sonofabitchin' motherfuckers!"

"*Major* potty mouth when she's pissed, eh?" Ben asks.

"Caught that, did ya?" Sera asks.

"Now I know how to tell if she's mad."

"Oh yeah," Sera tells Ben. "She'll cuss you out."

Jesse kisses the top of my head. "I'll be here with you every step of the way, Luce. I'll even go to the press conference with you if you want."

I look at him. "Are you for real?"

"Sure, why not? We've got nothing to hide, Lucy. We're adults who are involved. If we weren't celebrities no one would give a shit, but because we are everyone's up in our business. I understand. I hate when they fuck with my privacy too."

I nod and lean into Jesse, throwing my arms around his neck. He pulls me onto his lap.

"God, Jesse. I'm whiny right now and I'm sorry but when you see that press conference you'll understand. Even before I lost the cards they were so mean. Asking questions that were invasive, intrusive, and just disgusting. Not something I would share."

"I know. We got this. Okay?"

I nod against his chest. Frank smiles and I breathe a sigh of relief.

"Paps at the gate," Max tells us.

"Stupid fuckers. They can't get past here," Ben says.

"Good," I murmur.

As we near the mansion Sera whistles. "Whoa. I can totally see why you call this Casa Falling Down."

"I know, right?"

"Jesus," Jace says. "Do you get lost in here?"

"We did the first week," Ben says with a laugh.

We pull up to the front of the house and the guys grab the luggage from the trunk. When we enter the foyer, I see the rest of our luggage has already arrived.

"Excellent. All our stuff is here," Sera says.

"Good. Now let's get you set up. I'll show you where we're staying first. If you don't want to stay in that wing, you can stay in the one just across the way," Ben says, leading Sera and Jace up the stairs. They take a right while Jesse and I take a left.

"Jesse—"

"This way."

"Um."

He punches his code in and opens his bedroom door then sets my two suitcases down. Ethan comes in behind and sets the last two down.

"Lucy," he says with a wink before he walks back out.

"You want me to stay in your room?"

Jesse rubs a hand across the back of his neck. "Yeah, unless you'd rather stay somewhere else."

Holy—. For real. He's serious. He wants to try this for real.

I start to pace, taking in the comforting green, black, and blue throughout the room. Jesse grabs my hand and pulls me toward him. He hooks his hands behind my lower back and looks down at me.

"Tell me."

I rest my hands on his chest and draw circles with my index fingers. I bite my lip and when Jesse makes a scolding noise, I stop. I nearly roll my eyes but instead I muster up all my courage and blurt out my feelings.

"I'm scared."

"I'm fucking terrified."

I look up at him. "You don't do relationships."

"I know. What scares you most?"

"That once the novelty of me wears off and you get back on tour, the groupie whores will take over and I'll be kicked to the curb with a broken heart."

He nods. "I'm glad you're being honest and I can see that. I don't know how to do this, Lucy, but I want to see where this goes because I really like you. We have fun together, amazing sex, and we have so much in common.

I promise not to just kick you to the curb like that, Lucy. I don't make many promises because I don't like to break them, but I know this is one I won't break. I won't ever purposefully hurt you."

I nod and sigh. "I have to be honest too. I haven't been in a real relationship since high school." I meet his gaze. "I was involved with someone a couple years ago but that didn't last long. We never lived together or anything like that."

He nods.

"No other girl has ever been in this room?"

"Besides my mom and sisters, no."

"Wow. I wouldn't have guessed that."

"I'm going to be blunt, okay?"

I nod.

"The sl—women who came to parties here at the house, they knew it was just for a good time and we all knew they were using us for whatever purpose they had. In the beginning I didn't care, but when they started taking pictures and trying to make it more than it was, it got old real quick. I didn't want those-"

"Sluts."

He nods. "Sluts in my private space."

"Good to know you don't think of me like that."

"Luce. You're nothing like that. Not even your bad girl."

"Should I be insulted?"

"No. You're not slutty or skanky. You're sweet and kind and classy and seriously wild between the sheets."

I laugh. "I've never been accused of being wild between the sheets before."

"Wrong partners."

"Definitely."

"So, we're doing this."

I nod. "I guess we are."

We're silent for a few minutes, just looking at one another. I can tell he's thinking but I am too.

"Jesse?"

"Hmm?"

"Did you feel this way when I left Sunday?"

He nods.

"Is that why you were so quiet?"

He nods again.

I sigh. "You should have said something."

"I should have, but I couldn't risk you not feeling the same or not being ready for something more. I didn't want to ruin the perfect weekend we had."

"I have a request."

"Okay."

"From now on, no matter the consequences, if we have something important we want or need to talk about, we just do it. Get it out there. Knowing we've made this deal will allow for understanding on both our parts."

"I think that's a great idea. What are you thinking right now?"

I smile and shake my head. "I can't believe this. You're you and I'm in your room for the unforeseeable future. I think someone's drugged you or something because this can't be real."

"It's real. We're real."

I nod.

"We'll handle the press, get it out there that Blush is alive and kicking, introduce everyone, and I'll stand next to you holding your hand the entire time. And when you're done talking about Blush, I'll pull you close, just like this," he says as he pulls me closer, looking down at me. "And I'll dip my head like this," he adds against my lips. "Then I'll lift you up like this so no one misses the camera shot, you can wrap your legs around me just like that, and I'll kiss you just like this."

The kiss starts off with soft lips brushing against one another, then mouths opening and tongues coming together.

My fingers thread through Jesse's hair and his hands squeeze my ass as he holds me up. I moan when he dips his finger between my legs and runs it up along the seam of my jeans.

"Mmm," he says pulling back. "Well, maybe I won't kiss you *just* like that."

I laugh and pull his mouth back to mine as he carries me to his bed.

"Jesse Kingston's falling down…" he sings to the tune of London Bridge.

"Lucy Russo's falling down with a blush," I sing.

We both smile and then get wild between the sheets.

Chapter
fourteen

Jesse

Aﬁer a bout of mind-blowing sex with Lucy, I show her my closet. "Take whatever space you need."

"How can you only have that many clothes? It's not right that men can get away with that."

"I can't believe how many fucking clothes *you* have."

She shrugs, hanging up a dress. "I can't go out wearing the same thing all the time. I find myself in magazines more often than I'd like so I have to be fashionable."

He shakes his head. "Chicks."

"You men have it made. You suck."

"Only when you ask nicely," I tell her with a grin and a wink. She leaves herself open for those all the time. I can't help myself.

I can't help myself with a lot of things when it comes to Lucy, it seems. I've never entertained the idea of having a woman live with me. Ever. I'm not sure what's going on with me. I'm all kinds of fucked up. I mean, I'd even thought it through before I made the suggestion that they stay here and when I did I knew I wanted her in my bed.

It's not just that I haven't gotten enough of her yet (because I haven't, not even close), but I really like her being around. Watching her walk around my space, putting her clothes in my closet and in the dresser drawers I cleaned out for her, I feel good. I like it. Something's fucking wrong with me.

"Thank God. Clothes are put away. Shoes are put away. Now…" she trails off and walks toward the bed with what looks like a black electronic tablet.

"What's that?"

"This?" she holds it up.

I nod.

"It's my Kindle."

I just give her a stare. I have no fucking clue what a Kindle is.

She grins. "It's where I read and download books."

"Huh."

She brings it over and turns it on, showing me how she can hook straight to Amazon and one-click. She tells me about her one-click addiction. I just bet. If she's anywhere near as addicted to books as she is to clothes and shoes, I've no doubt she's got hundreds of books.

"How many books you got on there?"

She gives me a sidelong glance. She almost looks… guilty. She taps a button and shows me.

I let out a long whistle when I see she's got over fourteen hundred books. "Yeah, I'd say you have a one-click addiction. How many of those have you read?"

"Um, let me see." She taps a few buttons and some reader page opens. "Five hundred eighty-six."

"You'll never run out, that's for sure."

"Especially when Amazon is just a button away."

"Shopaholic. That's the only way to describe you."

"Not true. I think I only bought maybe one-fourth of the clothes and shoes I have. I'm content in shorts and a tank top or a sundress and flip-flops. My mom—"

I hold up a hand cutting her off. I've heard from Jace how her mom steamrolls her life.

"Enough said."

She nods, picking up a bag and heading to the bathroom.

"What's the plan for tonight?"

"Ben texted. We're going to order pizza and just hang out."

"That sounds good actually. Do you guys always do your own cooking or do you have someone to do that for you when you don't feel like it?"

"We cook a lot but not all the time. Mrs. Martinez is our main housekeeper and cook. She manages two other girls who basically run the household. Mr. Martinez is our gardener and fix-it guy if we can't do it ourselves."

"That's pretty cool."

I lean a shoulder against the doorjamb and tuck my hands in my pockets as she starts unpacking her toiletries.

"Yeah, they've been with us since the beginning. When we were able to, we hired them and got them out of the projects."

"How did you know them?"

"Xander's ex-girlfriend lived in that neighborhood and they took care of her. Her parents were crackheads."

"I see." With one hand in her bag she meets my gaze in the mirror. "Um, are you going to have problems with me putting my feminine products in your cabinet?" she asks, holding up a box of tampons.

I shrug. I could give a shit, to be honest.

"I don't care. Have you forgotten that I have a mom and two sisters? When we were younger we only had two bathrooms. Besides," I tell her, walking up behind her and wrapping my arms around her waist, resting my chin on top of her head. "This is your space as much as mine, now."

See? What the fuck is going on with me? Shit like that just keeps flying out of my mouth and the weird thing is, when I say it I mean it.

My phone chimes with a text. I kiss the top of her head and read it as she walks into the shower room.

"That was Ben. Pizza's here. They're all out on the patio."

"Let's go," she says, pulling me through the door.

I can't help but chuckle. "You in a hurry?"

"I'm hungry."

"Jump on," I tell her and I carry her piggy-back to where the others are. I just want to feel her legs wrapped around me, even if it's not in a sexual way. Her touching me does something crazy to my insides. This woman has gotten under my skin.

When we get to the patio, I take a seat then pull Lucy into my lap. Ben gives me a look and I just shake my head. I have no fucking idea. Xander smirks and I give him the finger.

"What kind of pizza did you get? Oh my God, Sera, are you seriously eating supreme?" Lucy says.

"Damn straight," she mumbles around her pizza. "No more modeling means I can put on those ten pounds they made me lose for modeling."

"You could stand to gain at least twenty," Ben says. She really could but I wouldn't have told her that. Ben's got no filter when it comes to that woman.

Sera sends him a glare. "Did I ask you?"

He shrugs. "You're too skinny. You look sick. People probably think you're anorexic or some shit."

She's still glaring. "They might *think* that about me but I'm positive they *know* you're a dick."

He throws his head back and laughs.

Lucy leans down and whispers, "What's going on?"

I shrug. "No clue. Sexual tension?"

She raises a brow then takes a bite of the sausage and mushroom pizza slice she snagged while I, on the other hand, inhale pizza loaded with tons of meat and cheese. Fucking manly pizza.

"Ethan, can you please pass me a soda?" Lucy asks him.

"Want me to mix you up a Captain and diet?"

"Oh my God, would you? That'd be so amazing."

He nods and walks behind the bar. "Sera? Want anything?"

"Captain and diet sounds good for me too."

"On it."

"What did Irene and Cage have to say about the press conference?" Sera asks and Lucy sighs.

She'd been stressed and freaking out when she conferenced them and when she hung up, she started pacing. That's when I grabbed her, stripped her naked, and made a feast out of her pussy. The woman tastes like the best kind of dessert. With the sluts that were around, I don't usually go down on them unless they're ones I've arranged to hook up with when we hit that city. Having a few regulars is fucking cool. I don't have to worry about being exploited and the chick knows what to expect, which is basically me fucking the hell out of her and then moving on.

But with Lucy, she's Lucy. Classy and beautiful and once I tasted her, I couldn't get enough. It's hot as hell how easily I can get her to come and I gave her two orgasms that had her back bowing up off the bed. Fuck yeah. I'm getting hard just thinking about it.

Then when I slipped inside of her, fuuuuck. Heaven. She's so incredibly tight that it's actually hard for me to get inside her. I'm so afraid I'm going to hurt her when I first push my dick inside her that I let her make the moves on how much she can take. But when I'm fully buried inside her, balls deep, that's when I'm back in control. I love watching her eyes half closed, her lips parted, her face and chest flushed with arousal. It's the prettiest sight I've ever seen other than when she comes. When she comes… I mentally shake my head. It's unlike anything I've ever seen or felt. Her face is completely calm, trusting, and giving. Her pussy clenches me so tight it's hard to move inside her, but I do and when her pussy spasms, she milks every last drop of cum from me. Maybe what's going on is I'm addicted to her pussy. I wish it was that simple. I know it's not and it's fucking scary as hell.

When Lucy fell asleep in the Jacuzzi the first night she was here, after I dried her off and tucked her in, I headed to where Ben and the guys were. I told them she was different and if any one of those fuckers made her feel cheap or used in any way, I'd cut their nuts off. Yeah, none of them knew what to do with that at first. Don't get me wrong, they knew that Lucy's different, but I'd gone all caveman (as Lucy would say) in a way they'd never seen before.

All I said was, "She matters," and they all nodded, accepting it just like that. It's not something any of us are used to but it is what it is.

"Did you have to go there while I was eating?" Lucy asks Sera. "You couldn't have waited until I was on my second drink?"

What were they talking about again? Oh yeah. Press conference.

Sera rolls her eyes. "No, I couldn't. If I have to be there, I need to know what the hell is going on."

"*Fine.*" Lucy sets her pizza down on her napkin. "We're holding a press conference tomorrow at Nichols Records, where they usually hold theirs?" She looks at me and I nod.

"I know where that is."

"This is good."

I just grunt and take another bite of pizza. I'm hungry and distracted by her ass wiggling on my cock.

Ethan hands her a drink and she gulps half of the glass. She coughs twice and I smirk.

"You might want to take it easy on those," Kennedy says. "Ethan usually makes his drinks three-quarters alcohol and one-quarter soda."

"Perfect."

"You don't want to be hungover for the press conference," I remind her, opening the beer Ben passes me.

"It's not until three in the afternoon so I can sleep in a bit. They want everyone there, from both bands, so I had to call Trace and Meggie. Trace wasn't at all surprised and Meggie can't wait to be photographed."

"She's so weird," Jace says.

"Nothing new."

"True."

It's cool there're four of them in Blush who knew each other growing up. It's like me, Ben and the guys. We've known each other since grade school, we're as close as brothers, and I'd trust them with my life. That's what I'd been hoping for, for Lucy and I'm pretty sure that's what she's got. Trace is a kick ass guy. Reliable and fucking insane on those drums. It was a stroke of luck that they'd been able to snag him for the interview. He'd just left his band days before and Xander only knew because he'd seen Trace in Nichols Records the day of the parting.

"After facing the wrath of the media, Trace and Meggie want to look through some of the songs we have and I want to look through theirs too. Cage reminded me we could use his studio and office space but Jesse offered the use of theirs instead," Lucy continues.

Wrath of the media. I nearly chuckle, but I don't. Honestly she gets so riled up about it, I wish I could step in and do it for her.

"Cool," Jace says.

She shrugs and picks up her pizza to take another bite. "I'm seriously dreading that damn press conference. I don't want to make an ass of myself again and I just know I'm going to," she whispers to me then lets out a sigh.

I rub my hand up and down her back. "We got this," I say with conviction as she meets my gaze. She pauses for a few seconds then nods.

The rest of the guys murmur their agreement and while I feel a bit of relief knowing they're going to be up there with me, I know she's going to have to answer their questions and that means she's going to be put on the spot, which means she's not going to react well.

"Thanks you guys."

"So," Sera says. Lucy shifts and raises a brow. "You're staying in Jesse's room?"

"Um..."

I just chuckle. "Relax, Luce. It's only Sera, not the press."

"I just... I'm not sure how much...?" she trails off.

"How much to tell her? Everything. It's family."

I shrug. "Yeah, she's staying in my room so really it's our room now."

Ben whistles. "Damn bro."

"No shit," Ethan says with a shake of his head.

Kennedy's mouth is hanging open.

"Dude, close your mouth. I don't want to see your chewed up fucking pizza."

Jace snorts. "I've gotta say, it seems so unreal, you know?"

"What do you mean?" Ethan asks.

"Just last week I was working in accounting wearing a fucking suit and tie and today I'm sitting on the patio of Casa Falling Down with the best fucking band *ever* and Lucy's sitting on the lap of the guy she majorly crushed on since she was twelve."

"Well, fuck," Ben says. "When you put it that way. But we're just guys who worked our asses off to get where we are. We caught a lucky break with Cage just as you all did."

"Mostly Lucy worked her ass off to get us here," Sera says.

"No thanks to her mom," Jace replies.

I squeeze her hip and she sighs. "It wasn't what I wanted to do, we all know this, but I did it. It wasn't exactly a hard job. I got on the set and pretended to be someone else and got paid a butt load of money to do it."

"But—" Sera starts.

Lucy cuts her off. "Stop. We've been through this a million times. Mom got her way from sixteen to now, but now it's us. Let's let the past stay there and be grateful because if we hadn't met Cage, like Ben said, we wouldn't be here."

Sera snickers. "You wouldn't be sitting on Jesse Kingston's lap and sleeping in his bed."

"Uh-uh. Our bed," I correct.

"Yeah, that," Sera says with a sigh.

"I gotta pee," Lucy says. I pull her down for a quick kiss before she heads inside.

"You know this is a dream come true for her, right?" Sera asks.

I shrug. Talking about the crush thing makes me uncomfortable. I don't mind being a crush or whatever chicks turn me into in their fantasies, but I don't want to be that for Lucy. Not anymore.

"I guess."

"Could be for him too," Ethan says.

Sera nods.

"She's definitely a dream," Xander says, winking at me.

"Shut up, fucker." I throw my bottle cap at him.

"What? I could've said wet dream, but I was respectful," he says, putting his hand over his heart.

I can see it, he's thinking about her, trying to imagine my woman naked.

"Knock it the fuck off or I'll beat your ass."

Xander laughs. "I can strip her down in my head any time I want to."

I nod. "You can, but you don't know what it really looks like under those clothes and it's so much more than your imagination."

"Well, fuck," he says and takes a drink of his beer. I smirk.

Lucy comes back out and slides back onto my lap. I kiss the side of her neck and she smiles. She slams down the other half of her drink and holds out her empty glass to Ethan who grins and takes it to make another.

"Wow, Lucy," Sera says. "Who would have thought?"

"Right?"

"I mean, all from a crush."

"Seriously."

"Then the chance meeting."

"Mhmm."

"Then the video."

"Yeah."

"Toss in a weekend of fabulous sex and now you're living together."

"Yup," she says around a bite of pizza then takes the drink Ethan hands her.

"But he's not just a crush," she tells Sera and I pull her back for a kiss.

"Oh, I know it," Sera says with a wink. "Trust me, I know."

I'm trying very hard not to hyperventilate right now with the phrase "living together" that Sera just used. I prefer "sharing a room" to "living together". It sounds less serious. It may have been my idea, but fuck if I know what the hell I'm doing.

Lucy takes a gulp of her drink and I'm pretty sure she's feeling the same way I am right now. I pull her close with one arm in a kind of open hug.

"Don't freak her out, Sera."

She just grins. "Why not? It's so fun. Look at her face."

I watch as Lucy purposefully wipes all expression from her face as she picks up another slice of pizza. She raises a brow. I think she's starting to feel a buzz from the very lethal Ethan drink. Lucy flips Sera the bird.

"Fucking actress," Ben says with a wink and Lucy grins.

I take a drink of my beer as she takes another drink of her rum (may as well call it what it is). Lucy burps really fucking loud and murmurs, "Excuse me," and pops the last bite of pizza in her mouth.

I freeze with my beer halfway to my lips. When I look up everyone's staring at her.

"What? I said excuse me," she says.

"How can something so loud come from such a small body?" Xander asks with a laugh.

She shrugs. "It's a gift and not one I share very often. That one kind of slipped out," she says with a blush, looking at me.

I chuckle. "Don't even worry about it, Luce. It's good to know you're human." And it really is because she's so fucking perfect in every way it's nice to see a bit of imperfection in her.

She nods. "Very human and very, very full." She leans back into my lap as I continue to eat my pizza.

"Make me a drink, bitches!" Meggie shouts as she comes walking out on the patio and I chuckle. This girl is nuts with her turquoise and pink colored hair, nose and lip rings, more ear piercings than I can count, and really kick ass tattoos.

"Dude," Trace says as he takes a seat. "Meat lovers plus." He reaches over and fist bumps me.

"Mrs. Martinez let you in?"

"Yeah," Meggie answers. "She's really kick ass. I like her."

"Me too," I say with a chuckle.

"Cage coming?" Lucy asks Sera who shrugs.

"I didn't even know these two were coming."

"Did you expect us not to party on the night Blush is formed? Get the fuck on with yourselves, bitches!" Ethan hands her a drink and passes a beer to Trace. They murmur their thanks.

I watch and Meggie takes a big gulp of her drink. "Holy fuck, Ethan. You're my favorite bartender ever. You're fucking hired!"

Lucy laughs. "Just like old times."

"No," Jace says. "Much better."

"True that," Sera says and raises her glass. We all raise our bottles and glasses. "To Blush, may we rock their asses off and to Falling Down for inspiring us to follow our passion."

"Here, here," Lucy says and taps her glass to my bottle. "Jesse," she whispers.

"Hmm?"

"I'm a little drunk I think," she slurs and flops back onto my chest.

"It's not surprising seeing as Ethan's drinks contain the equivalent of five or six shots and you've downed two of them in less than two hours."

She nods. "I like Ethan's drinks."

"Happy to serve," Ethan says, chuckling.

"She's a light-weight," Sera says.

"Well, she's so tiny and weighs next to nothing."

"I'd take some of Sera's tallness if I could. Being short isn't fun sometimes, 'specially when you're acting and you have to stand on a stool when you kiss the hero."

Trace busts out laughing. "Really?"

She nods. "It's really shitty. We have to stop filming, someone brings in a stool, I get up on it, then the cameras start rolling again, the hero walks toward me and then we kiss. Then when the kiss is over, cut!, remove the stool, and carry on about our business."

I chuckle. I don't know if she's telling the truth or making this up but it's funny as hell. "With everyone you acted with?"

"The ones over six feet. I'm only five-three so it's really difficult for the guy to kiss me without having to bend down, and when they bend down, the camera shot is skewed and they don't get both of us in the shot correctly. When I'm more even with the hero's mouth, they get the money shot of our lips pressing together, you know what I mean?"

I growl. I don't want to think about her kissing some other fucking guy, acting or not.

"Oh Jesse," she says, patting my face. "You're *the* best kisser ever. Oh my God, Sera." Lucy shakes her head. "You just can't know."

"I could—" Sera says with a smirk.

"Try it and die," Lucy slurs, pointing at Sera.

"Jesse..." she whispers.

"What's up, Cupcake?"

She sighs. "Do you think I'm too judgmental? I mean, I feel kinda bad for how I feel about the groupie whores. Some of them are probably very nice ladies and girls. And they might have reasons for being the way they are, you know? Looking for love in all the wrong places—as the song goes," she says with a snort. "I think maybe I'm being too harsh."

"Lucy," Kennedy says. "You can feel any way you like about people. It's everyone's right, and just knowing you're taking their reasoning into consideration, well, it just shows everyone you're thinking outside your comfort zone which tells us all you're trying to be fair."

Her jaw drops. "I think that's the most he's ever spoke."

"Probably," I laugh.

"Well, I'm glad to know that you don't think I'm a judgmental bitch. I'd hate that, you know? You're all so great and I love you guys."

"She's a chatty drunk," Meggie interjects.

"She is that," Jace agrees.

"Makes for a fun time," Xander says with a grin that says he's up to no good. "Hey Lucy?"

"What's up Xan my man?" she snorts and I can't help but laugh. She's so fucking cute.

"What's the one thing about Jesse that you like the most?" he asks her.

"Hmm. If you'd asked me this when I was twelve or even seventeen I'd have said his looks or his body because, hello! he's hella hot."

"You said it girl," Meggie cheers.

"And now?" Xander asks.

"I like that he's more than what everyone thinks he is."

"What do you mean?" Ben asks.

"Well," she flits a hand and sits up straight, "watching him in videos or on TV doing interviews or even on stage he seems kind of superficial, you know? I understand it's part of who he is, he keeps his private self private. He lets you see how kind and fun he is, but he hides a lot. But being able to see more of who he is has shown how deep and complex he is. He's a good guy. A manwhore, but a good guy."

"Awww, Cupcake, you had me up until 'manwhore' and you went and ruined it," I say, laughing with everyone else.

She pegged me straight on. She doesn't know everything about me yet. She may change her mind as she finds out.

I take another beer from Ethan and Lucy takes a bottled water.

"Thanks man."

Ethan nods and smiles at Lucy then shakes his head.

Yeah, she's definitely something else. I've got a feeling there's much more to Lucy than I've seen this past week. We've already seen her crumble at the thought of the press conference, a vulnerability and task that she hates with a passion. I'm really looking forward to seeing just who she is under that cool exterior now that I'm not on the outside looking in.

"Jesse," Lucy whispers loudly and Trace chuckles next to me.

"Yeah, babe."

"I'm getting sleepy."

"Okay." I stand up with Lucy. "It's ni-ni time for Lucy."

"Good, she needs to sleep that off or Irene will kick her ass," Sera says.

"Whatever," Lucy says, flitting a hand, nearly smacking me in the face. I chuckle and watch her nearly fall down.

"Come here, woman." I pick her up and she wraps her arms around my neck and her legs around my waist.

"You're so tall and strong. You're just so sexy, Jesse," she says before kissing my nose.

I grin.

"She's a cute drunk," Xander says with a smile.

"That she is."

"You really should keep her."

"I plan to. Goodnight everyone."

Chapter *fifteen*

Jesse

Everyone murmurs their 'goodnight' as we head up the stairs and to my room. I walk Lucy into the bathroom and sit her on the counter.

"What're you doing?"

"I'm going to brush your teeth," I tell her, putting toothpaste on her toothbrush. "Open." She opens her mouth and stares at me as I brush her teeth. "Spit." She does and I continue brushing her teeth clean. I fill a cup with water and hand it to her. "Rinse." She does. She's pretty good at following directions, even as trashed as she is. I hand her a full glass of water. "Drink up."

I brush my teeth and down a couple glasses of water.

"Need to take my makeup off," she says, reaching for a bottle of makeup remover and some cotton balls. She stands up, ties her hair up in a ponytail, and removes her makeup. Then she washes her face and stumbles as she's drying it. She's so fucking cute.

"Grab on."

She rewraps herself around me.

"I'm a monkey, I'm a little monkey," she starts to sing. "I cling to Jesseeeee when he carries meeeee."

I chuckle at her half-assed attempt at rhyming.

"I am a monkey. I can prove it like I proved it the other night on the patio, remember?"

"I remember really hot fucking sex on the patio where you blew my mind."

"Yeah, mmm. Wait. Monkey!"

I laugh.

"Okay, take your pants off."

I raise my brow. "Not even here twenty-four hours and already she starts with the bossiness," I tsk.

"No, no. I just want to show you. Pleeeeeeease Jesse?"

"You're an incredibly cute drunk, Lucy, and because you are, I'll do this for you." Hell, I'd do anything for her.

Bending forward, I unlace my boots and Lucy starts singing.

"I'm a monkey, hugging my Jesse. See?" her arms tight around my neck and her ankles hooked at the base of my back.

I chuckle and toe off my boots. "I see. Clever little monkey," I sing as I remove my pants and bend over again to pull them off.

"Monkey!" she sings.

"You singing about monkeys reminds me of the Coal Chamber remake of Shock the Monkey."

"Ozzy!" she shouts.

She starts singing it and I sing with her.

Cover me when I run
Cover me through the fire
Something knocked me out' the trees
Now I'm on my knees
Cover me, darling please

I carry her to the bed. I pull her shirt over her head and take off her bra. I slip her shoes off. I reach up and unbutton and unzip her pants. I start to pull and she lifts her hips helping me get them off. I let her sing the monkey parts.

Moooonkeeeeey, Moooonkeeeeey, Moooonkeeeeey
Don't you know you're going to shock the monkey

I quickly pull her peach lace boypants down her legs and there she is. Naked and beautiful and her tits are perfect.

"I like singing with you Jesse but I like it better when you're kissing me." She crawls up the bed on all fours and I groan at the sight of her naked ass, her pussy peeking at me from between her thighs. She pulls the covers down and flops back onto the pillows then wiggles her eyebrows.

I grin and pounce on her and she giggles. Best. Sound. Ever. Besides her moans, that is.

She rolls on top of me and presses her mouth to mine, not wasting any time before thrusting her tongue against mine.

"Mmm," she moans. "Jesse," she whispers as she kisses my neck.

"Hmm?"

She's straddling my lap, her breasts pressing against my chest, her nipples hard.

"I have a secret."

My hands drift down her body to cup her ass, pulling her pussy against my hard cock.

"Tell me," I say against her neck.

She tilts her head to the side, giving me better access and I take advantage, kissing and licking and gently sucking, careful not to leave marks that the media would use against her.

"I'm really horny when I drink," she whispers loudly.

"Oh yeah?"

"Mhmm." To prove her point she rubs her now wet pussy along the length of my dick.

"Damn, you're so wet."

"It's because you're so sexy and, oh yes, keep kissing there."

I chuckle and run a hand down her body, between her legs to cup her sex.

"Yes, touch me there, Jesse."

"Where do you want me to touch you, Luce?"

She doesn't respond and I don't move. She wiggles her hips in frustration.

"Tell me where you want me to touch you."

"I want your fingers inside my pussy."

Well, damn. I wasn't expecting her to be so graphic and fuck if my dick didn't just twitch when she said that.

I run a finger between her folds, parting her, gently rubbing over her clit, then down, down to circle her opening.

"You're dripping."

"I know, do something about it already!" she says in frustration and I laugh.

"Jesse," she growls, it sounds more like a baby lion but it's cute as hell.

She reaches between her legs and grabs my cock, positions it to her opening, and slides down before I even have a chance to react.

"Jesus," I say, holding her hips as she sits up straight, slowly sinking down, taking my length inside her. My mind goes blank when she squeezes my cock with her pussy.

"You're so big, Jesse."

I grunt as she wiggles her hips, impaling herself on the last inch of my erection.

"You're so tight. You feel fucking amazing, Lucy."

"Mmm," she says as she starts lifting and lowering her hips. She throws in the occasional hip swivel and I groan.

"Christ woman, you can fuck," I tell her as she picks up the pace. She really can. Shit, that hip swivel thing is fucking incredible.

She leans forward pressing her lips to mine and I reach up for her nipples. I pinch and finger them in the way I've found she likes and then she reaches for mine.

"Fuuuuuuck," I say as she gently tugs on my nipple rings. She's moving faster now, so god damn wet.

"You're going to make me come before I get you there if you keep on doing that, baby."

"Nuh-uh. You've got this," she says, tugging again.

My cock jerks inside her and she moans loud.

"Oh God, Jesse. That feels so good." She tugs again and my cock gives her what she wants. Jesus. How am I supposed to last with her pussy so wet, clenching so tight, her tugging on my nipple rings, and on top of that her moans are out-of-this-world sexy?

"Oh yes, Jesse, right there," she shortens her movements, hitting just the right spot and I slide my hand between her legs, my thumb circling her clit.

"Yes, Jesse," she shouts, her hips moving fast and fucking me hard, taking me deep, so fucking deep inside her pussy I'm afraid I'm going to hurt her. She tugs my nipple rings one more time and I lose it.

My hips lift off the bed meeting her thrusts and she cries out, "Yes! God, Jesse, so good." I grunt and then moan when she swivels those fucking sexy-as-hell hips.

"Fuck, Lucy, I'm going to come." The telltale tingling at the base of my spine, spreading to my balls and the base of my dick tells me I can't hold out much longer no matter how hard I try.

I thrust hard and fast, meeting her downward thrusts, pounding into her, I press my thumb harder against her clit and circle once, twice and she throws back her head and moans out my name.

She's still got a hold of my nipple rings and as she leans back, coming hard, she tugs and I'm done. I start coming with a shout, the orgasm fierce and long, it just keeps going and then she comes again, her pussy clenching my dick harder and I see stars. I shit you not, stars.

"Holy fuuuuuuck," I groan.

"Oh yes, Jesse, I can't stop coming."

I can't take it. The pleasure is so fucking intense even when our bodies still and she lies on top of me, her pussy spasms and my cock twitches. I need to fuck her again. It's just not enough. I need more. And then I feel it.

"Shit, Lucy."

She sits up, noting my tone. "What?"

"I didn't wear a condom." What the fuck is wrong with me? "I never *ever* forget a condom."

She giggles. "You did this time. It was kinda my fault."

I grunt. Fuck. Nope, that's all on me.

"It's okay. I'm on the shot and I'm clean." She looks at me warily.

"Um…"

"Fuck. I'm clean, Lucy. I just had a checkup and I'm good. Besides, I never fuck without wrapping up first."

"Except now," she says as I roll her over onto her back, my hips thrusting into her.

I nod. "Except now. I'd put a condom on but it's kind of like closing the barn door after the horse is out and holy shit does it feel good with you bare around me."

"You feel more?" she asks.

"Mhmm," I groan. "Condoms aren't all bad, but fuck, being able to feel your wetness around me, feeling the texture of your pussy walls; that gets dulled down with a condom. And your heat, damn."

I fuck her in slow, long strokes and she wraps her legs around my hips, locking her ankles at my lower back. In this position her head is even with my nipples and she leans up to lick one, tugging on the ring with her teeth.

"Lucyyyy," I moan.

"You feel so good, Jesse."

Her hips start to rise and fall, meeting up with mine, I take an extra second to grind my pelvis against her clit and it doesn't take long before she's moaning, her head thrashing from side to side.

"Faster, Jesse."

"Nuh-uh. Just like this. It feels too fucking good to rush."

"Torture, you're torturing me."

"Torture by cock. You shouldn't complain, Cupcake, the way your pussy's squeezing my dick you're going to be coming soon."

"Mmm, I need to come *now*," she demands.

"Soon. Just let it happen, enjoy the feel of my cock sliding in and out of you, how your tight walls grip me." I thrust deeper, nudging her cervix and all I want to do is pound into her, fuck her hard and deep, but I want this to last. It feels incredible. Like hot, wet velvet wrapped around my cock.

"Jesse," she moans. "Oh yes, yes Jesse," she chants as I thrust deep and hearing her calling my name in that breathy tone of pleasure triggers my need to get her off. I start moving faster.

"Yesssss Jesse."

"I want to feel you come all over my cock. Squeeze me tight and make me come with you. Christ, you're so hot and wet. I have to—" I break off as I thrust faster, deeper, her hips meeting mine again, her swivels matching up with my pelvic grinds and she screams out my name, literally screams, "Jessseeeeee!" and damn if I don't feel like a god damn caveman because I want to pound on my chest knowing I did that to her. The tightening of her walls around me pulls me from all coherent thought and I hammer into her and come with a roar into her neck.

"Fuuuuuuck." I come hard and it keeps going on and on, each thrust releasing more cum and more pleasure.

When she collapses back onto the bed, I fall on top of her, our bodies still shaking from the strength of our orgasms.

"Holy fuck," she whispers.

"Yeah," I whisper through my pants.

"I think they heard me screaming," she says with a giggle. "I heard them cheering."

I laugh into her neck. "That was so fucking hot, Lucy. You screaming my name."

"It was *so* good."

I grunt as I get up and head to the bathroom to wash up. I grab a clean washcloth and wet it with warm water then fill a cup with cold water and grab some ibuprofen.

I get back to the bed and kneel next to her.

"Spread your legs."

She eyes me warily but complies.

"Damn if that isn't a pretty fucking sight. Our cum mixed and leaking out your pussy. I almost hate to wash it away."

"If you don't, you're laying in the wet spot," she says with a laugh.

I raise my eyebrows and hand Lucy the water and pills and she murmurs her thanks as I gently wipe between her legs until she's clean. I toss the washcloth into the hamper and crawl back into bed, snuggling up to her from behind, wrapping my arm around her and burying my face in her neck.

"Mmm," she wiggles back against me. "I'm sore again."

I grin against her neck. There's that caveman again pounding on his chest.

She lets out a sigh.

"What is it?"

"It's really going to suck when this ends."

"Who says it has to?"

She shakes her head. "It will. This won't be enough when you're out on tour and I'm touring somewhere else."

I grunt, not knowing what to say but hating that what she said might be true. Fucking hell. I can't imagine fucking anyone but Lucy, but when we're drunk out on the road... I let the thought drift. Unless... huh. That thought has possibilities that make me feel better, good enough to pull Lucy back tighter into me. I smile into her hair as I drift off to sleep listening to her really cute drunk snuffle snore.

She wakes up, bolting upright and running for the bathroom. I follow and hold her hair back just as she throws up. And damn does she throw up. I reach over with my free hand to wet a cloth with cool water and hold it to the back of her neck as she pukes and pukes and pukes. Her stomach is a never-ending pit, I swear. She only ate three pieces of pizza. Jesus. Where is it all coming from?

I flush for her as she catches her breath and moans. I press the washcloth to her forehead.

"I'm sorry, Jesse."

"No, Lucy. Don't be sorry. It's okay. I'm sorry you feel so shitty."

"It was my dream that triggered it," she tells me, getting up on shaky legs. I lift her up onto the countertop and hand her a cup of mouthwash. She rinses, gargles, and spits. Then reaches for her toothbrush and toothpaste and brushes her teeth and tongue before rinsing her mouth.

"What was the dream?" I ask as she drinks a cup of water.

She sighs. "Fucking press conference. Nightmare."

"Damn, babe," I say, pulling her to my chest. "You really have a lot of anxiety over that, huh?"

"And then some. I'll show you," she says, "as soon as my wobbly legs get back to normal."

I chuckle. "You sure you're okay."

She nods.

"Up you go." I carry her to the bed.

"I need my laptop."

"Stay put. Where is it?" I ask, turning on the bedside lamp.

"In the laptop bag over by the window seat." I nod and grab it for her. I hand it to her and she pulls out the laptop, booting it up. When she pulls out a case and a pair of glasses and puts them on I can't hold back my surprise.

"Damn."

"What?" she asks, oblivious.

"All you need is one of those long tight skirts and a white silk shirt, and with those glasses you could be a naughty school teacher."

The glasses are retro-looking, kind of the cat frames from the 1950s, a dark brown color, and she looks sexy as hell.

She laughs. "You're such a perv," she says, shaking her head and typing in her password.

"Wait. Hold the phone! What's your password?"

"Nevermind," she blushes.

"I saw it, I just want to hear you say it."

"Never," she laughs.

"Say it. You know you want to."

"I really, really don't."

"So, that's how much you love me, huh? I'm your password? Name and birthday. JKingston0121."

"Oh boy. Don't let it go to your head or you won't fit through the door."

I chuckle. "You're crazy about me, admit it."

"You drive me crazy, yes, that you do. Okay, here we go," she says, changing the subject.

"What is this?" I ask as she pulls up a media file.

"My nightmare."

"Ah."

"Pardon me if I don't watch."

"You don't have to show me."

"I do. I want you to understand, about this anxiety. I'm really not being a baby."

I nod and she presses play. There she is, a younger version of Lucy standing behind a podium. She's smiling and reading from her cards. A bee buzzes around her head and she swats at it, lifting her hands and the wind takes her cards, blowing them all over the ground. I hear her gasp, but she recovers pretty well, looking nervous, wiping her hands on her skirt—then comes the Q&A portion.

They hammer question after question at her, not about her being in the movie that would go on to get her nominated for an Oscar, but rather about her being seen with the notorious womanizer she'd mentioned the other day. Question after question, even when she redirects them to the movie, they bombard her. I run a hand down my face.

"You can't be more than what, eighteen here?"

She nods. "It was only a couple months after we met, actually. I was young, unprepared, and obviously naïve."

"Where's your agent?"

"She'd got stung by a bee and she's allergic so she and my mom were inside the building giving her an injection so she didn't go into shock."

"Christ, Lucy. That never should have happened. It wouldn't have happened if—"

"Oh, I know, but it did. And every time I get up there in front of the press, they ask the personal questions even though I'm there for the professional ones. They don't care about my success or whatever movie I'm working on, they only care about anything that will humiliate or create drama."

I nod. Having seen more than enough, I turn off the video and power down the laptop.

"Now you understand."

I nod. "I didn't need to see that to support you and try to ease your anxiety, Luce."

"I know. I just wanted—needed you to see why I'm such a pathetic mess about this. I'm not as bad up there in front of them now, having walked the red carpet enough I've learned to talk around the questions I don't want to answer."

I nod. I would like to punch every one of those fuckers in the face, especially that one reporter. He was brutal. When she didn't give him the answer he wanted, he just kept asking and rephrasing until he was shut down by the other reporters.

"I'll be there, Lucy. I won't let that happen to you again. I promise."

She nods and takes her glasses off, putting them in the case, and setting it on the bedside table. I tuck her laptop into her bag and set it under the bedside table on my side and turn off the lamp.

"Come here." I pull her to me and she snuggles into me.

"What should I tell them, Jesse, when they ask about us?"

"What do you want to tell them?"

"Don't do that. Please. I'm asking you. We need to be on the same page with this."

I blow out a breath. "As far as I'm concerned, you can tell them everything. If you want to tell them you're living with me and you're sleeping in my bed, I'm all for it. I don't have anything to hide and I don't plan on hiding you."

She nods. "Then if they ask if we're involved, I'll tell them yes."

"Good."

"If they probe too much, I will evade. They don't need to know the depth of our relationship, just that there is one."

"Right. They don't need to know that we have toe-curling, spine-tingling sex where you scream my name at the top of your lungs and our band members cheer," I say with a grin and she giggles. Again, besides her moans and now her screams, her giggles: Best. Sound. Ever.

I kiss the top of her head. "I'm okay with whatever you want to tell them."

She sighs. "Thing is, I'm comfortable telling them we're involved. What I'm dreading is when the time comes that you go your way and I go mine and they start in about that."

If my earlier thought pans out, that may not even be an issue, but I'm not telling her that until I know if it's even possible.

"Why don't we worry about what's going on now, now; and deal with later, later. I won't leave you to deal with that alone if that's what happens."

She nods.

We lay there in silence for a few minutes before she lifts her head and pushes my hair out of my face.

"I really like you, Jesse."

I smile and damn if I don't feel like a big pussy because my heart jumped in my chest when she said that.

"I really like you too, Lucy."

She smiles and snuggles back into my chest.

"So…" I say

"Hmm?"

"You found my nipple rings."

She laughs. "Oh, I found them before but you had me positioned in a way where I couldn't play with them."

I grunt. "That's true. That was one hell of a weekend."

"Mhmm. I want to get a tattoo," she says.

"Do you know what you want? Where you want it?"

"I do." She laughs. "I thought for sure you were going to try to talk me out of it."

"That'd be pretty fucking hypocritical of me, don't you think, seeing as a large portion of my body is inked."

"Mhmm, but that doesn't stop some people."

I shrug. "You've got amazingly soft and flawless skin. It's beautiful as it is and it'll be beautiful if you choose to get ink."

She nods. "Thank you."

"I can set you up with my guy, the one that does all our ink."

"Really?"

"Sure. He's a fucking talented artist."

"I noticed, looking over your tattoos, and the guys'."

"Huh."

"What?"

"You should only look at mine," I say as jealousy rears its ugly head at the thought of her looking at another guy.

She giggles again. "You're so dumb. I just looked at their tattoos, I didn't stare at them like I do yours. I look at yours in a totally different way."

Well, that's better. Caveman, beating chest.

"Good. I like it when you only look at me," I tell her, rolling her to her back and brushing my lips over hers.

"Jesse," she says, putting her hand on my cheek. "There's no one else I want to look at."

I look down at her and my heart does that flip-flop thing again. I swallow hard and nod. I gaze into her eyes, reaching up to tuck a strand of hair behind her ear then running my knuckles down her cheek.

"I only see you, Lucy. Only you."

Chapter
sixteen

Lucy

In spite of all the support I'm receiving from everyone, I'm a nervous wreck—it doesn't help that my mother called to tell me she would be at the press conference. Shit.

"Who was it?" Sera asks, walking out of the bathroom.

I sigh. "Mom."

"No." Her eyes are wide, her mouth gaping.

"Oh yes, yes Regina will be there. God damn it! FUCKING COCKSUCKER!"

Jesse walks in chuckling. "She's swearing again," he says, walking over to me, pulling me to him, and giving me a toe-curling kiss.

"Wow. Yeah," I say, my vision unfocused.

"Holy shit, Jesse," Sera says with a laugh. "You're magic. Your kisses calm her down and blank out her mind. It's awesome."

Jesse grins.

"She does the same thing to him," Ben says with a chuckle.

"Legit," Jesse agrees and they fist bump.

"My mom is going to be there," I groan and throw myself on the bed face down.

"So what?" Ben asks.

"My mother is…"

"A bulldozer. A whirlwind. A tornado."

Ben nods. "Destroyer of all that is good?"

"And then some," Sera tells him.

"You've got an hour and we need to leave, Lucy," Jesse reminds me as they head into the media room.

"I know." I pout like a baby but I can't help myself. I don't want to do this. Don't. Want. To. If I stomp my foot, then my imitation of a three year old will be complete. Ugh. Suck it up, Luce. I walk to the bathroom and start applying my eye shadow when there's a knock at the door.

I walk over, enter the code, and on the other side stands my savior. I squeal, "Spenser!"

"Oh Lucy, I knew you needed me for this circus your mother's forcing on you."

"How did you know?"

He picks up the remote on the bedside table and turns on the TV where there's a picture of me, notes about a press conference, speculation about why I'm not acting anymore, speculation about Jesse, assumptions about everything.

Spenser flicks channel after channel. Same shit, different channel.

"Ugh, turn it off."

"Did I hear my name on the news?" Jesse asks, coming out of the game room.

"You did. Get used to it, not that you aren't already, being the sexy super rockstar that you are," I say, rubbing my hand over his amazing ass.

He grins. "There's no time for that so don't get me started."

"No, there's not, so *let's* get started," Spenser scolds. I take a seat in a chair by the windows.

"No, dressed first," he motions to the bathroom. I look at him and notice he's carrying a dress bag.

"Okay."

He closes the door behind him and locks it. "Everything you need is in this bag including bra and panties, shoes. Get moving. We're short on time."

I strip my clothes off and toss them into the laundry hamper before putting on lacy lemon yellow boypants and a strapless yellow bra.

"Yellow?"

"Mhmm. Looks fab with your dark brown hair."

"Okay."

He pulls out a yellow dress and slips it over my head before I even get to look at it. He zips up the back and it fits like a glove.

I look in the mirror and gasp. This dress is gorgeous. It's some form of cotton/spandex/nylon blend that is stretchy and unbelievably comfortable. The scooped neckline lands just above my breasts showing just a hint of cleavage. The yellow and white polka dot cap sleeves are so short they could almost be considered straps. There's a line of polka dots along the hem of the dress, which falls just above my knees. Next Spenser hands me a pair of sandals identical to the red ones I wore on the video shoot except these are yellow with white polka dots.

"You are a king, Spenser."

"Yes, yes, I know. Let's go out by the windows, natural light and all that."

I nod and carefully take a seat by the windows. Someone, likely Sera, put up a divider and I breathe a sigh of relief. I really don't want to be stared at right now. I'll get enough of that soon enough.

"This house is gorgeous. You lucky bitch."

"I don't care about the house."

"Oh I know, I wasn't just talking about the house," Spenser says and I see Jesse shift uncomfortably.

"Jesse Kingston your girlfriend has the most amazing rack," Spenser teases.

Jesse growls.

"If I were straight, I'd be feeling her up every chance I got, which would be a lot. Amazing tits, Lucy."

"Thank you?" I say with a laugh.

Spenser begins working his magic after he drapes a cape over me and I close my eyes and relax.

Another knock on the door and Jesse answers. Simone and Carmen enter as well as Meggie, Trace, Jace, Xander, Ethan, and Kennedy.

"Open those pretty eyes," Spenser says. "Just liquid liner with cat edge on the top, a little shadow, and falsies."

"Okay." Honestly I don't care. I know Spenser will make me look amazing and that's all I care about.

"Party in Jesse's bed!" Meggie says with a laugh.

"Oh, I'm sure he's had more than enough of those," Sera says.

I sigh and Jesse cringes.

"Not a good topic if you're trying to keep her calm for… you know," Ethan says.

"Noted," Meggie replies.

Sera introduces Spenser and the girls to Meggie and Trace. Unsurprisingly they've met before.

"Okay, we're ready for hair," Spenser announces, and Carmen and Simone motion for me to enter the bathroom.

They give me large spiral curls and then work my hair up into a half up-do, strategically styling my bangs to fall in just the right places.

Sera comes in with my jewelry. She slips the necklace on and locks the clasp. I put in the large yellow and white hoop earrings, the yellow and white bangle bracelets, and then my usual selection of rings.

"I should put a ring on my left hand and have the media buzzing like fucking bees."

"Do it!" Meggie yells and I laugh. I swear that girl has bionic hearing.

"How do I look?"

Spenser finishes my lipstick then tells me, "Gorgeous, of course. You'll have those fucktards eating out of your hand."

"From your lips to God's ears."

"Amen, sister," Carmen says.

Simone shrugs. "You'll be great."

I laugh nervously then exit the bedroom. Silence. I'm met with silence.

"Oh God, I look hideous. Spenser, I need to change," I say, panicking.

"No, no!" Jace says, holding my arm. "You look so beautiful, Lucy. I never liked yellow but it's perfect for you."

"Of course it is," Spenser says, rolling his eyes. "Wait until you see her in orange or fuchsia."

"The man knows his stuff," Jace says. He's leaning in to kiss my cheek and Spenser cuffs him on the back of his head.

"What the fuck?"

"No touching. No kissing. No licking." He looks to Jesse who's giving me a heated stare. "No fucking—of any kind!" he adds.

I laugh.

"Hold up," Carmen says. She hands me a pair of large white-framed sunglasses. "Retro baby," she says with a wink.

"Okay, I'm ready." Sera hands me a yellow and white polka dot purse and I just shake my head. Spenser is a genius.

"I don't think I'm paying them enough," I tell Sera and she laughs.

"You are too," Spenser scolds. "Now let's get moving."

"Wait, what? You're going too?"

"We are part of the band, are we not? We're the Blush blushers," he says, motioning to him, Carmen and Simone.

I nod. "You totally are."

"Let's go, baby. Can I hold her hand?" Jesse asks Spenser and I grin.

"That's *all* you'll be holding until this bullshit is over."

Jesse just smiles that sexy half-smile and his dimples wink at me.

I crook my finger at him and he leans in close. "I'm going to lick your dimples tonight."

"Cupcake, you can lick whatever you want," he replies with a wink.

Damn. Giving a press conference with wet panties. This will be a first.

So far, so good. I haven't tripped and fallen on my face.

"Good afternoon. I'd say it's nice to be here, but that'd be a lie." Everyone chuckles.

"I'd like to address the areas of speculation that have been making quite a few headlines without any real facts. First, I'm announcing, right here, right now, that I am on hiatus from the movie industry until further notice."

Murmurs rise from the crowd and I note the reporters taking notes.

"Questions will be answered after I finish my statement so if I may continue?"

Everyone quiets down.

"If an amazing role were to be placed into my lap with my costar being Milo Ventimiglia and the script had us kissing and frolicking between the sheets, I'd come back for that." That gets a laugh from everyone. "But seriously, if an exceptional script were to come my way and I was drawn to the character, I'd definitely step up for that—and I really would prefer Milo. But…" I say, leaving them hanging a moment, "for now I am going to focus on music. Serafina Manzini, my sister, and I both were in a band when we were in high school and we're resurrecting our old band, Blush. In addition to Sera and me, we're lucky to be joining up with Jace Warner, Megan Melody, and Trace Styx. In less than two weeks we'll be in the studio working on recording our first album with Cage Nichols of Nichols Records."

Sera, Meggie, Jace, and Trace step forward.

I take a sip of my water.

"Thank you for being patient while I tell you the part of this press conference that is most important to *me* and now I'll tell you what is most important to *you*."

Jesse steps up and grabs my hand. "The rumors are true, Jesse Kingston and I are involved. Do we know what the future holds? No more than you do. It's new and we're trying to enjoy spending as much time as we can together. I'm not sure what else to say about this that I'd be comfortable sharing with you, so we'll move on to questions."

"Ah, my favorite. Mr. Leonard." The jackhole who made my life a misery at my first press conference.

"Are you leaving acting because of Jesse Kingston?"

Jesse chuckles next to me and wraps his arm around my waist.

"No, afraid it's nothing that exciting. It's something that I've wanted to do for a very long time and I'm going for it."

I point to the next reporter. "Are you going to be in Falling Down's newest video?"

"As a matter of fact, I am, as is Sera. It's no secret that Sera and I enjoy being in music videos for Cage."

The band steps up behind us.

I point to another. "Is that how you met? Or is it true you met when you were a teenager?"

I laugh. "How do you all get this information?" Jesse shrugs. "It's true, when I was seventeen and making the big move out to L.A., I saw Jesse in the Chicago airport. I fangirled all over him, got his autograph, and a photo with him. We walked to where my flight was delayed to find out he was on the same flight." I shake my head when they all start murmuring again.

"No, we didn't sit together on the plane. He was in first class as he should be. Can you imagine this six-foot-three-inch man sitting in coach? Where would he put his legs?"

That brings a few chuckles.

"That was the last time I saw Jesse until the first day on set and in all honesty I was surprised. No one told us who we were going to be doing the video for, only that it was a big name band. And suddenly there was Jesse Kingston."

"Okay, hold up," Jesse interrupts. "I've got to tell them the whole story or they'll be upset if they hear it somewhere else."

I roll my eyes. "By all means," I gesture to the microphone.

"The band and I were prepped for the video, we'd gone over everything with Cage, and because we were so rushed that week, we didn't think to ask who the actress slash dancers were. It was rumored to be Lucy and Sera but we didn't know for sure. Not a big deal. We get along with chicks, right guys?" Jesse prompts the guys who all make leering faces and obscene noises.

"When we walked to the central part of the building where Cage had multiple sets worked up, we heard drums, guitar, and a voice that stopped us in our tracks. Okay, not right away because we were a little pissed that someone had the nerve to touch our equipment. Musicians are temperamental about sh—stuff like that. But the minute they started the next song, a ballad from a popular band," Jesse shakes his head, "we were stunned. When we finally moved forward, I turned the corner and was knocked on my ass. There was Luciana Russo sitting on a stool in front of a microphone, strumming my acoustic guitar, eyes closed, singing her soul out. We all just looked at each other, then over to Sera whaling on the drums like a pro, and that's when we decided to join in. Ben picked up his guitar and I stepped up to the mic. I've got to laugh here," and he does. "You should have seen the look on Lucy's face when she saw us. I thought she was going to either pass out or run away but she did neither. She finished the song with us and *then* she freaked out."

That brings about a bunch of laughs. "She hands me back my guitar and apologizes for touching my 'precious'. I knew who she was and she seemed kind of shocked about that. I'm not sure why. I mean she's a fu— freaking Academy Award-winning actress, right?"

"Jesse," I say with a blush.

"Anyway, we did the video and we had a good time, even if Lucy did insist on keeping it professional while we worked together."

"No matter how hard you tried to make it otherwise," I add with a grin.

I point to the next reporter. "Then you're not joining up with Falling Down?"

"Nope. We've re-formed Blush."

I point to another reporter. "Is it true you're living with Jesse?"

"I'm not comfortable commenting on the intimate details of our relationship until we figure them out for ourselves."

I point to the next reporter. "What's going to happen when Falling Down goes out on tour in a couple months? It's common knowledge that Jesse enjoys groupies."

I raise a brow. "You know, that's a great question and one I don't have an answer to. We actually just talked about this last night, right Jesse?"

He nods.

"I guess all I can say is when we know, you'll know. Hell, you might know before we do," I say with a wink to my fav reporter. I love Margo Phelan.

More questions about Jesse and I, ones that require answers about the intimate details I won't answer so I give them the same answer that I've made my standard. "I'm not comfortable commenting on the intimate details of our relationship until we figure them out for ourselves."

"Last question, Dave," I say to one of my favorite reporters.

"Have you considered having Blush and Falling Down tour together?"

My heart drops into my stomach and I laugh. "While that would be an incredible opportunity for our band, we're nowhere near the caliber of Falling Down. No-name bands don't usually end up out on tour with big-named ones like Falling Down."

"That's a shame," Dave says. "I'd have liked to have seen you two out on tour together."

I tilt my head in question.

Dave shrugs. "You seem happy together. Touring separately will likely screw that up."

I nod. "Likely." And that sucks ass. "I'll keep you updated. Thank you all for coming out this afternoon and listening as I tell you the facts of what's happening rather than continuing on with speculation. If something develops and you have questions regarding whatever it is, feel free to call my agent Irene McPherson. She'll set something up and I'll be as honest with you as I can."

With that I wave and Jesse hugs me to him, lifting me beneath my armpits so my face is level with his and I grin.

He pulls me in for a kiss and I wrap my arms around his neck, he wraps his arms around my lower back, holding me up in the air. I hear cameras clicking like crazy as we devour each other's mouths. Jesse pulls back, gives me one last soft, lingering kiss, then sets me down. I straighten my skirt and look to the crowd and fan myself. They all laugh and the cameras are whirling like crazy.

We interlock our fingers and head into the building with our friends and family behind us.

Once inside I let out a long breath of air and collapse my upper half over the reception desk. The receptionist laughs. Her black hair is cropped in a cute and messy pixie cut, her face round and stunning. Her eyes, a brilliant green, are what draw me in.

"That bad?"

"Actually, not as bad as I anticipated."

"That's good. The media can be a total pain in the ass."

I look at her nametag. "Celeste. It's good to meet you."

"You as well Miss Russo."

"None of that. I'm just Lucy."

"What are you up to?" Jesse asks.

"Shush. So, Celeste, you know a lot about bands, the music industry, touring, making records, what's needed as far as PR and stuff are concerned right?"

"Yeah. I've been doing this job the last seven years."

I nod and Jesse chuckles. "How attached are you to your job here?"

"Why are you asking?"

"Say I offer you a job as an assistant and PR person with a starting salary of," I reach for a pen and a piece of paper writing the number down and handing it to her.

"Are you for real?"

I shrug.

"Cage is going to kick your ass," Sera says with a laugh.

Our gazes are still locked and I can see her thinking this over, turning over the possibilities.

She nods. "I'm in. When do I start?"

"God damn it, Lucy," Cage bellows.

I turn to him sheepishly, though it's not for real and he knows it. "I'm sorry, Cage, she's just so brilliant."

"I know, that's why she works for me."

"Worked," Sera says with a laugh.

Cage sighs.

"You have so many professional super-assistants. My taking this one for myself won't hurt you."

"The hell it won't. She's the best I've got."

I shrug. "I figured. It's why I picked her."

"You little shit," Cage says, wrapping an arm around my waist and lifting me up in the air to give me a smacking kiss on the lips.

"You weirdo."

"No worries, Celeste. Lucy will take good care of you. If you'd like to start immediately," he sighs, "I'll work something out with Francine in personnel and get someone up here to *try* to fill your position."

"Never gonna happen," I say, folding my arms over my chest and Celeste laughs.

"Quit while you're ahead, Cupcake."

"True, true. I better shut up now." I give Celeste my phone number and she puts it in her phone then gives me a call back.

"Digits exchanged."

"Yep," I say. "I'll give you a call tomorrow and let you know what's up and we can discuss whatever we should be doing and all that."

She laughs as she grabs her purse.

"Cage, it's been a pleasure."

He chuckles. "You're not rid of me just yet. I'm their acting manager for their first album and tour."

She raises her eyebrows. "No kidding. Lucky you," she says to me and Sera.

"Right?"

"I'm outta here. Talk to you tomorrow."

Jesse wraps an arm around my shoulders. "Why did you pick her?"

I shrug. "Instinct. She wasn't intimidated by me or you. Did you notice she didn't fangirl all over you? Sure she looked her fill but she didn't even ask for an introduction or autograph. She knows her shit, I could tell by the spread of folders she has out there, so I took a chance."

Jesse nods.

"Alright people," Cage says, quieting everyone down. "The press conference went amazingly well. Great job Lucy. And Jesse, your filling in the rest of Lucy's story was perfect. Now we work on song choices and practicing together, getting comfortable with one another, and a week from Monday we record. I'd like to get your album out as soon as possible and get you on tour in the next three months."

"Whoa," Trace says. "Fuckin' cool."

I blow out a breath. "It's moving fast but this is good. If we move slowly I'll have too much time to think and go into panic mode."

Cage nods. "I know. Don't worry, Lucy. I've got everything planned out and I think you'll be pleased with the results."

"I have no doubt."

Meggie bounces on her feet. "You're Cage fucking Nichols, of course we'll be pleased."

He just smiles, never one to get a big head over compliments.

"We're staying at Casa Falling Down," Jace tells him, "and the guys said we could use their studio."

"Good, that's more convenient."

"If you need us, that's where we'll be," Sera tells Cage, running her tongue over her teeth.

"Alright. I'll be in touch. Stay out of trouble and out of the media if you can."

"Right," I say. "Now that they know Jesse and I are involved, they're going to be all over us."

He shrugs. "It'll die down when someone else does something gossip-worthy. Until then, play it cool but have fun."

"Okay. I'll call you tomorrow about the contracts. Irene got back to me earlier."

Cage nods. "Sounds good. Have a good day." He runs a hand over Sera's ass before he strides to the black elevators and promptly disappears.

"Oooh, the black elevator," I murmur.

"Do you think he's Batman?" Meggie asks.

I want to laugh but I can't.

"You know, I could see that," Ben says.

We all agree. Cage Nichols is Batman. Well, he certainly is one of my heroes.

"Let's go home," Jesse says, steering me toward the door. "Your parents are coming over."

I groan. "Jesseeeee."

"If you're whining over that you're really going to whine when I tell you Joey's coming too."

"Awww, damn it."

"All you need is a foot stomp to complete that temper tantrum," Meggie says.

"Do it and you'll be in trouble and you'll deserve a spanking."

I immediately stomp my feet. In fact, I stomp all the way out to the limo with Jesse laughing behind me.

Chapter
seventeen

Lucy

"I think your mom likes me," Jesse says with a wiggle of his eyebrows.
"That's only because you and Ben made your amazing spaghetti and we're freaking Italian. If you can cook Italian dishes like a God, it's going to get you in her good graces," I tell him.

"I don't care what it is, Jace told me she's a hard woman but she's softened up a bit."

I roll my eyes. "She acts tough, but she's really a softie underneath it all… and my dad makes sure of that."

Jesse grins as he takes a drink of his beer.

"Then there's the fact that you guys wouldn't let any of us help you clean up the kitchen or dishes. I think she's pretty much fallen in love with every one of you."

"We're awesome," Xander says as he plops into the chair next to me. "She knows it, she acknowledges it, she's brilliant. Isn't that right, Regina?"

"Of course I'm brilliant."

Again, I roll my eyes. Dear God they're all sucking up to my mother and she's loving it.

I pass her a spoon.

"What's this for?"

"So you can eat up the sweetness they're pouring all over you," I tell her exasperated.

"Oh Luciana, don't be jealous."

"Yeah, Lucy, don't be jealous," Xander says.

"I'm not jealous." I'm seriously not. I just think it's ridiculous the way they're carrying on with my mother because they're actually *afraid* of her.

"You seem jealous to me," Ben says.

"Oh for Christ's sake."

"Luciana, language."

"Yes, mama."

They all smirk at me and I flip them the bird.

"As I was saying, I'm not jealous. I'm amused."

"Amused?" Jesse asks, pulling me onto his lap.

"Mhmm. You see, it's really entertaining watching you all suck up to my mother to get on her good side because you're all *terrified* of her."

Sera laughs. "They so are."

"I'm not afr—" Jace is cut off when my mom motions him to her.

"Uh-huh," I snicker.

"Pathetic is what it is," Meggie says, bouncing around to Falling Down's latest album my mother insisted they play for her even though she isn't a fan of hard rock.

"It's amusing and a bit... endearing that they all want to get along with my mama. It shows me that they love me *so* much that they want to make me happy in every aspect of my life," I say with a laugh.

"Now who's shoveling sh—sweetness?" Kennedy asks.

"Hey now," I say, pretending to be affronted but I can't help but laugh, especially when Jesse starts tickling me.

He leans forward, turning my face to his, and pulling me close so our lips are a breath apart. "You're so fucking beautiful."

I blush and he smiles, running his fingers over my flushed cheeks.

"You always bring light with you wherever you go, but when you laugh, it's like rays of sunshine pouring over everyone, filling them with warmth and happiness."

I have no idea what to say to that. Jesse Kingston is waxing poetic and holy freaking hell.

"Jesse," I whisper. He presses his lips softly against mine, lingering for a few seconds, before pulling back.

"You can't know how that feels. I wish you could experience it."

"Oh, I don't know," I tell him. "I think I feel the same way when you're happy, when you get the full-on laugh. The best one is when you aren't expecting something, you get surprised and pause, then once you process it you throw your head back and laugh. The sound is full and rich and it flows through me, warming me from the inside out."

He just stares at me, his expression soft.

"Dude, hers was better than yours," Xander deadpans, blatantly eavesdropping.

I smile and Jesse smiles back. "Fucker."

"Jesse Kingston. Language!" my mother scolds.

"Yes, ma'am."

Now *that* I laugh at and Sera joins me. I giggle and tears start pouring down my cheeks, my stomach hurts so much that I can hardly breathe.

"Oh my, that was awesome. Where were the paparazzi when that was happening?"

"Can you imagine that on Entertainment Tonight?" Sera asks. "*Yes, ma'am.*"

"Dude, not even funny," Ben says. "We've been on there more times than we care to count and each time they've dragged us through the mud."

"Wow, really?" Meggie asks.

"Yep," Jesse tells her.

"Who'd you piss off?" I ask him.

He shrugs. "I dunno. No one that I know of. Why?"

"They're one of the only media groups that *doesn't* talk shit about me."

"True story," Sera says.

"Bet it doesn't stay that way for long," Ethan says with a frown.

I frown. "You'd think after today, with all the information we spoon fed those vultures, that they'd be more accommodating."

Xander snorts.

"I even offered to discuss things with them. *Me*, discuss my private life with the freaking press. I referred them to Irene who would set up a meeting if they wanted the true facts."

"That's just it, Luciana," my dad says. "They don't want the true facts. True facts are boring and don't make drama which doesn't make for good press which doesn't make good sales."

Cage grunts in agreement as he tips back his beer for a drink.

"Well, I tried. I went out there all professional and shit and gave them everything but what position Jesse and I were in last night and what color my lace boyshorts are."

"Lace boyshorts are hot," Xander tells me, wiggling his eyebrows.

"Lucy," my mother scolds.

"Mama, come on. It's the truth and you know it. Do you see anyone hounding Jesse or any of the guys from Falling Down for being manwhores? Did they go after Jesse after the night in the club? No and no. They came after *me*. Why do you think that is?"

"Because you're a good girl and you were fornicating with a bad boy in the middle of a dance club," Joey says from the doorway.

"Joey!" I walk to him and give him a hug. "How did you manage to get away? I thought you had a night shoot?"

"Amanda got sick from the heat," he says with disgust.

"Amanda Digby?"

He nods. "She's ridiculously simple-minded. She sat outside today, in the more than one hundred-degree weather, thinking just because she had one of those large umbrellas that blocked the sun that she was immune to the heat."

"Um… the sun maybe but not the heat," Sera says.

"Exactly. Idiot woman," Joey says, hugging Sera as I perch back on Jesse's lap.

"Want a beer?" Meggie asks.

"Holy shit! Meggie!" Joey shouts, lifting her in the air and twirling her around. "It's great to see you. What are you doing here?"

"I'm in Blush with your sister, Sera, Jace, and—"

I cough loudly and Meggie winks at me.

"That's great," Joey says. I introduce him to Jesse and the guys, he greets our mom and dad and Cage.

"Joey."

"Yeah?"

"I've got a bit of a surprise for you."

"What's that?" he asks.

Trace steps out from behind the bar where Joey wasn't able to see him—we'd planned this out earlier. Joey's eyes go huge.

"No fucking way!"

"Joseph Russo! Language!"

"Sorry mama but it's Trace fucking Styx!"

"Joseph!"

"Mama, you might just ignore the language for a little bit because he's going to be fangirling and likely swearing in his excitement. You know how he gets," I tell her.

"This is true. I'll ignore him."

I give her a look. It's not easy ignoring my brother. He's loud and boisterous in a party setting.

"What?" she asks.

"You can't ignore Joey."

"Oh sure I can. I've learned how to tone all of you out. Every last one of you, including your friends you had over in high school. Take Jace, for instance."

Jace squirms a bit in his chair, being put on the spot.

"No more than thirty minutes ago he started talking to Kennedy about the... sluts they... entertained a few nights ago. I tuned that right out. There are some things a mother doesn't need to hear and she learns very early on how to make that happen."

"Wow," Jace says, blushing.

"I'm not going to even lecture you men on the importance of respecting women," she says and they all shift in their chairs, all besides Jesse, who smirks.

"And you, Jesse Kingston. You better be the most respectful of them all. You are, after all, involved with my daughter—"

"And Nana Russo taught mama how to put hexes and curses on people," Sera says straight-faced.

"That she did. While I believe my mother-in-law was spawned from the devil incarnate, she has taught me many useful things."

Jesse takes a sip of his beer, totally relaxed. He shrugs. "I'm not concerned," he says. Everyone raises their eyebrows. "You know why?" he asks.

"Why's that?" I ask.

"Because I do respect you and if there comes a time when I treat you disrespectfully, I damn well deserve whatever your mom and nana bring on me."

I pat his cheek with my hand. "Oh you brave, stupid man."

Sera laughs.

I kiss his lips and he smirks. Oh, those dimples. My gaze zeroes in on them and his smirk turns into a knowing grin.

I lean forward and whisper in his ear, "Lick."

"Anywhere you want," he whispers back.

Evil. I shouldn't be thinking of licking Jesse's body from head to toe with my mama and daddy sitting no more than ten feet away, but damn if I'm not. Pure evil, that is Jesse Kingston.

Earlier Sera and I brought out the journals of songs we'd all written before, during, and after high school. Meggie and Trace were thumbing through a few of them, as were Xander and Ben.

"Who wrote this one?" Ben asks, trying to show me the page.

"I can't see that without my glasses. What's the title?"

"Blush."

Everyone gets quiet and I feel my cheeks heat up, my heart is pounding in my chest. "I did."

"Thought so," he replies. "It needs to go on your album."

"Why?" I ask incredulously.

"You know why."

"Now I want to hear it," Jesse says.

"No, really, you don't."

"Oh, I don't know," Sera says, running her tongue over her teeth. "I think he probably does."

"Bitch."

She laughs.

"What's going on?" Jesse asks.

"Nothing."

"If it's nothing, then you can sing it for me."

Shit. I sigh.

"Do you mind if I borrow your guitar for a few minutes, Kennedy?" Sera asks.

"Nope," he says as he stops strumming the chords and willingly hands it over to her. "Have at it."

Sera pulls up a chair next to mine and strums a few chords.

"I should really wait to sing until—"

Jesse shakes his head. "You're evading. Now you *have* to sing it so I can see what you're hiding."

I look down at my hands. "I apologize in advance."

"For what?"

"You'll see," Joey says with a chuckle.

"Shut up, Joseph. It's a lovely song," my mother says.

Well then. Here we go revealing… everything.

"Ready?" Sera asks. I nod and close my eyes, going to the place where nothing exists but music. I start to sing, with Sera singing backup on the chorus.

Every time I think of you, I blush
Every time I see you, I blush
Looking in your eyes, I blush
Knowing that I want you, I blush

Do you remember a time not so long ago
When we were strangers but said hello
You held my hand and looked into my eyes
The soul-deep feeling was no surprise

With how badly I want to kiss you, I blush
With how much I long for you, I blush
When I think of all the things I want to do to you, I blush
When I wish my dream would come true, I blush

Do you remember a time not so long ago
When we were strangers but said hello

You held my hand and looked into my eyes
The soul-deep feeling was no surprise

When I see you up on that stage, I blush
When I see you sing with your soul, I blush
When you reach out to the crowd like you do, I blush
Wishing it was me you were reaching out to, I blush

Do you remember a time not so long ago
When we were strangers but said hello
You held my hand and looked into my eyes
The soul-deep feeling was no surprise
I hope one day you'll know all the reasons why…
I blush

There's silence and I drop my head, my eyes still closed.

"Damn," Xander says. Ben, Ethan, Trace, Meggie, and Kennedy are in agreement—all the ones who haven't heard the song yet… all except Jesse.

"How old were you when you wrote that, Lucy?" Jesse asks softly.

"Eighteen," I say, then take a drink of my water and Jesse hands me a peppermint Life Saver.

"It wasn't long after we met you. You'd just finished an album and went on tour. We went to your concert here in L.A.," Sera tells him.

"You inspired her," my mother says. "Even at a very young age, before she met you."

"Mama," I scold.

Jesse turns me to face him.

I lift my chin and push back my shoulders as I meet his gaze. False bravado I'm good at. I am, after all, an Academy Award-winning actress.

"You felt that zing in Chicago, too."

It's not a question, not really, but I nod.

"It triggered a lot of shit," Joey blurts out.

I send my brother a glare. "Joey, shut up."

"What?" he asks.

Seriously. This is so embarrassing.

"I thought I'd met you somewhere before, I almost asked you. You seemed so familiar," Jesse tells me softly.

"Probably because she stalked you at every concert she could get to," Joey says with a laugh.

"Joseph," my father scolds. "Shut up."

Properly chastised, he goes back to fangirling all over Trace who seems to be eating it up.

I just look at Jesse. "You think I'm a weird stalker girl with some high school girl crush now, huh?" I ask.

"No. I think it might have started that way and it might have been what prompted our meeting in Chicago being a whole lot more personal than an artist and fan meeting, but I think Chicago is where things changed."

I see Sera nod and smile.

"You should have let me know you were coming to the concert. I would have gotten you VIP passes."

I shake my head. "No. It was better to not do that. I was way too young and I had a lot to learn. A lot. Besides, you had your manwhore status at that time and things between us would have never worked out."

"Hmm."

"Honestly, I don't know if they'll even work out now with us touring one way and you touring another. I wouldn't expect or even ask exclusivity of you during your tour. That wouldn't be fair."

"To who?" he asks, raising a brow, looking more than a little irritated.

"You."

"Hold up. You automatically think because I'm going to be going on tour that I wouldn't want to continue our relationship? That I'd rather fuck a bunch of groupie whores, as you put it?" he growls.

"I think it's time for us to move inside and give these two some privacy," Ben says. "Come on, Regina and Anthony, I'll give you the nickel tour."

Jesse and I sit there staring at each other as everyone clears off the patio.

Cage pauses. "That's going on the album. Your title track."

I nod and he heads inside, closing the door behind him.

"You can answer me now that they're gone," Jesse bites out.

I stand up and begin pacing. "What do you want from me? That—" I wave my hand, "touring, being wild, women, promiscuity—is your life. I walked into this with my eyes wide open, Jesse. I don't expect you to change your life for me."

"Why the fuck not?"

"What?" I look at him.

"Why don't you expect that?"

"Because you're *you*. You're a god damn *rockstar*. It's what you do."

He nods then runs his hand through his hair.

"Who fucked you over, Lucy?"

"Huh?" How the hell did he get that out of…

"Who was it that fucked you over?"

"I don't—"

"You do. Who was it that made you feel as if you didn't deserve to be treated with respect? Who was it that made you feel so inferior you don't have the right to ask for things you deserve?"

My heart is pounding so fast, my breath catches. I can't talk about this with him.

I shake my head.

He walks up to me, gently grabs my arms and gives me a soft shake. "Who did this to you?"

"It doesn't matter."

"Oh, there's where you're wrong, Lucy. It matters. It matters a whole fuck of a lot because whoever the prick is that did this, he broke you."

I gasp and tears fill my eyes. "Don't do this," I whisper, my body shaking.

"Why not? It's the truth, isn't it? When we were in Chicago you had this look where it almost seemed as if you claimed me the minute you felt that zing. Six years ago you were ready to make demands and we were strangers. Now we're in a relationship, we're fu—intimate, I've licked every inch of your body, and you won't ask that of me? Don't you think, being in a relationship with me, you'd have a *right* to ask that of me before we tour? I sure as fuck expect it from *you*."

The first tear falls. He wipes it with the pad of his thumb.

"What happened, Lucy? Who hurt you so badly you're shaking right now just at the mention of it?"

At his quiet, tender tone, I break. The dam bursts and he pulls me into his arms, holding me close. He sits back down and pulls me onto his lap, holding me as I sniffle.

"His—" My voice cracks and I clear my throat. "His name was Ian. We met on the set of *Fair Play*."

"Go on," he encourages gently.

"He was so nice when we first met: sweet, kind, attentive. We began dating. We'd go to dinner, movies, or the theater when we got a few days off from filming. After a little more than three months we went away for a weekend together, we went to the Keys, and, uh, we slept together."

Jesse nods, his lips pressed firmly together. "You were a virgin?"

I nod. "Yeah," I whisper.

"Did he hurt you?"

"No… not then." Jesse stiffens.

"When?"

"That weekend was really great. We spent a lot of time on the beach, doing touristy things. We were out of the hotel room more than in and I was glad he hadn't brought me there solely for sex, you know?"

He nods.

"Anyway, he continued being great for a couple weeks and then when his part in the film was over—mine wasn't, I was the female lead. He became resentful of my time away from him and in front of the camera. He made me feel guilty for going to work every morning," I say with a soft laugh. "Isn't that ridiculous?"

Jesse doesn't say anything but I really don't expect him to. I was asking that question of myself and my answer is yes. It is ridiculous.

"He became demanding of my time, jealous of my costar—"

"Because of the intimate scenes?"

"Uh, yeah. There was a lot of kissing and hugging, arms around one another, holding hands, and four sex scenes."

Jesse nods. "I remember the movie."

"It's not at all intimate when you're on set. There are people everywhere, some milling around doing their jobs, others just standing or sitting watching. You have to understand, when I'm playing a part, I *do* tend to lose myself in the character when the cameras are rolling. It's the only way I know. But it's the character, not Lucy, if you can understand that?"

"It's what makes you so good at what you do."

I shrug. "I guess. All I know is he assumed that I was enjoying all the attention my character received from my costar. Let's just call him H. You know who he is but I don't want to drag his name through this horror story."

"Horror," Jesse repeats and I nod.

"So, it was no secret that H and I got along well, we were friends, which makes working together that much easier, you know? And, of course, he's a beautiful man, inside and out, so, yeah, there was attraction there—superficial attraction. It was no hardship kissing him," I say with a small smile.

Jesse grunts. "I take it he didn't like that."

"No. He didn't. He became possessive, demanding of my time and—"

"And?" Jesse prompts when I pause.

I lift my eyes to meet his. "And," I whisper, "demanding of my body."

Jesse hisses out a breath.

"The first time—"

"The *first* time?" Jesse nearly yells.

"Shhh. They'll hear you and this isn't public knowledge." I sigh. "That was a shitty thing to say. They're not public, they're family but I'm not comfortable revealing this part of my life."

"I understand. But, God, Lucy," he rubs his hands up and down my arms.

"Let me just get this all out. I'd had a sex scene with H that day and it was one where we stripped completely down. Nothing showed as they covered my breasts and—" I sigh. "I just put a robe on after we were done shooting for the day, once we got the scene just right. It didn't help that it took a few takes so they could get multiple angles for editing and all that."

"He was on set? Watching?"

I nod. "It didn't faze me because I became Libby and H became David. When they call action, Luciana Russo doesn't exist on that set. I am whoever I'm scripted to be. When I headed back to my trailer, Ian followed along. I knew he was angry. H and I were all over each other even though it was just work."

"But he didn't see it that way."

"No. I explained it was the same as it was for him but he used my friendship with H against me, saying we were too close and if I wanted to be fucked, he'd show me how a real man did it. I'm sure you can imagine what came next."

He just gives one sharp nod.

"He left bruises on my body that wardrobe noticed when I was changing one day. They knew what happened but I didn't admit anything. I wanted to just forget it happened. I mean, it was my fault, right? At least that's what I thought then. I tried to break things off with him, but he begged and pleaded, apologized to me, and young, naïve Lucy reluctantly agreed to try. Needless to say, the good guy didn't last long. Then when I wanted to do something, how dare I ask, shouldn't that be up to him because I'd been off doing whatever all day and he was bored. He should be able to make the plans. I didn't want to argue about it, so I agreed. He became so controlling. It got so bad he wouldn't let me call my mom when I was off set because that was *his* time with me. A week later we had another sex scene."

"God, Lucy."

I close my eyes and snuggle into his chest, his arms wrapping tighter around me. "I hate telling this part. It's… just hard. The minute we got to the trailer, he shoved me so hard I fell to the floor. I hit my head on the edge of a cabinet and my head started bleeding. He grabbed my arm hard and jerked me up, then he took that forearm and slammed it over the edge of the kitchen table over and over, breaking both bones."

"Motherfucker."

"I tried yelling for help, knowing that the crew would be around soon because we'd quit for the day but he took the belt of my robe and gagged me. Then he raped me, brutally. Not once because that's not enough humiliation. Twice wasn't enough. He had to do it a third time, only this time—"

"Don't. I know what you're going to say."

At this point, I'm numb. "Why not? It's what happened. He sodomized me. He didn't care that I wasn't aroused at all, there was no prep. He went in dry and tore me so much each time, the pain from it got so bad I passed out. I guess that was a blessing. Anyway, the director, Mel, saw Ian coming out of my trailer with blood on his shirt. Ian didn't even notice it was there. He thought he was going to just walk off. He nearly did." I laugh mirthlessly.

"It took them some time to restrain him, so I laid there unconscious for who knows how long, bleeding all over the place, before they called the paramedics. I woke up in the hospital three days later with a broken arm, seven stitches in my head, and I don't know what they all did to fix the damage he'd done down... there. Apparently I'd lost a lot of blood. My mom flew up immediately. I worried about pregnancy because the prick didn't bother to wear a condom. I mean, that was good for DNA, but shit. I didn't want to be pregnant from that. Well, they had administered the morning after pill with my mom's consent. I'm not sure how. They must have shoved it down my throat or something since I was unconscious. I had to undergo STD and HIV testing on a regular basis for the next couple years but I still go through both every six months just because. I never quite recovered fully from that. I don't make demands of anyone and haven't since then. I tease being bossy but—" I shrug.

Jesse nods. "I'm so sorry this happened to you." He hugs me tight to him. "How did that not get leaked to the press?"

"There were only a handful of us on set that day because it was just the sex scene, and we were filming in Canada so not much press to worry about since the press that *was* there was following the other actors around. It was before I was popular."

"God," Jesse says, blowing out a breath.

"What is it?"

"I've been so rough with you."

"Don't do that, Jesse. You don't hurt me and if I had complaints about that, I guarantee you'd hear about it. I'm pretty sure you can tell I enjoy it. Remember the screaming?" I ask with a smile and he chuckles.

"I don't want you to treat me differently, Jesse. It was a long time ago. The only thing that still lingers is—my attitude is different, as you said. I'm passive and don't make demands or ask for things I'm not sure I have a right to. I'm afraid to," I whisper.

There's a knock on the patio door and I look over.

"Can we come out a minute?" Cage asks.

"Sure." I was thinking Cage and Sera but out comes everyone.

"Mama and daddy took off," Sera tells me, her expression soft, worried. "She'd like you to call her later."

"Okay. I'm okay."

She nods.

"What's up?" Jesse asks.

"We were in there talking about touring," Ben says, looking at me. "How would you feel about Blush opening for Falling Down?"

I freeze and Jesse smiles a smile so bright it lights up the sky. I swear, the entire sky.

"Are you fucking with me right now?" I ask. This would be the opportunity of a lifetime.

"Pretty sure if I was fucking with you my brother would be pounding the shit out of me."

"Damn straight."

"This isn't just up to me. It needs to be okay with Cage and after that it needs to be okay with Sera, Jace, Meggie, and Trace."

"I think it's a great idea," Cage says.

"Let's take a vote," Sera says with a knowing smirk.

"Not just Blush members but Falling Down members too. Be completely honest. No saying yes just because you feel loyal to Jesse or me. Base your decision on *you*," I tell them.

"Cool," Xander says. "I say hell yes. Who's in, raise 'em up."

All eight hands raise… then nine as Jesse raises his.

"Jesse."

"What do you say? What do you want to do? What do you want to do for *you*?" he asks, using my words.

"Touché." I smirk at him and lift my hand. "It'd be really stupid of me to pass up this opportunity. Everything's just falling into place."

"Fate," Sera says.

"Timing," Cage says at the same time.

"Is that the only reason you agreed? Because of the opportunity for the band?" Jesse asks.

"No."

He nods.

"And I'd like to ask you to not fuck the groupie whores—ever again.

Oh, fuck that. I'm telling you. If you want to be with me, no fucking anyone but me."

He chuckles.

"Because if you do, I'll have to chop your balls off and stuff them down your throat," Sera says sweetly.

"That's not going to be a problem. I don't want groupie whores. I just want you."

"Awww," Meggie says with a genuine sniffle. She's so weird.

"Cage?" I ask, looking into Jesse's eyes.

"Yeah, Luce."

"Are we allowed to fraternize with members of the other band while on tour?"

Jesse grins and everyone around us chuckles.

"Yeah, and I'm pretty sure if I'd have said no, you'd have done it anyway."

"Pretty much. We *are* talking about Jesse Kingston here."

"Fuck," Xander says.

"What's your problem?" Kennedy asks.

"We're going to have to listen to her scream on the bus."

I'm sure my face is the color of a tomato right now.

"It'll be alright, Lucy. You screaming just lets them know we're doing it right," Jesse says with a laugh.

"Gah," Sera says. "I'm riding on a different bus. I so don't want to hear my sister fucking her boyfriend."

I laugh. "Right about now I'm really glad my mom and dad have already left."

More laughing.

"There'll be enough room for everyone to be comfortable. You all can figure out who's on what bus," Cage says.

"Cage, can you give Dave the exclusive of this announcement?"

He raises his eyebrows.

"He was so great at the press conference, he deserves this."

"Done."

"Lucy?" Sera says.

"What's up?"

She's grinning. "You're so going to piss off Jesse's groupie whores."

I shrug. "They had their turn and it's over. He's mine now."

Jesse pulls me in for a kiss. "And she's mine."

"Fuckin' A. More sluts for me," Jace says.

"Pig," Sera scolds.

"You never know," he says with a shrug, "one of those sluts could be my future wife."

Complete silence and then we all start laughing, Jace laughing the loudest.

"Jesse," Ben says, nudging his arm.

"Hmm?"

"What are you going to do about the," his gaze flicks to me, then back to Jesse. "About the regulars?"

I roll my eyes. "Bitches better look out. That's all I've got to say. And you, Jesse Kingston, better send a skank-wide text to those whores and let them know that shit is over and then you better delete those sluts' numbers."

He grins at me. "Is this you teasing bossy?"

"Are you fucking with me right now?"

"Yeah," he says with a laugh.

"Here come the screams," Xander says with a laugh.

"Those aren't screams, those are whines and wails from all the skank-ass hoes crying because their favorite rockstar cock is unavailable to get them the attention they want," Sera says.

"True that," Trace says.

"Skank-ass hoes," I say with a laugh.

"Jesus," Cage says. "Fuckers, bitches, groupie whores, and skank-ass hoes. We'll be lucky to get through this tour without a brawl or a lawsuit."

"Damn straight," Xander yells. "Good times, fuckers!"

Cage leans back. "It has a good ring to it."

"What's that?" Jesse asks.

"The Falling Down-Blush tour."

We all look at each other.

Xander raises a fist. "Good times, fuckers!"

Chapter
eighteen

Jesse

Ten days later Blush has nearly all the songs ready for their album. They've been working steadily to get the right sound for the lyrics, learning how to work together, how to jam together, how to read one another, and so far they're doing pretty fucking good.

I'd rather be in the studio than in this fucked up stylist room Spenser, Carmen, and Simone set up but I knew I could trust them to not fuck up my hair.

"What can we do for you today, Jesse?" Carmen asks.

I tell her what I want.

She nods. "Spenser's going to want to do this one if that's what you want to have done," she says. I told her I was ready for a change and I am. This long hair bullshit on tour is too fucking hot.

"Well, hello Jesse," Spenser says. "Let's get you set up." He drapes a plastic cape over my lap and shoulders, snapping it in the back.

"Tell me what you're looking to do," he says. I relay to him what I'm looking for.

"This long hair under those lights while running across the stage is just too fucking hot. I said at the end of the last tour I wouldn't be touring again with hair this long."

"No problem. I've got you covered. I'm going to spritz your hair with water."

"Cool."

"Just letting you know."

He wets down my hair and then starts cutting. It doesn't even bother me, getting the hair cut off. I'd just gotten too lazy to get regular cuts but now that we've got Spenser and the girls around and going to be on tour with us, I won't have to worry about making an appointment with someone who'll either fuck up my hair or do the bullshit fangirl thing. Don't get me wrong, I love my fans. I do. But when I'm at a business establishment as a paying customer and instead of getting the services I made an appointment for I get squealed and gushed over, it tends to piss me off. Those are the types of fans that make me wary of everyone.

"Don't move. Time for clippers."

Damn, that was fast. It looks pretty fucking good. I thought the dude only did makeup, but hell, he's done a kick ass job with this cut.

"You look like the Jesse Kingston from back in the day," Simone says.

"Yeah. I feel like me again."

Spenser smiles. "Lucy has a wonderful effect on people, doesn't she?"

"She does. She makes you want to be real."

"Mhmm. That's our girl. Alright, you're done. Let me show you the back." He swivels the chair and hands me a mirror. It looks good. It's tapered up in the back and on the sides and spiky and mess on top. Simple style. I can work with this.

I nod.

"You won't need to put any products in other than this gel," he tells me, handing me a tube of goop, "unless you're going to be doing anything professional which we'll style for you anyway."

"Don't you even think of paying him," Carmen says. "Lucy pays us way too much as it is."

"You're valuable to her. She pays you what she thinks you're worth."

"She's such a great lady," Simone says, smiling.

"Yeah, and she's mine," I say with a wink.

"When are you going to pop the question?" Spenser asks.

I freeze. "What?"

"You know, propose."

"We just moved in together. I hadn't even thought about that. I doubt Lucy'd go for that now anyway."

"You're probably right. I don't think she's ready for that. She's pretty skittish. But if I was you, I'd get prepared, find a ring just so you have it in case one day you feel a sudden urge to ask her to be your wife."

"Oh, that's so romantic," Carmen says.

I start to break out in a sweat. I've gotta get out of here.

"I'm heading to the gym. See you later."

I swear I hear Spenser laugh as I book it out of there. He's probably jacking me around but he's right. Fuck. I mean, fucking hell, she's such a huge part of my life now. I love waking up with her and falling asleep with her. We spend as much time together as we can and I never get tired of her being around. She's smart, funny, and so fucking talented. I do miss her when she's not around, like now when she's practicing and rewriting notes while I'm getting my hair cut and lifting weights. I've only been away from her for an hour, if that, and I've done nothing but think about her. What the fuck?

I'm in love with her.

I plop down on the weight bench, stunned. When the hell did I fall in love with her?

"Nice hair."

I jump. Shit, I didn't hear Ben come in.

"Thanks."

"Dude, what's going on?" Ben asks.

"Nothing."

"Bullshit. You've got some fucked up look on your face."

I rub my hands over my face.

"Shit," I say, looking at Ben. We've never really had to talk to each other, somehow we've been able to communicate with just a look and right now he got my message as he sports a shit-eating grin.

"Finally."

"What?" I ask.

"You finally figured it out."

"What are you talking about?"

"You've been hooked on Lucy since you first fucking met her in Chicago, but when you heard her singing and saw her standing on that fake stage, you were sunk pal."

"Well, fuck. You didn't think to mention that to me?"

Ben laughs. "Would you have believed me if I had?"

"Probably not."

He nods and we sit in silence for a few minutes.

"What are you going to do about it?"

"I don't fucking know. Spenser dropped a not-so-subtle hint about asking Lucy to marry me. What the fuck? Marriage. I don't think we're ready for that. I know she's not for sure and I don't think I am either."

"Nah, don't rush it, bro."

"Yeah. Think I should find a ring just in case?"

Ben laughs. "I think it might be a good idea."

"Yeah, probably."

"You should probably tell her you love her first then go from there but, dude, take it slow."

I nod. "How do I tell her? I mean, fuck." I stand up and start pacing.

Ben laughs.

"I'm glad you find this funny, fucker."

"Sorry, I don't mean to laugh, you just look like you're in a bit of shock."

"Hell yeah I am. I just sat here and realized I'm in love with Luciana Russo, Academy Award-winning actress, god damn. Lead singer of Blush. She's so far out of my league it's not even funny."

"She is, but she loves you."

"Yeah?"

He nods. "I've seen her look at you the same way you look at her. She watches you when you're not looking. Sometimes she stares at you like you're a puzzle or riddle she's trying to solve."

"That's not very reassuring."

"It should be. It means she's taking the time to figure you out, too, that she loves you enough to want to try."

"Huh."

"Get your ass lifting and stop thinking about it," Ben says as he turns on the radio and Korn blares from the speakers. Kick ass.

An hour and a half later, Ben and I find ourselves in the middle of Tiffany's. I'm really liking this haircut. No one's recognized me so far. They look at me like I seem familiar but they haven't figured it out yet. It's perfect for ring shopping. What the fuck am I doing here? I'm not going to propose, not yet anyway. Just getting prepared before we get out on tour and life's too hectic to get away.

Marriage. What the fuck?

The jeweler closes the shop at our request. We really don't want to get mobbed by fans while I'm ring shopping and I really don't want Lucy to find out I went ring shopping when she's in the grocery line and sees the Enquirer. Shit. That would suck so bad.

Bart is his name, the jeweler. He pulls out a large display of diamonds.

"Nothing *too* big. She's so tiny," I tell Ben. "Right?"

"Yeah, big wouldn't look right on her," Ben replies as his phone rings.

"Yo," he answers. "Yeah, sure. Why don't you come down to Tiffany's on Santa Monica." He pulls the phone away from his ear as I hear a high-pitched squeal. "Stop it. Shut up. Yeah. No, we won't make a final decision until you get here. Yeah. Okay."

"Sera," Ben says. "She's borrowing my car but she's popping down here to help us pick."

"Jesus Christ, Ben."

"Chill. She asked if it was for later and I told her yeah. She knows."

"Good. I have no idea what to get her. I know platinum. I remember her telling me about this ring she saw and she said platinum is her favorite. She really doesn't like gold," I tell Bart who puts the gold rings back beneath the case and grabs more platinum.

"Jesus," Ben says. "How many carats is that thing?" He points to a huge square cut diamond ring that would probably have Lucy falling over.

"Sixteen carats."

"Crazy," Ben says.

"Some people enjoy the flashy," Bart says. "Personally I think understated always beats out overstated."

"Exactly," I say to Bart. "I knew you were perfect for this."

"Knock, knock," Sera says and Bart's assistant lets her in.

"Jesse, you sneaky bastard."

"Stop, Sera," Ben says. "He's already worked up."

Sera laughs. "This is so awesome."

"Bart here is our helper. We're going for understated not overstated and gaudy."

"Awww, you know our girl so well," Sera says.

I just grunt. I have no clue what to say to that. "Platinum. She likes platinum, she said."

"Yeah, platinum or silver."

"Are we looking for an engagement ring or a bridal set?" Bart asks and I have no fucking clue.

"I think when the time comes, she's going to want to pick out matching wedding bands so just the engagement ring," Sera murmurs.

I nod.

"Okay. Let's start with these," Bart says.

We look through the rings and they're not right. "These don't feel right for her. She's more... classic," I tell Bart and Sera grins at me.

"Exactly."

"Well," Bart says. "I think I have just the thing." He unlocks another display case and brings more rings over to us. "These are vintage style."

"Oh yeah," Ben says. "Those are more her."

I nod and look down and I see it immediately. I reach down and pick it up. Sera gasps, her hands fly to her mouth.

"Yeah, this is the one."

"Excellent choice," Bart says. "You've chosen the platinum tiara diamond ring with a princess cut diamond. With the accessory diamonds the total weight of diamonds is 3.42 carats."

"Get the matching band," Sera says. "She can have two wedding bands. This set is too perfect."

"I agree."

"Very good."

Bart starts talking about clarity and color and I don't know what the hell he's talking about but I nod along. All I know is this is Lucy's ring.

"With the wedding band, the total weight is 4.54 carats."

"Will that be too much?" I ask Sera.

"May I?" she asks Bart.

"Please."

She slips the rings on and oohs and ahhs. "It's beautiful, Jesse. Perfect. Not too heavy, not too flashy. The design of the platinum, the way it curves like that, she's going to love this. Look how it fits perfectly. Lucy and I wear the same size."

"Don't start crying," Ben barks. As if that's going to work. I send him a look like, are you fucking kidding me? And he shrugs.

"I can't help it. It's just so amazing. Bart, you keep things confidential, right?"

"Of course. We are very professional."

"I thought so. You look trustworthy." She slips the rings off and puts them on the velvet square on the counter. She reaches into her purse and pulls out her wallet.

"Here," she says, thrusting a picture of Lucy at Bart.

"Ah, yes. She's quite beautiful and an amazing actress."

"You should hear her sing," Ben tells him.

"I'm sure I will soon if the press conference was truthful."

"True facts, Bart. Lucy doesn't lie."

He nods.

"Here's the story. It's so romantic. When we were in seventh grade…" She launches into the entire story of the crush, the fangirling posters, the party for the video, concerts, Chicago, the video, and the living together.

"They are such idiots," she says.

"Hey," I protest.

"You are. I mean even I knew you were in love with each other the first day on the set."

"Me too," Ben says.

"Idiots. Anyway, soon they'll profess their love for one another, we'll record our album, then we'll tour with our new band and open for Falling Down. I have no idea when Jesse will propose to her, but it's like a fairytale romance."

"Yes, it certainly is," Bart says.

I hand him my credit card and he rings up the sale. I don't even pay attention to what he said the cost was. I don't give a fuck. Lucy's worth it.

Bart hands me the bag with the rings and certificates of authenticity and other crap I'll figure out later.

"Be sure to hold onto your dream, Mr. Kingston. It's not every day they come true," Bart says.

I nod. True story.

Sera agrees to hide the ring in her room since Lucy's in mine.

"I'll put it in my panty drawer. She won't ever go there."

"I don't even want to think about that," I tell her.

"I do," Ben says, following behind Sera.

"What are you doing, Ben?"

"Following you."

"Why?"

"Because I want to… *finger* your silk and lace."

Seriously. My brother.

I walk into the kitchen to grab a soda and there she is. She's in those sexy-as-hell tight black pants that come to just below her knees and cling to her sexy fucking body like a second skin. Her top is some short lacy thing and her belly button is peeking out at me, her piercing glinting in the sunlight.

"Woman, you look so fucking sexy right now," I say, wrapping my arms around her and kissing her breathless.

"Wow," she whispers. "I'm all for being separated for short periods of time if you're going to kiss me like that when you come back."

"I'll kiss you like that any time you want."

"Smooth talker. I absolutely love your hair short like that, Jesse!" She bites her lower lip. "It's so hot."

"Yeah?"

"Mmm. Seriously sexy."

Fuck yeah. "Later, I'm going to fuck you slow and easy, then after you come two or three times, I'm going to have you ride me fast and hard."

"Jesse," she whispers.

"Gets you wet when I tell you what I want to do to you, doesn't it?"

"Yes," she whispers and rubs her breasts against my chest.

"I fucking love how wet you get for me."

"I love how hard you get for me. How you lose control when you're inside me and you can't help yourself."

I grunt. I'm starting to get hard. I need to change the topic.

"Whatcha making?"

"Peanut butter Rice Krispies treats and I'll put melted chocolate over the top."

"I hope you're planning on making a shit load of them because the guys will sow them down fast."

"Mhmm. I plan on making six pans. It's why I'm melting the marshmallows in the Crockpot. Mrs. Martinez is helping me."

"Clever girl. How'd practice go?"

"It was great actually. We're going to have sixteen tracks on the album. We just need to pick one more but we had an idea we wanted to run by you."

"What's up?" I ask, picking her up underneath her thighs. She immediately wraps her legs around my waist and her arms around my neck. I make my way out to the patio and sit on one of the loungers under an umbrella.

"I was wondering if you and the guys would want to record a song with us."

"Absolutely. That'll be perfect, actually."

"Mhmm. I was thinking," she murmurs, running her fingers through my short hair, "we can end our set with that song and then you guys will already be on stage. It's the perfect transition."

"We'll have to work out how to have two sets of drums on the stage. Some of the venues aren't that big."

"Do you think Trace and Xander would be okay using the same set?"

"I'm not sure. You know how it is with equipment."

"I know," she shrugs. "We can figure it out. Besides we'll need to write a song and we've only got two days left."

"Yeah, with ten of us do you see that being a problem?"

She laughs. "No, not at all. I've been very creative since you became my boyfriend."

"Oh yeah?"

"Mhmm," she says, circling my nipples, dragging her fingernail over the ring giving it just a shiver of a tug.

"I have to tell you, Jesse, we all work so well together. Me, Sera, Jace, Meggie, and Trace. We already know how to complement each other and it's just fantastic."

"That's awesome, Luce. That's the hardest part, you know. Finding the chemistry in the band, seeing if you can all blend together, and it sounds like you do."

"The first test will come next week when we're recording. Then the ultimate test will be touring. I hope we make it through the four-month tour without killing each other or the band breaking up."

I chuckle. "You'll be just fine. I don't see Sera or Jace going anywhere. Meggie's already attached at the hip and Trace loves the sound and the laid back feel of the band."

She nods. "He told me he was worried there might be issues with drugs but then he saw how straight-laced we are and he relaxed." She sighs. "Do you think I'm uptight, Jesse? Is that what he meant by straight-laced?"

"No way. He just meant that you're not going to dip into the narcotics or opiate well."

"Yeah, no thanks. Not my scene."

I nod. "Mine either."

"I think it's amazing how well we get along, Jesse. It's been almost three weeks and you're my best friend."

"That's how it should be, babe. If we can't talk to each other about our bullshit, then there's something wrong."

"Truth. You're still okay with us staying here? We haven't even been looking for houses. I'm so—"

I cut her off with a press of my index finger to her lips.

"Stop. I want you here. The guys want you here. Mrs. Martinez already thinks you hung the moon and stars."

She almost preens when I mention Mrs. Martinez and I want to laugh, but I don't. It's important to her that there's no friction and I understand that need very well.

"I can't believe how much has happened in such a short time."

"Yeah."

She rests her head on my shoulder as she straddles my lap and I run my fingers through her hair. She sighs.

"This is nice."

"Mhmm," I say. My heart is beating a gazillion miles an hour and if she were to move her head just a little she'd hear it and wonder what the hell was wrong with me. Then I'd do something asinine like blurt out the fact that I love her instead of planning something romantic. But do I really want to plan out the way I tell her I love her?

I pull her closer.

"It's still early," Lucy says. "You think your friend could squeeze me in to give me a tattoo?"

"Now?"

She shrugs. "Why not? I've got nothing going on until later when we can all get together and knock out that song."

"I'll give him a call."

She runs her fingers through my now cropped short hair. "I really, really like your hair like this. Reminds me of the bad boy I crushed on."

"Yeah?" I say with a smirk. For some reason I think that's hot.

"Oh yeah," she murmurs seductively against my ear before sucking on the lobe.

"I think the bad boy you crushed on should meet your bad girl in our bed later tonight."

She sits up straight, surprise evident on her face. Then her expression quickly morphs into one of seduction and lust.

"I think that can be arranged."

I put a hand on the back of her head and pull her mouth to mine. I can't get enough of her. I slide my tongue against hers and moan at how fucking good she tastes. There is no taste in the world like Lucy and I never want to be without it.

Someone clears their throat from the doorway. I take my time ending the kiss. Fuckers keep interrupting.

"What's up, Xander?" Lucy asks.

"Not much. Any plans for this afternoon?"

"Lucy wants me to take her to Harley."

His brows raise nearly to his hairline and I chuckle.

"No shit?"

"No shit," she replies.

"What do you want to get?" Xander asks.

"Well, truthfully I'd like about six of them but I want to start with two."

"Two?" I ask.

"Yeah, one is small. I just want to get some butterflies behind my ear."

"That's hot," I tell her and she grins.

"Dude," Xander fist bumps me.

"What's the other one?" I ask her.

"I want to get this floral design along my side."

"How big?" Xander asks.

"From my hip bone to just under my armpit. It spreads a little onto my stomach and back."

"Cool. That might take a couple sessions."

"I'd rather just get it done if he can do it today so I can go back in a week or two and get some of the other ones I want."

Xander smiles. "And another rocker is born."

Lucy smiles proudly. "I couldn't get tattoos before because of acting but screw it. If something pops up and they want me for the part, they'll have to deal with the ink."

"I'll call Harley," Xander says. "Think Sera wants ink?"

"Yeah, she'll want to go along," Lucy tells him.

"You're going to be sore later."

"We'll have to improvise," she tells me with a wink.

I nod. Her brown eyes shimmer in the sunlight, the flecks of gold and black highlighted in the sun.

"You're so beautiful, Lucy."

Her expression is soft, her eyes full of so much emotion.

"Jesse," she whispers. "I—"

"Dude, he said he's got the afternoon free. I'll go grab Sera."

"Sounds good." When Xander walks away, I ask her, "What were you going to say?"

"It's nothing. I should probably pee and get ready to go."

I nod. "You should keep that on. It's loose and won't cling to the tat when you're done. Jeans will likely rub if it's going down that low."

She nods. "I just need to change my bra. A sports bra won't hurt but these lacy ones are a bitch."

"They're fucking sexy as hell, but I like them better on the floor. You've got amazing tits, and your body, those curves. I could lose myself in your heat."

"Damn, Jesse. You're getting me wet and horny."

"Yeah, I'm sporting a semi. I need to shut the fuck up."

She laughs. "Let's go get ready."

I follow her up the stairs. This woman is everything I never knew I wanted and exactly what I need. Fuck, I love her. I want to stand on top of the Hollywood sign and shout it out loud. I want to go all caveman and claim her, then beat on my chest. She's mine. Later.

"Jesse?" she asks, pulling on her sports bra.

"What's up babe?"

"Is it going to hurt?"

"Some. Not too bad. Like a cat scratch."

"That hurts!" she says.

"Honestly after a while you get kinda numb to it and forget it's even happening. For me the worst was the black outline. For Xander it was the coloring. We'll see which it is for you in about forty-five minutes."

She climbs up my body and I chuckle as I put my hands under her ass. "Monkey."

"You're so tall and I wanted to tell you something."

I nod. "Okay."

She places her hands on my cheeks, gently presses her lips to mine, then pulls back and meets my gaze. She pauses.

"You're just so incredible, Jesse," she says, shaking her head. Somehow I don't think that's what she wanted to say but I'm not going to call her out on it. Whatever's going on, she'll tell me when she's ready. If there's anything I've learned about this amazing woman who stole my heart it's that she can't be rushed because when she is, she runs. The last thing I want is for her to run from me. I can't seem to get her close enough as it is.

"You ready?"

"Yep," she says.

She goes to get down but I squeeze her ass. "I got you," I tell her.

"Yeah. You really do," she says. I'm about to tell her she's got me too, but Sera comes through the door chattering on about getting tattoos. Meggie falls in behind and I smile. We stopped locking the door during the day for this very reason—unless we're planning on getting naked.

"Grab my purse and Kindle?" she asks Sera.

"Got it."

I love having her in my life. Until her, I never knew what I was missing and I never want to go another day without it, without her.

Chapter
nineteen

Lucy

Wе enter the tattoo shop and Jesse pulls me close. My hands are sweating and I'm sure I've got a bad case of crazy eyes going on.

"You know you don't have to do this," Jesse says.

"Yeah, I do. First, because I want the tattoos. Second," I say, cutting a glance over to Ben and Xander, "if I don't, you know how bad I'm going to hear about it from Thing 1 and Thing 2 over there?"

Sera snickers. "Thing 1 and Thing 2."

"I'll show you my thing," Xander says with an evil grin.

"Jesse, what's up?" a very large, very tattooed man in jeans and a Falling Down concert shirt asks—I forgot to mention the very large beard and very long hair. The man is a whole lot of "very".

Jesse and the "very" man do some secret handshake.

"Harley, this is Lucy," Jesse says by way of introduction to the big man. "Lucy, this is Harley."

I hold out a hand. "It's nice to meet you."

"Oh, to hell with that," Harley says and grabs me up into a really tight bear hug and I squeak in surprise. "I've got to give the girlfriend of this never-going-to-have-a-girlfriend jackass a hug. You tamed the beast."

I laugh and hug him back. He's just a big teddy bear—who's very scary on the outside.

"Well, I don't know about taming him…" I say.

Two more tattooed guys walk up—way less scary than Harley—and shake hands with everyone. These two are hot. Meggie checks them out and I grin.

"These morons are Bret and Hunter. They'll take care of the rest of you while I get Girlfriend Kingston," Harley says, throwing his arm around me and leading me back to his station.

I grin at Jesse and he just shakes his head.

"Lock the door, Hunter."

"Got it, Harley."

"What are we going to do for you today, GK?"

GK? Oh, heh. Girlfriend Kingston.

"I want to get two tattoos, actually three, but I think I can only handle two right now."

Harley grins and nods. "Whatcha got in mind, doll?"

"I changed my mind, Jesse," I tell him, taking a seat in the victim chair.

He raises a brow.

"Instead of the butterfly behind the ear, I think I'm going to get a Blush tattoo for my upper back/shoulder area."

Sera squeals. "We need to have the same one!"

Meggie bounces on her toes and blows a bubble. "Count me in."

"The guys might be pissed," I say.

"Don't worry about it," Harley says. "I'll keep the design and they can come get theirs."

"You're such a sweetheart, Harley," I tell him and he blushes.

"Now tell me what you've got in mind…"

About thirty minutes later Harley's got a Blush tattoo designed and it's really freaking awesome—not that I got to see it. I may be pouting just a little bit. Sera, Meggie, Jesse, Ben, and Xander all got to see it along with Bret and Hunter. Yep, I'm the only one who didn't get to see it, but I feel kind of special because Harley said he designed it especially for me and wants it to be a surprise. It's a nice gesture, but what if I hate it? Jesse must sense my turmoil as I strip off my t-shirt and lay face down on the chair. He winks and squeezes my hand reassuring me I'll love it.

"You ready, GK?" Harley asks.

"Yep," I reply, turning on my Kindle.

"There's no way you're going to be able to focus on that," Xander tells me.

"You have no idea," I tell him.

"Here we go," Harley says and I feel the needle.

"Ouch, mother effing SOB!"

"Suck it up, GK. It's always hard until you get used to it."

"I could do so much with that statement," I tell them, "but I'm busy being tortured by a giant teddy bear."

"I take offense to that," Harley says as the guys chuckle.

I hear Sera squeak then growl.

"Ah, Sera's turn," Ben says, rubbing his hands together. "I've got to see it." With that, he's gone.

"Go keep Meggie company, Xander," I tell him.

He wiggles his eyebrows. "More than happy to."

"He's such a perv," I tell Jesse.

"Feel better?" Jesse asks.

"It was until you reminded me it was happening. Now you need to distract me."

He leans in close to my ear and whispers, "Tonight I'm going to take your clothes off, slowly. Then kiss you until you're breathless, work my way down your body to your sexy pussy and lick and taste and finger you until you come all over my face."

"Dude, you better stop. She's starting to wiggle," Harley says with a laugh.

"I just got started."

I let out a breathy sigh. "He's *really* good at that."

"More than I need to know."

About twenty minutes later, my Blush tattoo is done, cleaned, ointment put on along with a bandage.

"Alright. You sure you want the outline *and* the color for the side piece?"

I nod. "Otherwise I'll end up with just an outline. I know this one's going to hurt like a mofo and if we leave it half done it's always going to stay that way."

"Gotcha," Harley says. "I'm all for getting as much done as you can tolerate."

"That's a big piece, Luce."

"Yeah, I know, but it's so pretty."

"It suits you," Jesse says.

"Thanks." I smile at him and he leans down for a kiss.

"Stand up for me, GK."

I stand and he holds up the transfer.

"I thought so," he murmurs. "You're going to have pull your pants down a bit."

"Yeah baby," Xander shouts from wherever he is in the shop.

I pull one side down past my butt. "Panties too?" I ask.

"Mhmm," he replies.

"I'm missing out on Lucy's ass!" Xander exclaims.

"And bra," Jesse grumbles.

"Lucy's boobs!" Xander shouts.

"I'll just slip this arm out and hold it in the front. No worries, babe."

Jesse's head snaps up and he grins.

"What?"

He shakes his head.

"First time you called him by a nickname?" Harley asks.

I tilt my head and think. Jesse lifts a brow, still grinning.

"Wow, it is."

Jesse nods.

Harley wheels his chair next to me. "He likes it."

"So I see. I'll have to remember that." I give Jesse a wink.

"Alright, that's better." Harley holds up the transfer. "Lift your arm."

"Jesse?"

"Got it," he says, wiggling his eyebrows. He puts his hand over my bra covering my boob and gives a squeeze.

"Jesse," I scold and he chuckles.

I lift my arm and Harley applies the transfer which goes from my hip to a couple inches underneath my arm and one of the stems with a flower wraps over my breast.

"Holy shit," Meggie says, walking into the room as Harley helps me to the chair. Jesse sighs as his hand falls from my boob.

"Sorry, babe."

He grins. The endearment made up for the loss of boobage. Good to know.

"Don't freak me out, bitch." I flip Meggie off.

Meggie holds up her hands. "I won't, I won't. But it's huge."

"That's what she said," Xander howls in laughter.

I just roll my eyes at Xander but I'm laughing with him. He's such a goof.

"Here we go," Harley notifies me.

I nod. "All set."

The first swipe of the needle has me holding my breath but it's not enough so I let out a stream of expletives.

"You'd think she was just told she had to give a press conference," Sera chortles.

"This is brutal. Brutal!"

"Jesse, hand me her Kindle. I'll read her a little Tijan to distract her."

"Oh my God, thank you Sera. I was up to *such* a great part. I've got a bit of a girlie crush on Logan Kade."

"I see how it is. You get the real thing," Ben points at Jesse, "and you need a new crush."

I bite my lip. "I'd laugh but it hurts too bad. You'll see. He's such a player and his one-liners are awesome."

Sera starts to read and before you know it, everyone's got chairs pulled up listening to Fallen Crest Public.

After an hour or so Xander sneers, "What the fuck? I hope someone knocks those bitches on their asses."

"I'm sure it's going to happen," Harley answers. "There's no way Mason or Logan are going to let that shit slide."

I raise a brow at Sera who laughs behind her hand then goes back to reading. We've got big bad rockers and tattoo artists liking some Tijan.

"If you think this is bad, you should have read Fallen Crest Family with me. Sam's mom is a psycho."

"We'll have to read that with them next," Sera tells me with a smirk.

"Looks like we're all a bunch of Raisinettes," Jesse laughs.

I laugh with him. "Tijanettes, babe."

"New Tijanette members—rockers and tattoo artists. Tijan would be proud," Sera sniffles and wipes a fake tear.

"Weirdo."

Bret hands me a diet Coke with a straw and then a regular Coke to Harley.

"Thank you, Bret. I was getting a little dehydrated what with all the sweating from the pain and all," I tease.

Harley grunts. "I think we should 3D this fucker."

"That'd be wicked," Hunter agrees.

"Not today, though, right?" I ask, more than a little intimidated by what I've already taken on.

Harley chuckles. "No, not today. We won't color it all in either knowing you're coming back."

I nod.

Bret stands. "I'm going to order pizza. You all in?"

Everyone murmurs their agreement.

"Smoke break," Harley says.

"I don't smoke," I tell him.

"Me either but I need to stretch and piss."

"Well then. Have at it."

Jesse helps me stand, putting a hand over my boob as he does. Another squeeze.

"Don't get me all worked up," I scold Jesse who grins. "You're so sassy today."

"You bring it out of me." He leans in and gives me a soft kiss.

"Oh boy. You really need to stop that. I think to distract myself from your hotness, I should probably go pee. Please, can one of the pizza's be sausage and mushroom pizza? I can't stand all that meat that Jesse puts on his pizza and I don't do onions like on the supreme."

"No problemo. That's what Hunter eats too," Bret says exiting the store.

Ten minutes later Harley's back to inking up my skin. He's gotten a lot done in the time we've been here, which must be quite a while since it's starting to get dark. My side is numb from the needle.

"Harley, do your neck and back get sore? Does your hand get numb?" I ask.

"Sometimes the neck does. Back isn't so bad and no to the hand."

"I've got to agree with Jesse. The outline is worse than the color."

"I don't agree with that at all," Ben says.

"Of course you don't. You're not happy unless you're being contrary," Sera scolds.

"You gain any weight yet?"

"Fuck off, Ben."

"I'll meet you in your room later."

"You're living in a dream world, Benjamin," she says, imitating Morpheus from The Matrix.

I groan then whine, "Jesse."

"Luce, you're the one who wanted it done in one sitting."

"You're supposed to be sympathetic and loving and comforting. What kind of boyfriend are you?"

"The best kind. See me holding your hand while you break bones? I held your boob—twice—when you needed to adjust before, didn't I?"

I snort at that. "You can hold it later too."

"Dude," Xander interrupts. "Lucy's gonna have to be on top for a while. You don't wanna fuck up her ink."

Jesse shrugs. "Works for me."

"I just bet."

"So, Xander, were those groupie whores that I saw down your wing of corruption yours or did they belong to more than just you?"

"I'm good, Luce, but five girls is a bit much for me by myself. I shared."

"Lovely. Share the skanks, share the STDs. Such a generous friend."

Harley whistles. "Not liking the groupies, huh?"

"Not so much."

"You've just got good girl morals," Ben tells me.

I nod. "I do. I admit that. I've never been one for whoring around. Don't get me wrong, I've had hookups, they were just never one-nighters. They were more like mini-relationships."

Jesse growls, which I choose to ignore at the moment.

"That's the truth," Sera affirms. "She had to actually like the guy instead of just thinking he was pretty."

"I don't care if he's nice or not," Meggie says. "If he's hot and he's got a decent sized cock, I'm all for it."

"How can you tell if he's got a decent sized cock before—" I break off. "You know what? Nevermind. I'm going to just sit here oblivious to your whorish ways."

"You just reach down and grab the package. Jeez, Lucy. It's not that difficult."

I sigh. "I figured it out after I brought it up."

"You've never had a club hookup where you're grinding on a guy and he gets hard and you reach down to check it out?" Meggie asks.

Jesse coughs, hiding his laugh, and I grin.

"Well, the club part, yes. The reach down part, yes. The hookup, not that night but yes."

"Have you not watched the news lately? Did you not see their video?" Xander asks.

"Ha! Jesse Kingston you've corrupted our girl. Pull that video up, Xan."

"Maybe, but she corrupted me right back."

"Dude," Xander scoffs.

"There is no way for me to corrupt you, Jesse. You've already been corrupted in every way possible."

"Not true. You corrupted me into thinking relationships are good."

"No, no. You're the one who—"

He presses a finger to my lips then nods. "I did." My eyes widen and everyone gets quiet. Something's going on here. Something big. My heart starts to race. "I don't regret it either. In fact, I'm enjoying it. Who knew monogamy would be so fun?"

"It is with the right partner," Sera fills in.

"Mhmm," Jesse says then presses his lips to mine. He pulls back and tucks a stray strand of hair behind my ear, just looking at me and I start to wonder what he's looking at—or for.

"What's going on—" Xander starts to ask, looking up from his phone, and Sera elbows him.

"You okay, babe?" I ask.

He smiles and nods. "I just figured out that I'm feeling pretty good about it."

"Oh shit," Ben says and Sera elbows him too.

"About what?"

Jesse shrugs. "You. Me. Us." He pauses and runs his knuckles down my cheek. He leans in and his lips brush mine as he tells me, "Being in love with you."

Harley immediately pulls up the tattoo gun.

"What?" I whisper. I'd bolt upright but my boob's hanging out.

Sera and Meggie make noises in their throats.

"Yeah. I figured that out this morning. It took me a couple days to figure out what it was I was feeling, but I figured it out. You know, it's not something I've ever felt before."

My heart, I swear it's going to beat out of my chest like in a Bugs Bunny cartoon. Tears fill my eyes and I know my mouth is hanging open. I am seriously dumbfounded.

"You can't say that here, with everyone around and my ass and boob hanging out."

He throws his head back and laughs. "I probably could have waited until you were completely naked—"

"Bro, I'm surprised you lasted this long," Ben says.

Jesse wipes a tear from my cheek.

I breathe out a big breath. I look at him, then Sera and Meggie, back at Jesse.

"Are you—" I shake my head. "But how… oh my God." I stand up and Jesse cups my boob so there isn't a Janet Jackson moment much to Xander's displeasure. I sit on Jesse's lap and look him in the eyes.

I'm so shocked and taken off guard, I shake my head again.

"You crazy, silly man," I say, cupping his face in my hands. "I love you too."

"Yeah?" he asks with the widest grin I've ever seen.

I nod. "Yeah."

He pulls me to him and hugs me tight—and squeezes my boob.

"Dude, it's about time," Xander says. "I knew you were in love with each other for a while already."

"Whatever," Sera tells him. "This was the sweetest thing ever. I got to see Lucy's hottie Jesse tell her he loves her and her tell him back."

"In my wildest dreams I never imagined this moment coming true," I tell Jesse.

"Believe it," he reassures me, then squeezes my boob—again. "You better let Harley finish."

"It's cool, Jesse. It's not every day a rockstar confesses his love to a big time actress and she professes it back. You get a snapshot of that, Hunter?"

"Yep. This is one for the wall."

"Of course it is. My ass is hanging out and Jesse's squeezing my boob. Great picture," I say with a snort.

"Damn right. Now get your sexy ass back in my chair. We've got at least another hour to go."

Just as I'm about to get up and follow orders, there's a knock at the front door.

"Pizza bitches!" Meggie yells.

"Alright. We eat then we finish up."

"Sounds good. Have I thanked you yet, Harley, for doing this for me?"

"You have and you're welcome." He shakes his head. "Jesse Kingston's in love with Luciana Russo and she loves him back. What the hell is the world coming to?"

"Hey!" I protest.

"Baby doll, I'm afraid to tell you this, but you're way too good for that bum."

I laugh. "Oh shush you. Let's go eat."

Jesse and I grab some pizza and make our way back to Harley's station.

The rest of the group stays in the break room. Jesse pats his lap and I take a seat.

"I can't believe you told me you love me in front of everyone."

He shrugs. "You said it back in front of everyone."

"I did. You know what else?"

"Hmm?

"I meant it," I grin.

"Me too."

We both eat our pizza in silence, goofy grins on our faces.

"How long have you known you were in love with me?" he asks.

"Hmm. Thinking about it I'd have to say it probably started in Chicago. Do you have any idea how difficult it was to let you get on that plane and not stalk your sexy ass into first class?"

He chuckles. "I was kind of expecting it and I got a little disappointed when you didn't."

"Awww, you even liked me when I was seventeen-year-old jailbait."

"I did."

"Well, everything started in Chicago and grew from there. But when I *really* knew was when you asked us to move in with you and it didn't send me running in the other direction."

"We're so…"

"Weird," I finish for him and he laughs.

"Yeah. You know what though?"

"What's that?"

"I think I like that we're weird. It means we're like nobody else."

"Huh. That's true. Very profound Mr. Rockstar."

"I have my moments."

And this was one of those moments. A moment that had my heart skipping a beat. A moment where my chest felt so full of love and hope I thought I'd explode. A moment so touching and poignant and he didn't care that it wasn't just me in the room. He didn't care that his brother, my sister, our band mates and three tattoo artists were listening intently as he laid his heart in his hands for me to either accept or reject.

"It's weird, Jesse."

"What is?"

"You're so comfortable being in love with me. Are you the same Jesse Kingston who sat with me in front of the Beverly Wilshire and told me he didn't do relationships?"

"One in the same. I was talking out of my ass. I knew I wanted a relationship with you then. I knew that one night wasn't going to be enough."

I nod.

"I wanted more than sex from you. I wanted to know you… all of you and the more I got to know, the closer to the ledge I got until I just took the plunge."

"Don't break my heart, Jesse. You could and you'd destroy me."

"I don't plan on it. I was kind of hoping you'd stick around. I was hoping it so much that I was going to suggest to Cage we tour together but he beat me to it."

"Really?" I squeak.

He nods. "Mhmm. There's too much here between us to not see where this goes."

I sigh. "Who knew Jesse Kingston was a romantic?"

He shrugs. "Not me, but I knew you were. Especially when they forced you to sing Blush."

I groan. "That was supposed to be a surprise."

He chuckles. "I've got to say, it definitely was that."

"Have you thought about the new song at all?"

"Some."

"Me too."

"What've you got so far?"

"Well, I don't think it should be a ballad."

"I agree."

I grab my purse and pull out a piece of paper. Jesse raises a brow.

"What?" I ask.

He shakes his head. "Nothing. That's just a very musician thing to do."

"Well, duh, I *am* a musician."

"You are, but I'm still getting used to it. I'm used to you being an actress."

"Mhmm. You and everyone else. This is going to take some doing."

"What?"

"Proving myself. Right now the world is probably thinking this whole band thing is a big joke."

Jesse shrugs. "Fuck 'em."

I nod.

"What've you got for lyrics?"

"I don't have a melody yet, just the first line."

"Go."

"I met you in a dream last night."

"You walked straight toward me and into the light."

"Nice." I write that down. "All I saw was a silhouette of someone I might know."

"Step out of the light so I can see you. Go. Go."

Sera takes a seat. "I've seen you on screen, I've seen you on stage, I've seen you happy, and I've seen you rage."

Ben nods in approval. "I just want to know you, maybe if I show you."

"That I'm not the same, to me it's not a game," Xander adds while I quickly write the lyrics that pour from us. It goes around and around from one to the other and soon we have a song.

"Let's hear it," Harley says after directing me back into the chair.

"Here goes. Titled: Falling Down."

Jesse sings with me.

I met you in a dream last night
you walked straight toward me and into the light
All I saw was a silhouette of someone I might know
Step out of the light so I can see you. Go. Go.

I've seen you on screen
I've seen you on stage
I've seen you happy
And I've seen you rage

I just want to know you, maybe if I show you
That I'm not the same, to me it's not a game
You're real and I'm here, step out into the clear
Let's change it all, let's change it before we fall...

Down the empty black hole of nothingness
You've gotta admit, you're a mess
You can fix this if you want to try
I know you don't want to be that guy

Be more than you are right now
I'll help you, it's my vow
I don't know who you are but I've seen you in my dream
It's only real or it's fake, it's not always as it may seem

I just want to know you and see what's on the inside
What's on the outside doesn't matter so please don't hide
We can fix this if you want to try
I know you don't want to be that guy

Be more than you are right now
I'll help you, it's my vow
No more falling… down.

"Well, GK, you proved it to me with just that. Your band is going to knock some people on their ass when they stand there all skeptical and doubting and shit," Harley tells me.

"I hope so."

"Good melody, but it needs something more," Jesse tells me as I cringe at the feel of the needles working color deep into my skin.

"Yeah, Ethan, Kennedy, and Jace can figure that out. Text the lyrics Sera?"

"On it," she tells me as she takes the paper.

"I've gotta tell you lot, this has been the most fucking memorable day I've ever had in my shop. First, I've got Luciana fucking Russo in my chair and I get to see her ass and feel her boob."

"I knew you wanted to feel my woman's boob."

"Damn straight, Jesse. She's hot. And she's fucking famous. Academy Award-winning actress and shit."

I roll my eyes.

"Second, Serafina Manzini is here. You have no idea how many times I've—nevermind."

"Eww," I say with a laugh.

"Then we've got Meggie Melody. One of the best guitarists I've ever seen."

"Here, here," I cheer and Meggie takes a bow.

"I'm used to you Falling Down fuckers but not these ladies. Then on top of that, I've got a rockstar and Hollywood actress professing love while I tattoo her tit. It doesn't get any fucking better than this, I swear," Harley announces with pride.

I laugh thinking about Harley tattooing my boob while Jesse and I said our 'I love yous'.

"You fucker," Jesse chides Harley. "You were copping a feel while I was professing my love to my woman?"

Harley shrugs. "We've got to take the moments we're given, brother."

"True that," Xander says, and fist bumps work their way around the room.

"Are you guys for real right now?"

"What?" Ben asks.

"This is the weirdest day of my life and that's no lie. I can hear my mother. 'So tell me the moment Jesse told you he was in love with you. Well mama, it's like this. Harley, the amazing tattoo artist was inking me at the time and feeling me up when Jesse leaned forward and told me he was in love with me in a room full of people.'"

They all start laughing.

"I can see Regina now," Meggie says. "You better not mention the ink. Let her find out when she sees it, uh, this weekend."

"Oh shit. We were invited for… oh I am so fucked."

"Not yet, babe, but you will be when we get home. What?" Xander asks as we all glare at him. "It's what Jesse should have said right then. I can't help if he's not as quick witted as I am."

I roll my eyes—again.

This really is the weirdest day of my life—and the best because the man I love loves me back. As Harley said, it doesn't get any better than that.

Chapter
twenty

Lucy

"Oh my God. I'm a total masochist," I whine to Jace who rolls his eyes.

"Stop being such a pussy," Ethan scolds.

"Fuck off. Look at this," I say, lifting my shirt, showing them my now-complete tattoo. "This shit would hurt you too. Don't even deny it."

"It would but I wouldn't be pissing and moaning about it," Jace says.

"Jeez. What the hell is wrong with you guys? So harsh."

"Nothing," Jace says but I know that look. He's lying.

"Spill it."

"Don't worry about it."

"I'm always going to worry about things when it comes to you—all of you. What can I do? Can I help?"

Jace sighs and Kennedy eyes me skeptically.

"Just tell her for fuck's sake," Sera says.

"Do you know what's going on?"

"No, which is why I want them to tell already."

"Where's Jesse?" Ethan asks.

"He went to shower. Tell me."

"It might be better if I show you."

"Oh God," Meggie groans as Ethan picks up his laptop. "That's never good."

I sigh. "Nope, sure isn't. Not a shock though, is it?"

"Nope," Sera replies.

"How bad is it?" I look to Jace. He says nothing but his tight-lipped expression speaks volumes.

"Here's one of them," Ethan says.

"One of them?" I look at the screen and see a title that makes me gasp, want to cry, and want to apologize to the band members of Blush for my mere existence.

"Award-Winning Actress Attempts Rock Career," I read aloud. *"Award-winning actress Luciana Russo announced her bid to go forth seeking a career in music, putting acting on the back burner. For curiosity's sake we did a little digging and found that Miss Russo does indeed have a past rocking and rolling with two other band members of the group to be titled Blush. A high school acquaintance shared some early recordings of the younger version of Blush and instead of describing the tracks, we've put them up here for you to listen to. Be sure to share your feedback in the comments section below."*

"Dear Lord," Sera says as she presses the PLAY button.

"That's not us."

Jace shakes his head.

"Wait. Isn't that... what's her name again?"

"Whitney."

"Yes! That lying bitch," I curse. "Is there anything we can do? Sue her? Has anyone talked to Cage?"

"No, no, and no," Jace tells me.

"Fucking whore!" Sera shouts.

"Yeah!" I agree.

"Who's a whore?" Jesse asks, coming into the room.

I sigh and point to the laptop. He presses the PLAY button and cringes and laughs.

"That's not you."

"No shit," Sera says.

"Hmm. How far has this spread?" Jesse asks Ethan.

"Web-wide."

"Lovely," I say. "Now everyone thinks we totally suck. You might want to get someone else to open for your tour, guys, and you all," I say to Jace, Meggie, and Sera, "Might want to get a new lead singer."

"Fuck that," Jesse says. "I'm gonna place a quick call to Cage. I'll be back in a few." He leaves the room and Trace walks in.

"I'm not worried about it," Trace says with a shrug. "They'll see what we're about when we get our shit out there and in a few days we start recording. Knowing Cage, he's going to prioritize that shit to get it out there and prove the doubters wrong."

"Maybe," I tell him, "but there are ways to 'fix' voices and they'll still doubt. I mean look at that one girl's file that leaked where it was her real voice."

"Dude, that was epic," Xander says with a laugh.

"Yeah, but if they can fix her to sound as good as she does, they're going to think that they can do that to me as well."

"Concerts will solve that problem."

"Yeah, but Xander that's months away."

"True. But before we panic, let's see what Jesse and Cage work out. You need some lovin' from the Xan Man to make you feel better, beautiful girl? I'll even be gentle and let you be on top so your tat won't hurt," he teases, throwing an arm around my shoulders.

I laugh. "You're so generous."

"I know, what can I say? Anything to please the ladies."

"Uh-huh," Meggie says with a raised eyebrow. "You're a perv, you know that, right?"

"Yep. Proud of it. When did you lose the funky colors?"

She touches her now-red hair and shrugs. "Every now and again I do normal."

"Is that your normal color?" He narrows his eyes.

"Mhmm. Red head, carrot top, whatever you want to call me, go for it.”

"Why would I do that? I'm partial to redheads."

She snorts. "You're partial to anything with a vagina."

"Valid. But redheads top the list."

I roll my eyes. "Get your arm off of me when you're hitting on another woman. You have no manners, Xander."

He shrugs. "I don't need any. I get all the pussy I want."

I roll my eyes and press my lips together to stop myself from commenting on groupie whores with no morals.

"That's got to be tough for you," Kennedy states.

"You have no idea," I tell him and he chuckles.

"Well, alright. Got that all worked out with Cage," Jesse tells us as he comes back in the room.

"What'd he say?"

"We came up with a partial plan. He'll fill us in on the rest tomorrow. Here's what we've got so far…

Jesse unlocks the bedroom door and I breathe a sigh of relief as I slip off my flip-flops.

"I'd love to flop back on the bed but I'd end up screaming in agony," I tell him with a laugh.

"Why don't I wash your tattoos for you, then you can get ready for bed, and when you're done I'll put the goopy shit and a new bandage on for you."

I nod. "That sounds good." I walk into the bathroom with Jesse behind me. He helps me remove my shirt and sports bra. He washes his hands, then wets a washcloth and works some antibacterial soap into the cloth. He gently wipes and I hiss out a breath.

"I'm sorry, Luce. I'm trying to be as gentle as I can."

"I know. It's not your fault. It's just really tender."

He nods. "It will be for a couple days. Let me rinse it real quick."

"Okay."

He holds a towel below my tattoo and pours a small cup of warm water over the wound.

"Ahhh, that feels good."

"Mhmm. I brought you one of my shirts. I figured the bulkier the less it'll cling."

"Good idea. I knew I liked you for a reason."

"Funny girl with the amazing rack, you're looking for a spanking."

I can't hide the thrill that rushes through me or the wetness that pools between my thighs.

Jesse chuckles as he puts the aftercare product Harley gave me over my tattoos. It stings a little but not too bad. I'm not sure what I was thinking wanting the entire thing finished in one sitting. Well, yeah, I do. I was thinking I'd chicken out if I didn't get it all done at the first session. Harley decided to do a lot of the coloring but saved some of it for when I go back so he can shade and 3D it. I still haven't seen the Blush tattoo that Jesse just covered back up. Even if I'd tried to get a glimpse, there'd be no way without a mirror. Right now there'll be no twisting of my body to see my back. Likely I'd whine like a baby.

"There we go. I'll let you get set," he says and presses a kiss to my lips.

"Thank goodness Harley sent extra bandage thingies."

"He spoiled you like everyone else does."

"It's because I'm so adorable."

"That's exactly why."

"Thanks for cleaning that for me, babe."

He grins, still loving the endearments and I think it's amazing that simple names can make him feel a hundred feet tall. Even more amazing is the fact that he loves those nicknames coming from me.

I pull off my yoga pants and do my business, wash my face, and slowly pull Jesse's wife beater over my head. Yeah, this doesn't cover my boobs for shit but I'm guessing that was his plan. Sneaky shit.

Ugh, I'm so crabby. I can't get past the bullshit I've had to put up with for the last few months—starting with Aiden Jensen and still going with Whitney the whore. It wasn't my fault the guys thought she couldn't sing for shit and rejected her from the band. If she'd played an instrument she might have stood a chance—nah, she wouldn't have. No one liked or trusted her. She would stab you in the back first chance she got… today was proof of that.

Jesse knocks on the door.

"Mhmm," I say as I brush my teeth.

"That's what I need to do," he says, nodding to my toothbrush.

I wink then rinse my mouth.

"What plan did you and Cage come up with?"

He shakes his head, his mouth full of toothpaste. He spits. "Nothing's one hundred percent at this point. We'll talk about it tomorrow when we get to the studio."

I nod, frustration continuing to make me pissy.

Jesse rinses his mouth, then kisses my lips. "I don't like you all crabby, Luce."

I sigh. "I can't help it. Things were going well, you know? Finally it was quiet."

"You know what happens when it's quiet."

"Yeah, I know. The calm before the storm. I definitely want to bring a shit storm to Whitney."

"Don't worry. She'll get hers. Cage knows how to handle this kind of bullshit."

I just nod.

"Let's go to bed," he says, reaching for my hand. He opens the door and I step through first and gasp in surprise. Candles are everywhere. Small tea lights to humongous five wick candles are burning throughout the bedroom creating a shadowed romantic ambiance.

"Jesse," I whisper.

He walks to the bed and pulls my hand so I follow. He sits, his knees spread and pulls me in between. He grabs my other hand and pulls them both to his mouth, kissing them.

"Déjà vu—sort of," I say.

He's got that sexy half-grin going on that exaggerates those amazing dimples. He tilts his head to the side in question.

"It reminds me of when you kissed my hands in Chicago," I say with a shrug, a little embarrassed to mention it. He probably doesn't even remember doing that.

He nods. "You had this look on your face, kind of surprised and dreamy at the same time. Mine was more surprise. I wasn't expecting the electricity and heat that was between us. I'd never experienced anything like it before or after—until I saw you again. I should have known it was you the minute your voice punched me in the gut."

I smile. "Good to know my voice has that affect on you."

"Luce, I don't like when you're upset. Let's forget all the shit going on out there," he says pointing to the window, "and let's just… *be*, at least for tonight."

"That sounds like a very, very good plan."

"Of course it does. I came up with it."

This gets him an eye roll and he chuckles. "Let's get this off of you. You should really just sleep naked since you're bandaged up for the night anyway."

"True, I just don't want to get this all over the bed when I'm uncovered."

"Good thing Harley was all for keeping them covered tonight. This way I can stare at your amazing tits all night long if I want to."

I laugh. "You're so weird. They're just boobs."

"Oh, babe, these are not just boobs," he says, tossing the wife beater to the side and cupping my breasts. "These are works of art. I'm telling you, purely amazing."

"Whatever you say."

"Exactly," he murmurs then pulls me in for a kiss. It's soft and slow. He turns me and pulls me onto the bed, never breaking the kiss but making sure I don't bump my tattoos either. He's so gentle and sweet. I can't understand why he never wanted a relationship before. I guess I should be thanking my lucky stars because I was in the right place at the right time and it's me who he wants—as hard as that is to believe. It just doesn't seem real.

I lay back carefully, my head on the pillows and Jesse pulls off my panties, leaving me bare. His eyes roam over my body, starting at my waist and working their way down. His perusal moving upwards is much slower. Finally his gaze meets mine and he smirks.

"Definitely not 'just boobs'."

"It's not fair that you're clothed and I'm naked."

"Oh, I don't know," he says, grinning. "I'm kind of liking this arrangement."

"Jesse. I want to see you and touch you."

He considers this for a few seconds then reaches for the hem of his shirt. He tosses it aside as he stands and removes his jeans. No boxers.

"Are you serious?"

He laughs. "What?"

"If I had known that while we were at Harley's…"

"You'd have tried but there's no way. You were already too sore and I definitely didn't need you exerting yourself and bleeding all over so Harley could kick my ass."

"True. Do you go commando often?" I ask.

"Nah. I was just in a rush earlier. You should sit up, Luce, and not lay down until you have to later."

"Ah yes, I get to be on top," I say with a grin, pushing myself up onto my knees.

"You do. It's hot watching you ride me. The way your hips move, your back arches, your tits bounce. That sexy look you get on your face, and when I look down to watch you taking my cock inside you—there's nothing hotter."

My tongue sticks to the roof of my mouth. When he says things like that, I instantly go wet and if I'm already wet like I was a few minutes ago, I get drenched. It's not just what he says, it's how he says it. Soft and seductive in that deep growl.

He lays back, his head on the pillows and I lean down, running my hands up his feet to his calves, to his knees, to the inside of his thighs which draws out a twitch from his already hard cock.

"You know," I tell him, "if you'd been anyone else the first time I saw you naked, I'd have scrambled to put my clothes back on and ran the hell out of here."

He chuckles.

"You have to know you're huge, right? I mean, I don't have a whole lot of guys to compare it to, but damn Jesse."

"Let's not bring your previous fucks into our bedroom."

"This from the rockstar manwhore."

"They never made it to my bedroom, darlin'. Just you."

"Hmm. True. I never took a man home either."

He raises a brow at that. "Not exactly safe going back to a strange guy's place."

I shrug. "I was never really alone."

"Oh that had to suck."

I nod. "Having Max or Frank or one of the other guys around puts a damper on things."

"I just bet," he says, his breath hitching a bit as I lean forward and run my tongue along the length of his erection.

I wrap my hand around his cock, stroking from base to tip once, twice, three times, then lean forward to swirl my tongue around the head. He groans and reaches out to thread his fingers through my hair, getting frustrated at the messy bun, carefully removing the hair bands from my hair. He runs his fingers through my hair, massaging my scalp a few seconds and I moan around his cock as I take him deeper into my mouth. Finally he's able to thread his fingers into my hair, giving a gentle tug, controlling my movements when I go too fast for his liking.

I reach down to cup his balls, gently rolling them in my hand, pulling a groan from him. His fingers tighten in my hair and I suck him harder. He pulls my hair until I lift my head and his dick slides free with a pop.

"What's wrong?" I ask, hoping I didn't do anything wrong. I'm no pro at blow jobs but I thought I did pretty good last time I gave him one.

He shakes his head and smirks. "Nothing." He reaches down and with both hands under my armpits, pulls me up so I'm straddling his lap. "I just don't want to come that way. Not now anyway."

"Well, the way I see it, you could come in my mouth now and then come inside me later. I mean, I know for a fact you don't require much recovery time." Bless the man. He's got amazing stamina, an enormous cock, and the ability to be ready for the next round within fifteen minutes. He is, as he told me once, a sex god, but I will never *ever* admit this to him. His head is big enough as it is—both of them.

"I'll wait," he says, his hand trailing down my abdomen, his fingers between my legs, and then he touches me. Using just a fingertip, he lightly traces my slit, then back, back to my opening where he circles softly.

"You're always so wet for me."

"Unh," is the best I can do when he slides a finger inside.

"You doing alright? Not too much pain?"

I shake my head. "Ibuprofen, oh my God, Jesse," I gasp when he slides a second finger in, immediately hitting my sweet spot.

He smirks bigger, his dimple winking at me again. I have to. I lean forward and lick his dimple.

"There's my girl," he says.

"Mmm. I love your dimples. They're so sexy."

"Yeah?"

"Mhmm," I moan when his thumb begins circling my clit. I dip my tongue into the other dimple then press my lips to it in a soft kiss. What he's doing to me, oh my… I can't hold still. My hips lift and lower, riding his hand, pushing his fingers deeper into me, his thumb pressing harder against my clit.

"Your pussy's so hot. I can feel you tightening around my fingers but, baby," he says, pulling his fingers out from inside me. I gasp. "I don't want you to come yet."

I groan in frustration. "That's so mean."

Chapter
twenty one

Jesse

"Did you really think just because you were on top you would have control?" I ask her. She just gives me a look. "You really should know better by now. You'll come when I say you can come."

"But—"

"But nothing. Now move up here so my tongue can finish what my fingers started." There is no coming for her until I'm ready for her to come and her coming on my fingers just isn't enough right now. I need to taste her. I need her to come on my tongue, my face. I want her to scream and beg for more. Oh yeah, she'll be begging before I'm done. Top or bottom, it doesn't matter to me. I demand control in the bedroom. She knows it. From the pout on her lips, she'd been hoping I'd let her have control so she could come.

"Lucy, move up here. Now." My tone leaves no room for argument and she lifts to her knees, sliding her wet pussy along my chest. I hold in the groan threatening to slip through my lips.

"Fuck, Lucy. You're so wet I can feel it on my chest. Do you know how fucking hot that is?" My cock is so hard right now I could pound nails into a two-by-four, I shit you not. But I'll be damned if I'm going to take my pleasure before I give her at least two mind-numbing orgasms.

"There you go. Right over my mouth."

"This is embarrassing, Jesse," she tells me with a blush.

"It's no different than me going between your legs when you're on your back. Either way my face is buried in your pussy, licking and fucking you with my tongue."

"Maybe," she says skeptically.

"In about two seconds you're not going to give two fucks if you're kneeling above my face or not. You're going to be writhing, wanting to come."

She raises a brow.

I laugh, making sure to blow my breath across her pulsing clit. Yeah, I can actually see it throb. "You doubt me?" I ask.

Her eyes widen and she shakes her head.

I narrow my eyes. "I don't know. Seems like you're challenging me here, Luce. Like you think I can't deliver." She's really not, but fuck, I want to get her off hard.

"I'm not, I swear I'm not."

I grin. "Oh, I think you are. Remember what I said last time? Challenge accepted."

I grip her thighs and pull her pussy down on my mouth, licking and sucking up her wetness.

"So sweet. You taste so fucking good."

She moans when I suck on her clit then circle it quickly with my tongue, her body bucks. She's really fucking close.

"You're so god damn sexy," I tell her as I slip a finger inside her. She gasps and after working one finger in and out of her a couple times, I add a second. She throws her head back, her hair cascading down her back, her tits thrust forward and bouncing slightly as she rides my hand. It's the sexiest thing I've seen in my entire fucking life. I could look at her like this every day for the rest of my life.

What the fuck? I am not fucking going there. Not yet. Ring or not… no.

"That's it, baby," I say as I feel her walls clenching around my fingers, her thighs tensing and shaking. I curve my fingers and rub her sweet spot and she cries out.

"Oh yes, Jesse. Right there."

She reaches up and starts playing with her tits. It's all I can do not to flip her onto her back and fuck her hard. That's so fucking sexy.

"Mmm," I hum across her clit as I rub the flat of my tongue along her slit, up over her clit, then flick it with the tip of my tongue, fast and hard, my fingers working in and out of her, as she moves her hips with each thrust.

"Jesse!" she screams. "Oh my God. Yesss!"

Yeah baby. "Give it to me, Luce," I whisper, then tongue her clit some more. Her body's stiff, her orgasm has her pussy contracting around my fingers, and then she comes.

I wrap my mouth around her clit and opening and suck, then thrust my tongue into her. She screams again, and I work her clit with my mouth, thrusting my fingers into her, drawing out her second orgasm. God damn, this woman is so fucking hot. I nearly came from watching, feeling, and hearing her come. Jesus. I love that I can give that to her. No one's ever brought out this need, the need to bring her as much pleasure as I can, the need for her to know it's me who can give her this and no one else. No one. Else.

She falls forward, limp, and I lift her and move her down my body.

"We're not done, Lucy," I tell her and smack her ass. She moans. Ah, she let the dirty girl come out to play tonight. She lifts her head, but not her body.

"Up," I demand. She doesn't comply so I smack her ass again, the other side this time and damn if she doesn't slide her pussy along my cock. Her wetness rubbing all over me. *Fuck.*

"Lift." She does and I position my cock at her entrance. She sits up and looks at me, her eyes half closed, glazed over in passion.

"This part is you. Take what you can at your own pace."

Slowly she sinks down onto my cock, her wetness easing the way as she lowers herself down, down, until I'm balls deep inside her. Jesus.

"Shit, Luce. Do we need a condom?" I ask. This is her decision and one I won't take from her. Yeah, it feels in-fucking-credible being bare with her around me, but it's not just my decision to make and I will absolutely respect whatever choice she makes. No resentment, no attitude. Some guys might pull that shit, but if I'm going to be in this with her, I'm all in and that means respect in all aspects of our relationship.

When did I turn into such a pussy? Oh yeah, about six years ago when I met her in Chicago and lightning zapped through my body to my brain and cock when we shook hands. One of the scariest and best moments of my life.

"No, Jesse. We're okay."

"Sure?"

"Mhmm. You feel so good. God. How is it I feel like I could come again without moving when I just did—twice."

"Was that a question because the answer to that question is no one will ever own this body like I do. No one. No one will ever bring you the pleasure I do. Never." I lift my hips, nudging her deep, drawing a moan out of her, then she starts lifting and lowering her hips. My hands wrap around her sexy hips and, for the moment, I let her set the pace.

"You're so damn tight," I groan as she sinks down onto my dick just a little faster than before. I'm not going to last long at all if she keeps that up but I really think I could go twice I'm so fucking hot for her right now.

"Jesse," she whispers and I lose it.

"Lucy, I'm going to fuck you hard right now, I need to come, but then I want you to keep going." She nods, her eyes wide. Her head tilts back when I lift my hips to meet her down thrusts.

So hot, so wet, so tight. I slam into her hard and fast, her tits bouncing as she meets each movement, her moans driving me fucking crazy.

"Fuuuuuuck Lucy," I moan, my hands clenching her hips hard as my balls tighten up and cum erupts from my cock. *Shit.* Hard and hot and I've lost my fucking mind in this woman. And I'm still coming as her hips work my cock.

"So good, Lucy, keep going. Fuck. Fuck. Fuuuuuuck," I growl as I finally stop coming. *Shit.*

Her eyes are wide and I can't help but chuckle. She looks well and thoroughly fucked, a bit scared, a whole lot confused, and god damn if I don't love her with everything I've got.

"What the hell was that, Jesse?" she asks, lifting and lowering on my amazingly still-hard dick.

"A really fucking amazing orgasm. Shit," I say, blowing out a breath.

"How are you still hard?"

"Yeah, you do that to me darlin'. What can I say?" I ask as I lift my hips and thrust my cock deep into her. She moans.

"I love that sound, Lucy. The sound of your moans, knowing my cock has you feeling so good you can't hold it back."

Her cheeks flush even more than they were.

"It's a little late to be blushing, Luce. You had your mouth wrapped around my cock, my mouth was all over your pussy, and you've been riding me like a fucking pro for at least the last thirty minutes."

"Good point," she says with a grin, moving just a bit faster and adding that fucking swivel of her hips.

"Best fucking ride of my life, right here, right now."

"Happy to oblige," she says all cocky-like and I laugh.

"God, I fucking love you, Lucy."

Her eyes go wide again, then her expression softens. "I love you too," she says. "But it doesn't count during sex."

I reach up to cup her face in my hands. "Baby, with us, it always counts. I'll never say it just for the sake of saying it or because you fuck me stupid. I promise," I say, making an X over my heart.

She makes an X over her heart then holds up her pinky. "I'm a pinky swear kinda girl."

I nod and wrap my pinky around hers. I pull her down for a kiss. She pulls back before I'm ready for her to and I nearly protest.

"I'll never tell you I love you if I don't mean it," she whispers.

My heart leaps and some weird fucking feeling goes through my body. Almost as if I'm on a roller coaster and we're plunging down a thirty-story drop.

I nod and hold her gaze, her eyes shining with unshed tears. "I love you," I whisper against her lips.

"I love you," she whispers back, a tear sliding down her cheek. I catch it with the pad of my thumb. Yeah, it's a big moment, one where I'm happier than I've ever been—ever. And one where I'm scared as fuck. She could break me without meaning to, and it would be bad—so fucking bad.

"Baby, I need to—" I tell her and she nods. "Roll with me." I maneuver us where she's on her back, rolling on the side that is tat-free, and gently onto her back, making sure none of my weight rests on her.

She winces from the friction of the bed against her back.

"Here," I say, sliding my arm under the free side and she rolls to that side so I can do the same to the other side. "Okay?" I ask, my forearms beneath her body, waist to shoulders, my hands gripping her shoulders gently.

"Oh, that's so much better. The bed against my back stung."

I nod and slowly start moving in and out of her. There will be no rushing this. Not this time. I need to show her how I feel. Words just aren't enough.

"Jesse," she whispers, her hands cupping my face now, I steadily hold her gaze as I slowly, lazily slide my cock in and out of her.

Jesus, who knew you could feel like this? God, I feel like my heart is going to thump right out of my chest. The way she's looking at me— unbelievable.

"Lucy," I whisper, picking up the pace just a bit when I feel her getting wetter. "It's never—" I shake my head and swallow hard. "It's never been like this. I don't even know what this is. It's so much more than I-"

Tears slip down her face and I lean forward and sip them off of her face with my lips.

"Baby, don't cry. Please."

"Good tears, Jesse. Only good tears."

"Is there such a thing?"

She nods. "When my happy gets so big and my heart gets so full and I can't contain it, it has to come out somewhere."

I nod. "You're so beautiful, Lucy."

She laughs. "You're such a liar. I'm a really ugly crier."

"No. You could never be ugly. There's too much good in you. With red blotches and swollen eyes, you're still the most beautiful woman I've ever met."

"Jesse Kingston waxing poetic. Romantic candlelight. Telling me he loves me. Are you sure I'm not dreaming?"

"I promise you, this is no dream. If you don't believe the words," I say, and thrust a little harder, sweat running down my back as my body loves hers. The pleasure is so god damn intense I can barely hold on and when she arches her back, her hips pushing down to meet mine, her breath catching, I know she's close. Harder and faster I make love to her, wanting to watch the love run through her, wanting to pour my love into her.

"Jesse," she whispers. "Yes, right there." And she's there. I pick up the pace and I'm with her. I wait until her eyes unfocus and her pussy squeezes my cock before I let myself go, pouring everything I am into her.

"Lucy," I growl as each thrust pours more and more of my cum into her as her pussy milks it out of me. "God," I whisper.

"Unh," she shouts and I grin. She doesn't realize she does that, but I know what it means when she does. She did the same thing when we met in Chicago.

When her body stills, I roll us to our sides, our gazes still locked.

Her eyes drift closed.

"Hey, no hiding," I tell her quietly.

Her eyes open, full of tears. "It's just so much."

I nod. "But it's ours."

Her lips quiver. "It's ours," she whispers.

"I knew it'd be you," I confess.

"What'd be me," she asks, sniffling.

"I knew in Chicago that it'd be you that I loved."

"What?" she whispers.

I nod and tuck a strand of hair behind her ear. "I didn't want to leave you that day and if it hadn't been for the bodyguards I probably wouldn't have."

"I didn't want you to."

"I know. The timing was off then, just a bit. You were too young and I wasn't ready for you."

"And you're ready now?"

I consider that for a minute. "How can anyone be ready for… this? For you? I would have probably run away if I hadn't been smacked upside the head when you sang. You're so beautiful, you're an extremely talented actress, and you've got the voice of an angel—well, with a little devil mixed in," I say with a smirk and she giggles.

"Best. Sound. Ever."

"What?"

"When you giggle."

"I don't giggle."

I lift a brow. "You just did, Luce, and it's an amazing thing. Hearing you happy… yeah. Best sound ever—aside from you screaming my name out when you come because, baby, there is absolutely nothing better than when you do that."

She giggles again. Her eyes widen and she does it again.

"Well, Jesse Kingston, not only do you get me to fall in love with you," she tells me, running her fingertip down my cheek, "you also get me to giggle."

My heart swells when she tells me she's fallen in love with me. I swear it's going to burst. There's no way it can get much bigger than it is right now without exploding.

"I think you win, though."

"How's that?"

"Well, you captured my attention six years ago, enchanted me with your voice the first minute of our second meeting, left me wanting more after the first time we had sex—that never happens, I'm just saying. Then I wanted you around, in my life, in my bed—all the time. You got me to want a relationship and you opened my heart to love. I'd have to say you win."

She shakes her head, those damn tears slipping down her cheeks. I reach up and wipe them away. "No, Jesse. I think we both win, don't you?"

I know my smile is probably goofy and huge but I don't care. "Yeah, Lucy. I'd have to say we both win."

"Always on equal terms. That's how love should be. If it's not, then it's not love."

I nod. "Thank you," I whisper.

"For what?"

"Not using this against me, my—," I draw in a breath, "my vulnerability. It's difficult for me—to feel this without feeling weak or exposed."

"Oh, no, Jesse. Never. Never, ever would I do that. That's not love.

That's cruel and I could never be cruel to you. What—?" she breaks off, unsure if she should ask.

"It's okay. I'll tell you. There's a reason why I swore to never be in a relationship and it's a pretty fucking good one."

"Okay."

"You see, my parents never really loved each other. They hooked up at a party one night and one night turned into a series of nights that they fucked. They didn't care about each other. They just wanted to fuck."

She nods.

"So, when the condom broke and my mom found out she was pregnant, her parents flipped their shit. Being as she'd grown up with my dad, her parents knew his parents and next thing you know there's a shotgun wedding."

"Oh no."

"Yeah. I don't know why they stayed married. I guess at least the make-up sex was good. For as much as they fought, you'd think they'd have ended up with more than just me, Ben, and my twin sisters."

"Jesse," she whispers. Where I expected pity, there is none. This woman is incredible.

"That's why I swore to never be in a relationship. I don't want to be vulnerable, to have someone use my weaknesses against me like my parents did to each other. When they fought, it was so vicious. Anything they could use against the other, they did. They hurt each other, always trying to one-up the other to see who could hurt who more."

"That is most definitely not love and that isn't something you ever have to worry about from me, Jesse. I promise you that."

I nod. "I know and you're so amazing. I hope I don't do that to you. I don't know if I will, growing up with that—can I be different than they are?"

"You already are, baby. If you were like them, you'd use everything going bad in the press against me when you feel the least bit vulnerable—like now. But instead you help me find a way to make it better, to fix things. That's love, Jesse. You help, you don't hurt."

"I can't imagine ever not wanting to help make everything right for you. A happy Lucy makes for a very happy Jesse."

"And a very horny, Jesse," she says with a laugh.

"Mhmm. Speaking of." I get up from the bed and clean up in the bathroom. I wet a washcloth and walk back to the bed. "Slowly, baby, very slowly roll to your back?"

She nods.

"Open." She does and I clean her up, taking my time. It takes a whole lot of trust for her to open herself up like that, to expose herself by allowing me to take care of her like that. I'd never use that against her. I never wanted to take care of a woman before—like that or in any other way but with Lucy, things are so different, they have been from the first time she was in my bed.

I toss the cloth into the clothes hamper and wash my hands. When I get back into bed, she's lying on her side facing me, her hands tucked under her cheek.

I lean in and press a kiss to her lips, pouring my heart out to her, my brow pulling inward as I do. It's only when she returns my kiss that I allow all the tension in my body to release. It's her. She's my calm. She's my everything.

I pull back and look into her eyes. "I love you Lucy."

She smiles. "I love you Jesse."

"All is right in the world."

She giggles then gasps then giggles some more as if she can't help herself.

"You've always giggled."

"I did not."

"I hate to be the one to tell you, but you have. It's adorable, Luce. Don't think it's a bad thing. Your happiness is a gift."

She shakes her head. "You are so much more than I thought you were."

"Of course I am. You nearly fainted when you saw my cock."

She laughs and gives my shoulder a shove. I can't hold back my grin.

"Not what I meant. I meant I knew you were kind and caring from what I'd seen when you interacted with others in interviews or on stage. But I didn't know the full depth of it all."

"Are you sure this isn't just your crush, Lucy?" I don't know where the thought comes from, but I honestly *need* to know.

"What? No. I can see how you'd think it could be but please believe me when I tell you that my crush was superficial and what I feel now…" she pauses and meets my gaze steadily, "what I feel now… I feel so much of everything and it goes so deep that sometimes, like before, I don't know how to handle it or contain it—"

"And that's when your tears come." I nod. "Then I should probably tell you…"

"Tell me what?"

I kiss the tip of her nose. "Everything you feel, I feel."

"Only you don't ugly cry."

I laugh. "Lucy. You're beautiful. I love knowing that's what makes you cry."

"Oh, sure, now you like making me cry?"

"Oh my God, no. That's not what I meant—"

She laughs out loud and damn if she hasn't played me.

"Lucy, you're lucky you got your spankings already or I'd have to give you more." She's still laughing. "Know what? I think you need some more anyway."

"I probably do," she says as she snorts in laughter.

I can't help it, I smile and laugh with her. "I've turned into a total pussy, Lucy."

"You haven't. You look nothing like my vagina." She laughs so loud I swear they can hear her on the other side of the house.

"Woman, what's gotten into you?"

"This," she says as she reaches for my cock, which immediately rises to the occasion. Of course. I am the sex god, after all.

"Want some more?"

"Always."

"Far be it from me to deprive you," I tell her as she climbs on top of me, sinking down onto my cock, her breasts pressing against my chest as she kisses me stupid.

I understand now why she says "unh".

Chapter
twenty two

Jesse

She's still sleeping when I wake up. I need to piss. I go about my business and she's still out cold, the blanket tucked down around her waist revealing the bandaged tattoos and her fucking amazing tits. I'm not exaggerating here. They're perfectly round and firm. Her nipples are a rosy pink and I swear to you they look like they're begging me to suck on them. Okay, maybe I'm bullshitting a little bit but damn. My mouth waters at the thought of sucking on her nipples.

Shit, I'm getting hard. Hmm. It would take some careful maneuvering but it could be done.

I slide into the bed behind my girl tucking my lower body close to hers, lifting one of her legs over my thigh, and slowly pushing my cock into her opening. I'm not going in dry, fuck that. I'll just do this until she gets wet and pulls me in.

Damn, Lucy can sleep. She still isn't awake and the head of my cock slips inside her pussy. She does moan, though, so she'll be waking up soon. If not, I'll have to fuck her hard to wake her up. I'm not going to molest her in her sleep… not completely anyway.

Shit, she gets wet fast. I carefully lean forward, pressing my lips to her ear. "Baby, you're so wet for me even when you're sleeping."

She moans again and presses her hips back toward me.

"There's my girl. Come on, baby, wake up."

"Unh," she says and I chuckle. I slip my hand around to her front and circle her clit.

"Ummm, Jesse," she says, still asleep. Well, fuck, at least she knows it's me.

"Lucy." I thrust deeper into her, nearly two-thirds in now. "Wake up, baby." I pinch her clit and her body stiffens.

"Wow, Jesse," she says, her voice low and sexy. "Mmm, you can wake me up like this every morning."

"Fuck yeah," I say, thrusting deeper, almost all the way in. She rests her hand over mine between her legs and takes my index finger between her index and middle fingers, then circles her clit with my finger. Her head tilts back and rests on my shoulder.

"God damn, that's sexy. Your pussy just got super wet when you did that and—" I thrust deep, fully seating myself inside her, "oh yeah, you feel amazing."

"Jesse, more," she says.

Oh, I have more for her. I thrust slow but hard into her and I can already feel her pussy squeezing my cock. I'm not going to come yet, but she is. I let her circle her clit faster with my finger, I press down just a little harder and she moans long and loud.

"So close, Luce. Let go and come for me."

Her breath hitches. "I can't."

"Oh, I know you can and you will. Not once but twice, maybe three times before we're done." I thrust faster, rubbing her clit fast and hard, my cock hitting her deep and she cries out my name. I fucking love it when she calls out my name. That caveman's back inside me, beating on his fucking chest as her pussy spasms around my dick. God, I could come, but she feels so good. I'm not coming yet, not until she comes at least once more.

"There you go," I whisper.

"Mmm, Jesse," she moans. "I think I'm going to come again."

"Fuck yeah. Come all over my cock, Lucy. I love when you squeeze me tight and you get so fucking hot."

"Oh God, Jesse!" she screams this time.

Caveman. Beat. Chest. I want to roar but I settle for a growl.

"Jesus, you feel so good." I fuck her harder and she meets every damn one of my thrusts. My woman is amazing. She can do some serious fucking. Who would have thought from looking at her that beneath that gorgeous prim exterior is a minx, a sex goddess with a pussy made just for me? It has to be, because each time we have sex, it feels so fucking amazing, I swear I'll never get enough.

"Jesse," she breathes. "Fuck me harder."

Caveman.

More than happy to oblige, I grip her hips carefully to avoid the bandage, pull her ass back tight against my groin, and hammer into her.

"Yes, just like that. Incredible," she moans.

Beating on chest happening. Right now.

"Lucy, I'm going to come soon, I need you to get there. Rub your clit for me."

She licks her fingers and slips her hand between her legs.

"Dear God, that's fucking sexy. Circles Lucy, hard and fast. I can't hold off much longer and I want your pussy to squeeze every drop of cum out of me."

"Oh yeah, hard like that… Jesse…" she groans, her pussy gripping my cock so tight I almost can't come. I feel it, but it's not coming out until— growl.

"Lucy! Fuuuuuuck yeah," I groan. So good. So, so good. One last thrust, one last pump of cum and I still, my cock still twitching. Yeah, it's that good. So good that when it's over, I still feel it. Told you. My pussy.

"You know, Luce, I think you should know," I say, catching my breath, "if one of these times while we're having fucktastic sex like this I happen to have a heart attack, just know that I went extremely happy. Even if I go before I come, it was fucking awesome."

She laughs, her pussy squeezing my cock as she does. Damn.

"Shower?" I ask.

"Well, I have to avoid getting my back and side wet but yeah. It'd be great if you could help me."

"Of course. How sore are you?"

"My tats or my pussy?"

It hits me just right and I have to throw back my head and laugh. Shit, she's amazing.

"Let's start with your tats."

"Not as bad as yesterday but I think I'll avoid the spray of the shower."

"No need for that, Cupcake. We'll just adjust the spray to waterfall and it'll be like me pouring water over you."

"Oh my God. I want a shower like yours."

"You do. *This* is your shower."

"I mean when we find a house."

Oh fuck no. She's not going anywhere.

"*This* is your house."

She turns to look at me and I know I'm not looking happy right now because damn it, I'm not. She's not leaving. She's staying. She can't go anywhere. *What the fuck?*

"Jesse."

"Don't 'Jesse' me. Why the fuck do you want to leave?"

"I don't want to but come on—"

"No, you come on. You live *here*."

"But the guys—"

"Do you hear them complaining?"

"Well no."

I nod. "No complaints in private either. In fact, they seem pretty fucking happy having extra people around to hang with."

She bites her lower lip. I let her because it means she's trying to work this out in her mind.

"Careful now, this might sting." I gently peel off the bandages and toss them into the garbage.

I grab her hand and head to the shower. I turn on the water and let it warm up, then change the stream to waterfall.

"In we go," I tell her as I lift her into the shower with me. She wraps her legs around my waist and her arms around my neck.

"Jesse, I don't want to move."

"Mhmm," I say, still pissed off. "Let me wash your tats. They look pretty good."

She sighs as I lower her down to the floor. I twirl my finger, motioning for her to turn around and she does.

"Oh wow, that doesn't even hurt," she tells me, then tips her head back, letting the water wet down her sexy long dark hair.

"Good. I should wash that shit off so it doesn't get in your hair."

"Okay."

I soap up my hands and gently wash her flawless skin. Her mom's going to shit a brick when she sees those tats this weekend. I'll tell her it was my idea so Lucy doesn't get the brunt of Regina's wrath, although truth be told Reggie's bark is much worse than her bite. I think she's a little sweet on me, too. Who wouldn't be? I mean, I'm a fucking catch, right? I'm a sex god. I'm good looking. I'm a god damn rockstar. Women fall all over themselves to get to me, hell, men too if I'm honest. So why would Lucy want to find her own place?

I growl low in my throat and Lucy turns to me. "You okay?"

"Yep. I'm good." Lie. I'm not good. Not at all. I confess my love to her, make love to her five times last night and again this morning and she wants to bail. Maybe…

"Jesse, knock it the hell off."

"I don't know what you're talking about," I evade as I wash her other tat. "Damn, this Blush tat turned out great. Even the guys are going to love it. It's sexy but tasteful, feminine but not too girlie. Harley's a fucking genius."

"Will you help me look at it after we get you out of your bad case of pissy and we finish our shower?"

I can't help it. She's so fucking beautiful and sweet that even when she tries to look fierce she's just so lovable it does that funky thing to my heart.

"I don't have a bad case of pissy. Really. I'm good."

She raises a brow and watches me skeptically as I wash her front. It's completely non-sexual because I can tell when I wash between her legs she's sore. It's not a flinch or a grimace but just a bit of a frown. I'm really fucking proud of her though. Not many women can go six times in less than twelve hours, multiple orgasms each time. My girl is awesome.

"I need to shave my legs but I can't bend," she says with a pout.

"No problem, Cupcake," I tell her and pull on a tab sticking out of the side of the shower and a small bench comes out.

"Jesse. I think this is the best shower I've ever seen in my entire life."

Her enthusiasm and excitement make me laugh.

"Yeah?"

She nods, like a kid with a new toy. "What else can it do?"

"Let's wash your hair and shit and I'll show you."

I wash her hair, massaging her scalp a bit, then we rinse it. She does the conditioner thing, running her fingers through the long strands. I watch so I know how to do it if she gets sick or something and needs me—my heart seizes up in my chest. No. Lucy can't and won't ever get sick. Hell no. I can't stand the thought of it. What if—?

"Jesse? Breathe," she tells me with a tap to my cheek.

I blow out a breath and pull her to me. Nothing can happen to her. I just found her. I love her more than anything and if she were taken from me—no. It won't happen. Fate brought us together, it's going to keep us together.

"Are you okay, babe?" she asks.

"Yeah," I nod. "I'm good."

"Sure?"

"Mhmm." I wash my hair and body while she shaves her legs. Damn if that isn't sexy. What the hell? Who knew women shaving their legs was sexy? It's the motion, the glide of her hand with the razor, it's almost sensual. Jesus. I have it bad. I admit to being two hundred percent pussy whipped. The thing about that? I don't give a fuck. I like it. No one better mess with me about it either. I think of Ben and I just know he's going to. I'll have to punch him in the mouth when he does. He'll deserve it. Hell, he'll know it's coming the minute he opens his mouth.

I just watch as she finishes shaving her legs, so neat and precise. I suppose if she doesn't do it carefully she'll cut the shit out of herself and that shit hurts like a motherfucker.

"There. I just have to rinse," she says, turning to me. When she sees me staring at her, shoulder against the wall of the shower, arms crossed over my chest, she lifts her brows. "What?"

I just shake my head. How can I tell her she's so beautiful she steals my breath? That even watching her shave her legs is sexy. I'm turning into a fucking chick. I think I need to fight with Ben just to make sure my balls are still intact. *Shit.*

"Ready?" I ask as I get set to change the spray. "This might hurt your tats so brace for it."

She nods, almost bouncing in excitement. I grin. She's so damn cute.

I hit the button for FULL and all the jets shoot out water, ten total. They're positioned from all angles, including the sides.

"Ohhhh," she moans as the water beats on her back. "This is amazing."

"Let's try the next one," I say quickly, ridiculously jealous that the fucking jets can make her moan like that. I have no idea what the fuck is going on with me, but now I'm definitely going to have Ben punch me in the face. Maybe even Ethan too for good measure.

The next one is MIST and it's just as it sounds, a slow mist from all the jets.

"I don't like that one," she says, closing her eyes. "It's like being splashed in the face. I hate that."

"Next," I announce and press STREAM. It's just a regular shower, straight from the three nozzles overhead.

"That'll be great for rinsing my hair," she tells me.

"Next," I say, pressing STREAM-X. Regular streams come from all jets except the two that angle toward the face and she grins. "That's a nice one too."

I smirk. "You're so cute, Luce."

She flits a hand in my direction. "Next!"

"Brace yourself." I press MASSAGE.

The three overhead nozzles, pulse in a massaging stream.

"Shit!" she squeals.

"You alright?"

"Yeah, it just hit my tat on my shoulder."

"Okay, let me switch it quick." I press STEAM and steam comes from all ten nozzles and the exhaust fan kicks on to high.

"Oh, steam room."

"You ever go for a steam?"

She wrinkles her nose. "I tried it. I don't care for it really, not in the club anyway. This isn't so bad. It's not dry like the other."

"Yeah, I'm not a fan of the steam box either. If I want to sweat, I'll just lift weights or go for a run."

"Exactly."

"There are a couple more and I'll let you play around with them next time you shower."

"Cool. You don't mind?"

I pull her to me. "Lucy, I mean it when I say this is your house too. Please treat it as yours not just mine and the guys', okay?"

She nods.

"You don't see Sera, Jace, Meggie or even Trace having an issue with it, do you?"

"No, but—"

"But…" I pause. Wait. She's used to taking care of everyone, providing for everyone, that she's not sure how to react when someone does the same for her.

"Lucy?"

"Hmm?"

"You're used to taking care of everyone, right?"

"Well, yeah, I just always—"

"Okay. I get it but you can still take care of them from here, and seeing as we're in a relationship and we love each other, you're going to have to get used to someone taking care of you, too."

"I thought I was doing pretty well."

"You are. Don't get me wrong, you're doing great. I just didn't realize that was what was going on. You can talk to me, Lucy. You know that, right?"

"I do."

"Don't hesitate because you think I'll judge you. I never will. It's part of that pinky-swear and X over heart promise."

She nods.

"Trust me, Luce. Here's how much I trust you."

She just looks at me.

"I keep thinking all these fucking mushy romantic thoughts that would have Ben or the guys giving me shit and you know what?"

"What?" she asks.

"I don't give a fuck. I like it. I like feeling like this about you and I don't care who knows it. I like knowing you'll be here when I go to sleep at night and when I wake up in the morning. I like cooking for you. I like your reactions to each of the fucking different settings for this shower. That's how pathetic I am, how whipped I am, and I'm not too proud to tell you. A year ago I'd have probably thrown you out—no, that's not true either. It'd have been you and you're you and there's no wanting you gone. Period. Ever."

"Wow."

"Yeah. Word vomit."

She nods. I turn off the shower and we step out, drying off. She wraps a towel around her head like some turban or something.

"See? That right there? I think that's fucking adorable."

"What?" she asks.

"The turban thing you've got going on."

Her eyes are wide as she asks, "Jesse, you're all in, huh?"

I nod, head hanging, hands braced on my hips, only my head moving as I accept my fate.

"Me too," she tells me.

I lift my head up. "Yeah?"

She nods. "I'm used to taking care of everyone. I've always taken care of Sera, ever since her parents… well, since then. She was in such a bad way for so long and then she gave up her dream of music to model while I acted all because my mom wanted it. I made ridiculous amounts of money and she did as well, but I just bought the houses, paid the bills, paid for vacations, and made sure she was comfortable, happy, and never wanted for anything. I like doing that for everyone. Now there's Jace, Meggie, and Trace. I know they can all take care of themselves, but I just like to do it."

I nod. "It's a good thing. It's part of who you are. You nurture and take care of people, giving them what they need monetarily or emotionally. I saw that from the beginning. But, babe, you don't have to own your own house—hell, you already do. You can take care of everyone from here. I'd really like it if you'd stay. We can talk to the others later, especially Sera, and make sure she's good with staying here. The house is plenty big and she has tons of freedom here."

She nods. "You're amazing, Jesse. Thank you," she says, giving me a hug. I gently hug her back, careful not to hurt her sore areas.

"Want to see your tattoo now?"

Her head springs up. "Yes!"

I chuckle. "Okay. Let me find that mirror," I tell her, searching through drawers. "Ah, here we go. Ready?" I ask her.

She nods.

"Tell me which way to tilt." I hold up the mirror and she directs me. I know the minute she gets a clear image because she gasps.

"Oh my… Jesse this is perfect."

"Those are your lips from that one modeling thing you did. Harley found a picture online."

"Wow," she breathes. "It's perfect. Lips blowing out musical notes. I love the band name in blush and black over the top of everything. It makes me think that while the music is important, the band is more important and that's true. Without happiness and contentment in the band, the music would suck ass."

I nod. "Beautiful brilliant girl."

She smiles.

"Let's get that goopy shit on your tats and find you something comfortable yet respectable to wear."

"Respectable?"

"Well, as phenomenal as your tits are, I don't want the guys checking out my woman's rack. I'd have to punch someone and I'd rather avoid that if I can."

"It'd be Xander."

"Fucking A it would. He tried to check out your ass and tit at Harley's."

She laughs. "I know. There was no hiding my ass, I mean it was out there, but it's just a little area and not worth mentioning. But he tried so damn hard to see my boob. It was hilarious. Sera and I kept laughing at him."

I nod. "He's a perv."

"So are you," she says, challenging with the raise of a brow.

"I am, but I don't check out other dudes' women."

She rolls her eyes. "Please. When you were whoring you didn't give a shit who the chick was with."

I run a hand over the back of my neck, a bit ashamed of how I behaved. "I did."

"It's not okay but I get your reasoning now."

I nod. "Thanks."

She nods. "Now goop me up so I can dry my hair before it gets all funky."

I grab the tube and begin spreading the gunk over her tats.

Her gaze meets mine in the mirror when she drops the towel.

I groan when the phone rings in the other room. "Probably a good thing since you're already getting sore."

She nods, her eyes filled with want and desire.

I head to the bedroom and pick up my phone.

"Who is it?" she asks.

"Cage."

"Oh good."

"Yo," I say by way of answering.

He only says two words. "Show time."

Chapter
twenty three

Lucy

With everything that Whitney whore started, the media blew up calling me all kinds of vile names. All I could do at first was clench my fists. Then Cage came over and we all—both bands—had a meeting. Spenser, Carmen, Simone and even Mrs. Martinez sat in on the meeting. Everyone less than pleased with the latest turn of events.

My mother called and rescheduled the party for the following weekend, pending our recording schedule. Thank goodness. One less thing to worry about—well, two actually. First, I wouldn't have to listen to my mother go on and on about what a mistake I was making and how I should just stick with acting where there's less drama. Honestly sometimes I could shake her and tell her to wake up and smell the coffee. The life of an actress is where this all stems from. I haven't even broached into the career of a rocker yet. Gah. Second, she wouldn't see my tattoos—yet. I know it's petty and juvenile of me to hide this from her, but right now I can't be bothered to deal with any more bullshit. This is where Cage comes in.

Our savior. Our white knight. Our knight in shining armor. The man who has the answer to every situation. Cage came up with the perfect solution and as it's seven-thirty Monday morning, I'm ready to get this underway.

"You look relaxed," Jesse tells me.

I shrug. "Not really. I just want to get this done and resolve this bullshit."

He nods. "I can understand that. Your tats doing okay?"

"Yeah, they barely hurt anymore."

"You're such a hard ass," he says with a grin.

"Dimples," I say, standing on tippy toe getting nowhere near his face. He takes pity on me and leans down. I kiss one dimple, then the other. "You have no idea how sexy those dimples are."

"Luce, all I care about is *you* thinking they're sexy."

"It's seven-fucking-thirty. Get a room," Xander growls as he enters the kitchen.

I pour him a cup of coffee and hand it to him. He grunts. Same goes for Ethan, Kennedy, Jace, and Trace. Meggie bounces in and I'm hesitant on giving her coffee. What's she going to be like with caffeine in her system?

"Pour it, fucker," she scolds.

"Fine but no bouncing off the walls while we're recording."

She rolls her eyes, takes the cup of coffee, and leans against the counter.

Sera straggles in last looking gorgeous as always and I want to slap her. It's really not fair that she can practically roll out of bed and look like the super model she is.

I pour her coffee. "Bitch," I say. She flips me off.

"I'm totally feeling the love here," Trace says. Apparently sarcasm is everyone's friend.

"We should go," Frank says, stepping into the doorway.

Everyone files out and I note Gio and Mike are here as well as Max.

"What's going on?" I ask.

"We're taking two vehicles," Frank answers. "We could have gotten a stretch limo or hummer but we figured it was best not to draw extra attention to ourselves."

"Good idea," Jesse says.

"Who's riding with me?"

Jesse just looks at me.

"Besides you, of course." I smile brightly then take a long drink of my coffee, burning my tongue and roof of my mouth. Fuck. Not a good start to the day. I'm anxious and I hate feeling anxious.

"Sera and Meggie," Frank says.

"Dude," Xander says. "We're going to be in an all-dick vehicle. That fucking sucks."

"Get over it," Ethan scolds and climbs into their car.

"You think two black Town Cars following one another is going to be less conspicuous than a stretch limo?" I ask.

Frank raises his brows. "Wrong side of the bed this morning?"

I sigh. "I'm sorry. No. I'm just feeling anxious. I don't like feeling anxious, especially on such an important day, you know? I should be overjoyed and celebrating the fact we're finally starting to record, but instead I'm wigging out over this… this… shit."

He nods. "It'll be over soon."

"Until the next dramatic episode the media comes up with," Sera says.

"You'd think after six years of crap you'd be used to it by now," Meggie says.

"How often did you see my name in the media in a derogatory manner over those six years?"

She pauses. "Point taken."

I nod. "They even managed to hide some things I expected to be plastered on the front page yet Whitney whore is front and fucking center."

"I wonder how much they paid her," Sera says.

"A hundred grand," Jesse says.

My head whips to the side, my gaze meeting his. "What? How do you know that?"

He shrugs. "Was on one of the gossip sites."

"You were looking at the gossip sites? What are they saying?"

"I was and you're better off not knowing."

I groan and lean into his side when he puts an arm around me and pulls me close.

"It won't matter in another hour or two. She better hope that check cleared."

Sera snickers. "That'd be great if they held the check and canceled it."

Meggie snorts. "I always hated that bitch. You know she tried to steal Tommy Cavanaugh from right under my nose. She skanked through all the guys at your school so she had to come to mine for fresh ones who didn't know what a STD-ridden slut she was."

"Wow," Frank says with a chuckle.

"It's no joke," Meggie tells him. "She thought if she spread around the clap, they'd call it applause. She's got more crabs than Red Lobster. And last but certainly not least, she's got so much yeast she could open a bakery."

"Ack," I say, laughing and groaning and grossing out at the same time. "You were good until you mentioned yeast."

"Imagine how the guys feel when they get down there."

"Megs, you're so fucking sick," Sera tells her.

She shrugs. "I just hope the guys sniffed it before they licked it."

Jesse groans out a laugh. "Holy fuck that's disgusting."

"She did get around. It wouldn't surprise me if the whole thing was true," Sera confirms, then takes a drink of her coffee.

"Again, one of the weirdest conversations you've ever had this early in the morning," Frank says, shaking his head. "You've been having a lot of those lately."

I grunt and nod.

"Be glad Xander isn't here for this conversation," Jesse tells Frank.

"Can you imagine?" I ask.

"No. Do not even go there," Sera chides.

The car pulls up in front of Nichols Records and I'm surprised. Time flew by and the drive was fast. I look at the clock in the car. Eight thirty-four. Huh.

"We better get moving, we're on a tight schedule," Jesse tells me.

I nod. "Celeste is going to be meeting us here. Jesse, can you keep your horny band mates away from her?"

"I'll do my best, Cupcake, but I can't make any promises. You know how they are."

"I do, so thank you for whatever you can do."

"You bet."

He leans down and presses a soft kiss to my lips. "You're going to be great, Luce. Trust me, okay. Believe in your talent. Own that shit. Sing your fucking heart out, just like you did on the fake stage."

I nod. "I love you."

One side of his mouth kicks up in a half smile. "I love you too."

Meggie sighs then bats her eyelashes at me. "He is so very dreamy."

I laugh. "Oh fuck off you bitch."

"Nice mouth, Lucy. What if the press had been standing there?" Cage admonishes.

Now that I feel three inches tall…

"Sorry."

"You have to be careful. They're just looking for a reason now. You're a target with all the shit going on."

I nod. "I said sorry and I meant it."

He nods. "We've got to keep this under control and that means I'm going to be tough on you. I don't want to, but I have to. I don't like what's happening to you and since you're one of mine, I'm going to do what it takes to make sure it stops today."

"Thank you, Cage."

He nods. "Let's go. We're all set up." He gives me a sidelong glance. "*Celeste*, Spenser, Carmen, and Simone are already back there."

I cringe. "You know, I'd say I was sorry about stealing her, but that'd be a lie and I don't like to lie to people I care about."

He nods and smirks—just barely. All business today. I look at Sera who raises her eyebrows. I just shrug.

We get to the back room where Cage has us set up for the day and Spenser and the girls rush forward.

"Good. Nice choice in outfit."

I look down at my skinny jeans, black boots, and black Avenged Sevenfold tank layered with a pink one.

"Just a touch up on the hair and a smidge of liner on the eyes."

"Wow, I did pretty good today."

"Nicely done, Lucy. Sera—" he pauses. "Get in there with Simone now. You need serious work."

"And to think you called *me* a bitch."

"Huh," is all I can think to say.

Carmen comes at me with eyeliner and eye shadow, then runs a flat iron over my hair before a quick spritz of Spenser's magic spray.

Spenser works on Jace's hair a bit while Carmen heads over to Meggie. Sera walks out fifteen minutes later looking like a million bucks and Simone moves to Trace. She looks him up and down. His black hair is cut short, a lot like Jesse's is now. He's wearing a Volbeat t-shirt, worn jeans, and boots. He is the definition of a true rocker.

"Wow," she whispers.

"Pretty, isn't he?" I ask.

"Yeah. Those green eyes and those thick lashes. Whew," she mutters as she walks off and Trace grins.

"I'd kill for your eyelashes," I tell him.

"Kill for your boyfriend's," Spenser grumbles.

"Yeah, his too. Why is it men have such awesome eyelashes and we have to mascara the hell out of ours to try to even come close?" Meggie asks.

"No clue," Sera replies.

Celeste and I go over times and schedules and PR stuff. I have no idea what she's talking about so I hand her my phone with my calendar, itinerary, and email. She walks off to the conference room and takes a seat, getting right to work. I already love her.

Jesse catches my gaze and smirks.

"Lips!" Spenser announces.

"Kiss first," Jesse interrupts and gives me a gentle lingering kiss. "You've got this."

I nod. "We totally do."

"That's my girl."

Spenser whips out some pale pink lip gloss that smells like bubble gum.

"Hey Spense, you got any of that strawberry flavored lip gloss Lucy wore that one night…" I hear Jesse ask and I laugh.

"All right people, let's go," Cage directs and the members of Blush head into the sound room.

I grab the headset resting on the stool in front of my mic and wrap it around my neck.

"Here's what's happening. Right there," he points, "is the camera. There's another back by Trace and another over behind Meggie. All three will be on and all three will be live. We're going to keep it live for the first hour to give the public a taste of what you're made of."

"Those fuckers will be eating their words," Trace says with a nod at me. I smile and give him wink. He points his drumstick. "We got this shit."

I look to Jace who grins. "Whitney whore is going down." I breathe a sigh of relief at his words. I was so worried he was angry with me.

Meggie adjusts her guitar strap and bounces on her toes. A pink and purple guitar with her name written in cursive beneath the strings. Classic Megs.

Sera tilts her neck one way, then the other, cracking and stretching. Hot pink guitar slung over her shoulder, she lifts her arms and stretches out her back and sides. It's her routine. Next she leans forward, careful of her guitar as she touches her toes.

"Two minutes," I hear Cage say through the sound system. I hadn't even realized he left the room. I see Damian out there and he gives me a wink. I smile and wink back. He's such a sweet guy. It'll be fun touring with him when the time comes.

"One minute. Act natural. Either I or Nate here will tell you what's going on. Thirty seconds."

I adjust the headset, leaving one ear uncovered so I can hear what's going on around me.

Cage holds up three fingers, then two, then one. He mouths *live*.

"Let's start with *Breathe*," Nate tells us. "We'll play it straight through then see if we need adjustments. This isn't the way normal recording sessions go but it's what we've got for the first hour."

I nod and adjust the headset over my ears. "Trace count us off?"

He hits his sticks and we're off.

I felt your stare and I wanted to run
I felt your glare and under the mid-day sun
When I walked on by I saw your eyes close
When you breathed me in, I froze

My heart stops whenever you're near

My senses are crazed out of fear
Fear for my vulnerable very breakable heart
Falling for you wouldn't be smart

I breathe you in as I stand next to you
I breathe you in as you tell me what you feel is true
I breathe you in when you tell me it's love
I breathe you in but it's never enough

It's never enough.
I'll always want more than you can give
You'll always hurt me more than I can forgive
I want a love that's true

I'm sorry to say that isn't you
No matter how much
I breathe you in as I stand next to you
I breathe you in as you tell me what you feel is true

I breathe you in when you tell me it's love
I breathe you in but it's never enough.
It's never enough.
You can't give me love.
It'll never be enough

"Great job," Cage tells us as the last chord fades.

"Nice guys," I say, looking back.

"Hell fucking yeah," Trace says and I let out a laugh, Meggie, Sera, and Jace joining in. There's no censoring this feed.

I look at Jesse through the glass, who's standing with his arms crossed over his chest, one side of his mouth tipped up in a smile.

"Dimples," I mouth to him and he winks.

"Let's run it through again then we'll just sing through a couple songs. After that we'll record normally," Cage tells us.

"Sounds good." I take a drink of water. I nod to Trace letting him know I'm ready whenever they are and I, again, adjust the headset and wait for the count.

When Cage looks through the window and runs a hand across his neck we know they're cutting the feed. I breathe a sigh of relief. I hated every second of it. I don't know what the hell I'm doing in here or how recording is supposed to go and we had to do some fake shit just to prove ourselves.

I turn around, pulling off the headset.

"I'm sorry guys, I really am. This shouldn't be happening. None of it. We're here to play music not to have to deal with petty bullshit from some jealous girl who didn't get her way when she tried to steal my and Meggie's boyfriends in high school. I swear I feel like I'm twelve." I shake my head. "You don't deserve this. Not one second of it. I hope what we did today showed everyone what we've got and what we're made of. It was us. No gimmicks, no voice fixing crap. Just raw and uncut Blush. It's who we are and it's what we're going to bring to each and every concert. We have nothing to prove to anyone but ourselves. I'm done trying to fix what isn't broken. If another dramatic episode flares, so be it. We ignore it and do what we're here to do. We make music."

They all murmur their agreement and Trace hits his sticks together and yells, "Fuck yeah. Lucy fucking Russo can sing the hell out of any song put on her plate. If you couldn't, I wouldn't be here."

I nod. Trace goes on to praise the other band members and Meggie bounces with pride. I sit on the stool and take another drink of water. When I turn toward the glass, Jesse's got a big-ass grin on his face as do the rest of the guys, Spenser and the girls, Damian, Celeste, even Cage and Nate.

"Um, what did I miss?" I ask.

Cage points to the camera and I see the red light is still on. I smirk and shrug.

"Well America, you just saw Blush at its finest. This is us." I sweep an arm around to the others. "Take us as we are. We're just five normal people who want to make music and hopefully entertain you while we're doing it." I shrug.

"Three seconds, they say." I wink. "Have a good one people."

"We're out," Nate says with a chuckle. "I couldn't have planned that any better if I'd tried."

"Trace swore a lot."

"It's the internet. Fuck it," Cage says. "Let them fine me. That was brilliant." I shrug. "Take ten and then we really get to work."

I walk out of the sound room and Jesse hands me a peppermint Life Saver. "That was fucking awesome."

"It was okay. On *Bring Me Closer* I need to make the chorus edgier, you know?"

Jesse grins, his pride showing. "You guys are fucking kick ass. You all know your shit and not one of you gives less than two hundred percent."

"It's the only way I know."

He nods. "And that's why you're going to be a chart topper."

"They're going to give us a run for our money," Xander says.

"Fuck, we're screwed," Ethan says.

I laugh. "Shut up. There's no topping you guys."

Kennedy shrugs. "You just did."

"No, no. That was last night when I was on top…"

"Oh yeah," Jesse says, pulling me to him. "You know you could see part of your tats on camera."

"Oh boy. Mama Regina is going to have words for you later," Xander chortles.

"I'll tell her you got me drunk and talked me into it."

His laugh stops, his smile turns to a frown. "That's not even funny. Your mom's scary."

I nod. "She's going to have words for *you*, Xander."

"Lucy," he whines, trailing behind me as I head to the restroom.

What started out as a shit day has turned itself around within a matter of a couple hours, and Whitney whore is going to get what's coming to her. And to think I didn't have to even mention her. All I had to do was be me and bring it. Too bad what I brought was genuine and what she brought was bullshit.

I smirk and Xander gives me a look.

"What's going on in there, Luce?"

"Just thinking that while we just showed the world we're genuine and have nothing to hide, Whitney whore is going to be in a world of hurt. The

315 • Anne Mercier

media is going to crucify her."

"Yep. Especially after that jam session. There's no doubting Blush after that."

Nope. There's no doubting Blush. As Jesse would say, we've got this.

Chapter
twenty four

Jesse

"I have a confession," Lucy tells me.

"You only love me for my cock."

She snickers and swats a hand at me. "It is impressive but no."

"I knew it. You only love me for my Life Savers."

"Damn. You figured me out."

I nod. "I should have never shared my secret or my stash with you. It's all about the candy now," I say with mock hurt.

"Baby, you're sweeter than candy," she tells me with a wink.

"That was the corniest line I've ever heard," Jace tells her.

"I know, right? Wasn't it great?"

"You two are so weird, you realize this, right? It's not normal how naturally weird you are together."

"I happen to think we're a perfect pair of weirdness," she tells him. "Wait, what's that quote?" She looks to Sera who holds up her hands. "Don't even look at me."

She reaches in her pocket for her phone but comes up empty. "Shit. I forgot Celeste has my phone."

"Here, use mine," I tell her. She lifts her brows. "What?"

"Nothing," she says, shaking her head.

It's obviously something. "What is it?"

"I'm just surprised you handed over your phone like that. You didn't even look first to see if you had any texts."

"Do I?" I ask.

She swipes a finger across the screen then her lip curls. "*Yes.*"

Well that can't be good. She thrusts the phone in my face and I take it.

Heather. Oh fuck. I keep my expression blank as I swipe the screen and open the message. *Fuck.* Fuck. Fuuuuck.

"Well, this isn't going to go well so I might as well just get it out there."

Her lips are pressed together in a straight line and she nods once. Jace and Sera have expressions of panic and Xander raises his brow at me.

"Uh, well, the message is from Heather."

"Dude," Xander says, shaking his head.

"Who's Heather?" Sera asks while Lucy just looks out the window.

I'm not sure how to do this. God. I don't want to hurt her any more than she already is.

"One of the 'regulars'," Xander tells them.

Lucy stiffens and slides ever so slightly toward the edge of the sofa.

"What the *fuck* does she want?" Jace asks, leaning forward, his elbows resting on his knees, hands balled into fists, expression one that isn't friendly at all.

"What does who want?" Ben asks as he hands me a beer. He hands Lucy one of the Pinnacle vodka drinks.

"Thanks Ben. I'll need another one of these."

"But that one is—" he breaks off as she downs the entire bottle. "—full. Yo, Kennedy grab a couple more of those vodka drinks, would ya?"

"On it!"

Jace swears under his breath, clenching and unclenching his fists, Sera and Meggie send me death glares, and Frank sits back with his arms crossed over his chest.

"What the fuck is going on?" Ben asks.

"Oh nothing much," Meggie tells him. "Just some skank-ass hoe named Heather sent Jesse here a text and he seems awfully uncomfortable about it."

"Dude," Xander says again and shakes his head.

"Again, I'll ask. What the *fuck* does she want?" Jace bites out.

"We were supposed to meet up and I guess I forgot to cancel."

"You guess you forgot," Lucy whispers. "I bet you forgot to 'cancel'," she says making air quotes, "with the rest of them like you said you would too, huh?"

"I did. Fuck."

She nods, not looking at me.

"I see how this works," Sera says. "Lucy can't even so much as *look* at another guy without you getting all worked up and trying to piss on her leg, but you can't bother to text your whores and tell them you're no longer available? And delete their numbers like Lucy asked?"

"It's not like that. I forgot."

"Convenient, isn't it?" Lucy asks and takes one of the drinks from Kennedy and chugs this one as well.

"What the fuck?" he asks. I just hang my head. What can I say? I fucked up. Maybe I'll say just that.

"I fucked up."

Lucy laughs humorlessly. "I can't even talk to Damian about our tour and you still have your whores on speed dial." Silence for a few seconds. "You know what, Jesse? I don't think this is going to work for me."

"What do you mean?"

"Just what I said."

"You don't mean that."

"Oh yeah, I do. Let me explain something to you. You promised to send a mass text and get rid of those... women."

"And she's using the term loosely," Sera scathes.

"And you also promised to delete their numbers. Every last one. But did you do any of that? Nope. So I can only sit here and wonder why that is. I trusted you to do that."

"Fuck," Trace mutters under his breath.

"Let me tell you why I think that is. I think it's because while you *say* you want this," she says, pointing between me and her, "and while you claim to 'love' me," again with the fucking air quotes, "and while you made promises to me just this morning—" her breath hitches and my heart nosedives into my gut. I'm a fucking asshole.

She clears her throat. "While you made promises to me just this morning, I think deep down you didn't believe a word of it. You didn't believe in us so you kept your backups."

"No, that's not it at all."

"No? Then explain it to me."

"I forgot, Lucy. I was distracted with everything going on."

She nods. "I distracted you so much, you love me so much, you want only *me* so much that you can't send the text you promised to send to get rid of the whores you say you no longer want. Well, okay then. That's all settled. Yippee."

Jace cringes.

She stands up and I stand with her. She shoves me, catching me off guard, and I fall back into the sofa.

"What the fuck?"

"You stay here. I'm going to pack. Frank, please let Max know I'll need the car in about twenty minutes."

He nods and sends me a glare.

"None of you have to come with me. Actually I think I probably need to be alone."

"You know what? Fuck that, Luce," Jace says. "You go, we go. It's how we roll."

"Lucy, listen…"

"Sure. I'll listen as well as you listened when I asked you to delete the whores," she says, turning and walking away. "You have a right to expect and demand those things from me, you said. You fucking said that to me." She walks toward the stairs.

"Fuck!" I yell.

"Dude," Xander says. "What the fuck?"

"I fucking got distracted and caught up with Lucy and all the bullshit she's got going on."

She gasps.

"Fuck. I didn't mean it the way it sounded."

Her back still to me, she merely nods, her shoulders rigid. She starts up the stairs and her shoulders begin to shake as she walks a little faster.

"Dude," Xander says, giving me a shove. "Go, what the fuck are you waiting for?"

"I don't know."

Sera snorts. "You know what this is?" When I don't respond she shouts. "Do you?!"

"I do," Ben says with a look of disgust.

"This right here is Jesse being a fucking coward. Mr. I-Don't-Do-Relationships purposefully fucked up the best thing that ever happened to him and now he doesn't know what to do. Oh, boo fucking hoo, Jesse fucking Kingston doesn't know how to fix the relationship with the woman he swears he loves." She moves forward and stands right in front of me, then she gives me a shove. Hard. "You are a motherfucking coward and if you don't fix this now, you can find another band to go on tour with you because Lucy deserves a whole hell of a lot better than this and you fucking know it! She let you in. Do you know how hard that is for her? No, of course not. How would you know when you're too wrapped up in yourself to notice?" She shoves me again.

"I didn't do it on purpose."

"You fucking did and now you go fix it," Jace says, getting in my face. No one moves. No one. Then Xander stands up next to Jace, then Ethan, Kennedy, and Ben, then Meggie and Trace.

"Either you fix this," Xander says, "or I'm going for her because she's one hell of a woman and I'd be damn proud to call her mine."

"Get in line, dude," Trace says.

Kennedy and Ethan agree.

"Christ. I don't know how to fix this."

"You can't 'fix' this. She's a fucking person not an object. You show her what she needs to see," Ben tells me.

"I have no clue what that is."

"Then you're fucked, brother, and I'll be stepping up."

"The fuck you will," I say and head up the stairs, taking them two at a time. I take a breath and punch in the code. Tears fall steadily from Lucy's eyes as she pulls clothes from the dresser and puts them neatly into her suitcase. Shit. When she does things with precision, she's locked herself in.

"Lucy." She ignores me. "Lucy." I walk toward her and take her hand. She shrugs me off. "God damn it Lucy," I shout. "Don't make me grab you. I don't want to hurt your tats."

She laughs, mascara streaking down her cheeks. "Because that'd be horrible, right? To hurt me physically? But, hey, emotionally, let's fuck Lucy over. Noooo problem."

She takes another swig of her vodka drink. Just how many has she had?

"Please, Lucy. Just a few minutes, it's all I ask." I'll fucking beg if I need to. She can't leave me. I don't know what I'm doing, why I didn't delete them like she asked. God. I run my hands through my hair and pull.

"*Please.*"

She eyes me, then walks over to the bed and sits on the edge. "You have five minutes." She looks to the clock. "Starting now. Go."

Jesus.

"I'm going to be honest with you, Lucy, and tell you I don't know why I didn't send the text or delete them. I don't understand it. Maybe I was trying to hold onto something because I was afraid of what was ahead? Maybe I was afraid it wasn't real? I honestly don't know."

I pace back and forth in front of her. She doesn't even look at me, just steadily wipes the tears from her cheeks. It hurts my chest so fucking much knowing I made her hurt this bad. God. I feel sick. I did this. I did this to her. I am such a fucking asshole.

I drop down on my knees in front of her and her eyes go wide.

"Lucy, God, I am so sorry. Please don't cry. I'm a dick. I'm an asshole and I fucked up so bad. I know sorry isn't enough but it's all I've got. That and this," I say, taking my phone out, typing out a quick text. I read it aloud, "I've met someone and I'm in love with her. Don't call, don't write, don't text, and don't show up. We're done."

She doesn't look impressed. Even when I hit send. Not even when I delete each and every female in my contacts list that aren't business associates or family.

She tries so hard to choke back the sob that breaks loose and all I want to do is wrap her up in my arms and hold her, let her know how much I love her, but I know she won't believe me. I know she won't let me touch her. Fuck it. I'm going to try. I'm not going to take no for an answer. She is what I want and I'll be god damned if I'm going to let her walk away without a fight.

I toss the fucking phone on the bed and reach out to hold both her hands in mine. She tries to pull them away, but I hold tight.

"Stop," I tell her. She ignores me and I say it again, only louder and harsher. "Stop it right now, Lucy. God damn it. Listen to me."

"Why should I? You didn't listen to me… or you did, but it went in one ear and out the other."

I nod. "I deserve that and whatever else you've got for me. I'll gladly take it. God, Luce, I'm so fucking sorry. I don't know what I'm doing, how to do this. I've never had anyone to answer to and… fuck. Please don't go," I whisper, hanging my head. "I don't know if I was trying to sabotage what we have, to push you away, I honestly don't, but I can tell you I'm so fucking sorry. God, please don't cry, Lucy. Please."

Her shoulders shake as the tears keep falling.

"If you were looking to sabotage us," she says shakily, "you succeeded. I don't understand why you'd do that."

"Truth?"

She just gives me a look.

"I'm scared out of my fucking mind, Lucy. I don't know how to do this. I have no god damn clue. My parents, they're a piss poor example of how relationships work. No one I know has had a successful relationship, so who do I turn to when I need to figure out the answers?"

"The answer to that is me. Or it should have been."

I drop my head into her lap and wrap my arms around her waist. She tries to push me away, and she tries really fucking hard too.

"I'm not letting you go, Lucy. I can't. I can't let you go."

"Why? Obviously I'm not enough for you if you needed to keep those numbers."

"Lucy," I whisper. "You're so much more than I ever imagined I'd have in my life and I have no idea how to handle this. What we have between us, it's huge. The biggest. You, you're everything to me. Maybe I needed to push you to see how well you'd stick around, or to see if you'd end up hurting me like my parents hurt each other."

She nods.

"I swear to you with everything I am, I love you. I've never said those words to another living soul. Ever. I wouldn't say it if I didn't feel it in here," I say, thumping my fist against my chest. "Please talk to me."

At first she says nothing, but I can all but see the wheels turning as she thinks. She sighs out a shaky breath and wipes more tears. God, it's killing me knowing I hurt her like this. I'm a fucking prick. She deserves better than me.

And there it is.

My breath catches. *Fuck.*

"Figure it out?" she asks.

I nod.

"Why?"

"You deserve better than me. You are so fucking amazing at everything you do. You're kind, caring, generous, and you've got this big heart that you wear on your sleeve and share only with those closest to you. I think that's because you've been hurt one too many times and you feel the need to protect yourself. Me? I'm just a kid from the wrong side of the tracks who got lucky when a music producer dropped in for a drink at the bar we were performing at one night. It was a fucking dive. Peanut shells all over the floor mixed in with beer, ashes, and cigarettes. We didn't give a fuck. We just wanted to play and if we earned a couple bucks doing it. Well, then we found a way to feed ourselves, get some equipment we needed, or to pay for some studio time. Me and Ben, we were okay as far as food and clothes, Xander too, but Ethan and Kennedy? They had it bad. Their moms both crackheads. No food in the house ever. They spent most of their time at our house or Xan's. Xan's parents were doctors and weren't around much so we stayed there most of the time."

I sigh and look up into her eyes, reaching out to hold her hands in mine.

"You're pure, you're genuine, and you're so real I'm scared shitless. I'm just a street punk who doesn't know the first thing about love or relationships. I'm really great at keeping people at arm's length and likely that's part of what was going on here as well. I am so fucking sorry I hurt you. I don't want anyone but you, Lucy. Only you."

My breath hitches, my chest gets tight, and my vision blurs. "I can't stand knowing I hurt you. I am so, so sorry," I whisper. "I can't promise I won't fuck up again because, being me, I'm probably gonna. All I know, Luce, is that I fucking love you more than anything in this world. I can't imagine not being with you. Just the thought of not being with you rips my heart to shreds. I can't breathe, it hurts, Luce."

A tear slips from my eye and down my cheek. What...?

"Jesse," she whispers.

"I don't—" I try to speak but another tear slips.

"I won't say it's okay because it's not. I swore I'd never lie to you and I'm not going to start now and you can bet your ass I expect you to keep that same promise. But let me clue you in on what's going on."

I just look up at her, eyes wide, vision blurry. I'm so confused. My chest hurts and I can't breathe. I don't cry. What's happening to me?

"Jesse, I suspect for the first time in your life you feel remorse, pain, anguish, heartache."

"Is that what—I can't breathe." She runs a hand over my cheek.

"You've never let yourself care enough about anyone to leave yourself vulnerable and with that vulnerability comes heartache and pain when things go wrong. You finally let yourself *feel*."

"Well, this fucking sucks."

She laughs through tears. "I know. But the good outweighs the bad, doesn't it?"

I nod. It does. Nothing beats the feeling of loving Lucy. Nothing.

"I'm confused about what I should do here, Jesse. I want to leave on one hand but on the other I think my leaving would be a mistake, that I'd be giving up something that has the potential to be so, so wonderful."

"Please stay. Please believe me when I say I want no one but you."

She nods. "Do you want this? Me and you?"

"I do. I don't know what I'm doing, but I want to figure it out."

She breathes out a shuddering breath. "I won't lie to you, Jesse. I'm afraid, so afraid. I was scared before but now I'm terrified because I know how easily you can destroy me."

"That goes both ways, Lucy."

"Maybe so but what happens when we're on tour and the groupies swarm you? What happens when one of your 'regulars' shows up?" Those god damn air quotes again.

"I sign their shit and send them on their way. There are no regulars, Lucy. Only you."

"Can I trust that to be true? I can't ask you to promise to never hurt me again because that's an unrealistic request, but I'm going to ask you this: if you want out, if you want to go fuck around with someone else, you tell me and we call it quits *before* anything like that happens. If you respect me enough to do that, we could walk away being friendly. If you disrespect me and cheat on me, you'll be dead to me. That may sound harsh, but I won't tolerate cheating—and you already lied to me. That's not going to be easy to get past."

I nod. She's got valid points and I can't fault her for not trusting me now. I said I'd do something and didn't. If she did the same, I'd feel exactly as she is right now.

"We need to communicate, Jesse, no matter how difficult things are or how hard it is to talk about—even if it hurts one or both of us. If we try to talk it out, to work it out, at least we tried together."

I nod. "I can only ask you to be patient with me, Lucy. I don't know how to do this. I feel like a total pussy right now, begging you—my dad would laugh his ass off. Men don't beg women for anything and they sure as fuck don't cry. *Men don't feel.* Men use women to fuck, that's all they need to feel."

"God, Jesse. That explains so much. And I'd really like to meet your dad so I can kick him in the balls and elbow him in the face."

Amazingly, I laugh.

"I'm in this, Lucy. All-in. No going back. No excuses. No bullshit. Just me and you."

She nods. "If you hurt me again…"

"I won't. Not intentionally."

"This time was intentional whether you knew it or not."

I nod because it's fucking true. I'm a prick.

"I'm an asshole. I just need to get used to this. I never expected to be in love. Ever."

A few minutes go by and I know she's processing things, weighing things.

"Okay," she breathes.

"Okay?" My heart starts beating and I can breathe again.

She nods.

I wrap my arms around her, holding her close.

"I'm so fucking sorry."

"I know. Just don't do it again."

I nod and bury my face in her stomach, holding her close, carefully avoiding putting too much pressure on her tattoo.

"I love you, Lucy."

"I know you do. I love you too."

There's a knock on the door. "Yeah," I shout.

In they all come and I don't give a fuck if they think I'm a pussy for crying a few tears or getting down on my knees to beg forgiveness from the woman I love more than life itself.

This woman taught me to feel. She taught me to love. She taught me that some things are more important than pride, and she's that something.

Chapter
twenty five

Lucy

Recording the self-titled Blush album only took ten days. I'm not sure if that was normal or if Cage had people working extra to get this done as soon as possible, but it's done. While it was hard work, long hours, it was so much fun. I still shake my head when I think about Blush having an album. Dreams do come true. So far I've had two of them come true.

We're kind of rushing everything so we can tour with Falling Down. It's only been two months since we started the entire process with Cage, but so far we've finished recording, made a video, and have had a single released. We decided to not go with Blush for our first single. We wanted something hard and dirty instead of soft. We went with *Lick*. It's sexual, it's gritty, and it's hard. It's been well received, thank goodness. I guess after that live hour of recording and our little on-air discussion we had no clue was on-air, the media and the public decided we weren't a joke and that they were going to give us a chance.

In three weeks we go on tour with Falling Down. On. Tour. With. Falling. Down. I still can't believe it. Today, though, I'm getting scolded by my mother for getting my tattoos. This is the first chance we've had to get together for her cook out. I'm feigning sleep on a lounger so she leaves me alone.

"That 3D ink Harley added looks so wicked," Meggie says from a lounger next to me.

"Yeah, he's an incredible artist. He wouldn't let me pay him for the 3D. He said my payment would be getting his name out to the public. Apparently Jesse's not so good at PR."

"You aren't either, that's why you've got Celeste."

"Exactly. See? I'm brilliant at PR," I snicker and take a drink of soda.

"Where'd Jesse go?" Sera asks from my other side.

"I don't know. He was talking to daddy last I saw. Why? Do you need him for something?"

"No. He's just usually up your ass."

"Jealousy isn't becoming, sister dear."

"Oh, there's no jealousy in that statement. Besides, I'm quite content with the way things are going for me."

"Hmm. How are things going for you? Is it Cage? Or is it Ben?"

She shrugs. "Undecided. Cage is… not always available. Ben lives behind a stone fortress. I may start looking for someone less complicated."

"There's always Trace."

"Hmm. I've been considering that."

"I think he's been considering you as well," Meggie tells her.

"I can't believe we're playing Vegas tomorrow night," Jace says, sitting at the end of my lounger. "I'm so psyched."

"I'm nervous, so let's not discuss it. Let's discuss gambling before the concert."

"Yes, let's," Meggie chimes. "A little blackjack."

"Not for me. I'm strictly a slots girl," I admit. "I'm not so good with the cards. Seriously bad luck."

"She's not kidding," Sera adds. "It's pitiful."

"Gee, thanks."

Jace straightens up. "Oh man, here comes your mom."

"Fuck. I'm sleeping."

Sera snorts. Yeah, I know it's not going to work, but I need to try. I'm exhausted from listening to her carry on about tainting my flawless skin, how I'm never going to be able to model certain things, how I'll not be able to be in certain movies—although I'm pretty sure they have ways around tattoos. I know plenty of actors and actresses who have tattoos. But, whatever. Let her bitch herself out.

"Serafina, have you been eating enough? You still look so thin."

"Trust me, mama, I'm doing a whole lot of eating. Living with guys who can cook freaking gourmet meals ensures that I eat."

"Good, good. Those are good boys."

Sera snorts and I resist doing the same.

"You don't agree?"

"Oh, they are great guys. You just called them boys. They're all over six feet tall, heavily muscled, and inked."

"They are boys to me. They have no problem with me calling them boys. How is Luciana? She's tired from the media circus, I'm sure."

"She is. We're just glad the last couple months have been quiet so she can enjoy the process of recording, making a video for *us* instead of someone else, putting out the single, and now the album has hit the shelves so we can relax a little bit and just focus on practice and writing more music."

"Good, good. You all got the same tattoo, I noticed."

"It's the band tattoo, mama."

"I see this. Luciana has always wanted a tattoo like the one on her side."

"She never got it because of acting," Sera tells her.

"I know," she sighs. "It was a shock."

"I imagine," Jace says. "But it's kick ass ink."

"Ah, there's your father and Jesse. I wonder what those two have been up to."

"And there she goes, rushing off to find out," Meggie tells me.

"I think she's getting soft," I tell them. "Why can't she just be nice to me instead of nice about me to everyone else?"

"That's mama," Sera tells me.

"Mhmm."

"Time to eat," mama calls out.

Jace lets out a whoop like he used to when we were in high school.

Two hours and we have to leave. Mama's good about that, thank goodness. She knows work's important and she's the one who decided today is the day to have this gathering. I still don't get the point of it, other than to gather everyone in the same place at the same time and we do that every day—though without the parentals.

Jesse's already seated at the table, plate piled full of food. I can't stop the grin. The man eats like a horse—all of them do, and there isn't an ounce of fat on them. Sure they work out, but not every day. Bastards and their high metabolisms.

I load up my plate and am about to take a seat when Jesse reaches out and pulls me onto his lap.

"Well hello there," I say teasingly.

He nuzzles his nose behind my ear. "I missed you."

I set my plate down then turn and give him a lingering kiss. "You're the one who disappeared."

"I was hanging out with your dad. He's a great guy."

"Mhmm, he is," I say around a mouthful of food.

"Did your mom ease up on you?"

"Yeah, she did." I sigh. "Trace, can you pass me one of those whipped cream Pinnacle vodka drinks?"

"You got it."

"Uh-oh," Sera teases.

"What?" Jesse asks as I take the bottle from Trace and thank him.

"Let's just say Lucy likes those drinks a lot."

"They're so good. See, I mix this with a little root beer and it tastes just like a root beer float."

"I can see where that'd be dangerous," Jesse tells me.

"Mhmm. But we're at my parents and we have to leave for Vegas soon. I won't be getting drunk. I'll save that for tomorrow night after the show."

Jace chimes in with his usual, "Hell yeah!"

"Vegas baby!" Xander announces. He and Jace fist bump.

"Those two together…" I trail off, shaking my head.

"Never a dull moment, I'm sure," my dad says as he takes a seat across from us.

"That's for sure. I'm a bit sad I haven't gotten to see much of you today, daddy."

"That's alright, baby girl. We'll do this again in a couple weeks before you go on your tour."

"Jesse, if it's okay, why don't we have everyone over at our place?"

He smiles. "You know they're always welcome in our home."

I nod. "Good. I was thinking of inviting Joey."

Trace groans and I laugh.

"Sorry Trace, but maybe he'll bring a date and be distracted. For that matter, you should bring a date and be distracted then he'll leave you alone. The Russo manners won't allow for him to interrupt you on a date."

"That's right," my dad says with pride.

"Mama, you've outdone yourself. This is so good," I moan. Jesse runs his hand up my inner thigh, his index finger rubbing against the seam of my jean shorts. I turn to look at him, eyebrow raised.

He leans in close and whispers, "Your moan was so sexy I'm getting hard. Add your sexy ass wiggling on my lap…"

"So, you're getting me all hot because you are? That's not very nice seeing as there's no relief in sight," I pout.

"Mile high club," he grins and goes back to eating.

As Jace would say, *hell yeah*.

We take Falling Down's private jet to Las Vegas and mid-flight I get to thinking.

"Who did you have to pay off to get us this gig at the Hard Rock?" I ask Cage.

He lifts a brow. "I'm insulted."

"Uh-huh. Spill."

"I didn't have to pay anyone. The owner's a friend. If you remember," he tells me, then looks at Jesse and the other guys in Falling Down, "I got you a gig there too before you went on your first tour."

"I remember," Xander tells us. "The place was packed and we were nobodies. It was fucking awesome."

"Oh boy," Sera says, looking at me.

"What?" Xander asks.

She sighs. "Lucy's already turning green."

"I'm nervous. But no worries, considering we've never performed a live show together before, it's all good."

"Sarcasm is your best friend," Xander says as he sits down next to me where I'm sitting on Jesse's lap and throws an arm around my shoulder. "You've got nothing to worry about. You're going to kick ass and take names. And if you're nervous about this show, just think about the venues you'll be playing at when you open for us."

I narrow my eyes at him. "Gee, thanks for that."

He pats my shoulder and winks. "No problem."

"I think it'll be easier in the larger venues. With the lights you can't see too far out from the stage, right?"

Jesse chuckles. "Yeah, that's true, but you can hear them and there's no doubt about the number of people there."

"Can none of you placate me with bullshit today?"

"Baby doll?" Ethan asks.

"Hmm?"

"You got this shit. Relax. Enjoy it. And if you have trouble sleeping tonight, just fuck the hell out of Jesse. I'm sure he's got no problem with that."

I laugh. "I'm sure not."

Jesse wiggles his eyebrows.

"He's got amazing stamina and recovery time."

"Fuck you," Sera bitches. "I fucking knew it. He's all sexy and beautiful, his voice gets women's panties wet, and he fucks like a sex god. No wonder I can't find the right guy. It's all being packed into one man. Spread that shit around a little bit. Hell, I'll give up the panty-moistening voice and even a little of the pretty."

I bite my lip. "I'm sorry?"

"You fucking should be." She crosses her arms. "What's his recovery time?"

"I can't believe we're having this conversation in front of everyone,"

I tell Sera.

I look to Jesse and he just laughs and shrugs. "Um, sometimes he doesn't need any recovery time and the longest was around ten to fifteen minutes I think, but I'm pretty sure he could have gone sooner. He was just being kind and letting *me* recover."

"Dude," Xander praises and fist bumps Jesse.

"Again, fuck off," Sera curses. "I'm going to put Nana Russo's juju on your guy there so he has a severe case of limp dick."

"Can you at least wait until next week when I get my period?"

"Bitch."

I snort out a laugh, then laugh more at my snort.

The fasten seat belts sign lights up and I slide off Jesse's lap to the seat beside him and buckle up. He weaves his fingers through mine, grips my hand, bringing it to his lips and pressing a kiss to my knuckles.

I lean the side of my face against Jesse's shoulder, look up at him, batting my eyelashes, "You are so sexy, Jesse Kingston."

He taps my nose with his index finger. "I know."

"Oh boy."

He laughs.

The landing is smooth and there are cars waiting for us as well as security. Frank, Max, and the guys are getting some much deserved time off.

Celeste calls ahead, notifying the hotel we'll be there to check in shortly. Hanging around in the lobby of a hotel with the very recognizable members of Falling Down isn't a good plan. Celeste insists I draw more attention than they do, which is true in some places but definitely not in the Hard Rock Hotel.

I throw myself on the king-sized bed and kick off my flip-flops. Jesse takes care of the luggage then comes to join me.

"I'm going to have to fuck you stupid tonight, Jesse."

"Yeah, I don't have a problem with that," he tells me with a chuckle. "I'll tire you out, baby."

"I've no doubt."

His lips press against mine, his tongue sliding along the seam. I open for him and he kisses me slowly, leisurely, and I do believe he's going to be able to make good on that promise. Slow and leisurely sex with Jesse is a true test of my stamina. It's difficult to keep up with him at that pace, but I really enjoy trying.

He sits up and pulls me onto his lap. He takes off my top, then my bra. I stand up at his urging and he unsnaps and unzips my shorts, letting them drop to the floor. I remove his shirt and he helps me with his jeans and boxer briefs after taking off his boots.

His cock is already hard and I just… want. I drop to my knees and his eyebrows raise. I shrug and reach for him. His eyes glaze over with desire when I wrap my hand around the base of his erection, then lean forward to lick the head.

"Have I mentioned I fucking love your tongue?"

"Mmm, I can't say that you have."

"Well I do. Keep licking. Oh yeah, like that. Damn, that swirl thing drives me crazy."

He keeps talking and I want to grin, but more than I want to grin I want to drive him to the edge, so I take him deep into my mouth, sucking him hard, my tongue running along the vein on the bottom of his cock.

"So good. You suck me so fucking good."

He threads his fingers through my hair and guides my movements. As usual, I don't keep control for long—not that I mind. I like that he controls things in the bedroom. I'm not very assertive sexually and I'm really glad he doesn't mind.

I reach between his legs to cup his balls, rolling them gently and he grunts. He starts thrusting into my mouth and I get a taste of a burst of precum. His breathing is fast and ragged and I absolutely love that I can bring him this pleasure. I get aroused just knowing I can please him like this.

His thrusts increase in speed and I suck a little harder.

"Just like that. Yeah. Mmm," he murmurs.

I roll his balls again and meet his thrusts with my mouth, relaxing my throat so I don't gag when he hits it.

"Jesus. That thing you just did. Luce, I'm going to come."

I hum around his cock letting him know I'm good with that. His fingers tighten in my hair, his leg muscles tighten, and I know he's on the edge. I suck even harder, my cheeks and jaw already killing me, but I want him to have this.

"Harder. Just like that. Fuuuuuuck," he growls as the first spurt of cum lands on my tongue. I take him deep and he comes and comes and comes down the back of my throat. Shit, the man comes a long damn time and yet he's still semi hard.

I pull back and just shake my head. He pulls me up to my feet and tosses me on the bed. I let out a giggle of surprise. He crawls up the bed to where I'm laying and rips my panties off. Rips. Them. Off. That is so damn sexy.

Then he dips his fingers between my legs, testing if I'm ready. I could have told him I'm more than ready.

"Always so wet and ready for me," he says, swirling his fingers around my opening. He brings his fingers to his mouth and sucks them clean.

"Jesse," I whisper.

"So fucking good."

He leans over me, parting my legs, then slowly slides his hard length inside me. He moves slowly in and out of me, leisurely arousing me, rubbing against my clit, bringing me to my first orgasm within minutes. It's almost embarrassing how he does that so easily—almost.

He continues thrusting, his pace unhurried. He kisses me, his lips pressing against mine before slipping his tongue inside to rub against mine. With each lick of his tongue on mine, his cock slides inside me—so full and so hard. He slides deep, so deep, then grinds his pelvis against mine. The friction so, so good against my clit—already so hard and throbbing—the man does insane things to my body. When he pinches my nipples, I feel the pressure all the way to my core and I involuntarily clench around him, causing us both to moan.

"God, it feels so fucking good when you do that, Lucy. You're already so tight, but when you do that it's all I can do to not come."

"Mmm, Jesse," I moan. "Please, more."

"I'm not hurrying tonight, Lucy. I want to enjoy every single inch of your body, inside and out, and when I'm done I'm going to start all over again. I will give you this, though," he says and grinds himself deep, rubbing against that swollen bundle of nerves and I explode.

"Jesse…"

"Come on my cock, Luce. Give it to me. I want to feel your pussy squeeze me so fucking tight," he tells me with a grunt.

After bringing me to another orgasm, he claims another of his own.

He never pulls out, just keeps thrusting until he gets hard again. He flips me over and takes me from behind, hitting me deep and I come twice more before he rolls us to our sides. He takes me that way until I come again and beg him to stop.

"Jesse," I pant, "I can't come anymore. I can't, it's too much."

"It's never too much, baby. Feel how hard my cock is for you?"

I nod.

"Don't you want to come all over it, get it hot and creamy to drive me over the edge?"

I moan. His dirty talk drives me wild. My pussy comes to life, my clit begins to throb, and I swear the man's used Nana Russo's happy mojo on me.

His pace picks up when I squeeze him again and again.

"You don't play fair," he scolds. "I'm going to come before you."

"Good. I want to feel you come inside me, Jesse."

He grunts. "Fuuuuck."

"Oh my God," I moan, "I can feel your cum hitting—" and then I come with him, I might have let out a scream. I can't be sure. It was so, so good, my vision blurred and my ears started ringing.

When I'm gasping for breath, he rolls me onto my back and lifts my knees up around his shoulders. His movements steady and unhurried. He feels so good moving inside of me. His gaze never straying from mine. He's making love to me tonight, and my heart, my chest feels so full. I love this man so very much.

"Jesse," I whisper.

"Yeah, baby."

"I love you so much."

His gaze softens and he presses his lips against mine. "I love you too.

It's crazy how much I love you."

"I don't know what I did to deserve you, but I'm so happy."

"Ditto, baby."

It isn't until we both come once more that I tell him I'm exhausted.

He cleans us both up then lays down behind me, my back to his front, wrapping an arm around my waist before pulling me tight against him. He pulls the covers up over us and settles in with a sigh.

"I love you, Jesse."

He kisses my cheek. "I love you too, Luce."

I drift off to sleep cocooned by the body and arms of the man I've come to love more than I thought possible. Jesse Kingston has become my world and I'm the luckiest woman on the planet.

Chapter
twenty six

Lucy

"Great show," Cage tells me with a huge grin. "This is going to be one hell of a tour."

The crowd is still cheering.

"Encore?"

"Oh yeah," Trace says.

We head back out and I ask them what they want to sing. We've already run through our entire album, including the song Falling Down came out to perform with us.

"*I Miss The Misery* by Halestorm," Trace says.

We all nod. We know this one very, very well. It's one of the songs we play a lot during practices.

"You want more of us, Vegas?!" I shout, pulling the mic off the stand. They scream back.

"We might have a little something we could sing for you. What do you say?"

They shout back. I am loving this. I can't wait until we're at the arena venues.

"All right. The woman in this song is a total masochist but when you've got the right guy—all tall, dark, and sexy, incredible stamina in bed—"

"Stop talking about Jesse," Sera tells the crowd and everyone starts laughing.

"Hey, I can't help he's all that and more." Sera makes an obscene gesture and I laugh. "Here comes a little Halestorm for you."

We all start at the same time—vocals, guitars, drums. That's the part I love about this song. I work the stage, going from one side to the other, stopping to belt out some lyrics, pointing to the audience before moving on.

The song ends and the cheers continue.

"Thank you Las Vegas! You've been incredible tonight! Our tour starts in a couple weeks and we'll be back. I hope to see you then!" I blow kisses and toss out my water bottle and hand towel. Trace throws his drumsticks. Jace, Sera, and Meggie throw out a bunch of picks. One last kiss to the crowd and we walk off stage. I can't contain the smile and Jesse picks me up and swings me around.

"That fucking rocked."

"Hell yeah," Xander says and fist bumps us all.

"I've got to say, I'm looking forward to the larger venues now. That was so much fun."

Jesse nods. "You say that now, but the minute you set foot in the venue or do sound check, you're going to want to puke. Once you go on for real, you'll calm down fast just like tonight."

I nod. "We really did okay?"

"Jesus, Lucy," Cage says. "If you did any better, they'd have had a riot in here."

"I'd hug you, but I don't want to get your pretty suit full of my sweat."

"To hell with the suit," he says and pulls me in for a hug. "You do me proud," he whispers in my ear.

"You can't know what that means to me." Cage Nichols has worked with some of the biggest names in music and we did him proud.

"I know. You deserve this. Two weeks until the tour. Practices and PR every day until then, except for tomorrow due to travel," he tells us all. We nod our agreement.

"All right, boys and girls," Xander shouts. "Let's go party!"

We laugh. "Shower then party."

We walk down the strip, drinking, gambling, and being outrageously obnoxious. Amazingly Jesse and the guys only get recognized a couple times—likely due to Jesse's haircut that he hasn't shared with the world yet.

The guys are just as hammered as we are, stumbling around laughing. Around two in the morning I get the brilliant idea to scour the *entire* city of Las Vegas to find the *real* Elvis, because everybody knows Elvis isn't dead (rolls eyes at self).

I lose track of time somewhere around Caesar's Palace.

Oh my God, my head. Someone kill me. I crack open one eye, or try to, and it hurts like a mofo. I am never drinking that much again. Damn whipped cream Pinnacle and root beer. I take a deep breath and that hurts too. I groan. Jesus, what the hell time did we get in last night? I don't remember anything after looking for Elvis in Caesar's Palace. Fucking Elvis. That was some of the dumbest shit I've ever done. *Because everyone knows Elvis is alive.* Xander fist bumped me and it was on. He became my partner in crime.

I try again to open one eye to look at the clock. How the fuck is it possible for my eyeballs to hurt? Unh. Two fifteen in the afternoon. Wow, and I still feel this bad. I wonder how we got back to the hotel. Is Jesse even in bed with me?

I slowly and cautiously roll onto my back. One never knows if they're going to end up having a hangover accompanied by vomiting and with the queasiness I'm experiencing, I'm thinking I may be one of the unlucky pukers. I need some water and ibuprofen like yesterday. I turn my head and I see Jesse passed out cold.

I lift my hand to rub my eyes in hopes to open them both when my hand flops onto my face.

"Ow, what the fuck," I say. Something hard and sharp hits my face. Great, as if this hangover isn't enough. Now I'll have a bruise or some scrape or something on my forehead. At least I have two weeks for it to heal, whatever damage I've done with whatever the hell is on my finger. Did I get my nails done last night? Poke my eye with the acrylic? I move my thumb to touch my fingernails. Nope. God, even doing that hurts my head. How is that possible?

I'm going to have to open my eyes and it's going to hurt. I rub my eyes again—no damage done this time. Thankfully.

I open one eye then the other. There are clothes thrown all over the hotel room, my bra is hanging from the lampshade. Damn. I bet we had some really amazing drunk sex and I don't remember it. Just then a couple flashes of hard, pounding sex with Jesse flashes through my mind. Oh, those images… oh yeah. Wild monkey sex it was.

I breathe through the headache pain. It's evil. Never again.

"Unh," I murmur, trying to wake Jesse. He doesn't even flinch. Shit, the way he's so still, I hope he's not dead. Wouldn't that be just the way shit's been going for me lately? Apparently I swear a lot when I'm hungover too.

I reach out to go and shake him when a flash blinds me. What the fuck is that? I'm full of all kinds of questions—and right now I've got another one.

"Holy. Fucking. Shit." Is that a wedding ring? I wouldn't do something stupid like that. Besides, Sera was there to make sure I wouldn't, right? Right??

"Oh my God. Jesse!" I screech, shaking him, looking at the gorgeous diamond ring on my wedding ring finger. It really is so pretty—focus. Married! WHAT!

"Jesse, get up!"

"Wha?" he murmurs, his eyes closed as he lifts his head off the pillow.

"Wake up! You… Me… We… Oh my God!" I screech and my head pounds. Fuck.

"Stop screaming, Luce. What's going on?" he asks, so calmly, as he scratches his chest and opens his eyes. I look over at his hand, the one he's using to scratch his chest and gasp.

"What is it?"

"Unh," is all I can manage.

"Luce, why are you 'unh'ing?"

"Married," I whisper.

"What?" he asks, his eyes open now, very wide I might add.

"Left hand. Ring. *Married*," I whisper.

He looks at his left hand and goes completely still. He bolts upright and reaches for my left hand with his.

"How did you get that? That was in my…" he breaks off like he just remembered something, something vital that he's not sharing with me.

"Tell me. What…"

"Unh," he says and I start to panic.

"That about sums it up. Do you remember what happened?" I ask, taking a deep calming breath.

"Parts of it. It's coming to me slowly. How much do you remember?"

"Nothing after chasing fat Elvis through Caesar's Palace."

He chuckles. "That was fucking awesome."

I shrug. "I only wanted to search him for drugs. It's not a good way to die, overdosing on the toilet for the world to make fun of."

Jesse snorts then moans. "God, I think we drank bottle upon bottle of liquor last night."

"Tell me about it. Why are we wearing wedding rings, Jesse?" And why, all of a sudden, am I not panicking about this? A sense of calm has come over me. Weird. I'm sure the panic will come back later, once I get my hangover under control and it sinks in—and I think about telling my mother. Shit.

"Uh," he says, rubbing the back of his neck. That's never good. "We hit a couple more hotels and casinos looking for your Elvis and then we found a skinny Elvis. You insisted on telling him all about his fate. We headed to breakfast at Denny's."

"All of us, or just me and you?"

"All of us. When we got there you were so serious telling Elvis his fate. He was so grateful he asked if he could officiate our wedding."

I groan. "I don't remember any of this."

"Anyway, Elvis got permission from someone at Denny's to officiate our ceremony there. Apparently Denny's in Las Vegas also has a 24 hour wedding chapel."

"Huh. I guess that's convenient. Drunk people going for breakfast to sober up but don't quite get there before they decide to get married," I laugh. I can't help it. It's so hilarious.

Jesse laughs with me. "God, Lucy. I thought for sure you were going to be pissed off."

"I'm not pissed. Shocked, stunned, freaking out a little bit, but not pissed."

"Yeah. I was so fucked up I'm surprised I remember any of it. We laughed through the whole thing. You licked skinny Elvis's cheek."

"What the hell?"

He shrugs. "Who knows. We were hammered."

"Hammered doesn't begin to describe it."

"Fucking skinny Elvis was a riot."

"Where did you get this gorgeous ring?"

"Ah, that ring I've had for a while now."

"What?" I whisper. Is he serious? He's been wanting to marry me?

"Yeah, I got the ring because I knew I wanted to ask you to marry me—eventually—and if I had the ring handy and inspiration struck, well, I could ask you."

"Why didn't you ask me?"

"Would you have said yes?"

I hesitate. How can I not? That's a major life decision. Would I have said yes?

"I think I would have. We'd have had to talk about a lot of things and I think I'd have wanted to have a *little* longer of an engagement, at least through the tour." I groan again. "Oh God. The tour. The media. Shit. Cage."

"Yeah, about Cage. He was there."

"Seriously?"

He nods and grins. "He was all for it. He kept shouting *True love prevails*. Then he and Xander would fist bump."

"Wow. Cage Nichols?"

He nods. "Hammered. He was hilarious."

"I think I remember a little bit of that. Wow. Where did the wedding bands come from?"

"Elvis knew a jeweler down the street who opened for us to pick out bands."

"Skinny Elvis or fat Elvis?"

"Skinny Elvis. You freaked out fat Elvis so bad I thought he was going to get a restraining order."

"Oh come on. It wasn't that bad."

"Luce, you tackled him."

I rub a finger around my ring. "Well, he ran away and I didn't tackle him *hard*."

He chuckles.

"Anyway, the jeweler came in very handy. At least I helped pick out wedding bands. I remember that part."

"You did."

"I can't believe we got married—drunk married in Vegas with skinny Elvis at Denny's."

He nods.

"Jesus Christ, my mom is going to have a fit. Oh God. She's going to go on and on about how we don't have a prenuptial agreement and how it was irresponsible of us to get married without family there."

"Well, if you wanted to I suppose we could get the marriage annulled."

I gasp. "What?"

"I'm just saying, it's an option."

"From the looks of this room with my bra hanging from the lampshade and my panties on top of the TV, I'm pretty sure we had sex which means annulment is out of the question."

"If you wanted an annulment, we could pretend that didn't happen."

"Is that want you want?"

"Truthfully? No. I wouldn't have gotten married this quickly but really what do rings and a piece of paper change between us?"

Hmm. He's right. We live together. We work together. We're going on tour together. He's my best friend and I love him more than life itself.

"I don't want to annul the marriage, Jesse. I wouldn't have wanted to get married this soon but if you'd asked me to marry you, I'd have said yes. We could have been engaged for six months or a year. In that time we'd have gone on tour and got married after that."

"Since when do we do anything normal, Luce?"

"Valid point. I need ibuprofen and water. Then a pot of coffee. No prenup. You better not screw up, Mr. Rockstar."

"You either, Blush baby."

"Ugh. That nickname needs to go away."

He grunts. "Not going to happen."

"Who came up with that, anyway?"

"Your Vegas crowd and I guarantee that's going to catch on quick."

"Gah. The room looks like a tornado hit it."

He grins. "Not a tornado, just us. Wild drunk crazy monkey sex."

"Monkey!" I sing and he laughs. "I kinda figured with my bra on one side of the room, my panties ripped on the floor, and my jeans on the other side of the room, that it was a wild one," I giggle. "I do remember part of that." I gasp. "And I do remember you calling me 'wife'."

He nods. "I love you, Lucy, more than I ever thought I could love anyone. Each time I think I couldn't love you any more than I do at that moment, my heart goes and proves me wrong, you go and prove me wrong. I'm not sure how we'll handle this with the press or your mom, but I can't say I regret it."

"You say that now. Wait until I'm old and gray with saggy boobs and arthritis."

"You'll still be beautiful to me."

I throw myself at him and hug him tight. "God, you're so amazing, Jesse. I love you so, so much—husband."

He chuckles. "I love you too, wife."

"It's kinda weird."

"We'll adjust."

"We will. If I can adjust to living in the same house with Xander who is constantly panty-checking me, I can adjust to this."

He chuckles. "I'll be honest. I kinda like that you're wearing my ring and you've got my last name. Luciana Kingston."

"Mrs. Jesse Kingston. Do you know how many times I wrote that on my notebooks in high school?" I laugh.

"That's not weird at all," he tells me, his tone dripping with sarcasm.

"What? Maybe my writing it sealed our fate. I did make a list of wishes one day."

"What did you wish for?"

"I wished I'd meet you and we'd have a special connection."

"Came true."

"I wished we'd make music together, write songs, and sing together."

"Came true."

"Wow. Yeah. I wished you'd kiss me and, uh, we'd have crazy insane sex."

"Came true, but wild drunk crazy monkey sex."

I nod. This moment is profound. "Maybe my list was magic," I whisper.

"Maybe you've got Nana Russo's mojo."

"That's not supposed to work for personal gain."

He shrugs. "Whatever it is, it brought us together. Fate, the universe, Nana Russo's mojo."

"It's been a bumpy ride already. Hopefully the road smoothes out soon."

"Don't hold your breath, Cupcake. We've got a four-month tour coming up in two weeks—groupies, media, gossip—and to top that off, we've got your mom."

I sigh. "Again, why can't you bullshit me just once?"

"Because if I've got to go through all this with my eyes wide open, I'm dragging you right along with me."

"Awww. If that isn't true love, I don't know what is."

He snorts. "You grab the ibuprofen and water and I'll order us some coffee and breakfast."

"Bacon, please. And a Coke. Coke is the cure-all for hangovers."

"Who fed you that line?"

I shrug. "I don't remember."

"There is no cure-all for a hangover. See, if I were to feed you a line of bullshit, I could say wild monkey newlywed sex is the cure-all for a hangover."

"But you don't feed me lines of bullshit, you just drag me through whatever hell we've got to face."

He throws an arm around my shoulders. "At least we're facing it together, right?"

I nod. A positive thought comes to me and I almost bounce like Meggie. "That's true. That means I don't have to face my mom alone."

He groans.

"Isn't being married fun?"

The End

Want to read more Rockstars? Check out book 2 Blush Available now.

Acknowledgements

I'm not even sure where to begin. There are so many people to thank.

To Porter Natali: For being my biggest cheerleader and supporter, for talking me off the ledge more than once, and for not letting me give up. You are truly an amazing person.

My fantastic Betalicious Beauties: Eileen Robinson, Kerri Lofgren-Miller, Autumn Oertel, Heather Wishnia, Kim Carr, Jessica Butler, and Lisa Matheson Sylva. You ladies kept me going when I was ready to throw in the towel and pumped me up through the edits from hell. I am so very thankful for everything you've done and continue to do.

To Lisa Ravenscroft and Lydia, the HeaBook ShelfBlogger: Thank you SO much for your support and efforts for the Release Day Blitz and everything to do with Falling Down. You both are incredible and I can't tell you how much your help and support has meant to me.

A great big thank you to Jake Ingrassia, actor extraordinaire, for your help with regard to the movie and acting industry as well as technical terms I never would have known. Your character will be making an appearance in the next book... stay tuned.

To Milo Ventimiglia, M. Shadows, and Avenged Sevenfold for inspiring the storyline for the Rockstar series—Milo with his good looks and "working actor" mentality, M. Shadows because he's hot (laughs) and has an amazing voice, and Avenged Sevenfold with their fan-fucking-tastic music that keeps the creativity flowing.

To my sister and the tiny fan club of people from high school and work I'm proud to call friends: Thank you for being excited with me, supporting me, and buying the book. You all are awesome, hugs and love!

To those who I call friends in the social media community: I love you, I love you, I love you! You had no idea what the book was about or if it was any good but you jumped right on my bandwagon and pledged your support and vowed to buy my book.

To the amazing authors whom I admire and inspire me to no depths including, of course Tijan, L.B. Simmons, Jay McLean, Harper Bentley, and R.S. Grey. Thank you for letting me fangirl all over you.

A special thank you goes out to the lovely Tijan and the beautiful Jay McLean for allowing honorable mention of themselves and their characters in Falling Down.

Falling Down Mix Playlist

Slut Like You by P!nk
The Truth About Love by P!nk
Smooth Criminal by Alien Ant Farm
Can't Believe It by Flo Rida, Pitbull)
Timber by Ke$ha, Pitbull
Wild Wild Love by Pitbull,G.R.L.
Not A Bad Thing by Justin Timberlake
It Takes Two by Katy Perry
Do or Die by Afrojack, Thirty Seconds To Mars
Hard Out Here by Lily Allen
Milkshake by Kelis
Erotic City by Prince
Fall Down by will.i.am, Miley Cyrus
I Will Never Let You Down by Rita Ora
Domino by Jessie J
Kiss Me Slowly by Parachute
Traffic Light by Daughtry
Without Me by Eminem
Runaway Baby by Bruno Mars
Anywhere But Here by Safetysuit
Come Out and Play by The Offspring
Hashpipe by Weezer
Meant To Be by Parachute
Never Stop by Safetysuit
Sick by Adelitas Way
Stuck by Adelitas Way
Country Song by Seether
Stand Up by All That Remains
What If I Was Nothing by All That Remains
Best I Can by Art of Dying
Get Through This by Art of Dying
Best I can by Art of Dying
Scream by Avenged Sevenfold
Hail To The King by Avenged Sevenfold
This Means War by Avenged Sevenfold
Nightmare by Avenged Sevenfold
Welcome To The Family by Avenged Sevenfold
Face To The Floor by Chevelle

1000hp by Godsmack
Rise Up by Saliva
Remember Everything by Five Finger Death Punch
Far From Home by Five Finger Death Punch
Bad Company by Five Finger Death Punch
House of the Rising Sun by Five Finger Death Punch
Cold Night by You Me At Six
Stay With Me by You Me At Six
Crash by You Me At Six
Lipstick Lies by Oceans Divide
I Don't Apologize (1000 Pictures) by Otherwise
Tell Me I'm A Wreck by Every Avenue
Take Me Home Tonight by Every Avenue
Rent I Pay by Spoon
Gimme Something Good by Ryan Adams
For You I Will (Confidence) by Teddy Geiger
Shock The Monkey by Coal Chamber
Coming Undone by Korn
Twisted Transistor by Korn
Diamond Eyes by Deftones
Holy Diver by Killswitch Engage
Already Over by Red
Never Be The Same by Red
Walking On A Thin Line by Huey Lewis & The News
Your Song by Elton John
Lola by The Kinks
Born To Run by Bruce Springsteen
It's Only Rock 'n' Roll (But I Like it) by The Rolling Stones
Under Pressure by David Bowie, Queen
Brown-Eyed Girl by Van Morrison
I Miss The Misery by Halestorm
Bad Romance by Halestorm
Freak Like Me by Halestorm
Beautiful With You by Halestorm
I'm So Sick by Flyleaf
Fully Alive by Flyleaf
ALL AROUND ME BY FLYLEAF
THERE FOR YOU BY FLYLEAF

Contact Anne

I really am just a reader who writes stories sometimes, so never be afraid to drop me an email at Anne@AnneMercierAuthor.com. Anytime.

Website:

http://AnneMercierAuthor.com

Facebook Author Page:

https://www.facebook.com/AnneMercierAuthor/838272909530232

Facebook Page:

https://www.facebook.com/anne.mercier.24/100001421675299

Facebook Group:

https://www.facebook.com/groups/278767625659221/

Twitter:

https://twitter.com/Anne_Mercier_

Pinterest:

http://www.pinterest.com/AnneMercier24/

Spotify:

http://open.spotify.com/user/1286604532

Goodreads:

https://www.goodreads.com/author/show/5887184.Anne_Mercier

Made in the USA
Middletown, DE
30 April 2015